RODEO SUMMER

A Camden Ranch Novel

JILLIAN NEAL

Cover Design by

THE KILLION GROUP, INC.

Written by Jillian Neal

Cover Design by The Killion Group, Inc.

Copyright © 2016 Jillian Neal

Published by Realm Press

ISBN: 978-1-940174-34-1

Library of Congress Control Number: 2016934069

First Edition

First Printing – April 2016

To my Granddaddy Reese,
Thanks for all the tractor rides, for teaching me the trick to getting the honey out
of honeysuckle, and how life will make more sense if you sit down with a pot of
snap beans to pop while you think about it.
Thank you for the endless expanse of land where
I always seemed to be able to find my true self,
and for always being my favorite cowboy.

CHAPTER ONE

With adrenaline-spiked blood and tension locked tightly in his gut, Austin Camden dug his spurs into the bull, leaned in, and took one moment to clear his mind. The bull snorted and edged anxiously against the chute, trying to buck. Austin caught his right horn, making him snarl. "I don't think so, motherfucker. Simmer down and take it. You're getting rode."

With a half-smirk and a single nod to his own destiny, the quick creak of the chute-door hinge shot through his veins as he pulled up on the rope. The resin scent of his gloves coupled with the smell of dirt and sweat as he gulped a quick breath. The previously horizontal bull, named Mesquite Fever and known for his vicious temper, shot vertical in a quarter-second and was out of the gate.

Staring down at two thousand pounds of fight and fury underneath his sore ass, every ounce of anxiety evaporated into the roar of the Cody, Wyoming crowd, all shouting, "Camden!" Determination seized him, swallowing him whole. He wasn't going down, not yet. He wasn't leaving without the satisfaction that always seemed just out of reach. The bull spun into his hand, and Austin automatically counterbalanced. He leaned away from the spin, constantly anticipating the next motion of the bull.

He narrowed his eyes, locked his thighs around the beast, and let his training take over. Always the longest eight seconds of his life, but somehow, also the most rewarding. He was beginning to wonder if his life was measured in eight-second increments. On the bull, he was alive, heart thundering in his chest, blood surging through his veins, conviction in his soul. The rest of the time he simply existed, desperate and anxious for something he couldn't seem to find.

No one in his family understood what the hell he was doing. He didn't care. All that mattered was the next high, the next eight seconds. After that, maybe *he'd* be able to figure out what hell it was he wanted. Probably not, but this sure wasn't his last rodeo. He owed too many people too many things to quit now. Honing in on the energy of the beast, he leaned into the bucks and turns, letting his free hand work as a counterweight. His year wasn't ending in Cody. Not this time.

His fringed chaps, courtesy of his sponsors, slapped against the bull's hide. Sweat dewed under his hat and vest. He gripped his thighs tighter and clenched his jaw.

"Look at him go, folks. Camden has had a heck of a good season. Got the form of all of the rodeo greats. Unless he gets thrown tonight, he's lookin' to take it all home with a Cody buckle, and then it's on to Cheyenne. You're gonna be shoutin' 'Camden' in Vegas this season, no doubt." The crackled rasp of the announcer was drowned by the mighty roar of the crowds when the buzzer sounded.

Lowering his right hand and freeing his left from the rope, Austin bailed off of Mesquite Fever. Anger rose in the puffs of dirt surrounding him timed to the pounding hoofs of the bull. Damn thing chased Austin to the gate, horns first. Making good use of the half-second Jackson Sanders, his best friend and his personal bull-fighter, offered him, he scrambled up the fence and waved to the fans who'd leapt to their feet, still cheering his name. They sure as hell would be shouting "Camden" in Vegas. He wasn't going back to Pleasant Glen, Nebraska without the PBR champion buckle strapped to his waist. After that, he'd be able to figure out the rest of his life.

He couldn't halt the broad grin that spread across his features as his scores bellowed down from the old Buzzard's Roost judges' box directly above his head.

"Camden's ride on Mesquite Fever scores an 89.2. That brings his average to 195, and he's only got one more ride between him and the Cody buckle, ladies and gentlemen. He's forty points ahead of Travis Anders, his closest competition. Let's hear it for a champion rider."

The Buckle Bunnies Austin was beginning to think were permanent fixtures along the railings of the Cody Stampede Arena offered him lascivious grins and blew him kisses as he passed.

"You coming to Silver Dollar tonight, Austin? I'll meet you there," a gorgeous blonde with her rack tied up in a low cut midriff shirt and sporting a ridiculous pink cowgirl hat cooed seductively. His eyes ran the length of her bare torso and then down her tanned legs that went on for miles.

"Yeah, Austin. Come celebrate your win with us." A brunette nearby immediately leapt on the bandwagon.

It was flattering as hell, he had to admit. He'd been winning all season. The women, the sponsors, and his competition had all taken notice. Problem was the bunnies had lost their appeal somewhere between Ocala and Tulsa. Eventually blowing your load in any random woman readily willing to pony up for you proved completely meaningless. *Fuck*. What was wrong with him lately, anyway? Beautiful women were throwing themselves at him, and he wasn't interested. He should see a doctor. That fall he'd taken in San Antonio must've been worse than he realized.

His ego attempted a satisfactory explanation. He liked his sex with an edge and a woman with some wild heat coursing through her veins. Brains made a big difference, though he was certain his sixteen-year-old self would never have believed that. And he wanted someone with some curves and some experience to keep him warm and sated. The Bunnies, most of them city slickers that didn't know a Hereford from a horse, offered him no challenge and definitely no heat. They eventually all blended together into one boring fuck that felt good and then was over. He wanted and needed more, and that scared the shit out of him, not that he'd ever admit that. He didn't do fear. It wasn't in him.

"Yeah, I'll be at the Silver Dollar tonight. I'll see you there, darlin'."

He called himself stupid for even going, but his sponsors expected him to put on the bull riding show, and dammit, that's what he intended to do. You didn't make it to Vegas hiding out in your hotel room bored and anxiously counting the hours until your next ride so you could attempt to gain something worth having. He was going to be the Professional Bull Riding Champion, and he was going to make use of all of the money *and* all of the perks.

The icy glare shot from Travis Anders's eyes cut through the dusty heat swamping Cody that evening. Austin chuckled. Anders had been chasing him all season. Most bull riders could appreciate an outstanding ride even if it was done by their direct competition. Anders's sponsors were putting on the pressure, and he'd been a whiny douche ever since he got his ass bucked hard in Deadwood.

"Anders," Austin nodded as he waltzed by, making no effort to hide his smirk.

"Fuck off, Camden. Nobody likes a show-off."

"Show-off?" Austin laughed outright. "Don't get your panties in a wad, man. That wasn't even one of my better rides."

Heading back behind the chutes to get his extra gear, his grin continued to expand as his team met him with exuberant congratulations.

"Well done, cowboy. You made us proud." The corporate exec from Minton, Clifton Taft, shook his hand. Minton had given Austin another chance after his less-than-stellar year before. They were a small denim and chaps startup in Oklahoma, and he was making a name for them with every win. Their sales had skyrocketed in the last six weeks.

"There are men with luck and there are men with skill, Mr. Camden, and you've got both. The Ford Truck team is having drinks at Cassie's. Come as my personal guest." A top exec from Ford edged in front of Clifton. Austin saw his sponsor's face fall in defeat.

Austin accepted the Ford exec's handshake but shook his head. "Thanks for the invite. I'm honored, but I'm drinking with the Minton team tonight." He wouldn't turn his back on Minton, not for all the money in the world. They'd stuck by him since long before he was seeded in the top ten. Ford could flash cash all night long and show off their Rolexes and fancy cowboy hats, but Austin was as loyal as they came.

The guy from Ford faded into the crowd and headed Anders's way.

"You'da made him proud, man. That was one hell of a ride." Jackson simultaneously shook Austin's hand and slapped him on the back. He'd taken off his gear but his face was still painted for his bull-fighting duties.

"Yeah, well, thank you for the distraction. You're the best bull-fighter around. There's a reason we've been best friends since we were five." Austin tried to remove the image of Mesquite's horns bearing down on him from his mind. Jackson had saved his ass once again.

"Damn straight, I'm the best. Don't ever forget it, but I'm serious, Max woulda loved that. You rode the hell outta that motherfucker."

Austin managed a nod. Why did Jackson always have to bring up Max? Couldn't they leave that in the past? The haunting image of his own shattered reflection in the driver's side mirror of his first truck stabbed through his gut for the thousandth time since that horrible night twelve years ago. It was the first time he'd seen terror in his own eyes. Splatters of rain on the windshield dotted Matt's Huskers T-shirt just before the blood had seeped through the cotton. Austin could remember every detail of the moment that had all but destroyed his life. Ever since then, he'd been damned and determined never to let anything scare him. He'd never look in a mirror and see fear in his eyes again.

Jackson, Max, and Austin grew up in Pleasant Glen together. They were inseparable. Austin's father would let them ride the calves and break the green horses when they were old enough for that. When they were thirteen they worked all summer on Camden Ranch, Austin's family ranch, and used their combined savings to purchase a Mighty Bucky bronc simulator so they could really learn the techniques.

One stupid night when they were barely sixteen, they'd snuck out to the rodeo in Broken Bow. The rain had poured. The streets were slick. It hadn't occurred to them that they wouldn't hold the rodeo in the storm. The drunk driver never even stopped at the light two blocks from the arena.

Even if it hadn't been his fault, Austin had been driving, and he had never forgiven himself. He never would. With a quick glance skyward, he hoped somehow Max knew how much he and Jackson missed him, and that they'd never given up the rodeo dreams they all shared as kids.

"Let's get outta here," Austin urged.

"See ya at Silver Dollar. I promised the cute little blonde in the pink cowgirl hat a ride." Jackson smirked.

Beyond certain that she saw getting a ride from Jackson as a pathway to him, Austin kept his mouth shut. He'd much rather be on top of the bull, not in front of it. The bullfighters were fierce and nothing scared them, but the women never saw it that way.

Before he had time to worry over Jackson, he heard the gruff sneer of Brantley Preston drawing ever closer. *Of course, Preston'll have something to say about it.* "I want Mr. Camden's bull checked. He's been just a little too lucky this season." Brant passed Austin, followed by his Preston Cattle brownnosers.

Austin rolled his eyes. Brant was a prime, Grade-A asshole of epic proportion. He'd had it in for Austin ever since he'd seeded himself on a bull from K&H instead of Preston Cattle. His father was a former bull team owner turned stock supplier, and Brant was constantly looking to get his daddy's bulls sold into the competition.

His father, Brant Sr., was a wealthy rancher from Dallas. The fact that he was a shitty stock contractor was none of Austin's business. Not his fault they almost always supplied duds, until this year.

"You're so full of shit, Preston. Nothing wrong with that bull. Damn near did a handstand out of the chute," Austin huffed.

"It's interesting to me that your number with Dallas Devil hasn't come up. Why do you think that is?"

"You all draw the numbers and tell me who to ride, Brant. What's that saying? Somethin' 'bout if you can't ride, get the hell outta my way."

"I doubt you'll be quite so smug after Dallas Devil takes you down."

"Then either put me on him or shut the fuck up."

Six weeks ago, Preston Cattle had supplied a new bull to the PRCA. Dallas Devil was a massive rust-red ball of fury that flew out of the gates like a bat out of hell. Rank as they came, he'd already sent three riders to the hospital. Two of them were out for the season. A week ago in Tulsa he'd hooked a fighter. Austin showed no fear when he talked to Brant, but a tinge of nerves twisted up his spine.

"You'll be paired with him sometime, Camden, then we'll see whose name they're shouting in Vegas. Guaranteed the winning bull will be from Preston Cattle."

"I don't give a damn where the bull's from, Preston. The champion will be me."

Preston simpered while a photographer and reporter from the local Cody Enterprise asked Austin to pose for a front page picture.

After a long shower and a quick call home to do a little bragging, Austin sauntered into the Silver Dollar. His eyes adjusted quickly to the dimly-lit honkytonk, painted with neon splashes of light and low red and yellow stained glass chandeliers over the pool tables. It looked just like every other honkytonk bar in every other tourist-trap town he'd been in, dozens of them in the last eight states.

Following the cheers of his name, he forced a grin and joined Clifton and the other Minton reps at the bar. A shot of Jack slid down the bar, landing right in front of him from the capable hands of the bartender. Austin offered her a nod of appreciation before he downed the whiskey, reveling in the burn that ignited in his throat and scorched down his chest.

"When Mesquite spun twice I was terrified you were down the well, my friend. That was some nice ridin'." Scott Leonard, another of the Minton team, offered his congratulations.

"Wasn't as pretty as I like, but it got the job done." Austin preferred never to think he'd done his best. He didn't care for the idea that his greatest ride was behind him, and there was always room for improvement. Surely, if he'd really done his best he wouldn't still feel so damn lost.

"Hey Austin, that was an amazing ride." This time a trio of brunettes sauntered over. The one who spoke was already slurring. Her eyes danced like she'd had a month's worth of liquor in the last hour.

"Thanks, darlin'. Maybe you oughta slow it down." Reaching out instinctively, he caught her arm as she tripped closer to his bar stool. She giggled hysterically.

Sighing, Austin tried to hide his eye roll. One of the other women elbowed her friend. "Oh yeah. We were wondering if you'd do some shots with us...or maybe off of us." She hoisted her cleavage in his face and waggled her eyebrows.

Clifton and Scott shot him envious smirks. "I shoulda been a rider," Clifton teased. "Don't let us keep you from your fans, Austin."

Yeah, thanks. He was growing weary of trying to appease his sponsors by showing off with the bunnies. "Tempting offer, ladies," he lied. "I just got here. Night's still young. We'll see, but I gotta ride tomorrow night, and then I'm leaving for Cheyenne. Maybe another time."

Before he could fend off any other offers: "You are such a self-righteous asshole, Brant. Just give him to me!" screeched from the back of the bar.

Fear was laced in the name-calling. Austin got to his feet. He didn't have to guess which Brant had crossed the line, and so help him if Preston had done something to a woman, he'd skin him alive.

"Come on, baby, hit me. You know you want to," Brant taunted. He leaned down in the woman's face, asking for it.

Austin's brow furrowed. He lunged and caught the woman in question before she went after Preston with both hands. "Whoa there, sweetheart, I gotcha." He wrapped his arms around her slender waist, trapping her arms by her side, and tried not to notice how soft and warm she felt against him, or the fact that her sweet little ass nestled his cock right between her cheeks when he tightened his grip to keep her from scalping Brant Preston.

Having no idea what about her had triggered every protective instinct he possessed, he inhaled, desperate to absorb more of her. Her hair smelled of sweetened strawberries and cheap perfume. Her breasts rested against his forearm as he kept her pinned against him. His mind spun, absorbing the feel of her body in his arms. His pulse doubletimed, and his longing found a fix.

Some feeling he hadn't felt in months, in years maybe, welled in his soul. Something akin to contentment surged through him, settling him on his feet. She somehow reminded him what it felt like to be satisfied and to be...home.

"Let me go!"

"Fine, but let's not give him what he wants, okay? Simmer down for me."

She stomped hard on his foot with her well-worn cowgirl boots and attempted a ferocious growl. She sounded a great deal more like a frightened kitten. He gritted his teeth and pretended to be unaffected. She was trying so hard to be brave and stick it to Brant. Austin would never betray the frightened shivers he could feel against his chest. Damn, but he liked her spunk. He was also fairly certain he now had a broken toe. She wriggled again and tried to get her elbows in the game.

"If I let you go, do you promise not to hit Captain Douchebag?" He watched her try to hide a slight grin as she nodded. "All right." He released her and stepped between her and Brant in one quick move.

"What'd you do to her, Preston? You know acting like a pussy won't get you any."

"Fuck off, Camden. Always sticking your nose where it doesn't belong is gonna get you in trouble." Preston narrowed his eyes at the woman. She was still glaring at Brant with her arms crossed over her stunning cleavage.

Austin tried not to stare at her tits. The black tank top she was wearing didn't hide much. Her dark, dirty-blonde hair hung limply down her back, and her red-rimmed, whisky-colored eyes were trying to size him up. She'd been crying. He'd tear Brant Preston to pieces and bury him in a pile of cow shit. He ignored the thundering race of his heart as he offered her a slight smile. Damn, but she was beautiful. Broken...but beautiful. She made those Q-baby Wranglers, real cowgirls' favorites, look like they'd been painted on as part of a stunning masterpiece. She had the finest ass he'd ever seen, and that was saying something.

"Go back to your room, Summer. I'd hate to have to phone my lawyers to tell them that you were out drinking."

Summer? Austin took a closer inventory of the woman. *No way.* Realization settled on him slowly. Whatever was going on between her and Preston needed to end before she got herself in trouble. He didn't sound like he was joking. The threat was legit.

"Come on." Austin grabbed her hand, and with a slight tug he led her out of the Silver Dollar.

———

"What the hell do you think you're doing?" Summer tripped slightly, cursed her own clumsiness, and finally let Austin Camden pull her out of the bar. *Better question: What the hell am I doing?*

"I'm getting you away from Brant Preston. Guy's an asshat, unable to locate his half-inch dick in the dirt he stuck it in. Are you really Summer Sanchez?"

Summer rolled her eyes dramatically. "Brant's a jackass. Yeah, there's news. Somebody alert the press. Hello, I married the asshole."

"What?" Austin's mouth hung open. Summer tried not to notice the fire in his onyx eyes, or the way his Wranglers tugged and pulled against his extremely firm ass with each step he took, and how tight that white T-shirt was pulled against the lean muscles of his chest and torso. "You're married to that guy?"

"*Was* married. He's my ex. Why'd you stop me from hitting him? He deserves it, believe me." Irritation and thankfulness mixed in a confusing storm in the pit of her empty stomach.

"No doubt, sugar, but I have a policy—never give Brant Preston anything he wants. He was begging you to hit him. That can't be good."

The thankfulness won out over her irritation for the moment. Summer hated to admit he was right. Hitting Brant could have ended in disaster. Not that she couldn't take his little pansy-ass, but there was far too much at stake for her to give in to her temper now.

"Here." Austin opened the tailgate of his truck, a gorgeous luxury Silverado that looked brand new. He'd been winning all season. She was certain his bank accounts were choking with the bonuses he'd received, and just like every other rodeo cowboy, he was gonna spend it all before he made it to the next town. They were all so damn certain they had a pot full of gold waiting at the end of every line. It was gonna suck when he figured out that wasn't how life worked.

Summer watched Austin as he dug in the toolbox of the truck and located a bottle of whiskey. He patted the gate, urging her to join him.

Summer knew she should leave; not that she really had anywhere to go. "I haven't had anything to eat." Her half-whispered confession dissipated in the humid Wyoming air. She wasn't getting drunk with some guy she only knew because he'd been lighting up the rodeo circuit scoreboards all season long. There was no food in her system to buffer the effects of whiskey. "And I'm not some buckle bunny that's gonna go with you back to your room just because you were nice to her and gave her a drink."

"No, you're sure as hell not a buckle bunny, not by a long shot. So, why don't you tell me who you are? I'm not trying to get you drunk. I'm not an asshole. I just thought this might help us both simmer down." He lifted the whiskey bottle he still hadn't opened. "Some chick stomped on my foot, and it hurts like a bitch."

Laughing in spite of herself, Summer hopped up on the tailgate. "I guess I didn't answer that last question. Yes, I'm Summer Sanchez...or I used to be, and you're the one that wouldn't let me go."

"Not gonna apologize for that, but I will say I was sorry to hear about your father's passing. I followed his career since I was just a little kid. I saw you ride in Burwell a couple of years ago. You put on an impressive show. You still barrel racing?"

Summer felt her own jaw tighten. Guy sure asked a lot of questions. If she hadn't owed him so much, she'd have refused to answer any of them. As it stood, he'd effectively just saved her life, so she drew a deep breath and reached for the whiskey bottle. After downing a swallow, she shook her head. "No, I'm not racing anymore, and thanks for what you said about my father. I didn't really know him that well, and when I did know him he was an asshole." She shrugged.

And there it was, the concern and the sympathy she hated displayed in his gorgeous eyes fringed by deep black eyelashes that slowly blinked in the understanding that her dad may have been Mitchum Sanchez, rodeo king, greatest bareback bronc rider in the U.S., but he wasn't much of a father.

"I'm sorry," Austin offered her.

"Not your fault." She took another slight sip of the whiskey, still careful not to drink too much.

"Hey, uh, I'm sick to death of this bar, and honestly, this entire town. Wanna go see if we can find a steakhouse? Riding makes me hungry, so I'm starved. You just said you hadn't eaten."

Glancing around, Summer weighed her options. Austin Camden had the reputation of being a nice guy; a little cocky, but what bull rider wasn't? She studied him. Yeah, he was a nice guy, but there was a definite edge in his gaze. Intensity broadcast from every chiseled plane of his body. He radiated masculinity and sex appeal. Sure, she'd be safe enough with him, and she *was* starving, but her heart might not survive. He was far too tempting, and it had been so, so long.

They wouldn't be out too long. She could go by Brant's room to check on everything when they got back. Brant would probably be out all night long, asshole that he was. Her stomach answered before she could accept the invite. An embarrassingly loud growl rolled in her gut.

Laughing at her outright, Austin hopped off the tailgate. "Come on. Just dinner. I'm not asking for anything more than that. Let's get away from Brant and all the other shit going on in there." He gestured back to the bar.

"Yeah, okay, but just dinner."

CHAPTER TWO

Mesmerized, Austin watched Summer inhale the large cheeseburger and plateful of fries—the best fries he'd had outside of Nebraska. They'd made quick work of the jalapeno cheese things he'd ordered as an appetizer. Summer seemed to like the spice, and he grew more intrigued with her with each passing moment.

He'd spent the better part of ten minutes trying to get her to order the steak he knew she wanted. She'd refused. Stubborn. He grinned in spite of himself. Her eyes closed and a soft moan of satisfaction escaped her as she took the center bite of the burger.

Damn, damn, damn. He quelled a groan of his own just watching her. She hadn't been terribly forthcoming with information as of yet, but he was having more fun with her than he'd had in months.

"So, if you're not barrel racing anymore, did you just come to see the show?" he finally asked when she'd mopped up her beautiful mouth, licking her full, pink lips, making his Wranglers uncomfortably tight.

"I, uh, didn't make it to the rodeo tonight. I was...busy. I heard them announce your score though. Congratulations."

"Thanks. Your ex wanted my bull checked." Austin rolled his eyes.

"Yeah, well anytime somebody ain't rimming Brant's pansy ass he starts whining and pitching a fit like a two-year-old."

Austin couldn't help but chuckle at her vehemence and her filthy mouth. He was more than aware that he might've just stumbled upon the world's most perfect woman, for him anyway. His heart still couldn't seem to locate a steadying beat, and his entire body ached to hold her against him again.

"Good for you for pissing him off. I knew I liked you." A slight pink heat formed on her cheeks from her admittance.

A smirk formed rapidly on his features. So she liked him, did she? He'd sure take that. "You still living in New Mexico?"

Summer glanced at the well-worn carpeting in the steakhouse and then at a couple entering through the pane-glass doors. "No, not really."

Damn, girl wasn't giving anything away. Desperate to get something out of her, he considered. Maybe if he let a little slack out in the rope. Gave a little something to get something back. "You know, I never thought I'd be saying this, but honestly I can't wait to get back home. I miss the ranch. Never tell my old man I said that, though."

He earned a genuine chuckle. "Yeah, that was the part I always hated about barrel racing. I used to worry over Mama and the farm." Pain darkened her whiskey-brown eyes and stiffened her entire body. "We used to rent a little house on the McCallisters' farm in Bernalillo. Mama kept up with all of their youngins. They let me ride."

Her words were haunted and quick, like the sting was too much for her to bear. Austin reached and gently squeezed the hand she held in a tight fist against the table. His thumb soothed the tender skin he encountered. A wild spark of electricity shot up his arm and hit him squarely in the chest. His breath snared in his lungs. What the hell did this woman have that made him react this way? Pleased she'd finally given him something, he leaned in. "Is that why you quit racing? You needed to get back to your mama?"

"No." And there it was. One word. Nothing more. She shut him out again, just like that. Austin knew Mitchum had never married Summer's mother. In fact, no one knew Summer even existed until she'd ridden her own birth announcement, twenty years after the blessed event, into an arena in Santa Fe on a calico quarter horse right about the time her father was showing off his belt buckle.

She rounded the hell outta the third barrel, the crowd leapt to their feet, and she proved her birth name in every possible way. The next generation of Sanchez rode in like a bolt of lightning. Wild child, so everyone said. He wondered what her father had thought of that. Up until that moment, he'd assumed Mitchum had gotten her into rodeo, but after her declaration that she didn't know her father and her feeling that he was an asshole, he wondered just what Summer Sanchez was doing such a good job of trying to conceal.

"You didn't get hurt, did you?" Barrel racing was hard as hell. Something about her being thrown or injured made him restless. Panic churned in his gut.

After a dramatic eye roll she gave him an incredulous glare. "Do I look like I don't know how to ride, Camden?"

Chuckling and shaking his head, another smirk formed readily on his lips as he winked at her. "No, honey, you sure as hell look like you *know* how to ride."

She tried to conceal a slight grin and mean mugged him instead. "Everyone gets thrown, bound to happen sooner or later. You're gonna land on your ass sometime. Don't think you won't."

"I ride bulls for a livin', darlin'. I land on my ass most every night. I've broken every damn bone in my body, some of 'em twice. 'Sides, it's not the fall..."

"It's the way you get back up. Yeah, so I've been told."

Austin signaled the waitress and pointed to Summer's empty glass of Coke. "If I'm not being too forward, how the hell did a smart, beautiful woman that can ride a horse like nobody's business end up with the likes of Brantley Preston?"

Cocking her jaw to the side, she stared him down. "Guess I figured I hadn't done enough in my life to regret."

Before Austin could formulate a response, she threw another nervous glance around the relatively quiet steakhouse. "So, uh, where's your ranch? Who runs it for you while you're playing rodeo hero?"

"Damn, woman, conversations with you are like riding a roller-coaster that's come off the track. I'm from a little town in Nebraska no one's ever heard of. My whole family owns the ranch. My parents still run everything, but I have a litter of brothers and sisters, and heck, even a cousin and his wife, that run everything. I go back when the season's over."

"Not enough excitement working cattle? You gotta get your fix trying to kill yourself on a ballsy bull? Prove you're really living."

He couldn't figure out a thing about her, but she certainly had his number.

"Something like that...maybe."

There was some sense of distant understanding in the wildfire that glowed from her eyes. Like maybe, at one time, she'd had the same need for the fix.

"I kind of figured you were from Oklahoma, where your sponsors are."

So, she'd noticed him enough to know about Minton. Interesting.

"Yeah, everyone thinks that. I never bother to correct anyone. Let 'em think I'm from Tulsa. I don't give a damn. I'm not here to put Pleasant Glen on the map."

"Pleasant Glen." A sweet smile appeared on her beautiful lips. "That sounds nice."

"Yeah, it is nice. Grew up working my ass off. Never really realized there was anything outside of the Glen, to tell you the truth. I thought everybody got up at four and fed cattle, got soaked when it rained, tanned our own hides every summer out in the fields, and ate enough for four city-boys every night at supper. I was sure that's what everyone did."

"I kind of think everyone should." Summer bit her bottom lip as if she might've given too much away.

"Agreed." Austin wished the table between them away. He wanted to wrap her up in his arms. Tell her that whatever had her looking so damn sad he'd make it go away. Need weighted his entire body. His muscles ached with it.

"If you don't mind, I kind of need to get back to...my room," she spoke again without meeting his gaze. Lying? Maybe.

There were a few bites of filet left on his plate. Desire had kept him at half-mast for the entire meal. He didn't want their evening to be over just yet. He cut a hunk of the perfectly prepared steak. "All right, I'll take you back, but you have to try this first. It's delicious." He held the fork to her lips as she narrowed her eyes. "Come on, I'm not force feeding you gruel. It's a fucking filet."

Rolling her eyes, she parted those luscious lips and accepted the meat. Her eyes closed again as it filled her mouth. Austin clenched his own jaw and watched her work the steak in her mouth. His cock damn near severed the zipper of his old blue jeans.

"Damn, that is good," she admitted with a soft sexy sigh.

"I told you. Next time, I'm ordering for you Miss '*I just want a cheeseburger*.'"

"Next time?" She was quick to resurrect the guards she constantly clung to.

"Hell yeah. I plan on making bank tomorrow night at the finals. Come out and celebrate with me, then you're coming to Cheyenne, right? Everyone goes to Cheyenne."

"Yeah, I'm going to Cheyenne." She rolled her eyes.

Austin ignored her disdain, since it didn't seem directed at him. "Perfect, then I can court you all over Cheyenne Frontier Days. You were married to Brant Preston, so I'm assuming you have no idea what a real man is capable of, honey. Let me show you."

"Court me? What year are you livin' in? And my God, you're all the same. So, you just up and think I'm gonna follow you around Cheyenne licking your..."

Austin raised his left eyebrow in wicked intrigue. "What might you be thinking about licking, doll baby?"

She rolled her eyes. "Ugh, your bull-inflicted wounds and massaging your ego just because you bought me dinner?"

Refusing defeat, he shook his head. "This dinner has nothing to do with me wanting to get to know you better, Summer. What's wrong with that? Unless you got somebody else waiting somewhere I don't know about, or you really hate me as much as you'd like me to believe you do, why can't I take you out?"

"A lot of reasons, Austin, and I don't hate you." She choked over the last few words. The truth must've been difficult to swallow.

"Then give me a chance. I don't need my ego massaged or my

wounds licked. I have several other things I'd far rather your efforts go to if you're offering."

"I need to go."

You do not like him. He is not sexy and sweet, no matter how fucking good he looks in those Wranglers and boots. You do not want to see what's bulged behind that belt buckle. Summer drew another deep breath, trying to regain her balance. She almost whimpered out loud when her lungs filled with pine-scented, leather-infused, rosin-laced heat that was all Austin.

Against her own orders, her traitorous eyes stole another glance at his very impressive package, evident behind that belt buckle he wore so well. God, it would feel so good. A lifetime ago, or so it seemed, she would have jumped into his bed and let him show off all of his skills. There was no doubt he had them. Sexual prowess practically oozed from his pores. She would've met him at the door to his hotel room wearing nothing but cowgirl boots, a G-string, and a smile, and she would've loved every minute of it. She could've taught him a thing or two about taming a girl that liked it hot, hard, and wild in bed. A lifetime ago.

That girl had disappeared right along with everything else in her life. She stared out the windows of his fancy truck, trying to formulate a plan. Letting him know she didn't actually have a hotel room was not an option. His protective nature was more than evident in every motion of his body. She sensed it every time his hand gently eased to the small of her back to guide her into and out of the restaurant, the way he opened the truck door for her, and in the way he shot predatory glares at that guy in the steakhouse that had noticed her when they walked in.

"I'm staying at the Super 8," she lied with relative ease.

His brow furrowed. "You're not at the Cody? I thought everyone in for the rodeo was at the Cody."

"No...they were booked up."

A thousand questions played in his gorgeous black eyes, but he just nodded. She half wished he'd demand to know her story. Keeping it all shut up inside her head was slowly killing her. She was dissolving in the lies and constant war she'd created for herself. Maybe she should take him up on his offer to hang out in Cheyenne. It'd make the hours when Brant had J.J. go by faster. She liked talking to Austin. She even liked arguing with him. She wished she could've shared more, but that just wasn't smart. She had to stop thinking with her heart. That only got her into trouble.

He slowly pulled into the parking lot of the Super 8. "Can I walk you in? I swear I'm not trying to get in your bed, Summer. I'm trying to be a gentleman." He gently squeezed her thigh and stared into her eyes as if that might prove his manners and good breeding.

Yeah, a gentleman cowboy. I didn't think they even manufactured those anymore. "Thank you for dinner and everything, really, but I'm a big girl. I don't need anyone lookin' after me." Before he could argue, she leapt out of the truck. She felt the heat of his gaze as she quickly made her way inside the hotel lobby. He watched over her until she disappeared from his sight. Ducking down a corridor, she watched him sit in the parking lot staring at the door, contemplating following her, she suspected.

Just go, Austin, please. Her heart sped in her panic until his truck turned slowly and drove away. Mentally counting to 195, his overall score for Cody, she knew immediately why that number stuck in her head, she spun and headed back toward the front door. God, she really was an idiot.

"Ma'am, did you need some help?" the woman at the front desk inquired.

"No, thanks. I'm good." Another lie rolled off her tongue. It chafed at her throat. She was far from good. Heading out into the thick Wyoming summer air, she tried to steady her racing heart. Dodging the yellow glows cast by the streetlights, she headed towards The Cody Hotel. It was over a mile away. Austin would be there and in his room long before she arrived.

CHAPTER THREE

"Austin," Jackson's voice stabbed through Austin's drowning confusion as soon as he stepped inside the Cody Hotel.

"Yeah, man, what's up?" Truthfully, he couldn't have cared less. Summer consumed his every thought. What the hell was up with her anyway? He knew she liked him. She'd said that, and that sexy little blush that followed her statement was proof enough. Trained to notice the most minute detail of any situation he was in, since that's how you stayed alive on an angry bull, he'd caught her checking out his package more than once in the truck. He certainly hadn't needed any training to notice that her nipples tightened and her breath picked up pace when he'd squeezed her thigh, simply unable to keep his hands off of her any longer.

"Bunnies moved the party from the bar to the pool. Come on. They're waiting on you."

Austin shuddered and swallowed back bile. God, no more women throwing themselves at him. No more humid hotel pools that felt like dirty bath water. All he wanted was a cold shower and time to think. Technically, that wasn't true. All he wanted was Summer Sanchez in his room, in his bed, safe in his arms with her hot breath teasing his chest while he made her forget everything that had ever made her sad. As that wasn't currently an option, the cold shower scenario was the next best thing.

Before he could bail on Jackson, he spotted Brant Preston through the windows that enclosed the pool. He was sweet talking two of the bunnies who were hanging all over him. Hmm, maybe the pool wasn't a bad idea. He sure as hell wasn't getting in and the bunnies could have Brant, right after Austin used him to figure out how he'd gotten Summer Sanchez to be his for however long they'd been married.

An hour later, when Brant proved far too wasted to provide any coherent information, Austin made his escape from the hotel pool. He pried some chick named Sasha off of his forearm and sped toward the elevators.

When the doors opened on the upper floor, he stepped onto the plush carpeting and halted abruptly. *What the hell?* Rushing his steps, he headed toward Summer, seated on the floor with her head in her hands right outside Brant Preston's hotel room.

"Summer?" He stood in front of her. She wasn't escaping until she explained herself. "What the hell are you doing in front of Brant's suite?"

She lifted those eyes that he swore held the secrets of the whole damn universe and stared at him. The wildfire he'd seen there before was gone. Pain and fear broadcast from every square inch of her beautiful body.

"Talk, darlin'. Because I'm trying to keep my cool, but if I'm about to find out that you just walked way over a mile in the dark from the hotel you had me leave you at with ten-dozen half-drunk assholes out and about in this tourist-trap town looking for something sweet to take a'holt of, I'm gonna have something to say about it. I thought you hated Brant."

She swallowed, and he edged closer. Rubbing her hands over her eyes, she slumped and then returned her gaze to his. "I do hate Brant. I always did."

"Then why are you looking to get in his room?"

"I'm not." She stared up at him, narrowing her eyes defiantly. "I'm in front of Brant's room...because my little boy is in there."

If she'd backhanded him, he wouldn't have been more shocked. "Come again?"

The tremble of her shoulders marked her shuddered breath. "My baby, J.J., is in Brant's room, and I don't have a room...anywhere."

A volatile mixture of anger, protectiveness, and confusion swirled in his gut. "Get up." He held his hand out to help her off of the floor, but she didn't accept the help.

"Austin, I don't need some cowboy superhero to save me, okay?"

"Lucky for you my cape is at the dry cleaners. Now, get up."

When she didn't move, he leaned down and in one quick motion scooped under her arms and lifted her off of the hotel floor. "I have a suite with two beds. I also suspect that after the hike you decided you needed to take in eighty degree weather you might like a shower. I have one of those in my room, too. When you're finished with that, we're gonna talk. You may not need a superhero, Summer, but I'd say you sure as hell could use a friend. I'm taking the job."

"I can't..." she started to protest.

"Hush. You *can* sleep in a bed and take a shower. I will stay in my own bed. I'm not a douchebag, but I'm not taking no for an answer on this." With that he swept under her legs and carried her three doors down to his own room.

"You didn't have to carry me." She crossed her arms over her chest as soon as he got her inside.

"You're stubborn, and just in case you're wondering, you can't outrun me. Now, do you have bags somewhere? I have a hundred other questions, but we'll start there."

Her cheeks pinked with embarrassment, and Austin clenched his fists to keep from dragging her back into his arms and holding her until her confession made sense.

"I have *a* bag in my truck."

"Keys." He held out his hand. Begrudgingly, she dug in the pocket of those painted-on blue jeans that had been driving him wild all damn night and dropped a single key on an old Dodge keychain in his hand.

"Probably won't take you long to figure out which truck is mine."

"Good. Now, look at me."

She rolled her eyes but then landed them on him.

"You will be inside this hotel room when I get back, or so help me, when I find you, and I will, I'll turn you over my knee. I'm assuming that because your kid is across the hall you're not gonna skip town on me."

A huff of disdain lit the air between them. "You don't have to threaten me, Austin. I don't have anywhere to go. You could be nice. Thought you were a gentleman."

All right, so maybe he was being an ass, but every time he thought about her out in Cody in the dark of night after a rodeo with a thousand out-of-town cowboys in to watch the show and have a good time, it scared the shit out of him. God, what if she'd stumbled up on... He shut that thought down before his supper made a rapid reappearance. "I'll be right back."

When Austin reached the parking lot he headed right instinctively. "Damn it all to hell, Brant Preston, you are a motherfucking asshole," he spat in the stagnant air. The Dodge she'd hidden out near the hotel dumpsters should have been what was going in a compactor. If the thing cranked on the first turn, it'd cost God four miracles. He unlocked and then heaved the door open. *What kind of shit-sack lets the mother of his kid live without a fucking place to stay and drive this?* He located an old tack bag that contained a few pairs of jeans and a dozen tank tops and T-shirts. Panties and a bra were visible amongst the clothes. His mind spun, but he was too angry to really consider them. An economy-sized bottle of V-05 shampoo and conditioner along with dozens of hotel soaps were shoved in the front pockets where horse brushes were supposed to be stored, along with a small makeup bag.

The only thing in the truck worth owning was a car seat, facing backwards in the front seat. The rusted-out truck was manufactured four decades before the invent of an airbag, so that wasn't a problem.

Several blankets were crammed behind the bench seat. Another round of volatile fury rocketed through his veins as he considered the fact that she must've slept in the truck occasionally. He'd find Brant and fire-iron brand him until his personal Camden cattle marks were all over his sorry ass. Slamming the truck door, he ordered his temper to remain in control as he stomped back inside the hotel.

The universe was playing hot and fast with him that night,

however. Brant crossed his path on the way to one of the bunnies'
rooms on the first floor of the hotel. Austin clenched his jaw, but he
couldn't help himself. "Nice of you to bang your whores in their room
instead of in front of your kid, ass-wipe."

Brant spun, but the motion dizzied him. He held onto the wall to
remain upright. His confused blinks cost him precious time. "What'd
you say?"

"This." Austin drove his fist hard into Brant's gut using every ounce
of gall-driven fury the night had provided him, coupled with the kind
of strength it took to hold on to a bull for 8 seconds. Brant doubled
over with a sickly groan then slunk to the floor. Austin chuckled as
Brant tried to make out his face. He wouldn't even remember who'd
hit him come morning.

"Go to hell." Austin disappeared behind the closing elevator doors.
When he made it back to his own suite, Summer was standing with the
door open, staring at Brant's room.

After setting her bag on the desk, he spun and studied her. "How
old is J.J.?"

Her entire face lit in a beautiful smile. "He's eleven months. He's
crawling and pulling up. He wants to walk so bad he can't see straight,
but he hasn't quite figured it out yet."

Austin couldn't help but smile when she did. "Who watches J.J.
when Brant's...*working?*"

Summer all but gagged. "Brant's mama, who's a bigger bitch than
he is."

"Okay, I think I'm following along so far, honey, but why're you so
worried about him? Why do you keep watching Brant's room? Even
Preston wouldn't hurt his own kid."

"I know he wouldn't hurt him." Her smile disappeared. She trembled and squeezed her eyes shut, holding back tears with stubborn
resolve. Unable to remain rooted to the carpeting, Austin rushed to her
and wrapped her up in the strength of his arms like he'd wanted to do
all night long. All of the fight and fury he'd used to take out Brant left
him in an instant. He cradled her tenderly to him, let her bury her face
in his chest, and swayed.

"Shh, I've got you, okay? I'm right here, just tell me."

"I just…"

"You just?"

"It scares me when he isn't with me. Brant's mama is evil, Austin. She's awful. I don't know what she might do. I have a bad feeling."

Nodding, Austin considered. He knew a dozen pricks like Brant Preston. They'd pull a lot of shit to make other people's lives miserable, but they wouldn't hurt a kid. As for his mama, she must've raised Brant. Other than his parents coddling him up bad enough to turn him into a fucksqueak, he'd survived childhood.

Summer, however, had come up rough, without a daddy and working a farm that wasn't even hers. She also didn't even have a place to lay her head at night, so she had to be exhausted. It had to have been getting to her. You can't go on like that for long. Paranoia was clearly setting in.

"Okay, how does it work? You said when he isn't with me, so when *is* he with you?"

Pulling away from him, Summer sank down on one of the queen-sized beds in the room. "We were only married for three months. We divorced when I was pregnant with J.J. because he came home drunk one night and…"

Motherfucker, I should have stomped your balls through your ass and pulled them out your throat when I had the chance. Another round of rage spilled into Austin's blood stream. "And he what?"

Summer shook her head. Her jaw clenched and the fear haunted her eyes from the memory alone. All of Austin's guesses as to what Brant might've done made him sick.

"Anyway, Brant's trying to get full-custody of J.J. Right now, I get him a week and then he does. We go back and forth. If I miss a week, it looks bad to the courts. That's why I have to follow Brant around for all the rodeos. Brant's lawyer got him out of alimony because I filed for divorce. Child support covers a hotel room every other week but not much else. All of Brant's money is really his daddy's, but his mama's trying to make me run out of money so I can't pay my lawyer. It's all her doin'. I'm hoping that after Cheyenne, I can get a job in Dallas.

Find a place for us to live and settle down. That's what the courts want to see. I have to prove I can take care of J.J. and get him away from Brant's mother."

"When's it your turn with J.J. again?"

"He goes back and forth every Sunday night at six. I'll get him back in Cheyenne, the day before the events start." Finally meeting his eyes with her own, she gnawed her lip until Austin was concerned she was going to draw blood. "So, maybe if you wouldn't mind me sleeping here just for tonight, then I can drive on to Cheyenne tomorrow night. I'm staying with a friend there."

"Summer." Austin shook his head. "I'm not asking for anything other than for you to let me help you. I'd pay for you a room to yourself tonight if there was one available here, but there's not, and truth be told, I want you to stay with me. I need to know you're safe. I want to hear more about all of this, and like I told you, you need a friend. Will you please let me help take care of you and the baby? I stand to make full bonus in Cheyenne, and you know I'm walking out of Cody with bank. I've been winning all season, and I want to help."

"What do you want in return? No one's that nice." She drew her legs up and hugged them to her chest as if she might've been taking up too much room.

"Nothing, other than a chance to get to know you better. I don't know much about babies, but I'll figure it out." *She has a kid, dude, what the heck are you getting into?* One singular brain cell taunted him annoyingly. The rest of him felt the need to protect her with his life if it came to that. "Okay, maybe that's not totally true. Do I want more than a friendship with you? Hell, yeah. But what I want most is for us to see where this might go. I'm into you, Summer, after one meal. I think we could have something really good, sugar, but that's entirely up to you. You come to me if you want to do a little exploring. Otherwise just let me be there for you and for J.J."

For the first time in Austin's life, something was more important than looking for eight. Time extended beyond those eight-second increments he used for purposes of proving his worth. To his shock, it felt good. It felt right. He rode and existed entirely by his gut. This was what he was supposed to do. He could feel it. He'd never been more sure of anything. He just had to convince her of that. Some hint of the satisfaction he'd been searching for cemented in his soul.

A flash fire of intrigue lit once again in her eyes, but she quelled it quickly. "How are you into me? You don't even know me."

"My point exactly. I want to know you. I want to know you in my bed and out. I've never seen any point in not saying exactly what I'm thinking, so there you go. I want a chance, and I want to help. Everything beyond that is entirely up to you."

———

How the hell did I get here? Summer tried to let the steady flow of the shower water soothe her. She stood naked in front of the bathroom mirror, watching the white hotel shower curtain sway slightly. Her heart hammered in her chest, and she couldn't quite catch her breath in the humid bathroom.

None of this made any sense. She was staying in Austin Camden's hotel room, in front of a shower that she hadn't had to sneak in between the hotel maids' paths like she'd been doing all summer, and he'd readily admitted that he wanted more from her. He'd also seemed quite certain that even if she didn't want to jump in his bed, he still wanted to help her. *Who does that?* No one had ever wanted to help her.

Stepping into the shower and hiding herself behind the curtain made her able to accept the other complications with this situation she'd somehow stumbled into. She did want him. God, for just one night, she'd love nothing more than for Austin to make her forget the shit-hole that was currently her life.

Not that she didn't love and adore her son with everything she was, but it had been so long since she'd indulged her own wild soul. Slicked with the hotel soap, her hands glided over her breasts, landing in the underswells. Her nipples responded to the touch, almost as anxious as her mind to be tended. She tried not to notice the slight white stretch marks on the sides of her breasts. Tracking down her abdomen, she gave herself over to thoughts of Austin's hands making the same motion. Biting her bottom lip, she touched another set of marks on her hips, then swirled one finger through the wet curls covering her mound. Her clit all but begged her to parade out of the shower wrapped in nothing but a hand towel to take Austin up on his offer.

Doubting that he'd ever slept with a woman that was also a mother, she wasn't sure he'd know what to do with her scars. There were days she wore her stripes with pride. Her body had given her a child. The feminine strength and power of it all made her proud. Just like every cut, scrape, bruise and broken bone she'd endured barrel racing, the scars bore her something so precious they'd been more than worth it. At other times, like when Austin Camden was on the other side of the door, she wished her body more closely resembled something you might see in a magazine.

She shook her head and refused to pity herself. Other than the mercy fucks she'd given Brant, he'd had absolutely nothing to do with getting their baby into the world. Hell, he hadn't even shown up at the hospital when she'd delivered J.J. It was all her. He hadn't wanted anything to do with their son until his mother had gotten involved. *Just two more nights and you get J.J. back.* Then she'd be able to remember that everything was about the baby. He was all that mattered, not that she begrudged him that at all. It was just easier to trap away her own needs when J.J. was in her arms.

Impatience twisted in Austin's gut as he stared at the bathroom door. *You might as well shut it down, moron. She ain't putting out tonight.* He knew that. He reminded himself constantly, but he could hope, couldn't he?

His tongue wanted to know her taste. His hands need to feel those curves and the wet heat he could elicit from between her sweet thighs. *I could make her drip, make her sloppy for me.*

Thankful the shower water was still pouring full-stream, it covered the hungry groan he couldn't order away. He wanted to grip that sexy ass while he drove himself into her, leaving his own branding marks in every hidden-away place he longed to make his own. She had wildfire in her eyes and untamable lust in those luscious curves. He tried to remember that she had a kid. She was quite effectively someone's mother. Being J.J.'s mom sure as hell didn't mean she wasn't all woman, however.

His mind wandered over thoughts of when she'd last been worshipped and adored. Certainly never in Brant Preston's bed. He wouldn't know what to do with a woman like Summer if she'd written him an instruction manual.

She may not like your savage style, Camden. Don't get ahead of yourself. Before he could come up with some excuse for that, Summer stepped out of the bathroom. His mouth suddenly felt like the Mojave. Her wet hair clung to the white tank top she'd pulled on. The steam from the shower made the top all but translucent. Her rosy nipples were losing a seductive game of peek-a-boo, since her bra was tucked in the pile of dirty clothes she was clinging to like a security blanket. She made a valiant effort to keep herself covered.

When his eyes landed on the blue jeans she'd pulled on, his brow furrowed. Understanding hit him a moment later. "I'm gonna go ahead and assume that if I weren't sharing this room with you, you wouldn't be wearing them blue jeans to bed."

"I'm not sleeping in nothing but my panties with you, Austin. I really appreciate everything you're doing for me, but I'm not that kind of girl...anymore."

Anymore? What does that mean? "Does that mean I can't sleep in the buff?" He winked at her as he headed to the one drawer of the dresser where he'd shoved all his clothes. Locating a long V-neck undershirt, he handed it to her.

Shame rose violently in her eyes. "I can't take that."

"I brought every T-shirt I own with me when I left the ranch back in March. I have more than enough to share. I want you to really sleep, Summer. Be comfortable for me...and with me."

"Thanks," she muttered. Setting her dirty clothes in a pile on the floor, she accepted the T-shirt. "Are you really going to sleep naked?" The words seem to leap from her mouth before she could quite catch them.

Chuckling and giving her his wickedest grin, he waggled his eyebrows. "I'll be under the covers when you finish changing. You're welcome to come and see, darlin'."

"Cocky bastard," made its way through her extremely intrigued grin.

Delighted, Austin laughed outright. "Invitation is always open."

On her next emergence from the bathroom, he made no effort to hide his hungry groan. He caught a peek of some bikini panties when she rushed to her bed, but his T-shirt swamped her delectable little body. Her left shoulder was visible in the gaping collar and her breasts taunted the fabric.

She rolled her eyes at his appreciation.

"You do know you're drop-dead gorgeous, right?" he huffed.

"I'm not gorgeous." She shook her head and concealed the lower half of her body with the sheets and blankets on her bed. "I'm a mom." The last three words strangled in her throat.

Austin sat up and stared at her. "You being a mom doesn't make you not sexy as hell, Summer. Did Brant Preston put that shit in your mind? I shoulda pounded his ass twice."

"Twice?" she gasped. "Wait, does that mean you did once?"

Keep your mouth shut, Camden.

"Austin?"

"Mighta let my fist fly in the hallway when he was on his way to another room. He more than deserved it."

"Oh my God, Austin, you are aware he can keep you from riding, right? He's a jackass. He'd do it just to be a prick."

"Brant Preston can do whatever the hell he wants to me. He starts messing with you, I'll have something to say about it. I'll do the talking. He'll do the crying." He studied her eyes. Shock, appreciation, hope, and worth all fought for dominance in their whiskey depths.

She shook her head. "I know you want to help me. Thank you. I could never really say thank you enough. I know that, but..."

"That bothers you." He called her on it.

"What bothers me?"

"It bothers you that you don't think you can thank me enough." Austin stood from his bed, revealing the fact that he'd left his boxers on despite his teasing.

Sinking down beside her, he brushed her damp hair behind her shoulders. He longed to kiss the frown on her beautiful lips away, but he leashed his lust for the moment. "You don't have to thank me at all, honey. I just want to hang out with you, like I said. I don't expect anything in return. You've already thanked me enough."

"I haven't, and I can't, but please, Austin, don't get yourself thrown out of Cheyenne because of me." Her jaw clenched for a split second and she closed her eyes as if she were damming something back.

"What? Just say whatever you're thinking."

"Don't give up something you really want, something you've worked so hard to get, for me or anyone else. You'll regret it for the rest of your life."

"I'm not giving anything up for anyone, sweetness. Don't worry about me. Let me worry over you. That's what I want. You want to thank me for it? Come cheer me on tomorrow night and then hang out with me while we're in Cheyenne. We'll take J.J. around to see the sights."

"I'd really like that, but I can't afford a ticket for tomorrow night, or to any of the shows in Cheyenne." Regret ate at her words.

"Summer, honey," Austin rolled his eyes. He gently placed both hands on either side of her beautiful face and lifted her gaze to his. "You will come with me as my personal guest. If they want you to have a ticket, which they won't, I will buy you one. On that note, anytime we hang out I'm paying."

"Little chauvinistic don't you think?"

"Stubborn as hell. Damn, but you turn me on, woman. Chauvinistic? Maybe. But those are my rules."

"Did I really break your toe?" Debate played in her eyes, like she wasn't certain if she should feel badly about stomping on his foot. He laughed.

"I've had much worse, believe me. I'm a rodeo cowboy, honey, not a pussy. I'll be just fine. I'll take a kiss, though. That'd sure make it feel better."

Shaking her head at him, she narrowed her eyes with a hint of that seductive grin playing at the corners of her lush mouth. He wanted to kiss her more than he wanted to draw his next breath. "I'd love to come see you ride tomorrow night. I've been watching you from the gates for the last five rodeos. Be nice not to feel like a loser standing outside."

"You're never a loser no matter where you're standing, do you understand me?"

A single nod was her only response. He couldn't stand it. He couldn't bear the doubt she clung to, the shit she'd endured, that she somehow didn't understand how desirable she was.

Pulling his left hand away from her face, he used his right to trace the soft angles of her cheek. Leaning in, he paused for one second to appreciate the fact that her breathing quickened as soon as he touched her. He took her lips with a slow, greedy kiss. She tensed, but then melted into him.

She tasted like sweet strawberry wine. His tongue teased the seam of her mouth, and to his delight, she opened for him. He groaned into her mouth before his tongue moved with hers in an exploratory dance.

Her hands slipped down his shoulders and pulled at his biceps, like she desperately wanted more of him. His cock stirred anxiously as he wrapped her up tight against him. She clung to him. It was heavenly.

When she gasped for breath, he pulled back and whispered a few kisses on her swollen lips, then down her chin, not allowing himself to go any further, though he longed to sink his teeth into that section of skin where her neck and shoulder joined. She buried her face in his neck and he held her, cradling her, giving her a place to exist in any format she needed.

A full-minute later, she lifted her head and stared into his eyes. "Thought you were a gentleman, cowboy." She smirked, and another seductive round of heat bloomed across her cheeks.

Chuckling, he stood, certain she noted his tented boxers. If he sat there any longer, he was gonna push her much further than she was ready to go. "Gotta have a good-night kiss so you have sweet dreams. You deserve those. And a gentleman is nothing more than a patient wolf, darlin', never forget that. Go to sleep. I'll be right here if you need me."

Getting back in his bed alone was the hardest thing he'd ever done, and he rode bulls for a living. Sleep wasn't likely to come easy with her a mere three feet away from him and his every sense filled with her.

God, he needed another fix. Needed to get high on those lips. He envied the sheets of her bed. They were getting to enjoy her ass and pussy tucked between them. Had his kiss made her wet? Was she slick and fevered? Drenched for him? He longed to fill his lungs with the scent of her arousal while he filled his mouth with her juices. His jaw tensed as she leaned to turn off the lamp between them.

CHAPTER FOUR

Restless, Austin lifted his phone from the bedside table. 2:07 *I gotta go to sleep or I'm gonna be useless tomorrow.* He checked Summer once more. Her breathing was still steady. Deep in slumber, she was even drooling a little. A whispered chuckle escaped him. Good. She needed to sleep, and she clearly felt safe enough with him to let her worries go and really rest.

Laying back in his own bed, he ordered himself to sleep, but his thoughts existed in a tumbled mass in his mind. *"I just knew, right then, soon as I laid eyes on her."* His father, his grandfather, his great-grandfather, several of his great-uncles—all told basically the same tale.

His dad saw his mother in a broken down car on the side of the road, talked her into coming back to the ranch, and that had been that. He'd known from the moment he'd laid eyes on her. His grandfather's story was similar; saw his grandmother at the Montgomery Ward in Lincoln and he'd been sold, hook, line, and sinker. Hell, even his cousin Brock said he'd fallen in love with his wife, Hope, the moment she'd walked into a high school Chem lab. It'd taken him a decade to get his head out of his ass and do something about it, but the Camden legend had proven true once again.

Until the moment he'd wrapped his arms around Summer Sanchez's waist at the Silver Dollar Honkytonk, he'd thought the stories were some crap they all used to get their women to swoon over them. Life just didn't go that way. Or did it? He stared at Summer sleeping soundly in the bed next to his. Could it?

With a deep yawn, he willed the Camden family stories away and squeezed his eyes shut. He had to get some sleep.

The nightmare always started the same way. With his laughter interrupted by the sluice of the windshield wipers. Street lights collided with headlights from other cars as they joined the rain in the reflective assault on the windshield. The high pitched squeal ricocheted between his ears.

Summer gasped and leapt from the bed. *J.J.?* Frantically she scanned the room. Where was the portable crib? Her heart thundered against her ribcage. She started to scream. It took two seconds to remember where she was.

Austin's body jerked. He gripped the corner of the mattress. "*No!*" tore from his lips in a horrified peal, but he wasn't awake. Summer gripped her own chest. Emotion cinched her throat. She knew a thing or two about nightmares. *Poor guy.* She wanted to know what frightened him badly enough to make him react this way. She wanted to make it go away.

Without hesitation, she eased to his side and shook his broad shoulders. "Austin, wake up. It's okay." His right leg kicked something away. She didn't know what, but she shook harder, desperate to rescue him from whatever had him in its clutches. "Austin," she spoke with more tonality. "It's me. Wake up. You're okay."

He sat up, gasping for breath.

"Shh, it's okay." Summer embraced him, and to her shock, he clung to her like his life's blood depended on holding her close. Maybe she wasn't the only one that needed a friend. A moment later, he came to and jerked away from her.

"Sorry." He refused to meet her concerned gaze. Embarrassed, she knew. No rodeo bull rider wanted anyone to know that they were ever afraid. *Men.* She shook her head. They were all just little boys in bigger bodies.

Studying the still-tensed muscles of his pecs and shoulders and then the decadent roll of muscles down his back, she allowed that some of them were *much* better looking than others. But at heart, most of them, the non-assholes at least, still had the heart of a little boy and occasionally needed a little encouragement and a little tending.

He'd never admit to her that he'd been scared or tell her what the nightmare had been about. Not yet. But he was also still clinging to her forearm. Mm-hmm. She knew precisely what to do. "You okay?"

"I'm fine," he lied.

Don't roll your eyes. Don't do it. She nodded. "You didn't wake me up or anything. I couldn't sleep. Just kind of cold and…" The fear she summoned was always there. Accessing it wasn't difficult. And there he was. The terror in his darkened eyes evaporated immediately replaced with worry over her.

"Hey, come here to me." He reclined and pulled her onto his chest. She hid her mischievous grin. That worked quicker than she'd thought. He tucked them in with the sheets and blankets and dragged his fingers through her long hair. "That better, sugar?"

She sighed. God that felt good. The nerve endings on her scalp were elated with his magic fingers. He ignited feelings in her she had no business feeling, contentment being one.

"I've got you. Don't have to be anywhere in the mornin'. Just let me hold you while you sleep, okay?"

Okay, maybe her little ploy hadn't all been a lie. Sleeping in a cold bed all alone was nothing compared to being here, enveloped in his masculine heat with a pillow of firm muscle beneath her head, tucked safely in his well-developed arms.

Unable to help herself, she snuggled closer, inhaling deeply of his musk. She'd never felt safer, and she hardly knew Austin. She'd think about that in the morning. Right now, she was going to enjoy the feeling that they might really be able to take care of one another, for a little while at least.

The next time Summer awoke, she grinned. Austin was on his hands and toes on the carpet, wearing nothing but some old sweat-shorts, pumping out push-ups with ease. If that wasn't a mighty fine thing to wake up to, she didn't know what was.

She watched the chiseled muscles of his back contract and pull. Her gaze traveled down to his tight ass, clenching when he pushed his body upwards. She saved the best for last. She watched his arms, dear God those arms. Bull riders had to have mega-muscles to hang on for their lives, but they weren't like body builders whom she found unappealing. They had long, lean muscle, chiseled perfectly from their chests all the way to their hands.

Austin's biceps and forearms were a sight to behold, tensing as he lifted his body and lowered it back almost to the floor. She followed the masculine column of hair that ran down his arms until her gaze landed on his hands, wide, capable, strong, and then his fingers. Her breaths picked up pace when she thought about what he could most certainly do with his fingers.

"Like what you see, Ms. Sanchez?"

So, he was aware she was awake and watching him. "Working off some pent up *need* there, cowboy?"

He leapt to his feet, all traces of the fear that had consumed him in the middle of the night vanished, replaced with his devilish good looks and wicked grin. "Hell yeah, sunshine. I woke up with a beautiful woman tucked up against me, one who hasn't quite given me the go-ahead to wake her up the way I'd like to. Had to do something, and I already jacked off in the shower...twice."

"You're so full of shit," she came right back, but the lift of his left eyebrow and quirk of his lips said maybe he was that potent. Dear Lord, what must that be like? Her heart tripped over its next several beats. How exactly had he *wanted* to wake her up?

Her clit twitched against the fabric of *his* T-shirt, reminding her of how long it had been ignored. Could she somehow manage to both be a good mom to J.J. and to find out just what Austin Camden was made of?

"Get up, woman. I'm hungry. Let's go get breakfast, then I need to get my draw, find out which bull I'm riding tonight. After that, we'll go see what kind of trouble we can get into out here in Cody, Wyoming."

Grinning, she crawled out of bed, delighted that she didn't have to spend another day doing nothing more than walking listlessly around Cody, counting the moments until J.J. was hers again.

"I hope it's not Dallas Devil." The concern replaced her moment of excitement over his plans for the day. She was beyond certain that her asshole ex was doping that stupid bull. He didn't give a damn that cowboys were being hurt. Proving that he was giving Dallas Devil steriods would be next to impossible, but his daddy wanted a winning bull, and Brant wanted nothing more than to make his father happy. She'd been planning to snoop around the chutes in Cheyenne to see if she could get Brant caught. If she could get him in trouble, his claim on J.J. would come into question in court.

Austin planted a kiss on top of her head. "No worries. No matter which one it is, I whisper meat-packing horror stories to all of 'em before the chute opens." He winked at her as she cracked up. It felt so good to laugh again. She tried to recall the last time she'd done that.

Getting ready quickly, she took a moment to admire Austin's ass in a clean pair of Wranglers, along with his boots, his muscular chest in a button-down shirt, and the dirty Stetson that set off his chiseled jawline. A real cowboy. One that knew how to ride *and* how to work his ass off. One that was protective at all personal cost, even if he had a few demons that occasionally kept him from sleeping. And one that kissed with enough fire to brand her mouth all for himself. What woman could possibly resist that? She wasn't certain she could for much longer.

To her relief, when Austin pulled his papers that morning, he'd been paired with a bull named Perfect Storm. She'd never heard of that particular bull before, but he was owned by K&D so he was probably as safe as any bull could ever really be. Austin seemed pleased with his draw.

They had breakfast at Buffalo Bill's diner, along with a dozen other cowboys that were tired of the breakfast buffet at the Cody hotel. She'd watched in awe while Austin downed a mountain of flapjacks, three fried eggs, a slab of bacon, a platter of hash browns, and two cups of black coffee.

"Good thing you don't have to make weight to ride a bull," she harassed him.

"I told you I was hungry, sugar. I'm not a sissy-ass kid, or worse—a stock supplier from Dallas. I'm a cowboy. I eat." He'd chuckled as she watched him consume enough calories to get him through the day and giggled over his slight towards Brant.

When he finished, he grinned at her. "Now, what would the lady like to do today?"

"I don't care. You don't have to entertain me. I can find something to do on my own."

"Summer, honey, do you have some kind of hearing problem? How many times do I have to say I want to hang out with you today, tomorrow, and for the next two weeks in Cheyenne? After that, we'll see where we stand, but for now, please stop acting like I'm sacrificing something to be around you. From where I'm sitting, I have the best damn view in Wyoming and the best conversation going."

So, he wasn't thinking beyond Cheyenne. Summer told herself she should be relieved, but he refused to look at her. The husky tone of his voice shifted when he'd added that last part.

He was lying to her. She was almost sure of it. She and J.J. didn't need anyone else. Hanging out with Austin could be some kind of summer rodeo fling, like the ones she had before her daddy and Brant had come up with their ridiculous plan. Surely, he didn't really want more than that anyway.

As long as Austin was good with J.J., it would be fine. They could part ways when he won the Cheyenne buckle, which she was certain he would.

Once Austin wasn't around anymore, she could focus on getting a job. It would be for the best. Disappointment ate at her resolve. She called herself stupid for even imaging that Austin would want anything other than a fling. Lying to herself had taken on a numbing effect as of late anyway. She ignored the pain that bottomed out in her stomach. She would be fine, and so would he. It would never work out beyond Cheyenne.

———

That afternoon, Austin grinned as he guided Summer closer to the counter at Main Street Ice Cream. Every time he placed his hand somewhere on her body, electricity amplified in his veins. He couldn't wait to find out what touching something far more provocative than the small of her back, her hands, or her shoulders would be like.

Unable to hide his smirk, he turned to her. "Chocolate or vanilla, honey? What's your preference?"

Her jaw cocked to the side, meaning she'd picked up on his double entendre and precisely what he wanted to know. Those seductive whiskey eyes glimmered with challenge.

"Are those my only two choices, cowboy?" Her sassy tone spiked his blood.

"Hell no. I just need to know what you might like before I...order something for you."

"Uh huh. Well, to be perfectly honest, I'd say I'm more a vanilla sundae kind of girl. I like a lot of something extra in my vanilla. I want to know I've had...*ice cream* after I've had it. You know, chocolate syrup, some nuts, loads of candy, and maybe a hot red cherry or two on top. How 'bout yourself?"

He leaned in to let the low growl building in his chest sound in her ear. "You're killing me, babe."

"We're just talking about ice cream, right?" Her play at innocence and the soft purr of her voice was the sexiest damn thing he'd ever heard.

"Definitely not," his voice turned to the consistency of the gravel parking lot of the ice cream shop.

"Good." She stared him down, and he was momentarily concerned he was going to come in his jeans.

They edged forward in line and he wrapped his arms around her waist from behind her, crowding her, letting her feel every hardened plane of his hungry body. "I want you so fucking bad, Summer. I've wanted you from the moment I kept you from scalping your ex last night."

Turning her head, she lifted her darkened eyes to his. Need was penned on every curve of her delectable body. Her nipples made themselves known despite the bra and vintage Wrangler T-shirt she was wearing. Tight and needy. His mouth watered.

His hot breath caressed her right ear as he roved his hands over her hips and soft midsection. His voice was still husky from her earlier declaration as he whispered, "Tonight, sugar. After I ride, after I win, I'm taking you to my bed. I'll give you every single thing you need, and I'll take every single thing I've craved since the moment I laid eyes on you. Trust me, you'll know you've been fucked thoroughly come mornin' when you wake up naked in my arms."

She trembled against him, shivering in need. "Yes," panted from her. Her eyes closed momentarily, and she leaned back against him in a vow of surrender. It drove him wild.

"That's it, darlin'. You lay back against me. Let me hold you while you think about how good it's gonna be. Let it make you wet all for me. Feel my cock pressed up against your sweet little ass. Let it make you ache, because tonight I'll make it all feel better."

A soft moan escaped her. Austin forced a loud cough to keep the Cody ice cream parlor rated PG.

The juxtaposing heat of the Wyoming summer pierced the cold air spilling off of the freezers as the door to the shop swung open. Summer gasped and spun out of his arms when she heard an exasperated wail from a baby.

She rushed toward a woman who greatly resembled the long Pall Mall she was smoking—withered, painfully thin, with white-grey hair highlighted an odd orange color matching the blush she'd applied that made her appear to be bunking with Satan.

It took Austin half a second to realize that the woman had to be Brant Preston's mother and that the baby was J.J. He rushed to Summer's side when the woman held J.J. out of Summer's reach. Poor kid wailed and had his arms extended to his mother, kicking his legs in an effort to get away from his evil grandmother.

"Ms. Preston, please. He saw me. Let me hold him."

"Give her the kid," Austin bellowed angrily.

"It's Brantley's turn. We didn't know you were in here." Ms. Preston pursed her lips and took another long drag of the cigarette, despite the no smoking signs hung four places in the ice cream parlor.

"I asked you not to smoke around him. Now give him to me," Summer demanded.

"What kind of grandmother makes a kid cry? This seems like something the lawyers need to hear about, darlin'. Either that or he can tell his therapists all about grandma when he's a little older." Austin narrowed his eyes in on Ms. Preston.

With a huff, she shoved J.J. into Summer's arms. She cradled him close and rocked him back and forth. He stopped crying immediately. Austin grinned as he nuzzled his little face into Summer's chest, took tight hold of her T-shirt with one hand and wrapped the other around her neck.

"And just who do you think you are? That is Brantley Preston's child. This is none of your business," Ms. Preston smarted indignantly to Austin. She reminded him of a sashaying peacock on full display, but unaware of an incoming storm.

"Oh, come on, Ms. Preston, *everyone* knows who I am. Why don't you leave J.J. with his mama for a little while and go ask Brantley himself who I am? I feel certain he can tell you *all* about me. He's one of my biggest fans."

Summer bit her lips together to keep from laughing when Austin winked at her.

"Yes, well, Brant's not feeling well this morning. J.J. and I were out of the room so he can rest up for the finals tonight. He's presenting the buckles in the ceremony," Ms. Preston announced proudly, as if someone had just named her queen of the rodeo.

"Stomachache?" Austin smirked, and a giggle escaped Summer's lips. She cuddled J.J. closer, using him as a very effective cover for her laughter.

"Pardon me?"

"I was saying I heard Brant had a stomachache this mornin'. Must be something going around."

"Well, yes, he does, in fact. I suspect it's something he ate last night. He has a very sensitive stomach."

"Doubt that's it, but okay. And hey, tell Brant to buck up. I *really* want him to be there to present the buckles tonight. I want that more than you could ever know."

That did it. Summer began giggling hysterically. J.J. looked delighted with his mother's laughter. He beamed ear to ear and squeezed her tighter. Austin found himself longing for a moment. Longing for her, *definitely*. Longing for a family with her... *Whoa now, let's not get carried away just yet.* He patted J.J. on the back. "You don't get to hear near enough of that do you, little buddy?

To his delight, J.J. awarded him with one of his adorable grins as well. Two tiny teeth were visible on his lower gum line. Austin chuckled. The little guy's grin was a quick show of acceptance, then he hid his face in his mother's neck again. Summer beamed at their exchange.

After squeezing him to her and kissing his cheeks, she lifted her head. "I'd be happy to keep him today. I get him back tomorrow night anyway. Sounds like Brant's going to be *busy*. Please, Ms. Preston. I miss him so much."

The pleading desperation in her tone pricked Austin's heart. He put his arm around both Summer and J.J. and kissed the top of her head, but he hadn't figured out Brant's mama well enough to play her... yet. He would in time. He could read self-righteous bitches same way he read bulls. Shit all smelled the same.

"Oh you'd just love that wouldn't you. You won't be getting J.J. one moment longer than you're supposed to have him." Ms. Preston jerked the baby out of Summer's arms, spun, and flew out of the ice cream shop with J.J. screaming for his mama.

Austin envisioned a broom and flying monkeys following in her wake. Before he could fully process beyond that, Summer's jaw clenched as she dammed back tears of pure frustration. Austin wondered if she ever allowed herself to have them. Everyone always wanted women to be so damn strong. Far as he could tell, women were by far the stronger sex. Whoever decided that human beings shouldn't show emotion was a fucker.

Austin knew that sometimes the only answer to the world was tears, even if he'd never show his to anyone else. Fear wasn't something he indulged himself in, but sadness was different. Summer had been through hell. She'd earned every single tear she wanted to cry.

He wrapped his arms around her, letting her hide in his chest. "I've got you, okay? Wanna get out of here for a little while?" Her body shook from the internal war she was waging. "Baby, if you need to cry, go for it. It's fine. I'll hold you. I'll be right here." His own statement shocked him. Every vow he made to her still surprised him. What was she doing to him? He wasn't sure, and he didn't care. He was going with it. Being there for her felt right. That was all he needed to know.

"No," she defied angrily. "I just...don't want ice cream." Jerking out of his arms, she stomped out of the ice cream shop.

Okay, wait. Is ice cream still sex? Don't ask her that, moron. He raced after her, desperate to find something to make her smile again. She was right. Brant's mama *was* evil. The duo took the term *son of a bitch* to a whole new level. It was high time Brant and his mother took a long walk off a short pier, and he'd happily supply the pier.

"Summer," he called as he jogged a few paces before catching up to her on the sidewalk. "Come on. Talk to me."

She worked her jaw and glared back toward the hotel before turning to face him. "I'm sorry. She just makes me crazy. He doesn't understand what a jerk his father is. I'm sure he will someday, but he doesn't understand why I can't have him when he wants me. It kills me. He's not a tug-of-war rope, but he probably feels that way."

Austin pulled her back into the safety of his embrace. "I know it seems like he doesn't understand, but I kind of think he does. Kids are smart, a lot smarter than we want to believe. Let's just get through Cheyenne. Then you can get a job, settle in, and get the courts to realize what a piece of shit his daddy is. Maybe he won't have to see him all that often."

"I keep prayin' for that, but I don't know how I'd get so lucky. Seems impossible. I think that's why I always have this bad feeling about it. Brant's daddy has a ton of money. To the courts that's all that matters."

"Hey, come on. If you need money, let me help you. I haven't spent any of the money I've won, and not to sound like a brat-ass rich punk but my family does all right. We run a ton of cattle and have more land than we really know what to do with."

"Austin, I cannot let you do that. Plus, you bought that fancy truck. What do you mean you haven't spent any of your winnings?"

Unable to hide his chuckle, he wondered momentarily just how much assuming Ms. Summer Sanchez had done on his behalf. "You wanna go ahead and tell me everything else you're so sure of about me before I correct you, darlin'?"

She rolled her eyes then leveled a cold glare on him. He laughed. "So, the lady does *not* like to be told she's wrong. Sorry, cowgirl. You're up a creek without a paddle. Need me to come rescue you?"

"Shut up, Austin. Fine. When did you get your truck?"

"Three years ago. You ever tried to pull a full horse trailer, tractors, or a load of cattle in a tiny truck with half an engine?"

"That truck doesn't look like it's ever worked on a ranch." She cocked her jaw to the side and gave him a gotcha grin.

"Just so you know, if you argue with me while you're naked, I'll probably let you win."

Another eye roll.

"Sugar, I can show you the paperwork on the truck if I ever get you up to the ranch, 'til then you're just gonna have to believe me. I take care of my truck. We use the old trucks to run the feeders. I keep mine clean, and it hasn't been on the ranch in months. That makes it easier to keep up. But I learned to take care of all of my shit growing up. We worked for everything we got. So my truck, my house, my team, and most certainly my *girl*, I take excellent care of."

Summer knew he wasn't lying, but part of her still wanted to be right. She'd never met a rodeo cowboy that didn't blow all of his winnings long before he won again. And what was that taking her to the ranch and *his girl* thing? She'd thought he was lying that morning, but he'd just witnessed the shit-storm that was her life currently. Anyone with half a brain would run far away. That alone was why she had no business getting involved with Austin, no matter how badly she wanted to.

"Stop," he commanded as he gently lifted her face with his rope callused hands.

"Stop what?"

"Stop standing there deciding you shouldn't be with me or whatever because of what just happened with J.J. Your eyes give you away, sunshine, every single time. Stop trying to figure out the rest of your whole life in this one moment. For me, take it easy, please." With that directive, he spun behind her and proceeded to massage her shoulders with the might of his hands there on the sidewalk of Cody, Wyoming. Had it not felt so absolutely incredible, she would have called him on the decidedly eighth grade hallway-between-classes move.

It had just been so long since anyone's hands had been on her for the purposes of caring for her. She couldn't bring herself to harass him. Maybe he was right. Maybe she should stop worrying so much and just go with it. Up until the moment she'd had J.J., that's how she'd lived her life. Until her father had intervened with his grandiose plans, she'd done all right.

CHAPTER FIVE

"So, do you have a thing?" Summer inquired about an hour before they were due in the Cody Stampede Arena. She was trying to quell her own nerves. She'd seen more than one bull rider injured so badly they'd never walk again. One time, she'd seen one trampled to death. With every passing moment she spent with him, Austin's safety became more and more important.

Glancing in the mirror mounted over the dresser in his room, she studied her own eyes. Seeing something she hadn't found there in years almost frightened her. Despite the nervous energy swirling in her stomach, some sense of peace had settled in her eyes. Belonging... maybe? Before she gave it any more thought, Austin gave her that smirk that was sexy as sin.

"Pretty sure you already know I have a *thing*, baby doll. I'd show you, but then I'd be total shit on the bull, and I'm looking to get a nice check tonight."

"Do you ever think about anything but sex?"

"Not when I'm in the room with you. My mind and my *thing* get all wired together every time I get near you." He winked at her.

Another round of elation sped her heart. He kept saying things like that. She was ridiculously anxious for him to ride and get that stupid buckle so she could bring him back to the room.

There's nothing wrong with wanting to be the spoils of his war. She continuously reminded herself of this. He was kind, sweet, more than obviously interested, and Brant had J.J. for the night. No harm would come in enjoying herself with Austin. Forcing her mind to the things that had to happen before they went to bed, she rolled her eyes at him. "I meant like a thing you do before you ride. You know, for good luck or whatever."

He smirked. God she loved that look of his, like he knew her deepest, darkest desires, and couldn't wait to indulge her in them. "And what was your *thing* when you rode, Ms. Sanchez?"

She found herself laughing again. He made her feel things she barely recognized. That giddy sense of embarrassment and glee that came with a new relationship worked through her again. "I asked you first, cowboy."

Hemming for a half-second, he took her hands and pulled her closer. "I'm hoping some sweet kisses from you will become part of my *thing*. Other than that, I have a pair of spurs I'm pretty sure are good luck that I always wear and I loop the straps on my boots left then right. It's stupid, but sometimes I walk around the stadium before I ride to get my head in the game." He was winding tape around his wrists with a great deal of accuracy.

"I used to do that, too." Summer allowed the sadness she always felt when she recalled the circumstances of giving up the rodeo to diminish her glee over Austin's affections.

"Oh yeah?" Austin wrapped his arms around Summer again. Damn, but she was the perfect tonic for the case of nerves he was feeling tonight.

"Yeah." He felt her grin against his chest.

"What else did you do?"

"Mostly I walked around the stadiums, ate Hot Tamales candy, and listened to Miranda Lambert songs. Then I climbed on and had the time of my life."

"Should I pick you up some Hot Tamales, honey? Cause I'm really looking forward to you climbing on me and having the time of your life as soon as I have the Cody buckle in my hands tonight."

She shook her head as she pulled away from him. "I know you're scared."

"Wrong again, sunshine. I'm fine." Austin bristled. He didn't like her thinking that anything got to him. He wanted her to trust him before he took her to bed. Her declarations that she didn't want boring, vanilla sex had tied him in knots. Before they could engage in any of that, she had to trust him implicitly.

He was more than ready to spice up her love life, but for the moment, he probably needed to get his mind out of her crotch and into looking for eight.

"I know you're fine, but I used to do this, remember? I don't think less of you because you're scared. I just think you're human."

"I said I was fine, honey. Don't worry about me." Austin leaned down to adjust his bootstraps once more before they headed out.

"Nothing scares you, right?" She stared at him with defiant challenge lit in her eyes.

"No point in being scared. What's that gonna get you? I'm riding tonight, and I'm winning. Then I'm bringing you back here and we're gonna celebrate all night long. Nothing about any of that scares me. I don't do scared. If something about all of that frightens you, however, let's talk about that."

"I never did scared either, until I had J.J." Her truths crushed him. As bad as he wanted that damn buckle he was about to go out and get, he'd trade every single one he'd ever won to conquer the fear in her eyes. "If you don't want to be afraid of what might happen tonight when you're on a beast that could kill you, I'll do that part for you, but I'm not afraid of what happens after you're out of that arena. So there. I guess I kind of like you, cowboy, and I do want to hang out with you for the next few weeks if you're still offering."

A hearty dose of glee mixed in with the desire that had been swimming in his veins all day. "Damn, sugar, you're losing your edge. Be careful or you might actually agree to being my girl."

"Don't get ahead of yourself, Mr. Camden. I'm a handful."

"Oh, doll baby, I know. Why the hell do you think I want you so bad?"

The heat of their attraction seemed to radiate between them in that moment. She stared at him, her eyes dark and hungry. The hesitation lingered, but was dissipating as the moments extended between them.

If he didn't get her out of that hotel room, he was going to pick her up, sling her over his shoulder caveman-style, throw her in his bed, and fuck her until she couldn't walk. The Cody buckle be damned. "If you don't stop looking at me like that, I make you no promises that we'll ever make it to the arena."

She smirked, but before she could make another snide remark, he jerked her to him and took her lips in a blistering kiss that scorched a trail straight to his cock. Slapping her sexy little ass caught up in an old pair of ripped blue jeans, he pulled away from her and chased his breath. "Let's get out of here, darlin'. My patience is wearing mighty thin, and a lot of people are gonna be really pissed if I don't ride tonight."

"Well, we don't want to piss anyone off, do we?" she challenged.

"Let's get, Ms. Sanchez." He turned to head out, but Summer spun back and raced to her bag.

"You go on. I'll be right there. I just need to grab something."

Austin waited. She dug deep into the old tack bag and then extracted a round white clay medallion attached to a black ribbon. His brow furrowed as she placed the necklace around her neck and attempted to tie the ribbon ends together.

With a few quick steps he was behind her. "What's this?" He secured the necklace for her and took the opportunity to place a few suckled kisses along her neck and bare shoulders. Her shiver thrilled him.

"Just a necklace I wanted to wear."

Austin spun around her and lifted the medallion to study it. A beautiful image of a macaw was etched artfully in the clay and painted in brilliant shades of red, yellow, and orange on one side of the disk. He flipped it over and saw two parallel arrows on the back, along with the Zuni symbol for butterfly. There was a pair of crossed arrows at the bottom. *Friendship.*

Studying her eyes again, he couldn't quite believe what he saw there this time. "You have Pueblo blood, baby?"

"How did you know this was Pueblo?"

"Actually, it's Zuni, right?" He swallowed harshly. "Had a good friend coming up whose grandparents and aunts and uncles lived on one of the reservations. They're from the Hopi tribes. He and his parents moved to Pleasant Glen when he was little, but they went back to visit a lot. I went with him a few times."

"Oh."

Austin waited on more, but she'd clammed up again before his very eyes. "Oh?"

"Yeah, I'm part Pueblo-Zuni. My grandmother made it for me. I used to keep this in my pocket when I raced. I thought I'd wear it tonight." She shrugged.

For him. She was wearing it for him. Austin's heart thundered against his ribcage. In that moment, clasping her necklace, he swore he could hear Max's laughter over Austin's current situation. *"My name's Makya. It means eagle hunter, but your people can't say it right, so just call me Max. I'm gonna be a bull rider when I grow up."* Not wanting to dive into his typical explanation of how he could still hear Max's voice just then, he stared back at Summer.

"It's beautiful, just like you. I know the arrows mean protection. What does the macaw stand for?"

Her face flushed the color of an overly-ripe tomato. She glanced at the door, trying to escape the conversation. "It means summer." With that, she pulled the medallion out of his grasp and sped out into the hallway.

"And the butterfly?" Austin asked the empty room. Summer Sanchez had far too many secrets, and he was determined to uncover each and every one of them, starting with finding out how her Native American heritage fit in with the rest of her story. Her father, Mitchum, wasn't Zuni. She'd gotten her riding skill from him, but her heritage must have come from her mother's side. His long, agitated strides ate up the distance between them. He caught up to her just outside the doors to the hotel, laced her fingers through his, and escorted her to his truck.

————

Summer gripped Austin's arm tighter as he led her toward his team awaiting him at the chute that would hold Perfect Storm, his assigned bull.

The air was as thick as the crowds in the arena. She batted a fly away from her face and ordered her mouth to stay shut. She refused to beg him not to ride. They'd barely known each other one full day. Why was she so worried about him suddenly? *He's been winning all season. He'll be fine.* What was wrong with her? Her heart couldn't seem to locate a steady cadence and her stomach felt like it had been inhabited with angry hornets. *What if he gets hurt? Honestly, it's not if, it's when. Everyone said that when they talked about bull riding. Better question: why on earth do I want to get involved with a bull rider? It's just a fling.* She reminded herself again.

Breaths of memories entered her lungs. The rosin, the sweat, and the distinctive smell of horses and bulls took her back to all the times she'd been the one about to mount up and ride. She was going to smell like dirt and bulls by the time this was over, but knowing Austin, that was probably his favorite scent.

"This is my team, darlin'. Aaron Chalmers pulls my ropes. Cam Trenton keeps me from getting killed inside the chute. Gil and Mike are basically here to harass me, so I'm sure you'll get along with them well."

Summer grinned at his rag-tag team. They were all eyeing her suspiciously.

"And this is my best friend, Jackson Denton. We came up together. He spent every summer trying to throw me off of a Bucky," Austin explained.

Cam stepped up first and offered his hand. "You look mighty famil-iar. Have we met before?"

"This is Summer Sanchez. That name should ring a bell," Austin bragged.

Summer rolled her eyes. "That was a long time ago. It's no big deal. Do you care if I stay down here with you while he rides?"

"Way he's looking at you, sweetheart, I don't think he'd let you stay anywhere else. I'll tell you this, too, Austin's never had a girl he brought down here with him. You must be something special." Cam offered her a kind smile. *Okay, so I like Cam. Now to win over the rest of his team.*

"She definitely is." Austin winked at her, then wrapped his arm around her and whispered a kiss on her temple. That motion alone made her entire body long to strip him down, run her hands up and down his chiseled pecs, and let him have his way with her.

That's why you're getting involved with a bull rider. No one else has ever made you feel this way. Her mind took every available opportunity to remind her of the way Austin made her feel, the way he made her ache, the hunger he stirred within her that she'd been so certain was long gone.

"Summer." Jackson, the guy Austin had called his best friend since childhood gave her a dorky grin. It wasn't lost on her that his eyes hadn't made it up from her cleavage to her face as of yet. What, was he still twelve?

"She has a face, man," Austin huffed. "Eyes up."

"Yeah, tell me those aren't the first things you noticed," Jackson spoke through his teeth to keep Summer from hearing him. *Idiots.* She had a kid. She heard everything, always.

"Hey, if you want to know anything about this guy, I'm your man." When his eyes finally located hers, he managed his vow.

"Might take you up on that."

That male grunt of half-annoyance and half-amusement sounded from Austin's throat. "You wanna know anything about me, you ask me."

Before she could respond, another herd of people headed Austin's way. They were all wearing suits, as opposed to his team who looked like genuine cattle ranchers; Wranglers, dirty shirts, boots and cowboy hats. Austin stiffened slightly and pulled Summer closer. "Uh, this is the Minton team. Clifton Taft and Scott Leonard." He nodded to the suits. "This is Summer Sanchez. She's all mine."

Summer rolled her eyes and shook her head at Austin, but she couldn't order away the broad grin that stupidly spread across her face. Being *all his* sounded akin to heaven, even if she had only known him a day. She might as well enjoy it while it lasted.

"Ms. Sanchez," one of the men offered his hand. "Pleasure to meet you." His words didn't match the expression on his face, however. He looked bereaved. What the hell was his problem? "Why don't you come up with us to the Minton seats? You'd be welcome."

"Nah, I want her down here with me," Austin informed him quickly. The man ground his teeth as he forced a nod.

"We're looking for another win, Austin. Don't let us down." The other suit could speak as well, it seemed.

"No pressure or anything though." Summer made no effort to hide her disdain. She should probably work on that.

Austin's grin and the sexy gravel of his chuckle helped quell her temper just a little. He awarded her with another one of those winks. Why it delighted her so she had no idea, but she loved it almost as much as she loved the fact that he kept tightening his hold on her like he never wanted to let her go.

"I always do my best. Beyond that it's between me and the bull. I intend to bring home that buckle tonight, guys. Don't look so worried."

"No distractions though. Understood?" The second suit was officially on Summer's last fraying nerve. So that's what this was all about. They didn't want her to distract Austin from winning. No life outside of bull riding. She cocked her jaw to the side and debated telling the asshole to go eat a horseshoe. Austin raised his left eyebrow and narrowed his eyes.

"I haven't let you down yet, Scott. Let me say this as politely as I can: back off."

"Hey, I'm just looking out for everyone. We're bringing out the whole crew to see you in Cheyenne."

"Great. Can't wait to see everyone. For now, I need to get ready to ride. I'll see you at the buckle ceremony." Austin's dismissal was blunt. He left no room for argument. Summer liked him more and more with every word he spoke.

His chute team all muttered several choice words under their breath as Scott and Clifton dissolved into the crowds headed to the stands. "Punk-ass pricks. What got stuck in their craw?" Cam growled in a decidedly Southern accent.

"I did." Summer rolled her eyes.

"Forget it." Austin shot Cam a warning glare. "They like the money they're making. They don't want it to disappear. Don't guess it matters what happens to me as long as their sales stay up."

The injustice she felt for Austin bled quickly to worry. She shouldn't distract him. She didn't really have any rights to him, even if he kept telling everyone she was his girl.

"Stop thinking whatever you're thinking right now." Austin turned her and held her to his riding vest so he could whisper in her ear. "I want you down here. I want you at the chute. If I get turned toward the gate during the ride, I'll be looking for you, sugar. I want to see you smiling at me."

Summer's brow furrowed as she pulled away. How did he keep reading her mind?

"Those eyes, darlin'. They speak a language all their own. I intend to learn every word."

"Aren't you poetic, cowboy." She tried not to let his intention touch the places of her soul that were battered and bruised from the life she'd been trying to survive.

"Pretty sure that came from a country song, but I'll claim it." He laughed, and she couldn't help but join him.

The timed events went by quickly. With a front row seat for the barrel racing, she had no choice but to watch. Some of them were pretty good. She was better, but that no longer mattered. Before she'd quite prepared herself, tension sizzled along the bucking chutes from the riders. The air around her was choked with nerves. Her eyes zeroed in on Brant standing near chute two with his customary simpering grin as Dallas Devil was loaded in. Her ex-husband looked far too pleased. That was never a good sign.

Nausea roiled in her gut. Austin had been assigned to chute six. His bull hadn't been placed yet.

She gripped Austin's hand. "Just please be careful."

His responding smile took her breath away. By the time his lips connected with hers, she was woozy. A moan she'd tried to quiet spilled into his mouth as soon as she opened for his tongue. His hands gripped her shoulders then traveled to her back and pulled her in. His body consumed hers with the scorching brand of his tongue that sent heat spiraling throughout her.

In that moment, her bones felt as liquid as the heat now flowing rapidly between her legs. *More.* God, she wanted more, but he pulled away. She fought not to beg him to forget the stupid bull, and come back to the room with her. If he wanted a wild ride, she'd give him one. She'd give him most anything he wanted.

"I'll be fine, honey. I'm not gonna do anything that might keep me from bedding you as soon as possible." Another wink. My God, how could he possibly be so calm? She'd blame stupidity, but Austin was far from dumb. It wasn't him doing something that worried her, it was the bull.

Instinctively, she glanced back toward Brant. Having him in her sights kept the hysteria of what he might do next at bay. Staying one step ahead of Brant was always the key to survival. But the shock and fury that hardened his face as he glared at her was terrifying. She tucked back into Austin's embrace, hating herself for being afraid in the first place.

That kiss had apparently been Brant's first clue as to her and Austin's coupling. Austin had actually hit him the night before, and he really didn't remember who'd done it. He was such an idiot. She pressed her face to Austin's vest, trying to hide from the world around her.

Austin cradled her to him and brushed another kiss on top of her head. The safety of his muscled embrace and the heat that existed inside him chased away the icy clutches of fear that Brant always brought on. "What's wrong, darlin'? I've got you. I'll be gone less than a minute. I swear I'll be fine."

She managed a nod, but in that moment Austin must've spied Brant's glower. "So, he's what's wrong. I don't know what he did to you, Summer, and I honestly don't want to know. I have a pistol far too conveniently located for me not to react to him hurting you, but hear me say this, it will never happen again. Not as long as you're with me. I will keep you safe and treat you the way you should always have been treated."

"I know. Thank you. I don't understand how this is happening so fast. I feel like I've known you a lifetime. I feel safe with you. Doesn't that scare you? If the bulls don't, shouldn't this?"

Austin cradled her chin in his rope-roughened right hand and brought her gaze to his. "In my experience, darlin', all you need to change your entire life is eight seconds."

"You're sure you want me to be yours even with all of the shit I have going on right now?" There, she'd said it. The plaguing thought that had been eating at her all damn day.

"Summer, there have been very few things I've been more sure of than this. Relax and let's see where this goes, please. If you hate me come morning or hate me next week in Cheyenne, I still want to help you get J.J. Can we just take a deep breath and settle in for a little while?"

"Maybe, but every time I try to take a deep breath all I smell is bull sweat and shit." Her statement was both literal and figurative, and was a pretty good description of her life ever since rodeo season had begun in early spring.

Laughing, Austin shook his head at her. "I love your filthy mouth, darlin'. I'm hoping I get to hear some more of it tonight in our room, but for right now, I need to see how this is gonna go." He gestured his head to the first chute. A kid named Wes Kelly was seated on a bull and the timer was already ticking.

Summer swallowed harshly. In her three years on the circuit she'd seen four riders hooked, one break most every bone in his body when he got trampled, one killed, and more concussions than she could count even if she used both her and Austin's toes. Sweat-laced adrenaline permeated the air.

Her body jerked when the timer sounded and the door opened. She cringed as Wes flew off the bull on the first spin. He hit the ground hard and the bull turned to make a point. Summer allowed herself to breathe again when the bullfighters distracted the beast with relative ease. Austin shook his head. "Kid needs to be trained. That was less than a second."

The next man climbed the chute headed down onto Dallas Devil. Summer felt sick. Brant was doing something to that animal. She had no doubt. He hadn't been ridden more than five seconds all season, and he was angry and aggressive long before his flank strap or a rider was on.

"And tonight, Cody's own, Todd Lilmer, takes on Dallas Devil. The Devil hasn't allowed a rider eight all season long, folks. If Todd can tame the beast, he has a chance to take third right behind Austin Camden and Travis Anders. This is his chance for a spot in Cheyenne. Looks like he's gonna give it all he's got." The crackle of the ancient speakers didn't mask the announcer's obvious concern. Summer wondered if the announcer knew Todd personally.

The flashing red of the awaiting ambulances came into focus when Summer stared out toward the parking lot. Nausea twisted in her gut. She couldn't quite access the carefree girl she'd been in her barrel riding days. That took skill, guts, luck, and speed, but bull riding was man against beast. More often than not, the beast won.

There was a young women beaming at Todd and holding a little girl. Todd blew them both a kiss.

Summer longed to march over to her ex standing by the chute gate in complete safety and beat that evil grin off of his face. This rider had a family. What happened to them if he wasn't okay? Not that Brant would ever care. He didn't care about his own family. Why would he care about someone else's? All that mattered to Brant was pleasing his own father. Summer had met Brant Preston Senior a handful of times, one being at the wedding. He was an asshole, just like his son. Only difference was he held all the money in the family, and the rest of them all slopped up his shit to get any.

Clutching her chest, she let Austin hold her back to his vest. Her heart hammered rapidly and she couldn't seem to catch her breath.

"He'll be all right, sugar. Breathe for me." Austin's soothing voice sounded tunneled against the start buzzer. The gate shot open, and Dallas Devil bulleted out like the demon spawn he was. She gnawed her lip as Todd rode buck for buck.

"Shit," Austin cursed at the three-second mark when Dallas snarled and shifted hard right, bucking with all of his infuriated might. Todd slipped forward and bowed toward Dallas's horns.

Suddenly, Austin spun Summer against his chest blocking her view. He was a half-second too late though. She saw the bull's horn pierce Todd's throat, landing right between the covering offered him by his protective vest. Jerking her head back so she could see, Summer covered her mouth as Todd Lilmer hit the ground right under Dallas Devil's hooves.

The crowd was on their feet. The bullfighters were trying to get him away. Todd was on the ground, being trampled.

"Oh my God!" She couldn't watch anymore. She let Austin shield her from the carnage.

"He's all right." Austin's gasped breaths matched her own. "They're helping him up. Might have a broken hip. He's breathing though."

"What about his throat?" Summer tucked herself tighter into Austin's chest, certain most of the girlfriends of riders didn't react this way.

"Doc'll get him fixed up." Austin didn't sound certain enough for her to relax. The woman and the little girl were both in tears. Fear consumed their entire beings as they raced after the stretcher that had been lifted out of the ring.

The rides before Austin's seemed surreal. She couldn't quite understand why they kept happening. All she could see before her was Austin being hooked the way Todd had been.

She'd gotten thrown dozens of times when she was training to race. Difference in a horse and a bull was the horse didn't try to kill you after they threw you. Besides, back then no one really cared if she got hurt. Now, she had a little boy that depended on her. She had something worth living for. In that moment, Summer finally allowed herself to wonder what Austin was running from, or what he was running to. If he felt like he had anything worth living for, would he still climb on that damned bull to prove his worth?

She'd known the man twenty-four hours. How had he become so important to her? She didn't know, but maybe he was right. Maybe it did only take eight seconds. If she measured time in those increments, she'd known him long enough to be falling in love. Hadn't she? Is that what worrying like this was?

She wasn't certain she cared for love if this was it—not that it could've stopped her. She knew she loved her baby boy, and she worried about him like this, too. Before she could contemplate further, Austin was rosining his gloves. Her heart lurched to a hard stop and then resuscitated itself and flew the next moment.

"Austin..." She shook her head, but couldn't formulate a plea.

"Meet me wherever I climb out of this thing, sugar. I'll be fine."

His right leg crested the gate and his boots came down on top of Perfect Storm, who shifted against Austin's weight. Summer studied Austin's eyes and the chiseled planes of his jaw. She couldn't locate a single ounce of fear on his features.

He settled on the bull and exchanged hisses and grunts with the animal. Austin leaned down and whispered something to the bull. Summer assumed it was indeed a meat packing joke. She almost smiled.

She'd stubbornly refused to pray to a God that allowed horrible things to happen far too often ever since her ridiculous marriage to Brant Preston. But in that moment, as time seemed to slow and the seconds on the gate clock felt like hours, she breathed a prayer of protection over Austin. There was something to the two of them. She finally admitted it to herself. She couldn't lose him before they figured out what it might be.

Jackson and another bullfighter had replaced the fighters previously in the arena. They joined the crowd's raucous applause. The belled rope went over the bull.

"Current PBR champion, Austin Camden, is set to ride Perfect Storm. If we see him with a score higher than 78 tonight, folks, we'll be handing him the Cody buckle after the rodeo. On your feet for Camden, rider for Minton Chaps and Denim out of Oklahoma."

With a confident nod, Austin gripped the rope and the chute burst open. Summer's breath tangled in her throat. She could hold her breath for eight seconds, surely, so why did she feel like she was being gagged?

To her shock, Austin's free hand seemed to know the bull's next move with each passing moment. It guided him like the perfect compass. His muscles cinched and released in perfect time with each buck. He leaned right when the bull spun left with perfect skill and precision. Cam was standing beside her, screaming and jumping up and down.

"Beautiful ride! Look at him go!" The announcers bellowed. The entire stadium was chanting, "Camden!"

She'd never seen anyone master a bull the way he did. He was incredible. *She's all mine.* Biting her lip, she accepted her own fate. *She was all his, but he was hers as well.* She clasped the pendent her grandmother had crafted for her and held on tightly.

Five seconds, six seconds, seven seconds, she joined the screaming crowd, bouncing on her tiptoes.

My God, he was gorgeous. He arched his back into the next buck. Eight seconds. The buzzer reverberated against her soul. Cam wrapped her up in his exuberant arms and jumped with her. Laughing, she pulled away after a few jumps and raced to the gate 100 yards from where she'd been cheering him on.

Austin let go of the rope and rolled away from Perfect Storm. His ass would probably be bruised come morning from where he hit the dirt. She'd have to see if she could make that feel better.

When he crested the gate, she raced into his arms. He lifted her, spun her around, and planted a kiss on her lips that told the entire rodeo world she was taken.

"Camden's scores are coming in, folks, and if my eyes ain't lying to me, I believe that would be former title-winning barrel racer, Summer Sanchez, daughter of Rodeo King Mitchum Sanchez, he's got helping him celebrate his near perfect ride."

Summer never wanted him to stop kissing her. Electricity and bliss from the crowd banded them together. The jealous glares of the buckle bunnies welled a healthy dose of pride in her veins. He held her tighter. She flew with him in that moment, much longer than eight seconds, and she never wanted to come back down to earth.

"And it's a 92.8 for Camden. You're looking at the Cody champion, ladies and gentlemen. He's gonna be the one to beat for the PBR title this year, and I'm glad I'm not the one trying to best him. I'm not sure it can be done."

Austin couldn't believe his score any more than he could believe how good it felt to celebrate with Summer, who'd been cheering him on. Life didn't get much sweeter than this. Laughing, Summer held his face in her hands and kissed him again while the entire town of Cody, Wyoming, heralded his name.

"A ninety-two! Austin, that's incredible," she gasped.

"You're my lucky charm, darlin'. I told you I wouldn't do anything that'd keep me from celebrating with you tonight."

CHAPTER SIX

An hour later, Austin's cheeks started to ache from holding the smirk permanently affixed to his face. He couldn't have arranged this better if he'd tried. Standing in the wings of the makeshift area of Cassie's Honkytonk, set for the buckle ceremony with his arms around Summer watching Brant Preston squirm was perfection. Only thing better was going to be having the beautiful little spitfire in his arms, naked and willing, all for him as soon as he got her back to his room.

Brant and a few PRCA board members worked through the awards for the timed events provided by Preston Cattle.

A representative from the PBR joined Brant as Austin stepped forward. Brant simpered, and Summer's grin expanded further. *Perfection. This is the epitome of perfection.* A chuckle escaped Austin's lips.

"I'm Harrison Enrow from PBR, here with Clifton Taft from Minton Chaps." He gestured to Clif while he put his arm around Brant. "And I know Mr. Preston from Preston Cattle is thrilled to present this buckle to one of the most skilled riders we've seen in a long time. I've been head of the PBR for the last two decades, and I can think of only a handful of riders with Mr. Camden's ability. The Minton team picked well, and I know we're all anxious to see him perform this year in Vegas. Come on up here, Austin, and tell us who you have with you. Seems like I recall this pretty young lady receiving several buckles of her own."

"She's amazing, isn't she?" Austin winked at Summer, whose cheeks were glowing sunset pink. He wanted to kiss each of them just for an appetizer. "This is Summer Sanchez...*my girl*."

She cocked her jaw to the side and gave him another one of those eye rolls. Damn, but if he wasn't careful he was likely to fall head over heels for Summer and go right ahead and admit it *to* her.

Mr. Enrow beamed at Austin and then went on to recount the finer points of his ride.

Brant's lip curled, and his face screwed up like a bratty child that had finally been punished as he sidled closer. "You think you can just fuck my wife, Camden?" he hissed.

Pulling Summer closer, Austin's left eyebrow ticked upwards. He spoke through his teeth, still smiling like the cat that caught the canary. "Drivin' you crazy, ain't it, Preston? You didn't even know what you had when you had her, and we all know you don't have the *cojones* to keep a woman like her satisfied."

"You're a cocky bastard, Camden. I warned you last night. Don't think I won't see to it you go down for sticking your nose where it don't belong."

"Simmer down, Preston. You're stepping in shit in them fancy alligator boots. You lost your chance. I've got her now, and I know precisely how to handle my girl. I'll give her *everything* she needs."

"Austin!" Summer elbowed him rather hard.

Before she could scold him further, he was shaking Enrow's hand and accepting the buckle. One more notch in his season. Nothing stood between him and Cheyenne. Images of Vegas played in his mind, reflected off the overhead lights of the bar.

He had no trouble envisioning Summer standing by his side there as well. After he got the PBR title and buckle, they could spend a week or two living it up in on the strip. *You really gonna stick with her for the next four months?* His mind continued to taunt him. With one glance her way, in those sexy little jeans with heat still settled in her olive skin, the jeers disappeared entirely. He wanted her now; he'd deal with the next few months later.

Preston handed out the bronc riding buckles, and then the PRCA reps sent everyone to the dance floor.

"You are such an idiot," Summer fumed as Austin pulled her in his arms.

"You suck at dirty talk, darlin'. Try switchin' idiot for stud."

Narrowing her eyes, she played at laying her hand on his chest but pinched his right nipple instead, hard enough to leave a mark. Lust sizzled in his veins. His cock took notice of the slight pain and the mark she'd left behind.

Laughing at her outright, he waggled his eyebrows. "Careful, baby. Turnabout's fair play, and it's about all I can do not to take you out to my truck, lean you over the tailgate, and fuck you so hard you can't walk." That heat that set him on fire ignited in her eyes. "Mmm, you like that idea, don't you darlin'? Tell me," he coaxed as he began to sway her back and forth.

"Did you not hear what he said? Austin, you have no idea what Brant's capable of. Now you've gone and made me some kind of prize like some punk-ass caveman. I'm not a competition. I divorced him a year ago. I don't want to have anything to do with him, but Brant does *not* like to lose."

"I don't give a damn what Brant Preston likes, honey. And by the way, he's the one still calling you his wife. I didn't make you a competition. He did. So, let him be the ass-licker he is. You put those sweet little arms around me, feel me against you, and let me dance with you. We'll talk all you want about your ex tomorrow. Tonight, you're mine. All for me."

Annoyed and infuriated with Austin's asinine belief that Brant wouldn't do something terrible to him, Summer complied with his orders anyway. She called herself an idiot, something she'd taken to doing quite often since she'd agreed to dinner with the man holding her in his arms making her feel things she hadn't felt in a lifetime.

Her traitorous feet edged closer. She needed to be consumed by him. Her fear and anger dissipated in the humid air surrounding them.

She'd worry about what Brant might do in the morning. Tonight, she needed this.

"That's it." His voice was whiskey-smooth and evidence of his obvious desire for her felt rock hard against her abdomen. A shiver worked through her body. God, he was the personification of gorgeous male. Hard. Ready. His eyes dark, eager, and greedy. Certainty radiated in the solid wall of muscle her breasts were pressed against.

His strong arms made the perfect sanctuary from the world. They seemed to make the honkytonk, Brant, his sponsors, and the entire town of Cody disappear into the star-strewn summer night. Unable to help herself, she buried her face against his neck and reveled in his right hand kneading her ass and his left gently nestled at the nape of her neck. His thumb caressed her jawline.

"There's my girl." The words whispered through her long hair. "Riding makes me so damn horny, honey. Winning and having you in my arms. So much testosterone flowin' through me right now, I could go all night. You up for that?"

"Yes. God, yes, please." She barely managed the plea. Her body responded for her. Her breaths quickened. Her fingers gripped him tighter. Her nipples beaded against his chest, so stiff they hurt. Wet heat coated her panties. She'd never needed anything the way she needed him. It had been so long.

"So fucking sexy. I want to mark you, baby. Mark you all for me, with my mouth, then with my cum. I want your entire body aching and desperate to feel my fingers on you and inside of you. I want you needy for me. I told you, by the time I'm spent tonight, you'll sure as hell know you've been loved thoroughly. I don't do anything halfway, and sugar, you're all I want."

Continuing to allow her body to overrule her brain, she thrust her hips against the steel bulge she felt at his zipper line. She shuddered when his ridge pressed the zipper of her jeans against her panties, making contact with her clit. Her body demanded more. To the beat of the country song blaring from the cover band, she rubbed back and forth over him, dirty dancing the way she had when she was a horny teenager with something to prove.

His entire body tensed. She watched him close those gorgeous black eyes. Hot air hissed through his teeth.

"You like that, sugar? Feels good, doesn't it?" Gripping her ass firmly, he indulged her with another few thrusts, circling her pelvis around his impressive erection. Reckless desperation took her over. Her mind scrambled, and her body overheated. His every touch was tender but laced with intention that blistered through her skin.

Summer tried desperately to remember that there were at least a hundred people in that bar, that Brant might be watching them, getting angrier by the moment, but everyone else seemed to exist in an entirely different world. Nothing else mattered but her and Austin.

"You're so hungry for it aren't you, darlin'? Already needy for me. Tell me something. How wet is my girl? When I get you back to the room, I'll make you drip down your thighs before I give you what you're begging for. Make you so hot and slick you burn for me. Tell me, honey. Those sweet little panties already needin' to be taken off?" His words melted her completely. She held on to him for dear life, afraid if she attempted to stand on her own she might dissolve into the floor. Swallowing harshly, she attempted a smirk.

"Pretty sure I just came." The racy tone she'd intended was lost in the hum of her craving need.

"Oh yeah? Well, hold on tight, sugar. It's gonna be one hell of an evening." In one quick move, he pulled his cowboy hat off his head and captured her elusive breaths with his lips. Before she could abandon all pretenses and simply beg him to take her back to the hotel now, he nipped her bottom lip then sucked away the pain. Her heart flew into overdrive. His tongue explored her mouth like he'd never get enough of her. The crowds pressing around them, her own clothing, everything that kept her from being free in his arms set a choking constriction in her soul.

"Austin, please."

"I like you beggin', baby. So greedy for me. Tell me what you want."

Quite certain he was going to spontaneously combust on the dance floor of Cassie's Honkytonk, Austin managed to keep up his dirty talking game since it sure as hell set that wildfire he loved in Summer's eyes. They'd gone from their typical amber whiskey color to a deep russet, darkened by her hunger.

He needed to fuck her all night long and well into the morning, just to sate his soul long enough to eat, then he needed to do it all over again. Understanding that he'd never get enough danced in the fringes of his consciousness.

He leaned in again, desperate for another hit of her, like a beautiful drug he'd readily become a junkie for. Forcing himself to slow, he coaxed her tongue into his mouth, tasting her, devouring her lips like the sweetest candy. Another whimpered moan escaped her lungs while the beast he'd been trying to keep at bay roared inside him.

She pulled away, her lungs hungry for breath, and he fought not to order her lips back to his. "Austin, please. I need you."

A guttural groan accompanied the scorching kisses he trailed from her neck up to her right ear. "What do you need, darlin'?"

"You. Just please. I don't want to think anymore. I'm so tired of being afraid to live. Please. I need you to make me feel alive again, and I know you can. I have to stop telling myself I don't want you because I do. Take me back to your room and then just take me. Make everything else go away. I need *you*."

And there it was, the truth finally cemented between them. Before he could drag her from that bar out to his truck, Jackson tapped his shoulder. Fury ripped through him like a gasoline soaked fuse. "What the hell? I'm a little busy, Jackson," he snarled.

Laughing at him, Jackson smirked. "Yeah, the whole damn bar knows that. Minton's buying a round. They expect you to do the honors. I don't know who pissed in Clifton's Wheaties, but he ain't happy about this." He gestured to Summer.

"Yeah, well, he can fuck the hell off," Austin huffed.

"Maybe I should just go," Summer's eyes were seeking. Confusion played in their depths. Her lips were kiss-swollen and raw with heat, and her voice was breathy. Impatience saturated her tone. Her body swayed from the primal need he'd been tending for the last twenty-four hours.

"Hell no, honey. Come on. We'll do the toast or shot or whatever the hell they're wanting and then we're leaving."

Not willing to let her out of his sight, he grasped her hand and dragged her to the bar. The bartender was pouring up 7 and 7s, for luck, Austin supposed.

Every second he had to wait ate at him. He needed out of that damn bar and get Summer in bed, where he planned on keeping her. She was getting J.J. back the next night. He needed to make their evening alone enough to keep her begging for more. There was no reason they couldn't fuck while the baby slept, but he wanted her wild and uninhibited. Tonight, he'd have her just the way he wanted her, come hell or high water.

He accepted a tumbler from Scott and handed one to Summer. Her jaw clenched tightly. She stared Clifton down. As pissed as he was, Austin couldn't help but grin. His baby wasn't taking shit off anybody. He'd pay good money to watch her engage Clif in a verbal sparring match where she'd sure as hell dress him down one side and up the other.

Scott lifted his glass. "To Austin and the entire Minton team."

Austin joined in the toast and took a long sip of the drink. When he chose to drink, which wasn't often, he preferred straight whiskey or nothing at all. The weak 7 and 7 only served to irritate the churning fire in his gut.

Returning the half-empty tumbler to the bar he wrapped his arm over Summer's shoulders and turned her toward the door.

"I know you're looking to get out of here. No issues there. Could we just talk a second, Austin?" Scott's tenor took on a pleading edge.

Making no effort to hide his eye roll, Austin kept his arm around Summer. "You mind waiting in my truck for just a second. I'm not leaving you in here with him." He gestured his head to the table containing Brant Preston and the Preston Cattle team. No shock they'd been the only table in the bar not to join in the toast or the free booze.

"I guess not." Summer didn't sound too certain of that. Austin fought the urge to flip Scott off, throw her over his shoulder, and carry her away.

"Outside then," he directed Scott.

After helping Summer up into the passenger seat and turning on the engine and the air conditioner, Austin gently closed the truck door and spun to face Scott. "What's this all about?"

Scott lifted his cowboy hat and ran his hands through his hair. Nervous tension clung to the humid air surrounding them. "I don't know, man. Clifton's pissed about her. I told him you were in this, but honestly, I'm not sure that's true anymore."

"What the hell are you talking about? I've been hanging out with Summer for one fucking day, and I just had the best ride of my life. What's Clif's issue with any of that? Seems like he'd be kissing her boots."

"So this is all just a good time? Pick up lines, and drinks, and hooking up, and that's it?" Scott's questions bored into his brain.

"No, it's more than that."

It was just like two men not to realize that trucks aren't actually sound-proof. Summer's breath tangled in her lungs. *No?* He just told his sponsor that she was more than a hookup. What the hell was he thinking?

She fought the elation that rang in her ears. What were they doing, and more importantly why couldn't she find it in herself to put a stop to it all? Lowering her head, trying to blend into the leather seats of his fancy-ass truck, she continued to listen.

"Exactly. You've been with her for one day, Austin. You missed a team meeting this afternoon, and missed a practice session after that. Had her down at the chutes. The way you're looking at her, hanging all over her in a bar, Clif's worried you aren't in this anymore."

"Because I missed one meeting and a practice session I never agreed to. When we signed that contract back in February you never mentioned I couldn't have a life."

Summer racked her brain, but she knew Austin hadn't said anything about having a meeting or a practice session that day. Had he forgotten or did he choose to skip because he wanted to be with her? She closed her eyes. She needed time to slow down. Everything about her life before that moment tallied and whirled around her. She didn't understand what she was feeling or where this was going.

"Come on, Austin, you and I both know that bull riding takes everything you've got. I'm a very happily married man. My wife's meeting us in Cheyenne because I can't stand to be without her any longer. There are things that are far more important than buckles, man. I get it, but I don't think you can have both."

"It's been one fucking day, Scott. One day. I'm not proposing. I'm not moving her to the ranch. I haven't even slept with her yet. So what, I took the day off and hung out with a woman that gets me. Overreact much?"

"You moved her into your hotel room. And I said all of the same crap to myself when I met Liza. I could have it all. I could have the rodeo and her. She wouldn't keep me from anything. I knew about eight seconds in that I was full of shit. I stood in her bathroom one morning staring at myself in the mirror so I do recognize the look we all see on your face. Didn't even take me eight seconds to know you're lying to me and you're lying to yourself. You're full of shit, Austin. Enjoy your night."

Summer gripped the seat to keep from vaulting out of the truck and informing Scott that she had no intention of keeping Austin from winning in Vegas. They'd just barely started dating. She'd lived the rodeo life. She would not under any circumstances bring her son up as a rodeo gypsy.

As soon as she got full custody from Brant, she was going to find them a place and make him a home. Austin was just a fun, sweet, temporary distraction. After Cheyenne, they'd both move on. It took her a half second to compose herself when Austin flung himself into the truck, working his jaw furiously.

"What did he say?"

His eyes slid to hers, and he almost laughed, though the anger from Scott's accusations remained fixed in his gaze. "Not that stupid, honey. I know you heard us. There was a reason I brought him out to my truck to talk."

"Austin, maybe this is all moving too fast, or it's a bad idea or something. I don't know what we're doing. I don't want you to lose your sponsorship. I don't want you giving up anything for me. After Cheyenne, J.J. and I have to go back to Dallas..." She wasn't certain exactly what she was trying to tell him.

He turned in his seat to face her. The cab filled with the intoxicating scent of him, raw masculinity mixed with leather and the rosin that lived in his callused hands absorbed from his gloves. Her body and her mind went to war once more. God, she wanted him, but this could end in disaster for both of them.

"I don't give a damn about my sponsorship, and I'm not giving up one thing for you, Summer. If you really want me to stop, you just say the word. But I don't believe for one second that's what you're wanting, sweetness. Not for one moment. I see you sitting there trying to tell yourself we have no business getting involved, but you're failing that mission just as badly as I am. I want you, Summer. I want to see where this is taking us. Everything I've ever done in life I've gone by my gut. That's how I work. Everything about you, everything about this, feels right. I'm not giving anything up, but I know I'm getting something I've wanted for a long damn time. Forget Minton, and Scott, and Brant and whoever else it is you're worrying about. Just give me a chance, and let's see where we end up."

Dusty earth and gravel launched into the air behind his tires as he floored the truck and flew them back to the hotel.

CHAPTER SEVEN

They fell into the room lip-locked, jerking shirts out from each other's jeans, frantic to drown out the rest of the world. Austin hoisted that tank top that had been driving him to distraction all damn night over her head.

In one quick move, he popped the clasp of the bra making a valiant effort to contain her ample cleavage. Her breasts spilled forward, and a ravenous growl roared from his chest as her diamond-hard nipples throbbed against his palms.

He slid his hands down her sides, intent on stripping her jeans away, but she gripped his hands and halted his progress. "Austin, I should probably tell you..."

"Tell me what?" He jerked his hands from hers and unbuckled her belt. He forced his eyes to hers when she didn't respond. Fear and doubt clouded her gaze. "Hey, come here." He called himself an asshole for rushing her as he cradled her in his arms and tried not to feel the weight of her breasts against his chest.

"It's just, uh, I haven't really done this since way before J.J. was born, and..."

"And?" He lifted her chin so he could study her again.

She refused to look at him. "I have some marks and scar kind of things from carrying him."

Assuming if she'd gotten them from carrying J.J. they'd be located somewhere near her womb, he pulled her jeans apart and lowered them slightly. There were indeed a few faint purplish markings low along her abdomen and a few white lines marring her hips. Certain he wouldn't have noticed had she not pointed them out, he brushed kisses along each mark.

"Nothing about you is unattractive, sweetheart. My God, you're so fucking beautiful. I can't believe this worried you." Standing, he spun her so she was facing the mirror. He stood behind her. "Look at you. Look at us together." He cupped her breasts and let them spill through his fingers. "Your body drives me wild, Summer. I'm covered in scars and marks from every time a bull got a piece of me. You know what scars mean? They mean you lived, mean you survived, mean you fought, and you were the one that walked away. They all make up your life, and honey, my God, you are gorgeous. All I've wanted since I woke up with you in my arms this morning was to get you back in my bed. I only see two things that bother me."

"What?"

"One, your jeans and panties are still on, and I'm getting damned impatient with that. And this." He ran his hand down a long tattoo that she'd managed to keep hidden. A large, split feather ran upwards from her waist, with the two halves cradling her right breast.

"You don't like tats?" She sounded shocked by that.

"Uh, hell no, darlin'. If it's on your body, I fucking love it. It's sexy as sin. But remember, I know a fair amount about Native American symbols. I know what a split feather means, and the fact that you tattooed that on your side worries me."

"Why?" She continued to tremble against him as he kept her rooted in front of the mirror, desperate for her to see her own beauty. She was exquisite. Perfect curves. Beautiful breasts. Her nipples darkening, pert, and anxious. Her long hair teasing at her breasts. Perfect little hollows showing off slight muscles in her abs. Cute little belly button, half-in and half-out, surrounded by a smattering of freckles he wanted to kiss on his way to her pussy. Perfect, dimpled ass round and firm, accentuated by her hips. Sweet little pouch under her open zipper where her child had once resided. Natural. Just the way a woman was supposed to be. Why couldn't she see that?

"The split feather means wounded multiple times. What the hell happened to you, Summer? I want to know. I want to make you feel safe. I want to take care of you."

She spun to face him instead of the mirror. "It means wounded several times...but still fighting. Never forget that part. Every single man that's ever had anything to do with me has wounded me. Everyone except J.J. So, how about you just don't be another one."

"I have no intention of ever hurting you, and I'll never let anyone else hurt you again. Let's slow this down, okay?" He tried to quell the disappointment he couldn't help but feel. Slowing things down hadn't been his plan. Showing her exactly how he wanted her, making her feel beautiful, revealing her darkest desires and proving to her that he'd make her every fantasy come true had occupied all of this evening's agenda—right up until he'd seen the tattoo.

"No," she defied. The fire in her eyes exploded in a fierce blaze. "No, I don't want to slow it down. I don't want your sweet, gentle side. I know it's who you are. You've been showing me ever since you bought me dinner last night, but I know there's another side to you, too. I know there's a beast inside of you. I can see it when you ride. I can see you try to tame it when you look at me, when you touch me. That's what I want. I'm not some delicate little flower that wants you to be a gentleman in bed. I'm a fucking cowgirl, even if I don't ride anymore. I want to see you raw, and wild, and being a man. Believe me, I can take it, so give it to me. Let it all go. Show me the side you keep hidden from everyone else. I want the beast."

A low, ravenous groan thundered from his chest. All orders he'd been giving himself to slow it down were vanquished by her requests. Never before had a woman demanded what he so desperately craved. "Just remember you said that, baby. Cause I'm about to give you exactly what you asked for."

"Yes," she hissed as he lifted her into his arms and tossed her on the bed, removing her boots, socks, and jeans in three split-second steps.

He ripped the cheap satin panties from her. They were already half-torn, and impatience drove his every move.

"I'll buy you some more," he managed in a husky grunt. A loud moan of approval rang from Summer. Her body writhed and rolled against the sheets, so anxious. His mouth watered as he watched her tits bounce from the motion.

His laser-focused eyes tracked down her body. His mind listed every single thing he longed to do to her. He'd fuck those beautiful tits, squirt his cum all over her chest. Mark her thoroughly with his bites. Taunt her throbbing nipples until she begged. Show her who she now belonged to. Make her drink him so he could taste himself in her mouth. Suck and tease that sweet clit, make her scream until her throat was raw. Turn her over take her tight, puckered little ass slowly, gently, until she opened for him. Show her how intimate it could be between them. And, my God, he was gonna own every centimeter of her slick fevered pussy over and over again until she couldn't remember her own name, until all she knew was his.

He traced his fingers along her pouty slit, wet, full, and perfect. The essence of her, wild and ripe, filled his lungs as he fell to his knees and jerked her ass to the side of the mattress. "Legs over my shoulders, right now."

Austin's gruff commands sent another rush of wetness over Summer's pussy. They'd barely gotten started, and she'd never been more aroused. She'd never felt more beautiful or more willing.

"I said *now*, honey."

Lost in what he might request next, she'd forgotten to obey. Looping her legs over his broad shoulders, her body writhed in unbearable desperation to be owned.

"Watch me," he ordered. She lifted her head and simultaneously felt the wet rasp of his tongue bathing her slit. Barely able to breathe, she stared at his darkened eyes. His expression was loaded with undiluted sin as he began to coax and suckle at her clit.

A whimpered moan shook through her body. So close. She'd needed this for far too long. Just a little more. Unable to remain up on her elbows, she slid back to the mattress, entranced by his ardor for her pussy. His sucks grew in intensity and length. Drawing her clit into his mouth he allowed her one suck and then slowly, keenly pulled away, making her distend fully. He blew cold breath over her, making her exhale in racked groans as he denied her the orgasm she so desperately craved.

"Oh my God." She couldn't remain still. He rendered her mindless.

His hands clamped tight over her hipbones and ass. The boundless strength of his arms anchored her to the mattress. She couldn't move. "Be still and let me enjoy you, then I'll give you a taste of your candy."

Another intense moan was all she could manage. His inquisitive tongue tasted at her opening, slicked upwards for another drawing suck of her clit, then dipped lower to spin around her perineum.

"Oh, God, Austin, please, please." She had no idea why that felt so astoundingly good, but she knew she couldn't take much more. Apparently there was no spot on her body that he didn't want to claim. That knowledge alone nearly brought her to orgasm.

A persistent hum rang in her ears. His tongue reversed its path from her ass back to her opening, then to her clit where he indulged her with hot lashes.

"Please," she whimpered again.

A hungry growl reverberated against her. His eyes flashed with uninhibited carnality. She shook with need. Finally, mercifully, he sucked until she was certain she was flying. Her soul unhinged. Everything in her life that kept her shackled and bound sprung free. Pure, unadulterated pleasure erupted from her core and sizzled outward through her veins. She quaked, tightening her thighs against his five o'clock shadow, letting the friction amp her to unexplored heights. Every nerve ending from the top of her scalp to the bottom of her feet exulted in the climax. She cried out in broken syllables of gratification.

She became aware of the audible friction of Austin releasing his belt from its trappings and his jeans hitting the floor. Time seemed a variable concept. She was lost in elation. Awareness came back to her slowly. She felt his hot breath travel up her thighs as he crawled over her like a lion slowly tracking its prey.

"You taste so damn good, darlin'. Makes me fucking hungry for more. Taste us together." He fused his mouth to hers, parting the seam of her lips forcefully until she accepted and sucked her own flavor from his tongue. A hum of erotic approval purred in the back of her throat from the order.

She wiggled when his fingers moved back and forth from her clit to her opening, gathering more of the dew he was able to draw from her with ease. Their tongues tangled in an erotic dance until he lifted his head and traced her lips with his wet fingers. "Take more."

She accepted his fingers, sucking and enjoying the salty resin flavor of him more than her own essence. Liquid heat dripped down her thighs.

He pulled his hand away and gently stroked along her cheek bone, brushing her hair from her face. "You come so sweet, darlin'. So pretty. I want to watch this time. Show me how you bring yourself. Show me how my girl likes to be touched." With that directive, he took her hand in his and proceeded to suck her fingers until they were wet enough for his purposes.

Summer's stomach jolted at the thought of touching herself while he watched. Nervous energy twisted up her spine. She started to refuse, but chickening out was definitely not her style.

"Show me." His orders became more and more gruff when she didn't comply. Damn if that didn't just make her wetter. He placed his hands over hers and laid them on her breasts. "Imagine me doing every single thing you've ever fantasized about. Show me where you want my hands and where you want my first mark, so you know you're mine. Right now, honey."

The lust in his graveled tone mixed in a seductive cocktail with the wild girl she'd once been, the desire to be with him in every possible way, and the seductress she always wanted to be. Her many selves seemed to unite in him. He released her hands, and she began to grope her breasts. She wasn't gentle, showing him exactly how she wanted to be manhandled. A low, rumbled murmur escaped him. "You like it rough like that, sugar?"

Her body bucked off the mattress. She spread her legs farther, knowing he watched her every move and wanting to give him one hell of a show. "Yes," gasped from her lips.

"You're driving me wild. Where do you want my mouth, Summer? Show me."

She centered in on her nipples, stoking over them, twisting and pinching before moving back out to grasp the heft of her breasts.

"Am I sucking or biting?"

"Both."

"That's right, honey. Now keep going."

She let her hands glide down her abdomen, lost in the rumbled thunder of his moans. When she separated her swollen, tender pussy lips, getting her fingers wet and stroking her clit, a guttural growl echoed around her. She stroked faster. Her thighs tensed. She got closer, imagining Austin's dick moving back and forth instead of her fingers.

"So damn beautiful. My God. I can't wait much longer."

"Good," her breaths tensed with the word.

"Inside now. I want to watch."

Too far gone to argue, she slipped her ring and middle finger inside her overly-sensitized channel and used her thumb to continue tempting her clit.

Fucking hell, his little vixen was going to make him come long before he intended. She put on one hell of a show, but he could tell she was still nervous.

"You ready to come for me, honey?" He was unable to halt the commands that continually poured from his mouth, and damn if she didn't love to comply. Every word he spoke made her body twist with need. Her moans were intoxicating. That pretty little pussy was so wet he could fuck her all night long.

With another few strokes, she grunted in frustration. "Relax. Just let it come." She obviously needed a little help, and he was only too happy to step in.

He spun his tongue over each of her nipples, then nipped them forcefully. She gasped for breath. He left fiery trails with his tongue up her chest until he reached the apex of her shoulder, to the sweet spot where it joined her neck. He brushed a kiss there and she thrust her hips upward, desperate to be owned. *Perfection.*

"All mine." He sank his teeth into her satin skin and sucked until her body bowed. She came with a harsh cry of relent. "That's it." He watched her body tremble from the climaxes. "So damn beautiful. I need to be inside of you right fucking now."

Austin had intended to provide a little more foreplay. Next time, he told himself as he quickly rolled on a condom and centered his hips between her legs. He lowered his head to her right breast and drew it into the heat of his mouth as he spread her legs and thrust into her fully.

Her sweet little gasp was yet another thing he found perfect about her. She trembled against his size. "So tight aren't you, honey? It has been a while. I'm gonna go slow, just relax and let me make it feel good."

He pinned her arms over her head and slowly entered her again and again, gaining ground with each fervent pass, slicking his cock with her dew, feeling her wet curls tease at his sack. She drowned his cock in that warm honey she made so good for him. The silken walls of her pussy cradled tightly around him and began to nurse him rhythmically. He was fairly certain he'd died and gone to heaven.

Ignoring the momentary pressure and slight pain of being opened for the first time in far too long, Summer flexed her muscles around him. His eyes flashed as another loud growl thundered from low in his chest.

"Keep doing that, honey, and this'll be over way too soon."

"Then give me more."

"Gladly." He transitioned and began pistoning his hips, stroking that spot deep within her with every rapid thrust. Her entire body quaked. He kept her on the constant brink of another release. It hovered just out of reach, and he knew it.

She stared up at him, letting her eyes beg since he'd robbed her of words.

"Not yet, sweetheart. Not yet."

She wiggled back and forth, trying to provide her own friction. She was so close. It was right there.

"I said not yet. Stop trying to make yourself come. Don't think I won't stop and paddle your hot little ass. I'm gonna take good care of you, but you're gonna let it build for me."

A shuddered moan quaked from her lungs. She obeyed, giving herself over to the all-consuming feelings he provided. Euphoria sizzled in her veins. Every cell in her body pulsed, desperate for the explosive release he endlessly built.

Raw masculinity filled her lungs, primal and decisive. She ran her hands over his shoulders, loving the way his muscles rippled under her fingertips. Sweat dewed on his back. She pulled him closer, running her hands down the long, lean muscles contracting with the effort of his thrusts. She grasped his ass leaving marks with her fingernails, making him groan in elation. He loved it. She knew he would.

His commands in no way dampened the sense of security being in bed with him provided. She'd never experienced anything that felt so right. The connection between them grew with every thrust. She never wanted this to end.

Suddenly, he gripped her hips and thrust hard, burying himself to his hilt, and she spiraled over from the apex of the highest mountain. Her muscles cinched tightly around his cock. Her climax pulled his from him. A roar of satisfaction barreled through him. His lips took hers with greed as he gave another thrust deep within her.

When he lifted his head, they both gasped for breath, staring at one another in disbelief. Summer tried to decipher what she was feeling beyond the bliss-filled haze of euphoria he'd so generously provided.

"I'm not finished with you, honey. You make me so fucking hard. I told you I can go all night. You up for another round?"

Dear Lord. He wasn't kidding. How was this even possible? Her entire body had taken on the consistency of a jellyfish. She'd never in her life felt more bone-deep satisfaction, and he wanted to do it again. Summoning strength from somewhere she didn't even know existed, she managed to tense her pelvic muscles slightly. Indeed, he was rapidly stiffening inside of her. "Can I have just one second?"

"No problem." Gently, he withdrew and threw away what she assumed would be the first of many used condoms, given that he'd placed an entire box on the bedside table.

Slipping back down in the bed, he drew her up onto his chest and cradled her in his arms. All sense of her hard-lined lover disappeared, and her sweet, protective, cocky Austin returned. She had no concept of being cared for like this. All she knew was she wanted more.

"That was amazing. *You* are amazing." He cossetted her closer and whispered kisses in her hair. His callused hands gently moved over her body, settling her, contenting her. "I don't think I'll ever get enough of this, Summer. I've never been with anyone who makes me feel this way."

Apparently, if you wanted Austin Camden to confess his true feelings all you had to do was show him your deepest, darkest secrets and then provide him with a mind-blowing orgasm.

"I feel that way too, Austin, but after Cheyenne, J.J. and I have to..."

His index finger over her lips halted any further communication. "I don't want to hear about after Cheyenne right now. We'll deal with *after Cheyenne* later. Right now, I want you again. Minute's up, doll baby. I need more."

He turned her on her side and brushed kisses on the tender nape of her neck. A sigh escaped her as she closed her eyes. Every square inch of skin on her body was fevered and overly-sensitized. Once again, he knew. He was gentle this time. Blowing cool air along her shoulders before he peppered them with soft kisses. With a great deal of finesse, he positioned his right thigh between her legs, granting himself access to her pussy, still wet from her multiple releases.

"It's tender isn't it, baby?"

A nod was all she could manage. His fingers traced back and forth along her slit, not entering her, just preparing her for more.

"So sweet, you feel so good. I'll be gentle this time. I promise. Relax and open for me." Her body relaxed at his request. She seemed to have no control over any of her own responses, and she willingly allowed him to guide her every move. Settling back against him, she felt his left arm tunnel under her side and gently grasp her right breast.

He tucked her back safely against his chest, as his talented fingers entered her with a gentle explorative touch.

She trembled against him. A low thrum of approval sounded in her ear. He pressed in farther, and she was once again lost in the way he made her feel. Desired. Beautiful. Sexy. Loved? Maybe. She wasn't sure if that's what this was, and currently, she had no brain capacity with which to decide. Austin added another finger and located her G-spot.

"Oh, right there," she gasped.

A devilish chuckle sounded from him. "I know, sugar, and I'm gonna figure out where every single sweet spot is. I'm gonna know them all intimately."

As he continued to strum with his fingers, his lips returned to her shoulders and back. He suckled at her shoulder blade until he'd left a mark of ownership there as well. She came a moment later.

"Mmm, you like that don't you? You like it when I mark you?"

"Yes…" she panted for breath, "…more."

"My God, you are perfect," he grunted.

Before her mind stopped spinning from the confessions that came from her mouth and the orgasms he drew from her body, he had another condom on. "Nice and easy this time." He entered her slowly, just as he'd promised.

She still couldn't believe that he was hard again. Long, and stiff, and throbbing fiercely with need. All man and all hers. In and out, in perfect rhythm. When his fingers stroked over her clit, she cried out for him and for more. His thrusts picked up pace. She pressed back against him, letting him have her. This time his climax drove hers.

She shook with it, trembling constantly, unable to open her eyes or do anything but be consumed by him. He gripped her tightly, tensing with his release. When it freed him, he continued to cradle her tenderly in his arms, kissing over the hickeys he'd left on her shoulders, then got up to dispense with the condom and turn out the light.

Still dizzy and weak, she let him guide her up onto his chest. That sinfully-sexy chuckle of his made her grin, though she remained unable to open her eyes. She'd heard of being fucked to sleep, but it wasn't something she'd ever experienced before. Sated exhaustion overtook her.

"Go to sleep, sweetness. I'm pretty sure you're already about halfway there. I'm driving you to Cheyenne tomorrow, so get some rest."

Summer wanted to argue. He wasn't driving her. *She* was driving her. But she had no capacity with which to disagree, and she suspected that had been his plan. She'd deal with him in the morning. With a deep yawn, she passed out on his chest, certain her dreams couldn't be any better than what she'd just lived in reality.

Confusion and a slight sense of panic kept Austin from sleeping. He'd never been in love before. He'd heard the entire lineage of Camden men tell the stories about how they knew as soon as they saw the girl that she was the one. His parents would tell anyone willing to listen their story of fated love. He reviewed the tales in his head once again.

Did people really fall in love in one split second? Is that what he was in? *It took me about eight seconds to know I was full of shit.* Scott's words ricocheted around his head.

Austin shifted slightly, careful to keep Summer tucked safely against him. It was where she belonged. That thought reinforced the others. Okay, so maybe he was in love. That didn't mean he had to give up the rodeo. Hell, she grew up with a daddy in the rodeo, and she was a barrel racer. She knew how it all worked. They could travel together.

That isn't what she wants. He wasn't certain how he knew that, but he did. Same way he knew what to say to make her blush, knew where to kiss and touch her, knew how to ply her skin and where to suck her to make her come. He knew what to say to make her wetter, and how to argue with her just enough to give her the opportunity to show off her sexy stubborn side when that's what she needed.

Sleep continued to elude him. So, if he *was* in love, what happened next? His dad had never filled him in on *that* portion of the story. How had he gotten his mom out of that car and into his arms permanently? Maybe Austin should ask.

Summer's sweet breaths whispered through his chest hair. He grinned and tucked her closer still. She was so beautiful, and the perfect mix of sweet and sinful. His spiteful little vixen when that's what he wanted, and sweet as an angel when that's what he needed. Her frantic worry over him before he climbed on that bull added to his sense of completeness.

He hadn't fully admitted to himself that she was what he'd been looking for all this time, until he'd pressed his cock inside her and made them one. Then he knew. There was no more denial.

She stripped away all of his bravado and stupidity. She reached in his soul and touched the fear and pain he refused to ever acknowledge. The terror that he'd killed his best friend. The fear he was a disappointment to his family. The confusion over who the hell he really was and why he was still chasing a buckle that meant less and less to him by the moment. It all evaporated at her touch. She didn't heal him; no, it was as if those blistered lashes on his soul never existed at all when he was with her.

I kept trying to tell you it wasn't about the buckle, Max's voice echoed against the recesses of his mind. It had done that since the day of his funeral. Austin had never told anyone he could still hear Max, but sometimes he swore Max was doing his damnedest to get Austin where he was supposed to be going.

Before he could get lost in all of that, a loud knock sounded on his hotel room door. *What the fucking hell?* Summer didn't even stir. *Sweet baby.* He couldn't help but grin at his own work as he eased out from under her, tucked the covers softly around her, and slung on his jeans.

"What the fuck?" he hissed as he edged the door open, trying to keep the light from the hallway from disturbing his baby, content in his bed.

Brant Preston glared at him, holding a yawning baby J.J., who was trying to go back to sleep on his father's shoulder. Brant tensed, lifting his shoulder to stop J.J.'s efforts. Fury shot through Austin.

"Where's Summer?" Brant huffed.

"Fast asleep in my bed. She's worn out." Austin narrowed his eyes, waiting on Brant to understand exactly what he was implying.

"She needs to take him. He's sick or something. He was crying. It's her job to take care of him when I'm busy, and I don't want him back 'til after Cheyenne. I've got stuff to do."

Austin studied the baby. No sign of tears. He was breathing steady, looked comfy in the pajamas he was wearing. His confused lengthy blinks were telling. He hadn't been crying. He'd been woken up.

"He wasn't crying, and she's been trying to take care of him, but you and your mama won't let her. You woke him up, didn't you? Why? To get back at her for being with me? Did it really take you until one in the morning to come up with this brilliant plan? You're quick, Preston."

"Just get Summer."

"I don't think so, brain-boy." Austin considered. Summer swore that Brant would do something to get back at him for his goading about the two of them. He wouldn't put anything past Brant. Leaning back in the room, he grabbed his cell phone.

"What are you doing?" Brant demanded.

"Not being a dumbass. You should give it a try sometime. You want Summer to take the little guy for an extra week, then you call my cell phone and say that to my voicemail. I like to keep you from being the douchebag you are whenever I can. I want legal proof to make sure you're not gonna pull some shit trying to get her in trouble."

Simpering, Brant thrust J.J. into Austin's arms. He cradled the little guy on his shoulder and swayed him quite naturally. J.J. yawned and then tucked his head against Austin's neck. There, that wasn't too difficult. Maybe he could figure this out.

Austin switched the ringer off on his phone and stood listening to Brant stupidly explain that he'd given Summer permission to keep her own kid until the end of Cheyenne and not to bother him with J.J. When he ended the call, he edged to the side, trying to see into the hotel room, Austin moved with him, blocking anything from his view with the expanse of his chest. "She's mine, Preston. You don't get to see her like that anymore. It's all mine. For my eyes only."

"Good luck shacking up with my wife while you're babysitting my kid." Brant gestured to J.J. Austin longed to deck him again. The child in his arms was all that kept him from burying his fist into Brant's smug face.

"Leave." Austin spun and let the door close behind him. Staring down at J.J., he debated. Summer had spent the last six months sleeping in her truck or in hotel hallways off and on. She'd been exhausted long before he'd fucked her thoroughly. He wouldn't wake her up unless he couldn't figure something out. Currently, J.J. was sucking his thumb and working his way back to sleep. He seemed quite content with Austin.

Smiling at that, he settled in a chair and rocked J.J. back and forth gently. "Your daddy is an asshat." He cringed. "Okay, forget I said that." *Talking bad about the kid's dad. Not cool, Camden.* "So, listen," he whispered, "I'm kind of crazy about your mama. Think maybe we could share her? You can teach me whatever I need to know. I'll do anything you need, even the diaper thing, but fair warning, I don't have a lot of experience with that, so if you could wait 'til mornin', I'd be much obliged. I'll take good care of you both, I swear. I'm good at trials by fire. That's how I ended up bull riding. You just give me a shot, and we'll see if we can't talk mama into giving me one. Deal?"

J.J. made a soft sigh and then spoke a few quiet, gurgled sounds that Austin took to mean, "Deal." When "ma-ma" came out in broken syllables next, Austin grinned. "That's right. Mama's asleep over there. How about you and I go camp out with her?"

Standing, Austin eased back to the bed and arranged J.J. on his chest. Keeping one arm on the baby and wrapping the other protectively around Summer, his mind settled finally, and he fell sound asleep.

CHAPTER EIGHT

Blinking repeatedly, Summer tried to bring the image before her into focus. She was obviously still dreaming. She couldn't possibly be staring at her sweet baby boy cuddled up on Austin Camden's bare chest, both of them sound asleep. The perfection of the picture was almost more than she could stand.

She allowed herself one moment to imagine it, and since it was her fantasy, she ran wild with it. A family. Austin with his arm around her, standing on a porch somewhere, watching J.J. play in the grass. Maybe another one on the way. The dream spun again. Austin's hand on her round belly, smiling at her with pride. His lips kissing her swell, then looking up at her, and promising to love her forever.

The pain of something she could never have shattered the imagery her mind conjured with far too much ease. Unable to come up with something more creative, she reached down and pinched her own thigh. *Ouch. Okay, I'm not dreaming.* Scooting upward in the bed, she covered her exposed breasts with the sheets and blankets and contemplated who to awaken first.

Hazy sunshine was just coming up over the mountains and warming the town of Cody. Where was Brant? How did J.J. get there? And how was he in bed with her and Austin? Leaning, she brushed a kiss over J.J.'s plump cheek and then one on Austin's.

Austin's eyes blinked open. Almost instinctively, he gasped and checked J.J. on his chest. Relaxing after he was sure the baby was fine, he planted a kiss on his head and then gifted Summer with one of his devastatingly gorgeous grins. "Mornin', sunshine."

In that moment, she knew she was falling completely, hopelessly in love with the man gently cradling her baby boy. "Mornin'. How exactly did you get my son?"

"Well…" Austin yawned and readjusted, carefully keeping J.J. from being jostled, "…Brant showed up here at 1:00 a.m. demanding to see you. I politely told him to fuck off." He cringed and glanced down at the baby. "Is it okay to say that in front of him?" He looked so terrified, Summer giggled. She brushed another kiss on his cheek.

"Maybe just try to keep it to a minimum."

"No problem. Anyway, Brant was pissed you were with me and used J.J. as an excuse to interrupt us. Don't worry. He's not gonna pull anything. I made him leave a voicemail on my phone saying he was leaving J.J. with us and I also got him to say that he didn't want him back until after Cheyenne. We get him an extra week. I wanted you to rest, so little man and I chatted for a few then we went to sleep."

Austin's precautions and care warmed her entire being. Emotion cinched her throat. Swallowing harshly, she threw her arms around both of them. "He said that? He said I could have him for all of Cheyenne?"

Austin nodded, his grin expanding the width of his face.

"Thank you. You're amazing, you know that?"

Chuckling, he looked very pleased with her assessment.

"I told you Brant would do something," she sighed.

"He brought you J.J., and you just told me I was amazing. I'm pretty sure I've never seen you smiling this big. If this was his idea of revenge, he's dumber than I thought."

"Does Jean know Brant brought him here?"

"Going with Jean is Brant's mama?"

"Yeah," Summer nearly gagged.

"No idea, sugar. Not worried about it if she does. Having both of you in my arms is a pretty damn perfect way to wake up." Another cringe creased his forehead. "Got to get better about cursing."

"Do you really mean that?"

"About cursing?"

"No..." Summer rolled her eyes, "...about holding me and J.J."

"Hell yeah. Dammit, what is wrong with me? You may have to wash my mouth out with soap like my mama used to."

Summer doubled over, laughing hysterically. She couldn't think of anything more perfect either, and that should have scared her to death. But for the first time in a long time, she couldn't locate any fear.

Her laughter woke J.J., whose bottom lip protruded as he worked his way into a wail.

"Oh, I'm sorry, buddy. Come here." Summer lifted him from Austin's chest. He hugged her tightly, making every single confusing thing in her world settle. "Mama's got you."

Austin stared at her. The customary heat was in his eyes, but something about it was different that morning.

"What?" Summer somehow felt exposed.

"You're so beautiful." He leaned and brandished her mouth with a kiss that J.J. interrupted a moment later by latching his tiny hand onto Austin's morning stubble and taking a tight hold.

Laughing, Austin eased J.J.'s hand away. "Hey, man, we had a deal. You have to let me kiss her if we're gonna get her to give me a chance."

"You made a deal with J.J.?" Try though she might, she could not order the stupid grin from her own face. Elation bubbled in her stomach and sheer bliss radiated throughout her body.

"Yep, and I meant what I was saying. You're so damn beautiful. The way you are with him and then the way you are with me. I'm fallin' hard, woman."

The way he just said whatever he was thinking always threw her for a loop. Finding it much easier to talk with her son, whom she'd missed desperately for the last week, she situated him in her lap while she reclined back against the pillows. "And you, little man, what are you doing making deals with Austin? He's a slick rodeo cowboy. What did Mama tell you about those? Nothing but trouble."

"Don't tell him that." Austin sounded genuinely offended.

Shocked, Summer lifted her gaze from her son's hopeful blue eyes to Austin's onyx black ones. "I'm sorry. I was just kidding."

"No, you weren't, but we'll talk about that later. We need to get packed. I'm guessing the normal six-hour drive will be a good bit longer with little man on board."

"Austin, I'm driving J.J and myself to Cheyenne."

"In that piece of shit truck Brant lets you drive? Not on my watch, darlin'. As much as it pains me to say this, get your sexy nakedness out of my bed, and let's hit the road."

Rolling her eyes, Summer made little effort to quell her temper. "Brant does not *let* me do anything, cowboy. I'll do whatever the hell I want, and before I do anything else I need to change J.J.'s diaper. Did my idiot ex-husband bring his diaper bag?"

"So glad you cursed in front of him, too. Makes me feel better. Your idiot ex left me nothing but the little man, and Brant may not get a say anymore, but I do. You're not driving that truck from Cody to Cheyenne, through a half-dozen mountain ranges where if you break down in the middle of nowhere the only thing that might find you is a grizzly, or a mountain lion, and his friend the coyot'. That is, if you don't stumble up on a rattler while you're trying to carry J.J. to find a human being that you ain't gonna find. Now, you hang tight, I'll go find Brant and get J.J.'s stuff, then we'll get some breakfast and be on our way. I have to get registered tonight and do the cattle drive thing tomorrow morning."

Wishing she could stand up to argue with him, Summer fumed. She was naked, and Austin was between her and her tack bag. "At what point in all of this..." she gestured between herself and the broad hunk of man smirking at her with his arms crossed over his chest, looking ridiculously gorgeous with his rumpled hair, wearing nothing but low slung Wranglers, which only made her more irritated, "...did you decide you were the boss of me?"

"You sure as hell didn't seem to mind last night, sugar. Simmer down. You can yell at me some more when I get back." With that he swooped in and dropped a kiss on the top of her head. She swatted his direction, but he grabbed a T-shirt and ducked out of the way and escaped out the door.

"Ugh, he is so infuriating!" she huffed.

J.J. belly laughed at her outright then attempted to mimic her growl. He gave her a drooly kiss and set those blue eyes on her. He always looked at her like he could see all the way down into her soul. She assumed he probably could. After all, he was the only person who'd ever really held her heart. If she hadn't already been worried about making the trip in her truck, she might've been able to really be angry. As it stood, spending hours and hours with Austin, having his undivided attention, sounded like heaven.

"So, he's got you in on this gig too, huh? Sold mama out, didn't you?" She fanned kisses all over his cheeks, making him giggle again. "And I know, he's also sweet, and caring, and kind, and strong, and he took such good care of you...and he takes really good care of me in every possible way." She set J.J. on the carpet so he could crawl around while she got dressed.

In no time at all he was using her legs to pull himself up to a standing position. "What am I supposed to do, J? I can't fall in love. I don't even know *how* to do that. I have to take care of you, and you are *not* growing up on the rodeo circuit. No way. I'm gonna get us a little house, maybe a little tract of land. I can work at one of those horseback riding places. I could teach kids to ride and then you could learn, too. Maybe out in Nashville, or somewhere nice like that. Somewhere far, far away from Dallas. I'll make us a little money, and we'll be happy. Just the two of us."

Even if you get primary custody, Brant will still get to see him. Two weeks in the summer and two weeks at Christmas, just the way you grew up. She tried so hard to make herself believe that happiness was on their horizon, but when she considered life without Austin, her chest ached. Her bones felt hollow. She'd known him three days. How the hell had this happened? *When Brant has J.J. you'll be all alone.* Without Austin in the room with her, the fear returned with a vengeance.

"Open the door, motherfucker," Austin hissed through his teeth as he continued to pound on Brant's hotel room door.

Just as he was contemplating breaking the damn thing down, it swung open. Mrs. Preston glared at Austin like he'd just informed her that the color of her hair was best used for reflective hunting gear, not grey cover-up.

"I was just coming to see you, Mr. Camden." She pursed her lips like saying his name left a bad taste in her mouth. *Good.*

"Well, looks like I beat you to it. I need to get J.J.'s stuff before we head out."

"I've already packed the baby's things and loaded them into Brantley's truck. He didn't mean to bring J.J. to you last evening. He was just...agitated. I'll be taking the baby with me."

Chuckling, Austin lifted his cell phone and played Brant's message for his mother.

Her eyes goggled in fury. "And just what do you intend to do with that message?"

"I intend to keep it safely stored on my phone to make sure you don't pull any shit with Summer and that *we* get to keep J.J. the entire time all of us are enjoying Frontier Days in Cheyenne, *ma'am.* Now, why don't you and I mosey on down to Brantley's truck and get his stuff."

While Mrs. Preston spit and sputtered out some nonsensical argument, Austin smirked. "Truth be told, we don't do a lot of moseying where I come from, but I'd heard it was a common practice down there in Dallas, so I'll follow you."

An hour later, Austin was mopping pancake syrup off of J.J.'s hands. He'd devoured the eggs and pancakes Summer had cut into tiny bite sized pieces for him. Tired of debating his own motives and his own gut, Austin decided to go with it. He wanted Summer, not for a night or two, not for the next two weeks, but for a lifetime...maybe. If he was going to convince her to be with him, he had to vanquish his own doubts.

He recalled his cousin Brock and his older brother Luke harassing him back in early February. They'd been quick to call him on the fact that he didn't want to leave the ranch and go back on the circuit. He'd all but decided not to go until Minton called, and just like every season before, quitting before he gave it his all and tried his damnedest to get that PBR buckle felt like he was letting down Max. He owed Max that buckle. If she'd stick with him through Vegas, he'd give it up. He'd pay back his debt to Max and… and what? There was so much he had to figure out. First and foremost, he needed to know exactly what kind of life Miss Summer Sanchez really wanted.

Studying J.J., he tried to figure out if he was really ready for a built-in family. Reminding himself that if he wanted Summer, J.J. was part of the deal, he grinned. To his own surprise, he was rather pleased with that portion of the deal.

Geez, as soon as he introduced her to them, Luke and Brock and all of his brothers and sisters would torment him for his previous position on women, that one was just as good as another as long as she was curved in all the right places and didn't have too much baggage. Yeah, okay, so he was an asshole. A guy could change, right?

"I don't think Brant's feeding him enough when he's with him," Summer fussed. "And my idiot mother-in-law tries to give him shit like sliced olives and something called quinoa. It's disgusting. I tried it once at her house. She gets mad when J.J. won't eat it and won't let him have anything else." She sighed as she cut up the rest of her own egg to give J.J.

"Hey, you eat that. I'm stuffed. He can have mine." Austin quickly mimicked Summer's movements with one of his own eggs and provided it to J.J., who readily consumed it. The kid didn't look like he'd missed any meals, though Austin himself wouldn't eat olives or quinoa. And while he certainly wouldn't give something fit for a bird to a baby, he assumed J.J. was healthy enough. He was obviously much happier with his mama than his wicked grandmother. Kid knew what was up. No shock there.

When the little guy was yawning more than he was eating, Austin paid the bill and guided them out to his truck. Thankful he'd gotten the quad-cab, he helped Summer up into the passenger seat after she'd buckled J.J. into the car seat in the back.

"How exactly am I going to get *my* truck back?" Summer's grin said she was pleased he'd insisted on their new driving arrangements, though she was still feigning irritation.

"Let's make a deal on that," he carefully began his negotiations. Her brow furrowed, but she settled in and moved a little closer to him. As he backed out of the parking lot, he gave a nod to the great city of Cody and headed out on Sheridan Avenue.

"A deal on getting my truck back?"

"I'm somewhat willing to negotiate," he allowed.

"So, basically you're taking me prisoner?"

"I prefer the term *girlfriend* to prisoner."

Rolling her eyes, she sighed. "What's your deal, Austin?"

"I get the next two weeks to convince you that what we've got going on here is something big, bigger than I really ever even believed was a possibility. By the night I win the Cheyenne buckle, if I don't measure up as the guy you want taking care of you, I'll drive you back out here to get your truck." *I won't actually let you get in it and drive away, but no need to mention that right now.* "But if I show you that I can be the guy you want beside you, in bed with you, taking care of anything you need, taking care of J.J., you come back to the ranch with me. I'll buy you a new truck when we get there, one that actually runs without jumper cables and a prayer."

The frantic beat of his heart timed the silence as it extended between them. She stared out the window, then back at J.J., then down at her hands, and gnawed on her lip, but didn't answer. *Give her a minute. You've been pushy enough.* He almost missed the turn onto 20. Nerves he was only accustomed to feeling just before he climbed in the chutes ate at him.

"It's a long trip, darlin'. Six or seven hours, plus however many times you make me stop so you can pee. Go by a lot faster if you'll talk."

She finally turned her face in his direction. Terror fractured those beautiful eyes that drove him crazy. "I've had a kid. I'm sorry I have to pee a lot," she vaulted, using her irritation to cover the emotion.

"Hey, what's wrong? I didn't mean to scare you."

"No one's ever made me feel the way you make me feel, Austin. I don't know what this is, but you're right, it's something special. If it were just me, I'd jump at the chance to see where we might end up, but it's not. I don't want a rodeo hero. I don't want J.J. growing up never knowing where his home is because he's always on the road. Before I let someone in his life, I have to know that they're not going to become a part of it and have him get attached and then they disappear on him. I saw my dad four weeks a year, and when I was with him he was riding, so I still never saw him. They asked me to say something at his funeral. What the hell was I supposed to say? The only things I remembered were the women he got to babysit me so he could go to yet another rodeo show, and then how he ruined my entire life just before he died."

"I am not your father, Summer, so let me make you another deal. I got nothing but time between Cheyenne and Vegas. Minton might want me to ride at one or two smaller venues in Oklahoma, but that's not a requirement as long as I stay in the top 5 in Cheyenne. So, let's go have Frontier Day fun. I'll ride, I'll win, and then I'm done 'til November. You and J.J. come with me to Vegas, let me have my chance at the title, and I'll walk away. I'll be done forever."

"No, I will not let you give up the rodeo for me. You'll just end up resenting me and then hating me for it. You're at the top of your career, and you want to stick with it."

"I *want* you. Come on, Summer, give this a try for two weeks. That's all I'm asking. Let's figure out what we have here. It's too good to let go without really trying it out, and I'd never resent you for anything. I told you, I live by my gut. If I walk away from the circuit, it will be on my terms. No resentment. No looking back. Two weeks won't cost us anything, will it? Might gain us a whole lot."

Another stretch of silence. He took her hesitant nod as a good sign though his heart still couldn't locate a steady beat. "I just always swore I'd never fall for a *rodeo* hero."

"What kind of hero do you want, darlin'? Not Brant, I hope."

"No, not Brant. I never wanted Brant."

Now, they were getting somewhere. Before Austin could ask how the hell she'd ended up with Preston's ring on her finger, she continued. "I want a real hero, the everyday kind of hero. You know, the guys that when you see them with their wives they look excited to be with her. Proud of her even. They hold her hand or put their arm around her, the way you do me. And they listen to her when she talks. Think about her when they aren't with her. The kind of man that gets up and works hard for his family and doesn't complain. Then he comes home and throws the ball with his kids and plays with them. You know, one who's there for his kids no matter what they need and who doesn't lose his temper with them. Takes his wife to the hospital when she goes into labor and holds her hand the whole time, even if she's screaming and cursing at him from the pain. A cowboy that's happy being at home on the ranch instead of in a bar. One that's the same person on Saturday night that he is Sunday morning when he goes to church. *That* kind of hero."

"Look at me, Summer."

She lifted her eyes to his. The rising sun reflected the distant mountain ranges in her eyes. Her dreams were painted in their majesty.

"I come from a long line of those kind of heroes. I can be that for you."

"I don't know, Austin."

"Give me a chance."

"And you think we'll know in two weeks? That's all the time it will take?"

"I told you, your whole damn life can change in eight seconds. I already know what I want. You give me two weeks, I'll prove to you what kind of hero I can be."

"I'm in it now, I guess, so all right, two weeks, but you know Frontier Days are really only ten days long, right?"

"Yeah, I know, but I'm giving myself an extra few in case I miss something in the first ten."

"Fine, just please don't hurt me, Austin."

"I would never hurt you, honey, ever. You hold all the cards. This is your call. Fourteen days from now, you tell me where we're going from Cheyenne."

"I thought guys were supposed to be commitment-phobic," she huffed. A little of the tension broke, and Austin chuckled.

"I learned a long, long time ago that life's too damn short not to do whatever makes you happy. You, sweetness, make me happier than I've ever been. I'm going for it. I'm a bull rider for Christ's sake. I don't do anything halfway."

"Tell me something you've never told anyone else." Her sudden demand alarmed him. He had two weeks to prove himself. He couldn't screw anything up.

"Okay, let me think. I like to run my mouth all the time so I don't know if there's something I've never told *anyone*."

"Well, then tell me something that scares you or is important to you. You want me to fall in love with you, go back to your family's ranch and everything, and you want me to decide on all of that in two weeks, you better start talking, cowboy."

"Okay, uh…" He glanced her way. *This is your chance, Camden. Might as well hang on and go for the ride.* "I guess I could tell you about the worst day of my life. Would that work?"

"You got thrown didn't you? Almost got yourself killed or something? I don't like to think about that."

The things she said cut him to the quick. When she spoke without calculation, when she wasn't insistent on the plan she'd obviously come up with long before fate had seen fit to throw them together, when she was raw in her honesty, he felt her love, even if neither of them was quite ready to admit that just yet.

Lacing their fingers together, he lifted her hand and brushed a kiss along her knuckles. "I'm fine, sugar. I've been thrown more times than I can count, but what I'm about to tell you has nothing to do with a bull. How about I tell you this story and then you tell me how the hell you ended up with the likes of Brantley Preston."

Her forced smirk was sadder than any frown he'd ever seen. "So, we're both gonna start with the worst days of our lives then," she sighed.

"Don't have to talk about this if you don't want to." He'd gladly take the out. If so much wasn't at stake, he'd never have leapt right into this.

"I want to. I want to know everything about you. Maybe then I can figure out how the hell I got here in your truck, after having the most amazing sex of my entire life, actually considering getting in a relationship at the worst possible time I could ever imagine."

More than pleased with all of that, he smirked. "Most amazing, huh?" He chuckled. "I'm just getting started, sweetness. I have so much more planned for you. Every single night for the next two weeks,

I'm gonna show you what it can be like between us. I'll keep you so full, so satisfied you never want to walk away."

"Cocky much?" The tremble of her body shook through his groin like an earthquake. She could chastise all she wanted, but she couldn't quite hide how much that turned her on.

"Pretty sure you know I'm not stating anything that ain't a fact, darlin'."

Her face tinged that sunset pink that drove him wild, and she bit her lips together to keep from laughing.

J.J.'s excited gasp and cooing from the back had both of them glancing to check on him. Two bobtail deer, a buck and a doe, were racing along the side of the road. Summer beamed. "You see the deer, sweet boy? Aren't they pretty?"

J.J. readily answered his mother in a babbled string of syllables that made Austin grin as he slowed the truck. If the deer decided to cross the road, he didn't want to hit them. After a few more leaps, they turned back toward the mountains and sprinted away.

"Bye, bye, bye, bye," rang from the backseat. Austin and Summer laughed together.

When J.J. quieted down, Summer turned back to Austin. "Thought you were gonna tell me stories."

"Not a pretty story, Summer. You sure you want to hear this?"

She took his hand again and kept it in hers this time. "I have a lot of ugly stories, too."

Nodding, Austin drew a deep breath, buying himself a few seconds more. "Uh, do you remember me telling you about my friend that was Hopi-Pueblo?"

"Yeah, but what do you mean he *was*?"

"Well, there's a segue if I've ever been given one." The road before them was empty and extended on for miles and miles. He allowed himself one quick blink, trying to rid the images from his mind. *Just tell her the story and be done with it. You gotta let me go. Better things heading your way, man. She's sitting right beside you.*

Austin's chest clenched. Max's voice echoed in his own mind again. It used to only happen when he rode, or on Max's birthday or the anniversary of his death, when Austin forced himself to visit the grave.

It seemed to be happening daily lately. "Here goes, I guess. My parents got me a truck on my sixteenth birthday. We needed another one on the ranch. Luke was off at school and needed his truck there. We were short one."

Summer nodded her head, studying him closely. Summoning courage from her soft scent teasing his nostrils, he went on. "Anyway, Max, Jackson, and I had been crazy about the rodeo ever since we were little kids. Max was better than either Jackson or me, but we told each other bullshit stories about all being as famous as Lane, or Tuff, or your old man."

Summer's jaw tightened but she didn't speak.

"So, uh, we rode the green horses and the calves on Camden Ranch all the time. Got a Bucky when I was thirteen and we tried our damnedest to throw each other in the dirt with that. Attended every rodeo we could con somebody into taking us to, rode the practice bulls whenever we could. We were all in young rodeo in school. We grew up driving trucks all over the ranch, so turning sixteen wasn't a big deal like it is for city kids, I guess." He shrugged, trying to bandage the unhealable wound with details.

"What happened, Austin?" Her voice was soft, a soothing balm to the burn in his chest.

"Terry Don West was giving practice sessions before a rodeo in Broken Bow 'bout three days after my birthday, then he was gonna ride. Max had been invited because he'd won the title for our high school that year. We were all set to go, but our parents forbid us. Said it was way too far away for us to go alone. Broken Bow's about two hours from our ranch, give or take time it takes you to get to I-80. But we were sixteen, I had a truck, and nobody was gonna keep us away. Max was gonna ride come hell or high water. I swear if he'd lived he woulda had the title a half-dozen times by now. He was that good." He strangled over that admittance.

Summer squeezed his hand, leaned up in her seat, and brushed a kiss over his cheek. "You don't have to keep going."

"No, I want to tell you. You wanted something I don't talk about. This is it." He sighed. "We snuck out and took off for Broken Bow. It was pouring down rain, but like I said, we were dumbass teenagers. Made it all the way 'til I could see the arena. We were almost there."

Summer managed a single nod and squeezed his hand tighter.

"Uh, anyway, you know where this is heading. Guy named Peter Lynchfield had way too many shots and ran away from a fight he'd started at a bar nearby. He flew through the red light at seventy miles an hour and T-boned me. Max was killed on impact, so was Lynchfield."

"Oh my God, Austin, I'm so sorry."

Swallowing down the raw regret that haunted his entire adult life, he nodded. "Yeah, me too."

"So, when you ride, you ride for Max? That's what your nightmare was about."

He still wasn't accustomed to the fact that she seemed able to read the things written on his soul. "Yeah. I have them a lot. I have to get that buckle in Vegas. I owe Max a title, you know?"

"Max was Hopi?" She managed the emotion-strangled question.

"Yeah, his grandparents stayed on the reservation. His mom got a job teaching at Pleasant Glen Elementary School, and his dad worked as a ranch hand at a few ranches over from ours. They moved up there to give him a better life, a good education and everything."

"Did Max ever tell you the Pueblo Blessing?"

Austin tried to recall. He and Jackson used to sit for hours listening to Max's dad tell them Pueblo legends. They loved it. "The one about holding on?"

She nodded.

"Yeah, I heard it a few times. They read it at his funeral. It was on the program thing. I still have my copy somewhere at my house."

"I spent most every summer with my Grandmother on the Zuni reservation. We used to say it together every day before supper. Ever since Brant sued for full-custody, I've been saying it to myself. *'Hold on to what is good even if it is a handful of dirt. Hold on to what you believe even if it is a tree that stands by itself. Hold on to what you must do, even if it is a long way from here.'"

They spoke the last lines together. *"'Hold on to life even if it is easier to let it go. Hold onto my hand even if I have gone away from you.'"*

"Tell me about your grandmother, sweetheart. I want to know everything about you, too."

"Thought you wanted to hear how I ended up with Brant?" She gave him a sweet grin that he swore could warm the coldest Nebraskan winter night.

"I want to hear it all. We got nothing but time, so start at the beginning."

"I don't really like the beginning."

"Start there anyway."

Giving him her customary eye roll, she still complied. "I guess this will eventually get us to Brant, so fine. My mom was a buckle bunny back in the day."

Austin kept his eyes on the road giving no reaction other than a nod.

"My dad started out riding the New Mexico, Arizona, Texas, Oklahoma circuits. He kept Mom up in an apartment in Santa Fe. She and my grandma didn't get along. She didn't like the reservation and didn't want to do things the old ways. I kind of get that, I guess. After she got pregnant with me, Dad kept paying for the apartment but didn't really want me, so he stopped coming around after I was born."

"Summer, darlin', I am so sorry." Austin redacted his former admiration of Mitchum Sanchez.

"Don't be. Life's not fair or whatever. Anyway, when I was about two, Mama decided she was done waiting on handouts from Mitchum. She got herself a job as a nanny on the McCallister's Ranch in Bernalillo. They had a huge operation and a bunch of youngins, four brothers' worth of kids. I used to like my mom. I really did. It's just that she was always more interested in being my friend instead of my mom. Does that make sense?"

"She tell you to marry Brant for his money?"

"Mmm hmm," came out with a long sigh.

"Makes perfect sense. Keep going."

"Ray McCallister, the oldest McCallister brother, used to get really mad that my dad never came to see me. He got mom to file for more child support and said Mitchum should have visitation, since I was his. So, for two weeks every summer and two weeks in December I got shipped off to wherever Mitchum was riding. He'd leave me with sitters or the women he was shacking up with at the time. I never really saw him much, and when I was fifteen, I refused to see him anymore. He didn't even care. He never even called. He just asked his lawyer if that meant he still had to pay child support. I was so pissed, and I just never got over it. I'd come up riding the McCallister's horses most of the year, except when I was visiting the reservation.

"One day, Ray saw me riding and asked if I'd like to learn to barrel race. He said I was that good, even got me my own horse, Vixen. God, I loved that horse. My calico pony that could fly faster than lightning. I was convinced Vixen was the only thing in the world that got me, that moved as fast I always wanted to. Ray paid for me to take lessons, and sticking it to Mitchum drove me. I planned it all perfectly. Vixen and I practiced night and day from my fifteenth birthday 'til I was nineteen, and I was good enough to beat most anyone else.

"Mitchum never saw me coming. That rodeo in Santa Fe where he was showing off his buckle he had no idea I was gonna ride. Didn't even know I'd started competing. I was so sure I'd stick it to him for not loving me. Prove my worth on horseback. I was a dumbass teenager, too, I guess."

"He deserved a hell of a lot worse than an amazing daughter that could turn and burn."

"Yeah, well, he didn't think so. The papers went wild with his illegitimate daughter that he'd ignored her whole life riding better than he ever hoped to. The more titles I won, the worse he looked. Family values are pretty important to most ranch families. He stopped getting asked to come show off his buckles. They didn't want a deadbeat dad representing them. There are too many cowboys that do right by their families to need one like that. He was so pissed, and that made me deliriously happy, or I told myself it did, anyway.

"One day he called me up and offered to send me to college if I'd stop riding. I laughed at him. Told him unless he could come up with some college that had a major in barrel racing, he could kiss my ass. All in the world I wanted to do was ride Vixen and flirt with the sweet cowboys at the shows."

Austin grunted his annoyance at that thought, making her laugh.

"Anyway, about a week before my twenty-fourth birthday, he called me up and apologized. Said he was sorry about not coming to see me more and for being so mad about me riding. Said he was just jealous, and told me about the throat cancer. He'd chewed since he was ten, so I wasn't surprised, but for some reason the way he sounded scared me. He asked if I'd fly out to Dallas to visit him where he was getting treatments. He said he had a surprise for me, one that would help me with racing. Mama said I should go." She shrugged.

Austin's stomach turned. Dallas and Mitchum with a plan. Didn't take a genius to figure out where this had landed her.

"I showed up at the treatment facility thing, sat with him while he got chemo. I'd never seen him look weak before, and I felt so guilty for what I'd done to him. He wanted to go out to eat the next night with some friends of his he wanted me to meet. Brant and his daddy bought us dinner and offered to let me and Vixen come to their ranch to train. Said they could get me in better venues 'cause they were stock contractors and knew people.

"I was so stupid. Brant's daddy treated him like an idiot all through dinner. Said he was nothing more than a screw-up right to his face in front of us. I felt horrible for him. Even Mitch never spoke to me like that. Brant asked if I wanted to go get a drink later that night. He really wasn't so bad until his daddy put him over the stock contracts and he got so desperate to please his old man he forgot who he was, if he ever really knew.

"Mitch was in on it the whole time. Brant and I hooked up a few times. I ended up pregnant. Obviously, I couldn't ride anymore. His parents insisted on a wedding. I refused. Mitch said his biggest regret was not seeing me grow up and being there for me, and that if I thought I could possibly make it with Brant I ought to do it for the baby. Mama said I ought to marry him for his money and the big old house his daddy gave us. Said I could still ride every day after I had the baby. That's all I ever wanted to do, so what was the difference? Only, the day we got back from our honeymoon, I found out his daddy had sold Vixen." She shivered in her seat, and Austin fought not to turn around, drive to Dallas, and beat the shit out of Brant Preston Sr.

"I'm so sorry, sweetheart. Do you know where she is now?" He'd get her the horse back if it took all of his winnings.

"Yeah...a glue factory."

Austin shook his head, unable to believe what she'd been through.

"Mr. Preston got more and more demanding when the bulls Brant was supplying the rodeo weren't performing well. Brant started drinking. Kept coming home drunk and mouthing off about his mistresses. I'd catch him out in town with bunnies. I didn't really care until he brought one to our house. I cussed both of 'em out, but he hit me in the stomach. That was it. I wasn't gonna let my baby live with a daddy like that. I filed for divorce in my second trimester and moved out to the reservation with my grandmother. She took care of me the whole time I was pregnant.

"Brant's mama was furious with the divorce agreement. They didn't get to see J.J. but for two weeks in the summertime at my choosing because he'd been abusive. His daddy's lawyers got a judge to rewrite the custody documents where we went back and forth week after week. If I missed a week, I automatically lost him. It's been hell like this for the last six months. The next trial is supposed to be in September. My lawyer thinks she can get it back to the way it was, with Brant only getting him in the summer. I hope she can."

"Summer, if you need better lawyers, more lawyers, anything at all, I want to help. I've got plenty of money. Let me do something worthwhile with it, please."

"I think my lawyer can handle it. I'll know more closer to the trial."

"Wait, you said Mitchum was in on it. He told Brant to knock you up?"

"In one of our huge blow-ups that pretty much happened every damn day, Brant shouted that he should have never listened to my daddy. I asked him what the hell that was supposed to mean, and he came right out with the fact that Mitchum told him to keep forgetting the condoms. Didn't really occur to me until right then that good ol' Mitchum had up and started making rodeo appearances again now that I couldn't ride. That was during the few months where his treatments worked and he got stronger." She shook her head.

"My God, Summer, honey, I want to beat the shit out of the whole lot of 'em for you. I've a good mind to dig your daddy up and kill him again."

Her laughter was distant and hollowed. "Yeah, I've had that thought more than a time or two, but I got J.J., so the whole stupid disaster is kind of worth it, just so long as I get to keep him. That's all I really deserve, anyway."

"No, it isn't all you deserve, and I'm gonna prove that to you. You deserve to be worshipped, taken care of, and loved. You deserve to be able to ride every damn day if that's what you want, and a home, a place to call your own. You deserve a real man, not somebody's daddy's personal ass-wipe."

She studied him for several long moments. "Yeah, maybe, but it's not your job to save me, Austin. Mitchum, and Brant, and his daddy aren't your fault, and I don't need anyone's help."

"I don't think you need me to save you, Summer, but know this: if I *can* help you, it would be my privilege. Everyone needs help sometime."

"Thanks. Can we talk about something else? Thinking about the trial makes me sick to my stomach."

"Sure, baby. Anything you want."

"Tell me about your family or about Pleasant Glen. I like knowing people that had normal childhoods. Makes me feel like maybe at least J.J. has a chance at one."

"Coming up in the Glen was great for the most part. My family has a few black sheep, too. It wasn't all idyllic. I have an uncle that was an abusive alcoholic. My cousin Brock's dad. My old man and my grandpa ran him off the ranch. Brock's life kind of went off the rails. He made something of himself though. Came back and took over his part of the ranch. Married Hope last fall. They've got a kid on the way. My dad and my granddad and my great-granddad, all my great-uncles, every Camden before Brock's daddy was a hero, just like the kind you said you wanted. Salt of the earth kind of men. Kind of guy I hope to be someday.

"I have two older brothers and two younger sisters. I'm right in the middle. Luke and Holly, the oldest and the youngest, are the only two that went to school. Rest of us just want to be ranchers. Holl's working on her doctorate in Psychology at UN now. Swears she's leaving the

Glen and setting up shop in Lincoln or somewhere you don't have to drive through ten fences just to get to a paved road. That's what she's always telling us. Luke got a master's degree in Veterinary Medicine, but he didn't stay to finish the doctorate portion. He plays vet for the Glen since he knows more than anybody living there does, but mostly he's a cowboy.

"Grant owns part of the ranch and a few cornfields, as well. Swears the money's in the corn, but he runs a thousand head of cattle every year, too, so we're not real convinced. My sister Natalie got pissed when my dad gave Brock his daddy's portion of the ranch because he hadn't been there to work it with all of us. She gets that way. I don't know why. It ain't like she don't know what Brock went through because of my uncle. Anyway, she has a ton of acreage just like we all do. We all work it together, though.

"I grew up just like everyone else I knew. Riding horses, young rodeo, learning to pray right about the time report cards were due out, drinking whatever our older brothers could get a'holt of on Friday nights before the football games or the rodeos, depending on the season. Wearing out the tires on the ranch trucks racing 'em and spinning 'em out in the fields. Trying to talk girls into letting me get to third base in the truck beds, shit like that."

"Pretty sure you didn't have to talk too hard, cowboy."

"Hey, my dirty talkin' skills have improved in the last decade or so, sunshine. I had to get 'em perfected before I started trying to get you to let me get to third base." He winked at her just to watch her beam.

"I let you get a lot further than third base."

"Mmm, don't I know it. Plan on hitting several more home runs as soon as we get settled in Cheyenne and get the little one to bed."

"That so?"

"Yeah, honey. I'm already aching for you."

She shook her head at him then stared out the windows, taking in the magnificent Wyoming landscapes as they flew by. "Does your family ever get to see you ride?" she asked suddenly. "Oh, but I bet they're haying all summer aren't they?"

It deeply impressed Austin that she knew what was going on at the ranch in his absence. "They are haying, but actually Mama and Daddy and a few of 'em are coming to Cheyenne to see me and to have fun at Frontier Days. When we were growing up, we came to Cheyenne every year. You'll get to meet 'em. They should be in tomorrow afternoon sometime, but they're just staying a couple of nights."

Concern darkened her eyes, and she gnawed on her bottom lip.

"They'll love you, darlin'."

"I'm not exactly the kind of girl you take home to meet Mama." She instinctively glanced back at J.J.

"My mama's gonna love you and J.J. I can't wait for them to meet you."

"I'm not used to caring what other people think or trying to impress anyone. I don't know what you're doing to me, cowboy."

"You impressed the hell outta me as soon as I laid eyes on you, Ms. Sanchez."

"You just liked my rack." The naughty little grin she gave him had a direct connection to his groin.

He grunted his approval. "You do have fan-fucking-tastic tits, baby. My mouth and my cock need to spend way more time with 'em. I intend to do that tonight, as well, but that ain't the first thing that impressed the hell outta me."

"So, what impressed you enough to want to share your hotel room with me and then up and decide you might like me to move to Nebraska with you?"

"Your fire. Your soul. Your spunk. I felt it as soon as I grabbed a'holt of you. You knew there were things worth fightin' for. You're beautiful, Summer. I could spend the rest of my life just looking atcha, but I felt something as soon as I wrapped my arms around you. Besides, I'm the one that's supposed to be impressing you. You don't have to impress anyone. Soon as my mama meets you she'll try to get you to join her 'Get Austin to quit this bull riding nonsense' band."

"I might just do that." Summer laughed.

"See, you two will be thick as thieves. Dad and I will be screwed seven ways from Sunday."

She turned back to stare out the windows again, crossing and uncrossing her legs. Wiggling in her seat, she glanced back up at him sheepishly.

"There's a McDonald's about four miles from here, so go on with it."

"I have to pee," she admitted begrudgingly.

Laughing at her outright, Austin got in the right hand lane. He knew where 120 would ultimately take them. Knew the twists and turns, the landmarks he'd stop and show her, and where they could get out and have lunch. But the road fate had thrown him down faster than any damn bull had come out of the chute, he had no idea where that was heading, and if he were being truthful, that scared him worse than anything ever could.

CHAPTER NINE

When they were about a half hour outside of Thermopolis, somewhere between Manderson and Worland, basically in the middle of bumble-fuck, J.J.'s frustrated grunts turned into wails of anger.

"Oh, it's okay, J. We can stop in a little while." Summer unbuckled in her seat and leaned back to try and calm him. She offered him a pacifier, which he promptly tossed in his fury.

"Got his mama's temper, I see." Austin chuckled. "We can stop and get out for a little while. His ass is probably sore. I know mine is." He let two trucks pulling horse trailers, most certainly heading for Cheyenne, pass him and then pulled off at a large field between two family farms near a feed store.

J.J. quieted down as soon as Summer unbuckled him. He wiggled until she lowered him to the ground on his feet, held both of his hands and let him walk with assistance all over the field. Austin stayed with them, keeping a constant watchful eye for snakes and wildlife.

"What are you looking for?" Summer's concerned tone had him taking J.J.'s hands so he could be the steady hand for a little while.

"It's the middle of July in Wyoming, darlin'. The grass here is a little higher than I think is safe. It ain't my grass to mow, but I'll be damned if I'm gonna let you or the little guy stumble up on a red belly, or much worse, a prairie rattler. You have shorts on. Why don't you head on back to the truck for me? I'll walk with him, let him get some energy out, we'll chat, and then we can change him and get back on the road."

Summer leaned in and brushed a kiss on Austin's jaw. "Thank you for taking such good care of him. I'll be fine, though. I got bit twice when I was in New Mexico. Turned Vixen too tight, fell, and landed on a coral. Bit my ass through my jeans. Had to go to the hospital. Thankfully the denim took most of the venom."

Austin nodded his thankfulness as well. "I promise every time I bite your sexy ass, I'll only make it feel good, sugar." He winked at her as her olive cheeks blistered once again. "I've been bit a time or two, myself. Seemed like it happened every fucking time my dad told me to wear my chaps and not chinks anymore 'cause the snakes were gonna be coming out, and I chose not to listen."

Summer laughed with him as he let J.J. lead them around the open field. Austin's methodic scans of the grass seemed to make her happy. He hadn't been doing anything he wouldn't have normally done, but it was becoming more and more clear that Summer Sanchez had never had anyone looking out for her. That was all about to change.

———

They stopped for lunch at Stone's Throw in Thermopolis, a place Austin remembered going with his family whenever they made a trip out to Yellowstone. It was an upscale steakhouse and burger joint.

"You don't have to keep bringing us to nice places to eat, Austin. You've already impressed me, okay? I feel bad, you feeding us like this."

This time Austin rolled his eyes at her. "I'm pretty sure I've made myself more than clear. You're my girl, little man is my bud, I take good care of what's mine. Now sit down and pick out what you want to eat, or I'll order you a filet myself."

"Ohhh, a jalapeno cheeseburger. My mama used to make me those when I was pissed. She always said she shouldn't add heat to my temper, but they were my favorite." Summer all but moaned as she stared at the menu.

"Oh, I like you spicy, baby doll. Get all the heat you want. What will little man eat?"

"We can get him some chicken fingers. I'll cut 'em up real small. And he loves French fries."

Austin skipped the thirty-dollar filet, trying to make Summer more comfortable with him taking care of her, and went for a bacon cheeseburger with fries instead.

It was all just as delicious as he'd remembered. Glancing out the large plate-glass windows, he studied the impressive landscape of Thermopolis and another idea came to mind. "Hey, you wanna take J.J. out to see the hot springs? Pretty cool landscape, and he'd get a break from that car seat. Too late in the day for fishing, or I'd try to catch us something for supper."

Summer stared up at him like she couldn't quite believe he was real. When her loving gaze turned to her son, she grinned. "He'd love to watch you fish sometime. In a few years, he'll probably out-fish me. I like to fish, but I suck at it. I get impatient too fast and want to jump in the water as soon as it gets warm. Are you sure we have time to walk the springs? Don't you need to get on to Cheyenne and get registered?"

"We're making pretty good time. Have you ever seen Big Horn or the Painted Terraces? They're pretty cool."

"I always liked Cheyenne, so I'd pick these two weeks each summer to stay with Mitchum. He'd be off performing or whatever, and he always left me with a friend of my grandmother's. Her name is Ekta. She still lives there. J.J. and I were gonna stay with her, actually."

"Well, give Ekta my apologies, but I have very different plans for you. Invite Ekta out to the rodeo, though. My treat."

"Ekta isn't a big fan of cowboys. She hated my dad, even though he always let me stay with her."

"Ah, a friend of your grandmother that doesn't care for cowboys. Arapaho or Cheyenne?"

"Arapaho."

"Can't say I blame her for her thoughts on cowboys. We certainly didn't do her people right. Maybe I can at least show her that some of us are respectful. How'd your grandmother come to meet Ekta? Long way from Cheyenne to Albuquerque."

"I don't know how they met. I never thought to ask. They were friends when they were little girls. They still write letters back and forth all the time. I love them both." Another seductive round of heat colored Summer's cheeks as she abruptly stopped talking.

"Tell me. Whatever's going on in that pretty head of yours. Just say it."

"I have to at least take J.J. to see Ekta, so you might meet her and you'll find out anyway. Ekta calls me Whirlwind." She rolled her eyes as Austin laughed.

"Max's dad used to tell us about the Whirlwind Woman. Spirit that storms across the plains that brings visions and gifts to worthy men, or something like that."

"Worthy humans, not just men." Summer squeezed her eyes shut and laughed at her own expense.

"I'd say Ekta nailed it. You are my beautiful storm. And I must be some kinda worthy, because my God, the gifts you give me are something else, and the visions—let's just say you are a sight to behold."

"I was in the middle of a story, cowboy."

"Well pardon me, Whirlwind, go on with your story."

"Don't call me that. It's not true anymore, and I'm part Zuni, not Arapaho."

Austin sank his teeth into the delectable burger, making her no promises. It was far truer than she'd ever admit to herself. She was the most beautiful storm he'd ever seen. Her winds had consumed him thoroughly. The lightning in her eyes when his hands encountered her silky skin, the thunder of her moans, the quick rasp of her breath over his skin mightier than the gale force winds of Wyoming, and the fierce heat they created burned like a prairie fire, combustible and endless. He never wanted to tame her, never wanted to quell her flames. He just wanted to move with her across the plains.

"Anyway, when I was about fourteen, the last summer I agreed to go to Cheyenne with Mitchum, I was a wild child if there ever was one. Ekta brought me out here to the hot springs. She said the healing waters would soothe my spirit. She made me swim in them. I don't think it worked, though. When I got back to Bernalillo, I was even worse than I'd been before. My grandma would still bring me up to

Frontier Days every year, and we would stay with Ekta. I just refused to see Mitchum if he was there. So, long answer to your question, yes I've been to Thermopolis before, but I'd love to see them again. We could put J.J. in the stroller until we get somewhere he can play."

"Let's get, then." Austin left more than enough cash to cover their bill and guided Summer and J.J. outside. The wind whipped Summer's long hair across her chest and neck. He fought not to gather it in his hands and tug just enough to get her to expose that column of feminine perfection that ran from her slender neck to her breasts. He wanted to feast on her. *Tonight, Camden. You can have her all to yourself tonight. Right now, you need to figure out how to be a dad, real quick like.*

———

The water was too hot for J.J. to touch, which he didn't appreciate, but he gasped and oohed at the waterfalls. They located a playground and Austin aided him on the slides, the baby swings, and played with him in a tube with windows where Summer played peek-a-boo with them, much to J.J.'s delight. To his shock, Austin loved every minute of it almost as much as J.J. He was certain parenting got more difficult at times, but just then it seemed kind of fun.

The sun was settling down beyond the mountains behind them as they joined a long line of other trucks pulling into Cheyenne. "I talked Minton into putting me up in one of the ranch cabins. That'll give little man his own room, and you and me a bed big enough for you to ride me when I'm not riding a bull. Sound good to you?"

"Really? Wow. Those are expensive, but that would be so much fun. I love Frontier Days. Cheyenne always makes me feel like a teenager again. I know that's stupid, but I love how the whole town gets in on everything. All the decorations, and concerts, and the midway, and everything. Oh, and I'm pretty excited about riding you too, cowboy."

Austin grinned over her exuberance. He'd never heard her sound so excited about much of anything. "Good, darlin' 'cause I've had to go all damn day sitting beside you, holding your hand, breathing in that sexy way you smell, and doing nothing about it. My patience is wearing thin. I need a fix of my girl."

"Aww, you think I stink pretty," she laughed.

"Damn pretty, baby." He nodded to the statue of Lane Frost as they edged forward in traffic. Saluting the greats was in his blood. "Truth be told, I love Frontier Days, too. It was my favorite time of year as a kid. I loved it all, every moment of it."

"It's crazy to think we were here at the same time back then, isn't it? I wonder if we ever saw each other."

"I never saw you, Miss Sanchez. I sure as hell would remember if I had. Way you bowled me over in that bar in Cody. Guy don't get the wind ripped out of him, except by a bull or a girl. I'd a remembered if it had happened to me when I was a teenager."

Her expression said that explanation pleased her greatly, even if she did roll those whiskey eyes at him again. "I always stayed with Ekta, like I said. Mitchum occasionally gave me money to ride the rides, but I'd do everything that was free over and over again."

"You ever ride The Zipper?"

"I wanted to so bad, but I didn't have enough tickets."

"You're riding The Zipper before I steal you away to the Glen."

"That so?"

"Yes, ma'am, it is, and don't argue with me right now. I gotta get us checked in to the cabins, then go get my papers, find out my practice sessions, and all of that shit. You get me all turned on bein' stubborn, I'm gonna be worthless 'til I get my rocks off deep inside of you."

"The beast gettin' restless, cowboy?" That intoxicating storm of fire stirred in her darkening eyes.

Austin's growl reverberated off the windshield. He was glad J.J. had fallen asleep just outside of Cheyenne. "I'm barely keeping my hands off of you, Summer. Don't tempt me, darlin'. I can't take much more. I'll pull over, have my hands down those shorts, make you come just for me to watch and taste it on my fingers."

She stared him down. The lightning in her eyes struck the prairie gold and ignited in challenge. "Don't stop yourself on my account, cowboy. Put your hands all over me. Hasn't been easy sitting in here with you, either. I've been thinking about how good it was last night for the last 150 miles. I'm so wet for you I ache."

The long fuse of patience he'd been trying to extend all damn day met its end at her demands. Electricity sizzled in the air between them. Drawing a deep breath, he inhaled nothing but her potent musk. His cock made demands he could no longer deny.

Austin made the turn off for the ranch cabins where Minton was staying, but didn't pull up to the check in point. He guided the truck over the dirt roads that led out toward the lake and pastures as the sun gave off its last vestiges of light. Finding a secluded spot beneath the cover of a few river birch trees and a massive willow, he threw the truck in park and prayed J.J. would give them a little time.

"That so, sugar? Can't have my girl wet and needing me to make it better and not tend her. I'll always take care of you. Always. Now come here to me. Lay back against me with your head on my shoulder."

"Oh God, yes, please."

Lust-fueled fire churned through his veins. "You have to be quiet for me." He half-groaned in her ear as he pulled her into his arms. "Can you do that?"

She gave him a single nod before he captured her lips with his own. God, that sweet heat of her lips, parting for him fully, letting him taste and explore her mouth. It was more than he could stand. He had her shorts unbuttoned in a split second, exposing an entirely different set of lips so full of wet heat he longed to straddle her over his cock and make her ride him until he unloaded inside her.

"So wet, sugar." His fingers circled her clit, making her grind in the seat beside him. "Spread your legs and show me those sweet pussy curls."

He sucked away her whimpered moan with the blistering heat of his mouth then nipped her bottom lip. "Quiet, baby." Using one hand to cover her mouth, he speared the fingers of his other deep within her satin channel that was so slick he growled in her ear. His body shuddered involuntarily. My God, she was exquisite. Every rippled draw of her pussy against his fingers reminded him how astounding it felt to have his cock inside her. "Be quiet and let it feel good for me. Fuck my fingers, sweetness. Back and forth, just like that. When I get you to the cabin, I'm gonna lean you over the bed and let you pay me back, hard, just like my girl likes to be taken. I'm gonna own you, so be ready for me."

Another breathy moan sounded against his hand.

"Shh, darlin'."

She shuddered against him, fevered tight and desperate.

"It's right there isn't it? So close I can feel it comin' for me." Giving her the friction she required, he pulled his fingers almost out and back in hard and fast. She shook in his arms. Her breath tangled in her lungs. Her body tensed against him. "Gotta remember to breathe, sugar. There it is. That's it." She released in racked gasps of breath, choked and haggard.

When she stilled, he gently eased his fingers from her opening and dragged them upwards with a gentle stroke over her clit that made her shiver. "Now watch me," he whispered as he brought his fingers to his mouth and devoured her nectar. The sweet sexy spice drove him wild. He wanted to gorge himself on her juices, certain he'd never get enough.

She turned and buried her face in his neck. He wrapped his arms around her and allowed her recover in his embrace.

"I love being in your arms. I feel so safe here." Her words were barely a whisper, like an admittance she wasn't certain she should state out loud.

"I will always keep you safe, Summer, and I love having you in my arms. I love being with you. I'm gonna prove that to you if it's the last thing I do."

They were momentarily bathed in the harsh glow of headlights from a truck passing by their hideaway. The moment dissolved around them. She slid away from him and refastened her shorts. "Told you Cheyenne made me feel like a teenager again."

Chuckling, Austin slowly backed the truck out of the cover of the trees. "These are gonna be the best damn Frontier Days I've ever had."

CHAPTER TEN

Summer heaved another one of Austin's suitcases from the back of the truck and had it half way up the few steps of their tiny and completely perfect ranch cabin before he caught her.

"Just what exactly do you think you're doing, woman? By the way, I need to know your middle name so I can scold you the right way."

"I'm unloading the truck, cowboy." She thrust the suitcase into his arms a little harder than was probably necessary. Her mind was still spinning from that orgasm he'd expertly conducted in the front seat of his truck. "And my middle name is Malia, but you barking out all my names is *not* how I prefer to be scolded." She loved the way his onyx eyes displayed every color of a bonfire when she said things like that. The way his muscles tensed and he licked his bottom lip like it was all he could do not to devour her whole. She sensed the beast he tried so hard to keep caged inside his soul rattle the chains, anxious and hungry. It drove her wild.

Setting the suitcase on the wraparound porch, he made it to her in two quick steps. "Malia—rebellious. I'd say your mama nailed that one right off, wouldn't you? Now, question remains, what am I gonna do about you not letting me take care of you when you know good and well that's my job?"

"You were setting up the portable crib. I'm perfectly capable of carrying bags, Austin. I keep telling you I don't need anyone lookin' after me."

His eyes flashed with a hint of danger that ran her internal thermometer right back to hot with fevered need, even if he had just gotten her off a half hour ago. She locked her knees and clenched her jaw to keep from showing him how badly she wanted another round with him.

When the strength of his capable right hand, hardened from years of gripping the handhold of a bull, connected with her ass, a breathy moan escaped her. She bowed toward him. Her hands collided with the wall of chiseled muscle that constructed his chest, on the next strike. He kept his darkened eyes zeroed in on hers, watching her reactions.

Before she could dare him to do it again, "Ma-ma-ma-ma" began babbling from the little nook where Austin had set up J.J.'s crib, and a large family with a bunch of kids staying in the three cabins next door sauntered up. As Summer was certain they would not approve of her and Austin's erotic foreplay, she gripped his bicep and let him haul her up to the porch and steady her.

"Later, I want more of that," she whispered, just before offering the mother and father of the family a grin.

Austin managed to turn his craving grunt into a half-cough.

"Excuse me just one second, baby's waking up from his nap." Summer raced to J.J.'s crib, made quick work of scooping him up, kissing him all over, making him laugh hysterically, and then changing his diaper before she returned to the porch. Austin took him from her arms as soon as she appeared. J.J. looked delighted. He smacked Austin's face in a sign of love.

"As soon as Jeb and John heard Austin Camden was staying in the cabin near ours they wanted to come over. I hope we're not intruding on anything," the mother of the brood was commenting.

"Oh no, ma'am, it's fine. Austin loves meeting his fans." She gave Austin a quick wink while he shook his head and tried not to appear flattered.

"We can't wait to see you ride, Mr. Camden. We have tickets for all of the bull riding shows." One of the younger boys sidled closer to Austin.

"Oh yeah? Well, I tell you what." Austin leaned down, balancing J.J. in his arms but getting on the little guy's level. "I'm doing the behind-the-chutes tour next week. You come down there and see me then, and I'll see if we can't show you some of the bulls and broncs, maybe even get you some Camden hats or flags or something so you can wear 'em to the shows."

"Really?" The little boy turned back to his father, looking like Austin had just given him gold. "Can we go, Dad, please?"

The man chuckled. "Heck, yeah, buddy. We'll be there. We'll let you two get back to unpacking. It was nice to meet you." The whole family waved as they made their way back to their respective cabins.

"Damn, they're nice. Now I'll feel bad if I make you scream too loud and we end up corrupting those kids," Austin lamented.

Unable to help herself since she'd been thinking something very similar, Summer giggled hysterically. "They have to learn sometime, right?"

Shaking his head at her, Austin handed J.J. back and unloaded the rest of the bags from the truck. When he checked his watch for the third time, Summer rolled her eyes. "Would you just go get checked in. I'll unpack everything and then J.J. and I are going to go get some groceries."

"Why don't you just come with me? It won't take long. When I'm finished, we can get some supper and groceries or whatever."

"Because if I put J.J. back in the car seat or you try to put me back in that truck we'll both pitch a big ol' fit that'll make you wish you hadn't. Now go. I'll be fine. I'm gonna make us dinner here. Look, we have a whole kitchen." She gestured to the small-but-functional kitchen just inside the back door of the cabin.

"All right, fine," he tossed her the keys to the truck, "but I'll walk. You take the truck. I don't want you out wandering around by yourself. Sun's down and town's full of tourists."

"Yes, because cowboys, ranch families, and vendors selling Rice Krispy Treat balls covered in chocolate cleverly called 'Wyoming Bison Balls' are so intimidating. I'm a cowgirl, sweetheart. I don't take any shit off of anyone. Never forget that. Although I will say, you offering to let me drive your truck is even more flattering than your offer to up and move us to the ranch. I know the deep affection cowboys have for their trucks." She tossed the keys back to him.

A grunt of frustration accompanied his eye roll. "Stubborn as hell, and damn if you don't turn me on. Fine, but use this," he thrust a credit card in her hand, "and don't buy any of them bison balls. You want your mouth full of balls, I'll take care of that as soon as I get back. Open wide and use your tongue."

Before she could react to that, he popped a kiss on her head, then one on J.J.'s cheek, and headed out. Sighing, she laid his credit card on the table beside the bed. "I don't need your money, Austin, and I'd probably get arrested for using a credit card without my name on it, anyway." She spoke to the ether and to J.J., who was taking in his surroundings while gumming his fingers. "You ready to go, little man? There's a little mercantile around here. It isn't far. Wanna ride in your stroller?"

Moving quickly, she set him on the western rug in the sitting area, popped open the stroller outside, then rushed back in to retrieve J.J before he could get into anything. The path leading back to the cabin check-in lodge was well lit and led directly to the main street teeming with people arriving for Frontier Days. Summer felt perfectly safe.

Glancing back at the cabin, admiring the welcoming glow of the front porch lights she'd left on, she tried to sort through everything that had happened in the last three days. J.J. was cooing softly as they strolled. She grinned. What she wouldn't give to just stop time right here, right now. Tucked up in a cozy cottage with Austin Camden claiming her as his, J.J. safely with them. No Brant, no Prestons, no Dallas, plenty of food, a nice warm bed, a shower whenever she wanted one, none of the problems that had plagued her for the last several months. *But this isn't real life.* He'd seriously asked her to move in with him. Who does that after just three days? Austin.

She wished she could be that confident about anything. Confidence like that had to come from not regretting most every decision you'd ever made, but how could he be so certain they could make this work? Didn't he understand that J.J. would always have to come first?

Her mind spun with all the things that could go wrong, with meeting his family, getting to see Ekta, Austin riding several times over the next two weeks. It all staged a vicious uprising with that feeling of complete contentment she felt when she was in the little cabin with Austin and J.J. Neither side seemed willing to wave the white flag. She had no idea what she was going to do, or where she'd find herself at the end of Cheyenne.

She was trying to enjoy it while it lasted, but worries plagued her constantly. What if his family didn't approve of her? What if they got into some kind of big fight or something? Where would that land her? What if this all didn't have a happy ending? Nothing else in her life ever had. She reminded herself of the last time she'd felt like she had the world on a string. Just a few years before, she'd been certain the Frontier Day barrel racing buckle was going to be hers. Not everything worked out just because you wanted it to. Austin was right about one thing, though: it did only take eight seconds for your life to completely change.

———

"Hey, remember me? Your best friend since birth, the one you were supposed to let follow you to Cheyenne since I'm carrying half your crap in my truck, and the one that's saved your ass more times than he can count?" Jackson whined as soon as Austin's boots hit the gravel parking lot of the PBR tent area.

"Damn, man, I'm sorry, I forgot. Little distracted lately, but it's all good."

"Yeah, whatever. Let's go grab something to eat once you have your papers."

"Can't. Summer's making me supper. Got plans tonight. I'll catch up with you tomorrow, though. Family's due in around lunchtime."

"She's cookin' for you now? Damn, she must be some kinda good in bed for you to be playing house after just a few days."

"Think I'll keep all that between me and my sheets, if it's all the same to you. And I ain't just playing. I'm thinking of making this a permanent thing. I know it's quick, but..." He shrugged, not about to profess his feelings to Jackson.

"You've clearly lost your fucking mind," Jackson scoffed. "Scott said she used to be married to Brant Preston. Can't believe your sucking up his sloppy seconds."

Unmitigated rage rocketed through Austin. He grabbed Jackson's dirty T-shirt and jerked him forward. "Summer isn't anyone's sloppy seconds. She's mine. You got that? If you don't like it, you can fuck the hell off. I'm gonna let you remain standing upright because we used to be friends, and there's three chicks over there making eyes at you like you're a piece of prime rib and they ain't eaten in a while. But if you ever talk about Summer like that again, I'll pound your pussy ass into the dirt and I won't feel sorry for ya."

"Damn, Austin, what the hell is wrong with you? It's like I don't even know you anymore. What happened to you?"

Letting the flare of his temper burn out, Austin made himself consider the question. "I don't know, but somethin' good. That's all I can say. I don't want it to end this time. Beyond that, I don't know." Bound and determined to get back to Summer, he headed inside the tent to get in line for his paperwork and instructions for the next two weeks.

Jackson followed after him. "You gonna marry her?" bellowed from him.

Refusing to answer, Austin's eyes landed on none other than Summer's illustrious ex and the team from Preston Cattle, in registering their bulls. Something had happened and Brant was scrambling too much to have paid attention to Jackson's question...Austin hoped.

"Bull did what we all want bulls to do, sir. I don't know why you're over here talking to me. Preston Cattle will pay for the loader's emergency room trip," Brant negotiated.

"What the hell happened?" Austin let his momentary irritation with Jackson go.

"Heard a loader got hooked just getting Dallas Devil in the trailers. He's bad off. Bull's mean as a striped snake, and something ain't quite right with him. Starting to show some signs."

"You think they're doping him?" Austin and Jackson both spoke through their teeth.

"Don't know for sure, but he's ornery as all get out. Vet in Cody tried to tranq him so they could load him, didn't do no good. I ain't looking forward to fighting him, I'll say that."

Three PBR reps weren't taking Brant's pandering. They moved in and talked faster. Shaking his head, Austin approached the line of folding tables where the Frontier Day reps were checking riders in.

"Austin Camden," he provided when the woman lifted her head from her paperwork to eye him.

"Ah, yes, we've been anxiously awaiting your arrival, Mr. Camden. Good luck at Frontier Days. Your fans precede you. I've been asked all day long if you'd arrived."

Austin chuckled, not certain how to respond to that. His mind continued to whirl over what kinds of trouble could come Summer's way if Brant was caught giving Dallas Devil steroids. The PBR didn't mess around with shit like that. Preston and all of his blessed money could go down for it. *He deserves whatever he's got coming and more.* So long as Brant's fallout didn't implode near Summer and J.J., he didn't give a damn. He'd take care of them. They didn't need Brant's money, and J.J. would be better off without a father like that.

The woman cleared her throat, regaining his attention. "All right, Mr. Camden, here are your practice times. The practice arena is about a mile that way." She gestured south. "You'll be doing two behind-the-chute tours. You'll need to be on horseback tomorrow morning before sunup for the drive. Cowboys are meeting at the pasture north of Cheyenne on I-25. You can't miss it. Parade is at 11:00. Your rides are listed there." She pointed to the schedule she'd placed in his hands. You'll be paired with your bull the morning of your rides and your draw will be available either here or at the PRCA tent after 8:00 a.m. Be sure not to miss the big pancake breakfasts. All of the concerts this year are in this brochure, riders and their dates get in free with your Frontier Days badge.

"There will be music and dancing at the Buckin' A Saloon each night, along with the rides and fun on the carnival midway. You can purchase your armbands there. The first round of competition, the cinch shoot-out, is tomorrow night, but I'm betting you already knew that. Other than that, let us know if you need anything while you're in Cheyenne."

"Thanks. Will do." Austin tipped his hat to the woman while keeping his eye on Brant standing outside of the tent. He must have talked his way out of the suspicions about Dallas Devil. Seemed to Austin that Preston was biding his time waiting on someone. Didn't take a genius to figure out who that might be.

"You smell trouble? Cause I sure as hell smell trouble," Jackson huffed. "Better thank your lucky stars that I'd rather fight Brant than you, after your spouting off a few minutes ago."

"Yeah, yeah, okay, I'm sorry I threatened you, but keep your mouth shut about Summer. She means something to me."

"Yeah, okay, fine. Just don't turn into some kinda pussy-whipped puppy for her. At least not before you win the buckle this year, okay?"

"You got it. Now, should we just assume he's gonna be a prick and go ahead and beat the shit out of him, or should we hear him out first?"

"Better hear him out since you got PBR reps all over the place."

They headed out of the tent. Brant narrowed his beady eyes and sauntered closer, leaving less than five feet between them. Austin's biceps flexed of their own accord. Jackson, who'd always loved to fight ever since they were kids, chuckled and gave Brant a gleeful grin.

"You seem to think you have something that rightfully belongs to me, Camden." The inevitable and idiotic words that were supposed to fuel Austin's rage spewed from Brant's stupid mouth. The cool night air between them weighted with tension.

Laughing at him outright, Austin smirked. "Two things wrong with your dumbass thought processes, Preston."

"Only two?" Jackson feigned shock.

"True. Okay, two things wrong with your attempt at getting me to fight your sorry ass. First off, women don't belong to anyone but themselves unless they say otherwise, but I get that concept is probably over your head. Secondly, seems to me that since I'm the one with her in my bed, you've got very little left to lose. Since I'm not stupid enough to jump in a fight that might cost me something, why don't you take your pansy ass on back to Dallas? You aren't worth the gunpowder it'd take to blow you to hell. Get your mama to lick up your wounds for you. I don't have to fight you for her. It's always lady's choice, and she chose me."

"You scared, Camden?"

"Aww, come on, Austin, he's asking for it," Jackson jeered.

"I don't do scared, Preston, but I'm also not a dumbass. I take good care of what's mine. Beating you seven ways from Sunday, while enjoyable as fuck, just ain't worth it."

Before another round of quips could be exchanged, Scott and Clifton approached, eyeing everyone cautiously. "Everything okay, Austin?" Scott turned and stared Brant down. Seemed if it came to blows, Minton would step up on Austin's account.

"Yeah, Brant's just got his panties in a wad. Needs to simmer down."

"Sounds like a plan," Clif huffed. "Get out of here, Brant. You're both grown men. I don't have to guess what this is about. We may be in Cheyenne, but this ain't the Wild West. Divorce papers are about the biggest sign of closure you could ever ask for."

Shocked and impressed, Austin couldn't help but smile. Brant rolled his eyes, mumbled something about it not being over, and headed toward the Buckin' A Saloon.

"Truce?" Scott offered Austin his hand.

"You got it, and thank you. Nothing's changed where we're concerned. I may have a girl I'd like to keep, but I'm gonna get Minton that buckle."

"We got greedy, and we're sorry. Here, thought you might like this." Scott held up a small, navy blue onesie about J.J.'s size. The image on the front was of a bull rider. Camden was imprinted over the bull, and Minton Chaps was on the back. He handed off a matching baseball cap and two matching T-shirts for Summer. Clif added a pair of toddler Wranglers.

"Little small for me." Austin laughed.

"Have a feeling you wouldn't mind Summer's little cowboy wearing this tomorrow night. My wife picked it out. I have two kids, still don't know how to buy baby clothes," Scott allowed.

"I appreciate it. They'll be there rooting me on. Family's coming in, too. Should be fun."

"Please tell Summer she's welcome in the Minton box if she doesn't want the baby down at the chutes, and we look forward to meeting your folks. We're all doing the cattle drive tomorrow morning, so we'll see you then." Clif offered them a wave before he and Scott headed back the direction they'd came. Austin folded the baby clothes up and surveyed the first night of Frontier Days. By tomorrow evening, the arena would be jam-packed with people anxious to see who made it through the first round of competitions, attending concerts, riding the midway rides, and enjoying their vacations. Half the competition field would be cut on the first night. Austin could hardly wait.

"What are you gonna do about Brant? You know he ain't gonna back down. Guys like that have their heads shoved so far up their ass all they can do is spew shit," Jackson commented when Scott and Clint were out of ear shot.

"No joke. As long as he doesn't come anywhere near Summer or J.J. he can keep right on being a shit fountain. I don't give a damn. He wants to tangle with me, I'll show him the stupidity of taking on a bull rider."

"Let me know if you need my help. You know I'll back you up. But, uh, those girls that were out here before we went in the tent are still over there, so I'm gonna see if they might like someone to show 'em around Cheyenne."

"You have a four-way tonight, I *am* gonna wanna hear about it," Austin called.

"Finally, a *you* I recognize. I thought she'd done you in, man." Jackson waved and headed off toward the girls smiling at him rather ostentatiously.

Traffic was at a standstill as Austin attempted to make his way back to the ranch cabins. Allowing his mind to spin while he pumped the brakes anxiously, he worked through how he could possibly have fallen for Summer Sanchez so quickly.

Clearly, it was serious enough that Brant was up in arms, and both Scott and Clif recognized something was different. They'd seen him take more than one bunny to his hotel room in the last few months, and they'd never said a word. Since Austin couldn't recall any of their names, he wasn't shocked.

If he were being completely honest, he'd admit that he'd had a thing for Summer Sanchez since he'd first seen her ride four years ago. He hadn't had the courage to chat her up after the rodeo that night, but things were different now. So, the odds weren't in their favor. Didn't have to ride bulls long to know that odds meant nothing. He'd figure a way to make this work. Nothing else was even an option in his book. She was too good to ever give up.

Dropping by the drug store on his way, he picked up some lube, two more boxes of condoms, along with a new toothbrush, some razors, and a small stuffed animal calico horse for J.J. to play with.

When he finally made his way back to the cabin and rushed inside, the sight before him filled his heart as much as it swelled his cock. He doubted their neighbors would appreciate the music volume, but he couldn't have cared less. The empty recess that had been his life before disappeared completely.

He stared as Summer stood at the small oven, a spatula in her hand over a sizzling skillet. She was rocking her hips back and forth to the beat of Miranda Lambert belting out "Gunpowder and Lead" on the radio.

Damn, damn, damn, if that wasn't a sight he'd donate his left nut to come home to every single day of his life, he didn't know what was. Her short-shorts were hugging her sexy ass, and the tank top she was wearing didn't quite conceal the hickeys he'd left on her shoulder. Her hair was pulled up in a messy ponytail, with a few wayward strands playing on the nape of her neck as she swayed. She was the epitome of perfection. J.J. was seated in his portable highchair at the table, singing along nonsensically in between his Cheerio consumption.

Silently moving through the sitting room, he set the drug store bag on the table and slid in behind Summer. She startled and gasped, making him laugh.

"Keep dancin', darlin'." His hands grasped her hips, she started to sway more provocatively. "Hot as hell and all mine." He took another nip at her shoulder and swayed with her before he grasped those luscious tits and massaged.

She spun in his arms, delight consuming her entire being, as his grasp travelled from her tits to her ass. "You think you can just grab whatever you want, cowboy?" she flirted shamelessly.

"Hell yeah, I do, and don't pretend you don't like it."

"I do like it." She leaned up on her tiptoes, and Austin sank his lips to hers in a kiss that could've set then entire cabin ablaze. When they broke apart, she spun back to the ground beef, peppers, and onions she was cooking. Refried beans were in a skillet beside the frying pan.

"What are we cooking, Miss Sanchez?"

"I'm making you my Frito pie. It's a New Mexico specialty, nice and hot. Have you ever had it before?"

"Nope, but I like Fritos, and I like pie, and I already told you I like your spiciness, so I only see this going good places."

"It's almost done. Did you get registered?"

"Yup, everything's set. Hey, you know Miranda's gonna be here doing a concert Friday night." He gestured to the radio.

"Are you serious? I love her."

"I was aware, and I happen to have an all-access pass to the concerts, sweet thang, that is, if you'd like to go."

"I wish we could. I don't have anyone to keep J.J."

Feeling like an idiot, Austin grimaced. "Shoulda thought of that. Sorry."

"S'okay. It's not like you've been around him all that much."

"No, it's not okay. I don't want you thinkin' I don't want him here with us, or that I'd forgotten about him. I just wasn't thinking. I got excited when I saw Miranda's name on the concert list 'cause I knew you'd want to go. I didn't think beyond that."

"Austin, it's fine. That was really sweet of you. You can still go if you want."

"I don't want to go anywhere without you, babe. What are you even saying that for?"

"I just don't want you to miss anything because of us." She shrugged and began piling Fritos on paper plates.

"Hey," Austin cradled her back to his chest again as she worked. "I have everything I want in this room with me." He carefully included J.J. "If you're here, I'm pretty much in heaven. Sure as hell not missing

anything. Besides, I can't run my hands over all of my favorite things..."
his hands made another path up to her breasts, to her neck, then back
down over her crotch and ass, "...at a concert."

Laughing, Summer wiggled away from him and continued fixing
their plates. "You'd be surprised what I might let you get away with at a
Miranda concert, cowboy."

A rumbled growl escaped Austin's lungs. "I'm pretty sure she plays
Lincoln on occasion. If not there, I'll take you to Denver. Everybody
plays Denver."

A few minutes later, Austin dug into the Frito pie and groaned.
"Damn, that's good." He ate with more vigor. It was outstanding.

"Told you it was good. It's better with homegrown peppers. I used
to help Mama and Ms. McCallister can 'em. I know how. Someday, I
want a garden where I can grow my own."

"You think you could find somewhere to garden on a
120,000-acre ranch?"

"Whoa! Are you serious? That's huge."

"I gotta do it. *That's what she said.*" He winked at her as she rolled
her eyes.

"I had no idea your family's ranch was that big."

"I told you, we run a ton of cattle. I wasn't exaggerating, honey."

"I know. I just wasn't expecting that."

"How 'bout it? Think I can till you up a garden somewhere there?"

"Three days."

"What's that mean?" He didn't have to ask, but felt like making her
explain.

"We've known each other three days. You said I had two weeks to
decide, which still isn't really enough time, so let's not start garden
planning just yet."

"When you know, you know."

"You don't know."

"I *do* know, and you like to argue."

"I talked to Ekta while you were gone."

"Nice subject change. Very smooth," he huffed. Why couldn't she
just say she wanted to keep what they had right then? Why couldn't
she believe in him for a half-second? *You said two weeks, stop being an ass*

or she's not gonna give you two more days. Popping the tension out of his neck, he drew a deep breath. "What did Ekta say?"

"She wants me to come over tomorrow afternoon for a little while, and she said to bring the hawk, which I think is you."

"I'm a predatory bird?"

"Ekta said it, not me, and she's always saying shit like that. She means it with love."

"Well, I have to drive cattle early tomorrow morning, and then I thought we'd take little man to the parade. My family should be here by lunchtime, but we don't have to hang with them if you don't want to. They didn't give out any practice sessions before the first rounds, so we can go see Ekta whenever you want."

"Austin, we should hang out with your family. They're coming all the way out here to see you. I'll see if we can go to Ekta's another day."

"Nah, it's fine, sugar." Austin made himself another plate of Fritos and meat. "Dad'll want to spend hours in the old frontier town talking to the play-actors about life in the Wild West then telling us how we're all pussies now 'cause we have indoor plumbing. Then he'll tell us about how he had to walk to school through five feet of snow uphill both ways and got beat with a switch by the teachers just 'cause it was good for him. We won't be missing much. He tells the same stories 'least a half dozen times a year. We can just catch 'em next go 'round."

When she began giggling again, he instantly decided Summer's laughter was about the sweetest sound in the entire world. "Your dad sounds like how real dads are supposed to sound."

"Yeah, he's got the dad-thing down pat. Definite hero material by your qualifications." Her grin seized the air in his lungs.

"I can't wait to meet him."

"I can't wait for them to meet you. Luke texted me while I was out, said he and Holly are coming, too. Holl will probably stage some kind of suffragette reenactment in old frontier town. While Dad's chatting up the guy that plays Wyatt Earp about the shootout in Tombstone, Luke and I will have to sweet talk the woman playing Miss Kitty at the saloon into helping us break her out of frontier jail."

That did it; Summer doubled over laughing hysterically. "I think I'm gonna like Holly."

Austin rolled his eyes. "She's a hot mess."

"Are you one of those overly-protective big brothers that threatens any guy that hits on her?"

"I mighta done that a time or two, but only if I really don't like the guy, or I think he's being pushy. Plus, I don't have to worry about her here. She'll tell anyone who'll listen that cowboys are dumber than stumps, and she don't want anything to do with any of us."

"Your sister grew up on a ranch and hates cowboys?" Her brow furrowed.

"Told you she was a mess."

Summer stood and walked around the small kitchen table. Austin slid his chair back, and she seated herself in his lap, making his entire day. "Your sister doesn't know what she's missing out on, and you don't have to sweet talk Miss Kitty. I'll help you break her out of jail." She nestled her head in the crook of his neck and drew her legs up until she was curled up against him. Austin reveled in the contentment of having her safe in his arms. "I know you think you're certain about us, Austin. I didn't mean to change the subject like that. I'm just scared, and I'm not certain about any of this, okay?"

"Yeah, it's okay." He swallowed down hearty portions of need and nerves. "How about if I'm certain for both of us 'til you feel like you can be certain *with* me? That work?"

"Yeah, I like that plan. I'll try to be sure soon. I'm just not so good at the trust thing, and it's not just me I have to worry about anymore." She glanced over at J.J., who was banging his fists on his highchair tray, smashing his food with a great deal of vigor. "You scare me. I think you're too good to be true."

"I'll prove myself to you one way or another, Summer."

"Yeah, I'm starting to think you just might."

CHAPTER ELEVEN

Austin cleaned up the pots and pans she'd used to cook with, cleared the table, and hand washed the dishes while Summer got J.J. ready for his bath. *So this is how it's supposed to be.* Summer told herself not to get used to this, but it just felt so good. Being taken care of was addictive. She was running water in the bathtub when Austin appeared again.

"Can I help?"

"Sure. Thanks. Can you take his clothes off while I get the baby soap and stuff from his bag?"

"Oh, that reminds me." He disappeared for a moment and then reappeared, carrying J.J. in from the portable crib that was doubling nicely as a playpen, along with a pile of baby clothes. "Scott and Clif gave me these while I was registering. Pretty sure they're peace-offerings." He set J.J. on the bathroom counter and blocked him from crawling off with his body as he held up a Camden hat and outfit for J.J.

"I shouldn't let this work because Scott acted like a complete prick last night, but they're really cute," Summer admitted as she held up the baby Wranglers.

Austin chuckled and went about removing the current T-shirt and Walmart-brand baby jeans J.J. was wearing. They needed a good washing after playing on the playground in Thermopolis. She'd have to remember to pick up some detergent next time she was out.

Austin joined her on her knees beside the tub when she sat J.J. in the water. He loved to take baths and immediately splashed out his glee. Water covered Summer's T-shirt, and Austin laughed.

"Oh, I like bath time."

"Well, you did make a deal with him. Maybe he's helping you out, cowboy."

"Good work, little man." Austin winked at him.

Summer made quick work of washing J.J.'s adorable little fat rolls. "Hey, would you mind grabbing me a cup from the kitchen so I can do his hair? I forgot it."

"Sure, be right back."

When Austin returned with a large plastic Cheyenne Frontier Day cup circa 1997, J.J. had located his penis and was pulling on it, much to Summer's chagrin.

"That's normal, right?" She had to ask someone that owned one. He kept doing it, and it worried her.

Laughing, Austin nodded. "Don't have a lot of experience with little ones, but I'm gonna go with totally normal, nothing to worry about. It's fun to pull on. He doesn't know not to do it in front of people yet. Holly can probably tell you all of the psycho-babble that you're wanting to hear about how it's a healthy developmental stage or something. Ask her tomorrow, but there's nothing wrong with him."

"I kept telling myself that, but it's just nice to hear a normal guy say it. Should I tell him to stop?"

"You're not gonna stop him, honey. Not now and not in a few years. Why make it a big deal? It's part of life. Leave him be."

Summer washed J.J.'s hair. He shivered and gasped when she carefully poured a cupful of water back over his hair to wash the dust and dirt out. She let the water out of the tub, which she hated to do because it always made him cry.

Austin took over. "Okay, little man, I know the bath water is fun, but you're gonna freeze in there eventually." He lifted J.J. from the tub and wrapped him up in a towel while Summer retrieved his pajamas. She returned quickly and handed Austin a diaper.

"Tell me what to do." He looked like he was preparing for battle.

She giggled and gave him quick instructions. J.J. relocated his earlier play thing. Shaking his head, Austin fixed the diaper around him, effectively ending playtime. "I get it, man, I really do, but maybe try not to do it in from of Mama so much. Kinda wigs girls out until... well never mind. We'll go over all of that later. Way, way later. For now, let's do this pajama thing. Make me look good, now. Mama's watching. I need to impress her."

Summer laughed. Momentary joy and all-consuming hopefulness pervaded her soul. It felt so good to hope. Austin seemed certain he wanted both of them forever. Did he really want to be a stepfather for J.J.? It seemed like he really did want to take both of them on. Someone that would be there for him for all of the insanity that came with growing up.

Shocking her yet again, Austin plucked the bottle of milk Summer had prepared from her hands, carried J.J. into the sitting room, fed him the bottle, and read him a story out of an old copy of American Cowboy he found on the table beside him. It was an article on PRCA changes in rodeo rules from 2009. Austin would stop occasionally and explain his opinion on the ruling to the baby, until J.J. willingly let the soothing thrum of Austin's voice carry him off to sleep.

Summer followed them as Austin gently laid J.J. in the crib and stepped away to admire his work. "You're amazing," she whispered as she threw her arms around him, hugging him tightly.

"Maybe I'm getting this hero thing down all right. Still have a lot to learn, but there's lots of days left for learnin'. What shall we do now, Ms. Sanchez? I'm pretty good at getting you to bed, too." He ticked that left eyebrow upward and gave her his sexy smirk that she swore all but melted her panties every single time.

"Don't you have to be up before sunrise to drive cattle, cowboy?" God, she loved flirting with him, loved that determined look he got in his eyes when she played hard to get, loved that he made no qualms about taking her when he wanted her.

"Getting up before sunrise to drive cattle ain't nothing new, darlin'. That's my life when I'm not playing rodeo hero. If you think having to be up early is gonna keep me from bedding you every single night until

I'm spent and you're so weak all you can do is sleep in my arms, you got several other thinks coming."

"Oh yeah?"

"Yeah, how 'bout I show you?"

Summer shimmied out of her tank top and tossed it in his face as she headed toward the bedroom. His echoed groan sounded off the paneled walls, reaching her before he did. He stopped at the door, leaned against the jam, and crossed his arms. "Now take them shorts off for me, nice and slow."

She spun back to face him, but he shook his head and made a circle motion with his index finger. The hot, leaded intention in his gaze burned away any insecurities she'd ever had about her body. Every demand made her feel beautiful.

Turning back, she slowly slid the shorts over the expanse of her ass, but kept her panties in place. She shook her hips back and forth as she worked, loving the fire she could feel from his gaze and the way his audible breaths quickened with every inch she revealed.

When she stepped out of the shorts, she turned back again to note the way his entire body was tense and trained in on her with scope-honed attention. "Take your bra off for me, sweetness." She performed that task quickly, desperate to get this party started. "Drop it and grab those titties. Let me see you play with 'em for me." She scooped the heft of her breasts and let them spill through her own fingers. His guttural groan pulsed through her veins and tightened in her pussy. After a few passes, she moaned more from his actions than her own. In a few quick motions, he shed his T-shirt, jeans, boots, and boxers. His massive cock sprang free. He gripped it firmly, stroking up and down as she groped her own breasts. "Now those sweet little satin panties. They still have your cum on 'em from earlier, or did you change?"

"I didn't change." Her voice was a breathless whisper. His onyx eyes gleamed in the glow of the moonlight slicing through the trees. The low flame in them emboldened to a roaring blaze. "Good. Nice and slow, then throw those in my face." She complied. He caught the panties, brought them to his face, and inhaled deeply. "So fucking sweet."

A whimpered moan escaped her. She licked her lips. She still hadn't gotten a chance to taste him, and the desire to know his flavor flooded her mouth.

"Oh, you like that, do ya, doll baby?" Keeping the panties in his right hand, he stepped fully into the room and kicked the door shut. She watched him wrap her underwear around his cock and tug. He shuddered from the sensation, and it was all she could do not to beg him to give her a taste when he came.

"Oh my God, yes."

"You want me to keep going? Want me to come all over your pretty panties, baby? 'Cause if that's what you want, lay down on that bed for me. When I blow, I'm unloading all over you. I'll mark what's mine, and every square inch of your beautiful body belongs to me."

"That's not what I want…right now anyway." She had no issue with his marking her. In fact, the idea of it made her body long to wear his cum, but right now, she had other plans. She didn't mind being owned by Austin, but that road went both ways.

Stepping up to him, she ran her hands from the tensed muscles in his neck, over his Adam's apple, feeling him swallow down his own need as he jerked off with more vigor.

She splayed her hands over his pecs, loving the expanse of chest hair she encountered. God, he was all male perfection, a cowboy with greed chiseled in every plane of his hardened body. She traced the disks of nipples with her thumbs, reveling in his rumbled groan. Leaning in, she kissed from his collarbone southward, using her tongue and then her teeth until he was so close, she gripped his hand and tossed the panties, now covered in his pre-cum, aside.

"Save it for me. I want to drink you. I want to hear you roar my name when I slide you down my throat and swallow it all."

"Then you better fucking get on those knees, honey, 'cause I'm out of patience."

Moaning over his demands, she sank her teeth into a hollowed plane below his collarbone and sucked, marking him for herself as well. She left more over his right breastplate, down his abs, following the hairline, and left a final mark at his hipbone, then she fell to her knees, listening to his rasping growls as she drew his cock into her mouth.

"More," he pressed in slowly, shuddering as he moved. His right hand braided in her hair, drawing her in again, then back out, he guided her as she cupped his sac gently. "Suck hard, baby. I'm right there," he begged as she drew him in tightly, hollowed her cheeks, and tasted the sexy, salty tang of him. She spun her tongue around his head, cleaning him of his essence before she buried him in again, so hungry for him to fill her mouth with everything he was.

His flavors saturated her senses; to her shock she'd never been more turned on. She took him to his root, swallowed with him at her throat, and he came with a thundering cry of her name she was worried would not only wake J.J. but the entire campgrounds. Hot cum shot in hard spurts down her throat as she continued to swallow. Low, guttural groans hummed from him as he shuddered and jerked.

Licking the last drip with a long drawn suck, she stood and he cradled her in his arms still swaying unsteadily from his climax. "Damn, but you are perfection. Seems to me I got to come and you didn't though, darlin'. That ain't how we play. On your elbows and knees on that bed. Shake it for me so I can spank that sexy ass for making me come before you."

A breathy moan escaped her as she bolted for the bed, following orders readily.

His fingers plunged in her without warning. "So wet, sugar. Sucking my cock made you horny for me, didn't it?"

"Yes," she panted, feeling her body cinch around his fingers. The noise of his approval from deep in his throat sounded in her ear as he leaned over her, pushing his fingers deeper.

"You ready for me? I need you again. I told you I'd never get enough."

"Now," she ordered. She heard the tear of the condom wrapper. Shaking her hips back and forth, she willed him to move faster. The rasp of wiry hair from his thighs slapped the back of hers as he grasped her hips.

"Take it all for me, just like that." He buried himself in her fully, filling her to capacity. She pressed back against him. It felt too good not to take everything she could get. His hand smacked her ass. She gripped a nearby pillow and buried her face in the mattress to cover a scream of pure pleasure.

"More, please." She loved everything he gave her, the raw abandon, the trust, the unbound freedom she could still taste on her lips. She loved him.

The realization took center stage as he made another deep thrust, accompanied with another smack on her ass. Her entire body quivered. Her legs shook violently. Her mind begged for the release he was withholding. In and out, hard and fast, over and over. Her right ass cheek burned, and finally he gave her what she longed for. She screamed out his name as the orgasm seared through her on his next strike.

His hands gripped her waist as he buried himself in past his hilt and gained another orgasm of his own. She'd heard women talk about men that could go more than once. She thought they were lying. That was before she'd met Austin.

———

Eventually, she was tucked safely and naked in his arms and he was turning off the lamplight. "You are perfection, Summer. I've never met another woman like you."

"I love…" she bit her lip. He tightened his hold on her. Her heated breaths tangled with his. Hope was palpable between them.

"Say it."

"I love being here with you." She turned and tried to let her eyes say what she couldn't verbalize. She bit her lip and tried again. "I love…" she choked, "…um, I love how hard you get so fast after the first time."

Shaking his head at her, he sighed. "Well, I'm pretty sure I love *you*. I told you, I don't do scared, so I'm saying it. And I love being here with you, too. Just so you know, I've never been able to recover so fast like that. It's you, baby. It's all you. It's us together, actually. You make me a better man, because I want to be that for you."

"I know you do." She buried her face in his chest and tried with all her might not to be afraid, but she couldn't. There was too much at stake.

"You ready to go to sleep?" He gently, patiently even, pulled his fingers through her hair and whispered kisses on the top of her head, letting her hide in him.

"When I was a teenager and staying here with Ekta, I used to sneak out at night and go hang out in town. When I got back, I'd watch her old movies. I told you being here. It makes me feel like a kid again."

"Pretty sure we don't have to sneak out anymore, and I think J.J.'s pretty happy in his crib so I'm gonna suggest we leave him be, but we sure as hell can watch a movie."

"There are some in the sitting room. All John Wayne, but that could be fun."

"Go get whatever you want. I've seen 'em all. You wore me slap out, sweetness, so I make you no promises I'll make it until the bullets start flying, but I'll try."

"It's okay. You have to get up early anyway."

He tipped her chin up with his callused hand and brushed his lips across hers. A soft moan escaped her when he turned his head and blistered her mouth with his goodnight kiss.

———

Austin awoke long before sunrise. The feel of Summer's curves moving against him with her steady breaths settled his brain but stirred his cock. Glancing down at his own chest, he smirked. The marks she'd branded him with glistened a deep purple in the fading moonlight. Damn, but he loved them being there, loved that she wanted to imprint him as hers.

Checking the clock by the bed, the idea he'd been debating cemented in his mind. He eased the covers down her beautiful body and swirled his tongue between her breasts, tasting the sweet tang of sweat gathered there. Nuzzling the side of her left breast, he sucked along the underswell, leaving love bites of his own along her luscious tits. Damn, how had he not spent more time here?

Her sleepy moan racked readily in his balls as he swept his tongue over the tightening buds of her nipples. The flavor of her filled his mouth as he began to suck.

She lifted her head, her hair in a wild mane around her beautiful face. Her body soft and smooth, heated from his advances. That sexy smirk formed on her full lips as she watched him nip and suckle.

"Mornin', darlin'. If you haven't figured it out yet, I want you."

"Mmm, yeah, I got that all on my own. Thought you had to go drive cattle down a highway." Her sleepy voice held a sexy rasp that churned impatience through his bloodstream.

"So, I'll be quick." He drew the stiff peak of her left breast into the fiery heat of his mouth and sucked with fervor, watching her abdomen quiver and quake. "Spread those pretty legs for me. I need a fix before I go."

CHAPTER TWELVE

Glancing at the clock in his truck again, Austin cursed. He hadn't quite had time for that second round with Summer, but damn if he could have left when she was soaking wet, shaking, and begging him for more. Trucks lined the fields where cowboys were already saddled up and ready to go. He had to park damn near a mile away from the horses.

Half-running, he made it five minutes before they were releasing the steers. Jackson, Cam, Aaron, Clifton, and Scott were already mounted, but were holding a saddled horse without a rider between them. They all glared at him as he approached.

Cam smirked. "Well, you look good and fucked, so do we at least get to hear about the obvious reasons you're so late?"

"Sorry." He pulled his hat lower and made quick work of mounting while he endured the chastising he supposed he'd deserved. The horse was skittish, not quite broke yet. *Great.*

Austin settled in and stroked her side, trying to get her to stop jerking back and forth. He pulled up on the reins and clicked his mouth as the steers were released. He fell in behind the herd, driving hard with guttural commands that flowed naturally from him. He'd been doing this his entire life. Horse would have to get over it. She jerked a few times, but seemed to figure out that Austin wasn't putting up with it when he dug his spurs in.

Clif and Jackson headed north to the other side of the fence to make sure none got away. Scott hung back to gather any stragglers.

There were more than six hundred Corriente steers heading towards Frontier Park for the rodeo, but there were over fifty cowboys on horseback and it was just a few miles, so it shouldn't be too difficult. Refusing to do anything halfway, Austin scanned the herds along the road, anticipating where they were heading next. He began his counting before remembering that these weren't his herds. He'd never see them again.

Corriente were basically bred to be roped in rodeos and weren't good for much else, except maybe being escape artists. Sinewy things whose meat wasn't worth the effort could jump a fence during a drive right before your eyes. Driving was in Austin's blood. It was all he'd ever known, and he took pride in everything he did, just like his daddy taught him.

Letting his gut take over, he made another careful scan of the herds. Something wasn't right. Hair on the back of his neck stood. Another thorough scan revealed nothing out of sorts, but Austin couldn't shake the ominous feeling.

His eyes landed on Brant and a few of his cohorts from Preston. They were mounted, trying to gallop like the idiots they were, and carrying coils of rope that were highly unnecessary, and he doubted they had any clue how to use. As long as Brant was there, Summer was fine, so Austin told himself to relax.

A few steers lagged and then made their getaway from the herd. Austin and Cam headed their way, calling and directing them back. Nerves twisted up Austin's spine with every hoof-fall of his horse. His stomach roiled, probably since he hadn't gotten his ass out of bed in time to have breakfast. Cam cut right to get two that had stopped to consume some grass, while Austin headed due south now to get four that were still traveling. He'd done this hundreds of times. Why the hell was he nervous?

Keeping constant watch on the steers, something moved in his peripheral vision. Jerking his head to the side, he pulled up on the reins as Brant Preston and his horse thundered dangerously closer.

"Kee, aww," bellowed from Brant, and the quarter horse he was on broke out in a sprint from twenty feet away. Austin cut away, but his horse reared vertical on its hooves, kicking wildly moments before Brant's horse clipped its muzzle. Austin landed flat on his ass on the drought-hardened Wyoming earth.

Laughter filled the air as Brant bolted from the scene, following the path Austin's horse was now blazing through the prairie.

"Are you all right?" Cam dismounted and helped Austin up.

"I'm gonna beat that motherfucker into the ground and feed him his own nads for breakfast."

"Guess that means you're all right. Hang on, I got a rope. Horse'll slow up in a minute, and I'll get him."

By the time Cam had managed to get Austin's horse, other cowboys had to step in to get the steers, and Austin looked like an idiot that had never been on horseback. The drive was half over before they were racing to catch up. If one more well-intentioned cowboy asked him if he was all right, Austin was gonna lose his mind.

When everyone dismounted at the event arena, Brant, coward that he was, stayed firmly tucked in with the pack of good-for-nothing pussies from Preston Cattle and in eyesight of plenty of PBR and PRCA reps. The smirk permanently affixed on his stupid face only amped the rage consuming Austin.

"You gonna tell Summer what happened?" Cam handed him a pack of jerky and a bottle of Dr. Pepper he'd picked up from the convenience store.

"We should've whipped his ass last night. Then he wouldn't have been able to get on that horse this morning," Jackson huffed.

Austin downed a long sip of the soda and shook his head. "Don't say anything to Summer. She's already scared of him. I don't need her freaking out about this."

"You're good to ride tonight, though, right?" Clif was pacing. Scott kept crossing and uncrossing his arms. It was getting to Austin. He wished they'd cut it out.

"My ass is sore. What else is new? I'm a fucking bull rider. I'm fine."

"I pulled your day sheet for you. You're riding a bull called *Ransom Paid* from Summit," Scott provided.

"Great. If all goes well today, I'll murder Preston, take my family out to lunch, hang out with my girl, then I'll qualify."

"Simmer down, Austin. He wants you riled. That's why he did this. He wants you out of the competition. Can't stand for you to win the buckle *and* his ex-wife."

"Yeah, well, life's really gonna suck for him then, cause I'm going home with both."

"Then let that drive you. Go in there with something to earn, calm and driven. If you climb on the bull angry and unfocused you'll be heading home a lot quicker than any of us want."

Austin offered nothing more than an irritated grunt as he stalked back to his truck. Brant turned from his cocoon of morons as Austin passed. "Ass sore, Camden?"

Unmitigated gall throbbed in his muscles. His jaw clenched, and his eyes flashed with fury as he turned to stare Brant Preston down. *He wants you riled.* Scott's words managed to quell a little of his temper. They joined his own personal motto when it came to the ass-licker in question. *Never give him what he wants.*

Sporting a pompous grin, he nodded. "Yeah, it is. Got thrown off a horse of all things. No worries, though. Gonna go home and let Summer make everything feel better. She always knows just what to do. Makes everything feel *so* fucking good." He edged closer to Brant. "You know what they say, right, Preston? Time heals all wounds, especially a really, really *good* time." He went as far as to tip his hat to the son-of-a-bitch before he turned and headed to his truck.

By the time he made it back to the ranch cabin he and Summer had made a temporary home, he thought he'd done a half-decent job of looking unaffected. She called him on it before he made it to the porch she was sitting on rocking J.J. "What the hell happened to you?"

Ignoring her question, he took the steps two at a time and made it to her in a split second. He leaned to brush a kiss on her lips, but she blocked his mouth with her hand. "Tell me what happened first."

"I can't even get a kiss?"

"Not until you tell me why you look like a hornet stung your sac."

"Damn, woman. Don't say shit like that. Makes me squirm."

"Talk, cowboy."

"Nothing happened. I'm fine. You ready to go to the parade?"

"Full of shit answers will get you nowhere."

Rolling his eyes, Austin eased into the rocker beside hers but said nothing.

"You are not more stubborn than I am. You will not win this," she warned.

"No one's more stubborn than you are, darlin'."

When her eyes narrowed and she cocked her jaw to the side, he knew he was in for it. When she started to stand, he held up his hands in surrender. "Brant happened."

She settled back in the rocker and held J.J. tighter. Her eyes closed. "I knew he was going to do something. Did he hurt you?"

"No, he didn't hurt me," Austin huffed.

"Oh God, did he get you disqualified? He did, didn't he? I'll go talk to him. I'll figure something out."

"You will keep your little ass in that chair, and you will never go anywhere near Brant Preston ever again. You hear me?" The thought of Summer being in Brant's general vacinity stabbed terror through his chest. He took one long moment to reconcile the fact that she had become the one and only thing that mattered to him. That buckle meant less and less with every passing moment. All he wanted was her.

"Just tell me what happened," she demanded.

"He was being a prick just like always. Drove his horse into mine before I saw him coming. My horse freaked, and I got thrown. My pride hurts a whole lot more than anything else, so can we drop the whole damn thing, please?"

"I'm so sorry, Austin. I told you he wouldn't let this go. This isn't a good idea."

On his feet instantly, he jerked Summer up out of the rocking chair. "This," he gestured between them, "is the best thing that has ever happened to me. Don't you dare sit there for one half second and let your shit-for-brains ex make you think that he can control us. That's what he wants. He wants you scared and cowering from him. That's how he gets his way, and I won't have it. No one gets to treat you that way. Ever. He's a bully, plain and simple, and if he keeps this shit up, when the time is right, I'll give him the fight he's wanting, but it'll be *me* and him, not *you* and him."

"You will do no such thing. You're not fighting him for me. That's your pride and your temper talkin' anyway. You're smarter than that. You have no idea what the Prestons are capable of, and I won't let you get hurt for me."

"I'm not hurt, Summer. I'm just fine. The only way he could ever hurt me is if he managed to drive you out of my arms. I will not let the likes of Brant Preston keep me from you."

The terrorizing fear he'd seen in her eyes the first time he'd taken her to dinner returned in an instant. It had disappeared as soon as he'd taken her to his bed. Dammit, he wouldn't let her ex do this to her. Not anymore.

"You promise you're not hurt?" She swallowed harshly.

Gently, he wrapped his arms around both her and J.J. "Sweetheart, I get thrown off of two thousand pound bulls on the regular. I'm fine, and what he really wants is me all riled up so I screw up at the qualifications tonight. First thing I ever said to you was never to give Brant Preston what he wants, so that's what we're gonna do. We're gonna get little man ready and take him into town, go to the parade, meet my folks, and have a grand time at Frontier Days. Brant can lick my ass tonight when I hit the dirt after my eight second ride, then he can watch me spend all my winnings on you."

———

Keeping J.J. secured on his shoulders so he could see the passing parade floats, Austin grinned when he saw them. "There they are."

"There who are?" Summer scanned the teeming crowds surrounding them.

"Look, coming up there. One in front is Holly. That's my cousin Brock and his wife Hope, and Luke's bringing up the rear. Mom and Dad are probably checking in wherever they're staying."

"Shouldn't we go over there? They're looking for you."

"Nah, see that look on my baby sister's face? She wants to surprise me."

"It's weird how you read people like that," Summer fussed.

Chuckling, Austin lifted the baby off of his shoulders, settling him in his arms instead, and kissed Summer's cheek. "You seem to like me reading you in bed, sweetness. I told you, I live by my gut. There's not a better radar system. When I know something, I know something."

Another minute passed, and Holly beamed and pointed their direction. She ducked through the crowds. Austin braced ready for her to spring, but she stopped short and he offered her a grin.

"Uh, bro, you know kidnapping's illegal right?" Holly squeezed him fiercely. She always did. "Hey, little guy," she added, tickling J.J.'s belly, making him squirm to get away from her.

Rolling his eyes, Austin brushed a kiss on J.J.'s fat cheek. "Yeah, I know, but I found him, figured he'd make a great next-generation bull rider, so I took him."

Summer shook her head at him. That sunset glow bloomed across her cheeks again. Releasing Holly, Austin wrapped his arm around Summer instead.

Brock and Luke were both smirking, and Hope was beaming ear to ear while rubbing her baby bump that had doubled in size since the last time Austin had been home. "All right, this is my big brother Luke, my cousin Brock, his wife Hope, and my kid sister Holly. Everyone, this is Summer Sanchez, my girl, and her son J.J."

Luke's mouth hung open stupidly, and Brock was trying to cover his laughter.

"It's so nice to meet you, Summer." Hope, of course, threw her arms around Summer, nearly choking her in her exuberance.

"Oh, goodness, uh, it's nice to meet you, too. When are you due?" She gestured to Hope's bump.

"October 23rd."

"I'm glad you two came out. Wasn't sure you were gonna," Austin commented.

Recovering from his laughter, Brock linked his hand with Hope's. *"My girl,"* he goaded, "wanted to see what Frontier Days were all about.

She's never been to a rodeo. I figured this was the best one to see. 'Course, if you get your ass thrown tonight, I'll never get her to another one, so if you could not get yourself hooked, I'd be much obliged."

"I'll make that a priority strictly for Hope's enjoyment."

Hope elbowed her husband, and Summer chuckled.

Luke extended his hand to Summer. "Ms. Sanchez, saw you ride a few times. Hell of a barrel racer. Not sure why you're hanging out with my brother, but it's an honor to meet you."

The heat in Summer's cheeks intensified. Austin had hoped she'd be comfortable around his family, not embarrassed. "Thanks. That's sweet of you to say. Hard to race when you have a little one, and Austin's not so bad. God, he stinks when he gets outta them chutes, though."

Everyone erupted in laughter. Delighted she'd come out of her shell, Austin planted a firm kiss on her cheek. "You like my stink, darlin', don't even deny it."

Before anymore quips could be made, Austin's parents were upon them. His father glanced from Austin, to the baby, to Summer, and back again. "Oh, dear Lord in heaven, Jess, he's only been gone four months, right? It ain't been longer than that?" His father sounded genuinely frightened.

Austin laughed. "Mom, Dad, this is Summer Sanchez and her little boy, J.J. Summer, this is my mom, Jessie and my dad, Ev. You all get to know each other 'cause I'm bringing 'em home with me."

Summer's eyes goggled, and every single Camden lip sealed in shocked silence.

"Austin!" Summer gasped.

"It's so nice to meet you, Summer," Austin's mother stepped in to save the day. She embraced Summer readily. "When Everett brought me to the ranch the day we met, he eloquently announced to his parents that he'd up and found me on the side of the road and wasn't letting me leave. 'Course, he hadn't said any of that to me, which made it a rather awkward supper. His mama kept staring at me like she was half-worried I'd been dropped in the back fields by a spaceship. Austin comes by it honest. I tried to teach it out of him, but he's stubborn as one of them bulls he insists on throwing himself off of. He likes to give me gray hairs."

In that moment, Austin watched Summer fall in love with his mother. Summer threw her arms around her once again and let his mama mother her. Smiling, he let the feeling of being with his family, a portion of them anyway, soothe his weary soul.

"May I?" Jessie extended her arms for J.J.

"Oh, sure." Summer nodded. Austin handed J.J. to her and she slid seamlessly into the role of stepgrandmother.

"Ms. Sanchez, I'd heard you'd quit racing. Shame, too. Came up watchin' your old man as well. You were better." Austin's father winked at her and gave her a quick hug.

"Oh, thanks." Summer seemed to still be reeling from Austin's announcement. He was sure he'd hear about it later, but he'd never seen any reason not to shoot straight with people.

"Lot a story there, Dad." Austin shook his head.

"Figure there's a lot of story right here, son." Ev nodded to Summer.

Austin watched his mama study the lot of her family. "Well, Hope, baby, you need to get off your feet, and I need a cup of coffee something fierce. Summer, why don't we leave the men here, and we'll go heap pregnancy advice on Hope, 'cause heaven knows she don't get enough of it every single place she goes back home. If one more person slobbers all over her bump, I'm gonna smack 'em. Only I get to do that." She patted Hope's belly, making everyone laugh.

"Oh, I better not." Summer looked positively terrified to leave. "J.J. needs to go down for his nap soon."

Wrapping her up in his arms, blocking her from everyone and everything around them, and keeping her from escaping, Austin kissed the top of her head and whispered, "She wants to get to know you, sugar. Relax for me. You don't have to go if you don't want to. Hope probably holds memorial services for flies she has to swat. She's that kind, and Holly'll just tell you every embarrassing thing I did as a kid. I promise no one's gonna make you do anything you don't want to do. Deep breath."

Obviously panicked that Summer was uncomfortable, Hope bit her lip as she studied them. "I'd love to talk to you about J.J. We're having a little boy, too. I keep hearing about all of the trouble Brock, Austin, and Luke got into when they were growing up. I'm getting worried." Everyone offered her nervous chuckles. Time advanced around them, but for the moment it seemed to stop for the Camdens.

Summer pulled away from his embrace and managed a half nod. "Okay, sure." *Sure*, was most certainly not something she was feeling, and everyone knew it.

"You go on. I'll take little man back to the cabin and put him down for his nap. You all can head back when you're done. I'm sure there are plenty of Camden trucks here now."

"Are you sure?" Summer pled.

Lifting J.J. back out of his mother's arms, Austin lifted him high in the air and brought him back in one quick motion. J.J. belly laughed and applauded before he threw his arms around Austin's neck and hugged him. "He look unhappy to you?"

"No, he loves you." Summer's expression said she wasn't happy with that fact. He prayed his mother might help convince her that maybe all of this was fate.

CHAPTER THIRTEEN

A half-hour later, Luke, Brock, and Ev watched in stunned disbelief as Austin gently laid J.J. in the portable crib. He was sound asleep.

Standing at the small refrigerator in the ranch cabin, Ev shook his head. "You got anything stronger than root beer? I need a drink."

"Sorry, Dad. Didn't really think I should be drinkin' around J.J. Saloons will be open in a few hours." Austin settled on the old plaid-wool sofa and tried to figure out how to explain what had happened between him and Summer to his family.

With a grunt of annoyance, Ev took a root beer and joined his sons and nephew in the small sitting room. "Talk," he demanded.

"Met her in Cody. I don't know, Dad, kinda felt like I fell in love with her as soon as I saw her trying to scalp Brant Preston in the Silver Dollar Bar. Didn't you always say that was a Camden thing? You knew you wanted Mom as soon as you saw her on the side of the road? Grandpa wanted Gran as soon as he laid eyes on her in Montgomery Ward or something? Great-granddaddy Camden fell for Mimi when he saw her protesting for women's suffrage."

"That happen to you with Hope?" Luke sounded deeply concerned. Austin noted the faraway look in his eye, but he didn't comment.

Brock sighed. "Kinda, I guess. I knew I wanted her as soon as she walked into class, but things were *real* complicated for a real long time, as you know. I guess I always knew I wanted her in my life. We were best friends from the moment we met. I will say that. Maybe it *is* a Camden thing."

"Took me a few days to talk your mama into staying on the ranch though, Austin. You're already playing daddy to her kid and sharing her bed." Ev sighed.

"Sharing her bed has nothing to do with why I'm crazy about her, Dad."

"I'm sure it ain't hurting your feelings too bad either, though." Luke rolled his eyes.

"No, it definitely ain't." Austin would never deny that.

"So, Summer's up and ready to move to the ranch with you?" his father demanded. "Whose idea was that exactly?"

"Mine. She's not after anything, Dad. She hasn't even agreed to it, anyway. I can't seem to convince her that I want her, despite all the complications. I made her a deal that I'd prove myself for the next two weeks while we're here, and if I succeed she comes back with me. For the past few months, she's been a rodeo gypsy because of her ex and J.J. Not like she's got a home to go back to."

Squeezing his eyes shut and rubbing his temples, never a good sign, Ev was quiet for a moment. "Look at me, son." Austin stared his father down. "Your entire life, if someone told you that you couldn't have something, that was the one thing you went after with everything you were. You look me in the eye, and you promise me that you don't want Summer just because she told you that you can't have her. Because that girl's been hurt bad. I can see it in her eyes. Don't know how. Don't know when, but hurt and scared as a horse that ain't been tended nicely. She has a little boy that deserves someone full time, every time, day-in, day-out, even when it's the damn hardest thing in the world to do. This isn't something you can walk away from like you've done four-dozen other women across this great country."

"I know that, Dad. Okay, I know. She has been hurt by her old man, and by her ex-husband, and by life itself. I'm not in this lookin' to get out. I know what she wants, and I know what she needs. I'm in this to stay. If you'da told me back in April that I'd want to come home with a girl I was lookin' to keep and a kid, I know I would have laughed in your face. I know you're shocked. Hell, I'm still in shock, but I want this more than I've ever wanted anything, even more than that damn buckle I've been chasin' half my life."

"You'd give up the circuit for her?" His father's test didn't even make him bat an eye.

"In a heartbeat."

"Right now?"

"No, but she don't want me to right now. I owe Minton and I owe Max a showdown in Vegas, and you know it."

"You don't owe Max anything, Austin, but that's the ghost you've been chasin'. It ain't ever been that buckle. What if something changed and Summer wanted you to quit right now?"

"Why would she want that? There's not that many events between Cheyenne and Vegas. I'll be right there with her setting up a life most of the time. I'll take both of 'em with me when I compete."

"Let's just say she did."

"Fine, yes, I'd walk away, but that ain't me. I don't back down from something I've committed to. You taught me that."

"Yeah, I taught you that, and you need to remember that lesson more when it comes to Summer and J.J. than anything else."

"Noted." Austin was growing weary of this interrogation.

"Wait. Why was she trying to fight Preston? Ain't he the head of that huge stock supplier outta Dallas? He's been in the papers with that bull of his. PBR thinks he's doping him or something?" Luke had processed enough of the story to have recalled that bit of information.

"Brantley Jr. is the kid. His old man runs Preston Cattle. Both of 'em are shit sacks. Wouldn't surprise me if they are amping that bull. But," Austin sighed, "Brant Jr. is J.J.'s dad. He's Summer's ex."

"Preston hadn't been a name thought of too fondly by the entire Midwest for a long while, son. Cowboys got land, and they got cattle, and they got horses and homes, but ain't none of that matters if they don't got a worthy reputation. How'd she get mixed up with the likes of them?"

"Her father basically handed her off, trying to get her out of the rodeo because she was stealing his thunder. It went downhill from there. It's a damned mess. She's trying to get full custody of J.J. because Brant is an abusive asshole. I intend to help her do that."

"He hurt her?" Brock edged forward on the couch, immediately ready to defend Summer. He'd grown up with an abusive father and didn't take too kindly to anyone that lived by the school of thought that you get your way with your fists.

"Several times. Don't worry though, I'll take care of Brant Jr. when the time comes. All I can do not to stomp his ass into the ground with my boots every time I see the rat-bastard."

"You need any help you let us know. I'll get Grant out here if we need him," Luke readily vowed.

"Simmer down, all of you. I'm gonna go ahead and assume that you tearing Brant Preston limb from limb might not help Summer get J.J.," his father reminded them. "And I'm not real excited about the Camdens and the Prestons reenacting the Hatfields and the McCoys."

"There's fights worth fightin', Dad," Austin vowed.

"Agreed, and if she's who you want, son, I'll do everything in my power to help you two make a life on the ranch. Your mama and I will be there for both of you every step of the way, you know that, but you got to play your cards right, Austin. She might not want this as badly as you do."

"She does. I know. I can tell. She's just scared and hurt, like you said. If you want to help me, then help. Tell me how you convinced Mama to stay there with you."

His father adjusted his cowboy hat that he'd balanced on his knee, and considered. "Well, your mama, I mean...you know ain't nobody on God's green planet that's gonna tell her what to do. I tried to show her I'd be there for her no matter what. Took care of her. Taught her about the ranch and listened to her when she told me about being a buyer for that fancy department store. She wanted to learn to shoot, so I taught her. I just gave it everything I could, finally begged her not to leave. She did, you know. She went back to Denver for a little while. Scared the shit outta me. She kept saying she was coming back, but I was sick worried she wouldn't. Day she showed up, I kept her in my arms, wouldn't let her go 'til she said she'd marry me."

Austin turned on Brock. "How 'bout you? How'd you get Hope to stay with you?"

"Well, that was different. Hope and I had been friends for so long, and she was more convinced than I was that I could keep her happy. I had no idea she'd want to move back to the ranch. My wife is an angel sent straight to me from Heaven, and there ain't no other way to explain it."

"All right, well, I have two weeks to convince her, so you got any advice?"

Brock hemmed for a moment before he nodded. "I'm happy to help, man. You know that. I guess it's like Uncle Ev was just saying, listen to whatever she wants to talk about. You gotta listen even when she ain't talking, actually. Women are like that. They'll make comments about out-of-the-blue shit, and you gotta put it all together like a puzzle. Like Hope wanting to come out here. Couple weeks ago, she started talking about how she was feeling much better now that the nausea's gone. Then she made a few comments about getting out of the Glen for a few days. I finally put it all together when she reminded me that she'd never been to a rodeo or seen you ride."

Austin considered all of that. "Summer keeps talking about how being back in Cheyenne reminds her of being a teenager. That something I should be paying attention to?"

Ev rolled his eyes. "He's always been real quick-like."

Luke and Brock chuckled.

"Yeah, if she only gave you two weeks to convince her to move in with you, I'd listen to most any clue she might give up," Brock vowed.

"Agreed." A dozen ideas began to formulate in Austin's head. It was completely understandable that after a year of nothing but stress she might want a night to feel free as a bird again. He could do that, if he could get her to agree. "Hey, Dad, do you think you and Mom might keep J.J. for us tomorrow night, if Summer agrees?"

"We do have a little experience with youngins. It's fine by me, but she might not want to leave him with us. She barely knows us."

"Hope and I will help," Brock readily agreed.

"Yeah, I'll convince Holly, and we'll help, too," Luke sighed. "Surely the six of us can keep up with one barely-walking toddler."

"He's really good. Don't cry too much. Loves his mama something fierce." Austin grinned as he eased back to the nook near the bathroom to check on J.J., who was still sound asleep sucking the thumb of the arm he had clutching the horse Austin had purchased for him.

———

Summer couldn't remember the last time she'd laughed this hard. As much as she was enjoying Austin's family, part of her wished they weren't so great. It would make her end of Cheyenne decision much easier.

"So, Austin's never lived with anyone before? Another girlfriend or anything?" She couldn't help but wonder, and his mama kept encouraging her to ask anything.

"Honey, you are something I've been praying for since that boy was about sixteen years old. I knew it'd take a woman like you to bring my baby boy home. He's been roaming the earth for more years than I care to count looking for something he couldn't seem to find. Fate has a funny way of working things out. When I saw the way he was with J.J. and wrapping his arms around you I finally understood. He's been looking for you."

"Wow, no pressure or anything, Mama." Holly shook her head.

Summer continued, "Do you really think that? Do you think fate intervenes like that?"

"Yes," Hope leapt back into the conversation. "Someday, I'll tell you about how Brock and I ended up together, but trust me, fate intervenes when you least expect it, and sometimes in an explosive way."

Summer considered that. "He told me about Max and the wreck." The words tumbling around in her head took flight from her tongue.

"He told you?" Holly set down her coffee and stared at Summer in shock.

"Yeah, but maybe I shouldn't have told you he told me. I'm sorry. I'll apologize to him when we get back," she pledged to his mama.

She smiled. "Honey, we were there. He won't mind you telling us. I regret every day of my life telling them they couldn't go. He'll never believe it wasn't his fault. If I had it to do over, Ev and I woulda taken 'em out there, but that's the thing about hindsight. It's 20/20, and sometimes it leaves scars you can't erase."

"I can't believe he told you. He never talks about it. Gets up and leaves the room if anyone even mentions Max. So, I guess what I'm saying to you is welcome to the family, Summer. I'm Holly and I can totally kick Austin's ass if the need should ever arise."

They both laughed at her secondary introduction. "I think I can handle that if I ever needed to," Summer smirked.

"And that is precisely the kind of woman my son needs." Jessie lifted her half-empty diner coffee mug for a toast.

Glancing at the large clock hung on the wall of the coffee shop, Summer grimaced. She hated to be rude. "Um, I'm so sorry to have to leave. I've had such a good time. It's just I have a friend that lives a little ways out, and I promised her J.J. and I would visit this afternoon. I want to get back in plenty of time to take care of Austin before he rides."

When Holly started laughing, Summer cringed. She felt heat flood her features. "Uh, I didn't mean it that way. I swear." She withered in her chair and longed to bolt out the door, but Austin's mother grasped her hand.

"Sweetheart, trust me, if I thought you could take Austin to bed and keep him off of that damned bull tonight I'd keep J.J. and lock you two in a room and not let you out. I appreciate you wanting to take care of him, however you meant it. Besides..." she winked, "...people like to say that good cookin' is the way to a man's heart, and that certainly doesn't hurt your chances, but you and I both know it's gonna take more than that to rope Austin. So, girl, you do whatever it is you need to do, because I want you on Camden Ranch as much as my son."

Wow. Okay, these people really make their minds up fast. Clearly, Austin didn't only get that particular trait from his father.

"Thank you. It's just a lot to consider with J.J. and everything." Before Summer could make her escape, the coffee-infused air seemed to be vacuumed from her lungs. She shivered when she felt him standing behind her. His presence was oppressive and heavy-laden with the fear he longed to inflict. Jessie, Holly, and Hope lifted their eyes in confusion.

"I need to talk to you, Summer, about our son. Let's step outside." His hand landed hard on her shoulder, and she instinctively jerked away from him.

Brant's voice chafed her skin and irked her blood. She spun in her seat and glared at him. "You can go straight to hell where you came from, Brant. I'm not going anywhere with you, and our son is just fine."

"With your new little boy toy, I'm assuming." He simpered.

"Excuse me, young man, we were in the middle of a conversation before you so rudely interrupted to call my son a boy toy. I'm not sure if you've ever seen Austin shoot, and since you're still with us I'm gonna go with no, but he got his marksmanship from me. I can shoot a blowfly off a bull's ass from three hundred yards off my front porch with a cup of coffee in one hand and not spill a drop. You're already on my nerves, sweet thang. If I was you, I'd get before you get gotten," Jessie commanded hotly.

Summer laughed mostly to annoy the fuck out of Brant, but my God, she loved Austin's mama.

Holly turned to Brant pursing her lips. "Would you say that you learned your asshole-ish behavior from your mama? Do you feel she overly-dominated your childhood and now you have to show out as an adult because of regression issues? Or was it your father that taught you to be an abusive douchebag? *Or* are you just one of those kind of guys that stupidly believe that if you act like a dick yours will get bigger? Lots of that going around these days."

Summer bit her lips together but couldn't help herself. "He's got a healthy dose of all of those things actually. Poor thing don't know his ass from a hole in the ground."

"As if that wasn't obvious from the moment he walked in here. Take a long walk a long way from Summer, Mr. Preston, but don't be fooled, I've got my sights on you, son." Jessie narrowed her eyes.

"My God you really are as stupid as I always knew you were, Summer. Not good for anything but spinning around barrels. How'd that end up for you? I'm not intimidated by a bunch of squawking hens. We need to discuss who you're leaving our son with...without my permission."

"I don't need your *permission* to do anything, Brant. You never could figure that out, could you? Heard you couldn't get Austin to fight you last night, like the dumbass you are, so you rode your horse into his this mornin'. Don't that sound like a real man? Letting a horse fight your ridiculous battles for you."

"I'll just let my lawyers know that you've left J.J. with someone I don't approve of," Brant snarled.

Calling his lawyers was always his final threat. Largely, since Summer had been so afraid of losing her son, she'd give in to his demands. That's why he continued to use the idle threat. Maybe it was sitting at a table full of strong women, or maybe it was finally being in the arms of a real man that really seemed to love her for her, but she'd officially arrived at the end of her rope. Brant wasn't jerking her around anymore. "Great, and I'll let mine know that you've threatened Austin repeatedly and were not only abusive with me and with J.J., but now you've expanded to animals. That should make you look good when we go to trial."

"I think I'll just talk to Dad about this." Brant backed toward the door. Austin was right. He was nothing more than a bully, and she wasn't taking his shit anymore.

"You do that." Summer rolled her eyes.

The bell on the diner door announced his departure.

"Mmm, mm, mm, I take it that's J.J.'s daddy. The one you were telling us about." Jessie shook her head.

"Yes, ma'am. I'm so sorry about that. He's been steering clear of me because of Austin. Brant's afraid of him. I'm sure he was delighted to see me in here without him."

"Well, sounds like we need to get you back to my son."

"Oh, it's okay. You all stay. I can walk back."

"You will do no such thing. Not with him out there," Hope vowed.

Everyone stood and escorted her out to Jessie's Suburban.

Unable to help herself, she raced into Austin's arms as soon as she spotted him sitting on the porch with his brother.

"Hey there, darlin'." He sounded pleasantly surprised. "You okay?" The way his embrace was always full-bodied and all-consuming was intoxicating. His safety and his love radiated from his entire being. Letting her feel the strength of his upper body, he cradled her gently in his arms. Her heart wanted desperately to tell him that she didn't need the full two weeks. She wanted to move to his family's ranch right now. Her brain argued contentiously however. She knew that just wasn't a possibility.

"We met Brant," his mother explained. Austin tightened his hold of her. She buried her face in his chest, wishing the rest of the world would disappear for a little while.

"He say something to you?" Fury perforated his normally controlled, graveled tone.

"I'm fine," she lied, and he knew it. Afraid he might actually call her on it in front of his family since it seemed he'd say most anything in front of them, she tried to plead with her eyes for him to just let it go. "Where's J.J.?"

Austin continued to study her. "He's still asleep. Dad and Brock are watching TV. They're keeping an eye on him. I took good care of him. I always will."

"I know. It's just Ekta's expecting me."

"We are talking about whatever he said to you later, you understand me?" He lowered his voice to a barely audible whisper.

Summer nodded. "Yeah, I know."

"Luke wants to see the chutes and the arena before the crowds start to gather for the qualifications tonight. You okay with him riding to Ekta's with us? Then we'll run back to the arena and come pick you up whenever you're ready to leave."

"Sure, that's fine." Summer turned her head and offered Luke a smile. His single nod perfectly matched the one Austin frequently gave people, and he returned her smile.

Luke was a little taller than Austin and had very similar features. His hair was dark just like his brother's, but his eyes were a royal blue, where Austin's were as dark as charcoal. "Just let me get J.J. I probably shouldn't have left him."

CHAPTER FOURTEEN

Before Austin broached the subject of them leaving J.J. with his folks, he needed to know what the hell Brant had run his mouth about. Whatever it was, he had Summer running scared again. She was trying so hard not to show it, trying to be brave just like always. He kept his arm around her as they walked out to his truck. When she started to climb in the back with the baby, he wrapped his arm around her waist to halt her progress. "Luke can cram his ass in the back. You're sitting up front with me."

Luke rolled his eyes but didn't complain.

Summer directed them off of the main street through Cheyenne where all of the festivities were being held farther out of town. Austin navigated them over some rough terrain, and then they were upon a tiny log cabin near the south end of the river.

An elderly Arapaho woman was sweeping the porch. Her waist-length gray hair framed the wrinkles on her face. Summer leapt from the truck as Austin put it in park and the woman beamed.

"The whirlwind returns." Ekta embraced Summer, hugging her and swaying her back and forth. Austin released J.J. from his seat and lifted him out.

"Whirlwind?" Luke spoke through his teeth.

Austin matched his low intonation. "Tell ya later."

Keeping Summer's hand in hers, Ekta met Austin and Luke between the porch and the truck. "And I see we've reached the end of our lariat and we've met both the hawk and the buzzard, Whirlwind. You have to let go of the rope, my child."

"Uh," Summer's voice shook. "Ekta this is Austin and his brother, Luke." She lifted J.J. out of Austin's arms.

"Yes, but their purpose is to be the hawk and the buzzard."

"Am I the buzzard or the hawk?" Luke quizzed softly.

"I'm the hawk," Austin answered more audibly.

Ekta gave him a knowing smile. "Indeed you are. She's needed you for some time. Had to construct that rope though. She's always wanted to climb even when she shouldn't have. Now, sweet Austin, make your wings strong. She needs your strength to make it back safely."

"Okay, am I the only one that has no fucking clue what she's talking about?" Luke huffed under his breath.

"No, you're not," Summer sighed. "But she'll tell me after you leave."

"Do not worry, buzzard, your time to be the hawk is nearing on the horizon. There is a Sapana for you awaiting your strength and your wings, as well. One you already know, if I'm not mistaken. Yes, you know her as yours, but you must figure out how to guide her home. That will not prove easy, I fear," Ekta explained, but her gaze hadn't left Austin the entire time she'd been talking. He was beginning to feel a little like the contents of a petri dish.

"Uh, I think we're gonna get out of here. You sure you're okay, honey?" Austin asked.

"I'm fine." Summer shook her head at Ekta, but the beaming grin still hadn't left her face.

"Just call me whenever you're ready for me to pick you up. I have to be at the arena at 7:00."

"We'll just stay a little while. You two have fun." She brushed a kiss on Austin's cheek. J.J. followed suit, delighting both of them.

"You know it isn't nice to make people think you're insane as soon as they meet you. You should at least wait until they're not afraid to leave me with you anymore," Summer sighed as soon as Austin backed the truck out and drove away.

"Your hawk believes in his spirit that I know of what I speak. His concern is for his flight, which he feels coming."

Summer rolled her eyes and followed Ekta into her tiny wooden cottage, one of the only places on earth where she always felt welcome. "Okay, tell me what the heck you're talking about. I know you want to. Why do you keep calling Austin a hawk?"

"Have I never told you the story of Sapana, Whirlwind?"

"If you'd told me the story I might have some idea why my boyfriend is supposed to be a hawk." *Boyfriend.* It was the first time she'd called him that. A smile formed on her features. She knew she shouldn't like the way that sounded as much as she did.

"So much more than a boyfriend, Whirlwind. So much more."

"Talk, Ekta. You're freaking me out."

"Calm, Whirlwind. I made tea. Put J.J. on the rug and let him play, then I'll tell you Sapana's story."

"He doesn't stay on the rug anymore. He crawls everywhere and pulls up."

"You say this like I have not raised children." Ekta directed Summer to a basket full of toys on her rug. Studying the space, Summer understood that J.J. could crawl to his heart's content. There was nothing he could harm or that could harm him.

She settled him by the basket and accepted the mug of tea Ekta provided her.

"Many moons ago, there was a young woman, Sapana, who went from her teepee village out to gather firewood. She was the most beautiful girl from her village."

"So, this story obviously isn't about me," Summer quipped.

Ekta placed her index finger over Summer's mouth. If it had been anyone else, Summer would have bitten them.

"You don't have to see your own beauty for others to recognize it, Whirlwind. Stop spinning and whipping the prairies and listen. While Sapana and her friends were out, Sapana saw a porcupine. She immediately decided to catch the porcupine, never one to think of the pain she might inflict upon herself trying to do so. She wanted the quills, much like some girls want rodeo buckles." Ekta winked at her. Summer ground her teeth.

"The porcupine began climbing a tall cottonwood tree. Of course, Sapana followed. She tried to strike the porcupine with a stick, but the animal climbed, constantly just out of her reach. Always obstinate no matter the task, Sapana climbed higher and higher until her friends begged her to come back down to the earth. Naturally, being her, she refused.

"She climbed higher and higher chasing the elusive porcupine. She climbed until she could no longer even hope to see the ground below her, and suddenly the treetop vanished and she found herself in the midst of a camp circle. The porcupine turned into an old man."

Summer's brow furrowed. "Keep going."

"Patience, Whirlwind. This is important. Porcupines are very fond of their quills, but they will use them to protect themselves. It is important that you remember they will use them *only* to protect themselves. If you try to grab hold, you will get pricked. Remember that, Whirlwind. The porcupine-man forced Sapana to marry him."

"And there it is. I take it porcupine-dude is Brant in this particular legend that's supposed to reflect my life."

"Seeing yourself as Sapana already, are you? Such a smart girl. The porcupine-man put Sapana to work that very day, scraping and stretching buffalo hides to make him robes. Sapana worried constantly about how she would ever get back home. She missed the green grass and the trees that had once been her world. The porcupine-man refused to allow Sapana to ever discuss her village or how she might return to it. Every day he would leave Sapana to go hunt. He never failed to leave her a list of work. In the mornings, she was to dig for wild turnips, and in the evenings she was to work on the hides he brought home. Each morning he would warn her not to dig too deep when she found turnips. One morning, she stumbled upon an unusually large turnip. With a great deal of difficulty, she managed to loosen the turnip with her digging stick."

"He made her dig with a stick? Asshole. Maybe he *is* Brant."

"Whirlwind." Ekta pursed her lips.

"Sorry, sorry, go ahead."

"When she pried the turnip loose she was shocked to find that it left a hole large enough for her to see her way back down to earth. She quickly returned the turnip and covered the hole, understanding why *Brant* never wanted her to dig too deeply, for he knew what she would find."

"I thought his name was porcupine-man."

"Did you really, child? On her way back to the teepee, she came up with a plan. Porcupine-man always made her scrape and soften the hides he returned with so she could make him robes. After she completed his robes, there were always sinew strips left over. She decided she would hide the sinew under her bed until she had enough to make a lariat."

Summer shifted uncomfortably. In her experience, Ekta's stories almost always applied to her life in an all too familiar way.

"For months, *Summer* hid sinew strips away."

"I thought her name was Sapana."

Ekta smirked. "When she believed she had enough of the straps to make a rope long enough to carry her back to earth, she waited for porcupine-man to leave for the hunt and she set to work. She pulled up the turnip, laid her digging stick across the opening, and tied one end of the sinew lariat to her stick and the other around her waist. Slowly, she lowered herself by uncoiling the lariat. Down, down, down she went. A long time went by before she could see the tops of the trees from her village, and then she ran out of rope."

"Figures that'd be my luck," Summer sighed.

"Ah, but there is more to Sapana's tale, my child. She hung for a very long time swinging to and fro, back and forth, unable to climb back up the sinew lariat and too high to jump down. Suddenly, the lariat began to shake violently and stones flew by her body. The porcupine-man had returned from his hunt and had located Sapana. Porcupine-man was furious that she'd tried to escape him. Another stone nearly struck her head.

"Just when Sapana was certain she could not be rescued, a buzzard circled beneath her. She told the buzzard what had happened to her. He flew to her and instructed her to step on his back and promised that he would carry her to her earth. 'Let go of the lariat. I've got you,' he assured her. Seeing no other options, Sapana untied the lariat from her waist and got on the buzzard's back. But the buzzard was not her warrior, you see. She was too heavy for him. Then a hawk approached and buzzard explained that the girl needed to be returned to earth. Hawk flew with Sapana until he reached her people, and he returned her safely with buzzard's help. To this day, when Sapana's tribe hunts, they leave a buffalo for hawk and buzzard as a way to thank them for returning their beloved Sapana to them."

Summer swallowed harshly. "So, Austin is going to have to save me. *Great.*"

"Ah, but there is more to your tale than Sapana's, my dear. In your tale the rescuing hawk has been flying for so long he's forgotten why he started flying in the first place. When he rescues you, he will remember how to go back home, because his home is yours, Whirlwind. The hawk has forgotten his way. You will show him. If you will allow it, my child, you will save each other, but it is all up to you. Just know this—you cannot hang on that lariat forever. Brant's aim with the rocks improves with time."

"Ugh, why does everything have to be up to me? Why can't something just be easy? Why can't Sapana have just not chased the damn porcupine, found herself a nice cowboy, and settled down?"

"Interesting question, Whirlwind. Why couldn't she?"

"Because I'm an idiot," Summer sighed.

"No, you're not unintelligent, but you and your hawk do have a habit of chasing entirely the wrong things. Both you and Sapana tend to see the tree they want to cut down instead of the answer in the forest."

———

"So, you're not only bedding Summer Sanchez, but you're also gonna move her into your house?" Luke asked Austin again.

"Bro, how many times do I need to explain this to you? She's fucking awesome. I'm in love. I know I said I'd never fall, but I did. Just have to get Preston to stay the hell away. I plan on walking out of the arena tonight ten thousand dollars richer. I'd say that'd buy a pretty damn nice engagement ring, not to mention the millions I've racked up this season."

"I feel it bears mentioning before you up and spend all of your bank on a ring that barrel racers are generally a little wild and completely crazy."

"Yeah, she's perfect. That's what I've been trying to tell you." Austin laughed.

As they searched for a parking place near the arena, Luke jerked Austin's shirt to the side, reveling several of the hickeys Summer had left on him the night before. He shook his head. "Figures. I somehow suspect she has more."

Austin smirked and waggled his eyebrows.

"I hope you know what you're doing. Whole thing seems nuts to me, and I really don't want to be a scavenger bird in this like that woman kept calling me, if it's all the same to you."

"Ekta took good care of Summer when Mitchum used to ride here every year. Summer adores her. I don't give a shit if she is crazy. I'm just glad somebody was there for her at some point in her life."

"Speaking of riding here, shouldn't you be getting your head out of Summer Sanchez's crotch and be getting it into qualifying on a bull tonight?"

"I'm in it. Should have seen my last ride in Cody when I knew she was waiting on me outside the chutes. Ninety-fucking-two. My best ride yet. She's my good luck charm."

"Okay, fine, geez, she all you're ever gonna talk about again?"

"Sorry, guess I am obsessin'." Austin tried to feel bad that he'd dominated conversation the whole day with talk of Summer. His brother wouldn't be in town too long, but convincing Summer to be his permanently took up all of his brain capacity. "Uh, how's the ranch?"

"Hay's mostly in. Grant and Natalie are finishing it up, but Gilbert's ranch is heading for the auction block."

"What?" The news effectively jerked Austin out of thoughts of he and Summer making Camden Ranch their permanent home.

The Gilberts had owned the small 7,000-acre ranch next to the Camdens since long before either Luke or Austin had been born.

"Yeah, you remember back last winter when their barn burned?" Luke reminded him.

Austin nodded.

"Bunch of bad investments near about bankrupted them just before that. Looks like arson, but it was an inside job."

"No way. Ames Gilbert is as honest as the day is long. He wouldn't torch his own barn for cash."

"No one thinks it was Ames. Seems Derrick put his daddy's money in oil a month or two before OPEC slashed the price per barrel instead of in corn, where everybody with half a brain knew the money was gonna be. He freaked and decided he'd get the insurance money for the barn, try to reinvest in something else. Whole town's up in arms over it. They couldn't get enough for their last shipment of cattle to save 'em. Going up for sale first of September."

"Damn, that's a shame. Derrick has always been an idiot, though. Remember when we were in middle school and he stuck marbles to bullets and started throwing 'em in the fucking gym? Guy's a moron."

"Yeah, well remember in high school when he downed a fifth of his daddy's good bourbon and drove his truck into the pond by our house?"

Austin and Luke laughed at the memory of Derrick Gilbert sitting by the pond, singing *God Blessed Texas* over and over again, at three in the morning, staring at his old Dodge Ram bed-up in the water.

"Who could forget that? Ames tried to make him work our ranch 'til he paid for the damages, but he kept screwing things up and Dad fired him."

"Dad thinks we should buy the land before it goes to auction. He hates to see it go for prices that low."

"You interested?" Austin asked.

"Might be. You want to split it with me, or are you planning on spending all of your money on Summer and your new life?"

"My new life will be just like my old life, but significantly improved since she'll be there riding beside me or waiting on me to get back from workin'...preferably naked in our bed."

Luke's customary annoyed grunt came just before his eye roll. "You're full of shit, you know that, right?"

"You're the second guy to say that to me, but you're both wrong. I finally feel like I figured out what the hell I'm on this planet for."

"Fine. Are you interested in buying the Gilbert's land with me or not?"

"Yeah, maybe. Let me get home and get settled in. We have 'til September, right?"

"Few other families looking at it, but Grant said you can't grow corn on it, so..." Luke shrugged.

"I still need to figure out what it might take to get J.J. away from Brant permanently. I'm guessing she needs a better lawyer. That's gonna take some money."

"It ever cross your mind that she might see you as a sugar daddy that could get her what she's wanting since you've been winning all season?"

"It ever cross your mind that I ride bulls for a livin' and if you ever say something like that about her again, I'll kick you out of this truck and beat your ass six ways from Sunday?"

Luke shook his head, but he also shut his mouth.

Austin dropped Luke back off at the Best Western, where his family had four rooms. He grilled his mother, Hope, and Holly until Holly spilled the entire ridiculous situation with Brant while they'd been having coffee. She'd gone on and on about how Brant's father probably caused him to feel emasculated or some shit with other words Austin didn't understand. He'd deal with Preston later. Sounded to him like Summer had stood up for herself without using her fists. He thanked his lucky stars for that before he headed back out toward the river to retrieve Summer and J.J. He smiled to himself, thinking how much he enjoyed that he was the guy picking her up.

Summer stormed out to the truck before he'd even had a chance to stomp on the emergency brake. She had J.J. in his car seat and was up beside him, kissing on him, before he could ask what the hell had gotten her sassy-ass up in arms.

The fact that she was kissing him while looking highly irritated confused the hell out of him. *Women.* Why did they have to be so dang hard to figure?

"Head in my Wranglers says to keep kissing you. Head above my beltline says to ask you if you wanna tell me why you look madder than a wet cat."

She settled down in the seat beside him. "I'm kissing you because I missed you, and I don't know, I guess I'm kind of glad you're back."

Laughing at her outright, Austin nodded. "Your ringing endorsements always make a guy feel appreciated, and I missed you too, sweetness. Now, what's got my girl so ornery? Since you were kissing me and didn't backhand me when you got in the truck, I'm assuming it isn't me. You and Ekta have a come to Jesus meetin' about something, or are we still pissed at Brant?"

"I'm always pissed at Brant, but it ain't him this time."

"All right, I s'pose I could ask J.J. He isn't much more forthcoming with information than his mama is currently, however."

"I'm just... I don't know...mad at myself, honestly."

Shocked she'd come out with that, he debated how to proceed. "Anything I might could do to get you to stop being mad at yourself?"

"No."

"Wanna tell me what brought on this round of self-abuse?"

As he backed away from Ekta's cabin, Summer crossed her arms over her drool-worthy chest and stared at the onslaught of cottonwood trees like they'd greatly offended her. "Ekta says you're going to have to save me, and that pisses me the hell off. Why can't I have a boyfriend that doesn't have to save me? Why can't I just save myself?"

"What exactly am I going to be saving you from?"

"The porcupine-man."

"The what?"

"Brant, I guess. It was this long story about you, and me, and Brant, and how I brought all of my trouble on myself, which I already knew, and now apparently I'm draggin' you into it. I don't want to do that. I'm just so tired of regretting most of my life."

"Summer." Austin hit the brakes and pulled off on the side of the dirt road. "Look at me." Her whiskey gold eyes stared up into his. "Tell me the story."

At the end of the long, drawn tale about Sapana and the hawk, Austin drew a deep breath. The motion of Summer's body scared the shit out of him. She was about a half-second away from bolting from his truck, grabbing J.J., and never looking back.

Better talk fast, brother, she's officially freaking out.

Austin shot an annoyed glanced skyward. He didn't need Max telling him that.

"All right, well, I kind of already did save you, didn't I?" He had no idea where this idea had come from but it was the best he could come up with, so he was going with it.

"What?" She turned back to him. "What do you mean?"

"I saved you in the Silver Dollar that night. If I hadn't stepped in, you woulda beaten the tar out of Brant, and as much as he deserves it, that would have been real bad for your custody case. I already saved you. And not that I'm patting myself on the back or anything, but I did give you a place to stay and a ride to Cheyenne, 'cause trust me, that truck of yours wouldn't have made it out here. So, I've already saved you, and you didn't seem to hate it too bad. It's over and done with, and trust me, darlin', you already saved me, too."

Summer's brow furrowed. "But why would Ekta tell me the story after it happened?"

"She's known you since you were a kid. I'm betting she already figured that you'd be mad about me trying to save you."

"She said something about me showing you how to go home."

"So, there you go. I'm not going home without you, Summer. You *are* showing me the way home. I've been out on this circuit for half my life. I never wanted to go home because when I'm there, everything I see reminds me of Max, and I feel guilty all over again. Now, I want to go home because I want to have a home with you. The story is past tense. We saved each other. They fell madly in love at the rodeo, even though it only took a few days, and they lived happily ever after. That don't sound too bad, right?"

"No, it doesn't sound too bad at all. I'm just not sure that's what she was telling me."

"You're the one that's being stubborn about the whole thing. I know what I want, and she's sitting right beside me in this truck. You know what you want, too, but you're terrified to admit it. I know it's scary, sugar, but sounds to me like Ekta's trying to tell you that you're supposed to fly with me. That's precisely what happened in the story, isn't it?"

"I guess so."

Austin was certain she still had her doubts, but she no longer looked like she was going to bolt. In fact, she studied him like she was finally seriously considering his offer to take her to the ranch and make her all his. He'd take anything he could get on that front. Maybe he should call Ekta up and thank her for making up some crazy story about a hawk to tell Summer.

"Mom and Holly couldn't stop talking about how much they loved you. Did you have fun with them?"

"Yeah, I had a really good time. They're all so sweet." A genuine, beautiful smile formed on her features. Austin had to remember to keep his eyes on the road. Looking at her grinning like that was prettier than any sunrise he'd ever be witness to.

"Mom didn't tell you too many embarrassing stories, did she?" He chuckled at his own expense. He'd gladly tell her anything she wanted to know.

"Well, I did finally ask about J.J.'s recent fascination when he's nekkid. Holly said it's perfectly normal, and your mom told me you played with yours so much when you were little she was worried you were gonna pull it off." Summer dissolved in hysterical giggles. Austin amended his recent thought on telling her anything she wanted to know. It hadn't occurred to him that his mother remembered things about his younger years that he had no hope of recalling.

Fire blistered his face. Dammit, he was too old to blush. "I'll have to thank her for sharing that with you."

Summer leaned and brushed a kiss across his fevered cheek. "You're an amazing guy, Austin. It made me stop worrying about J.J. If he turns out like you, then I did a good job being his mama."

"You're a fantastic mom, babe. No worries there."

"I try. I always feel like I'm screwing something up, though."

"I kind of think kids don't need you to be perfect. Dad says they just need you to be there for everything, especially when they screw up."

"I hope he's right."

CHAPTER FIFTEEN

Dipping low, Austin did a few deep knee bends trying to work in the Cheyenne Frontier Days chaps all the riders were wearing that night. Clearly, someone who'd never actually had to wear chaps had come up with this plan.

He vastly preferred his old ones from Minton; at least they were worn in the right way, felt like a second skin. Despite the annoyance over the new chaps, he was more than pleased that Summer seemed to have settled on the idea that she'd already been saved and she'd survived it, maybe even liked it—not that she'd ever admit that out loud. She'd even asked him a few questions about his house in Nebraska and about the kind of cattle they raised. If she didn't have the habit of making her mind up just to change it, he'd have been darn near ecstatic.

"Sucks you have to wear new chaps to ride in." Summer watched him bob up and down. "Hey, you know how I used to soften mine? It works like a charm."

"I'm listenin', sweetness."

"Here, take 'em off and give 'em to me."

Austin did as he was told and watched Summer grab an old horse brush from a tack basket near the bull riding locker room under the

Cheyenne Arena. When she returned, she proceeded to lay his chaps out on one of the metal benches, and rough them up using the brush and a great deal of vigor.

"Fucking gorgeous and smart as a whip, too. I still don't know I got so lucky." He couldn't help it. He swelled with pride watching her help him get ready.

"It won't be as good as an old pair, but it gets them close," she explained as she rubbed the inseam vigorously. Only a real cowgirl would know that's where they pinched the worst when they're new. His grin expanded.

"I can do it, darlin'." He held his hand out for the brush.

"No, you keep stretching. I got this."

Luke, Brock, and Austin's father made their way into the locker room using the passes Austin had secured for them.

"What's she doing?" Luke quizzed as he watched Summer work.

"Breaking in a new pair of chaps for me."

"Damn, that's genius," Brock admired.

Summer grinned. "I went through a lot of chaps when I rode. New ones suck."

"Amen to that," Austin agreed.

"All right, I'm gonna head up to the seats with the girls. Son, please be careful. Just be walking when you get off of that thing for me," his father urged.

"I'll do my best, Dad." Austin accepted the hug from his father and watched him head out toward the stands. Luke and Brock wanted to play chute team so they were staying. "All right, you two, I gotta do the walk out in just a few because, you know, I'm the shit and all," he goaded. Summer, Brock, and Luke all rolled their eyes at him. Only Summer grinned, but she was the only one that mattered. "I want my good luck kiss so you two get. Chute number nine. Doubt the bull's loaded yet, but should be soon."

"Yeah, yeah, we'll see you down there," Luke huffed.

As soon as they made their escape, Austin pinned Summer up against the painted concrete brick walls, kissing her like a man on fire. He needed that sweet heat she gave him with reckless abandon. Her soft moan as he tempted her lips with his tongue until she opened for him fed his hunger. It was gonna be one hell of a night. Desperate for more of her, he nipped her bottom lip, loving the way she arched those beautiful tits into his chest when he did that. When he sucked away the slight pain, another moan filled his mouth.

"Please don't do anything that might keep you from being in bed with me tonight. God, I need you with me, Austin, not in the hospital. Just please be careful."

Her words always spoke directly to his groin. Lust raced up his spine. He swore every hair on his body stood on end. He traced up her slender waist and discreetly teased the underswells of her breasts with his thumbs.

"Trust me, darlin', only thing that's gonna happen tonight after I make bank is I'm gonna take you back to our cabin and take you to bed. God, you smell so damn good." Taking another kiss and another nip, he inhaled again of that sweet sexy spice that was all Summer as her body swayed between him and the wall.

He pulled her closer, locked his arms around her and nuzzled his face against her neck. "Soon as I get you back, I'm gonna bury my face in you, darlin', 'til I feel your juices dripping down my throat. I'm gonna make you grind that pussy in my face and beg me until I lap up everything I make you give me, and that will only be the first course. So much I wanna do with you tonight, sugar. No fucking bull's gonna stop me."

"You promise me." She shuddered in his arms. Her nipples tightened against his chest from his spoken desires. His cock throbbed its approval.

She wanted a promise that he wouldn't get hurt. That really wasn't a promise he could make. Before that moment, he'd never even considered the pain and inherent risk that came with his current profession affecting someone else. "Oh, I promise I'll fuck you so thoroughly tonight you'll be screaming for me. Have no doubt about that, sugar."

"That's not what I meant..."

He kissed the words from her lips. He didn't want to make promises to her he didn't know if he'd be able to keep. Getting her to trust him was of the utmost importance. Her defiant nod said she knew he wouldn't make that promise. She forced a grin and pulled the Zuni macaw necklace out from behind her Camden T-shirt.

"Thank you for wearing that for me, baby. You're all the luck I need. Just knowing you're gonna meet me outside that gate when I get off and that little man is up in the stands with my mama wearing a Camden shirt means more to me than you'll ever know."

Fear darkened her eyes to a deep chestnut. "I'll be there. I promise."

"Then let's do this. I've got plans for you tonight." He refastened his chaps, wrapped his arm over her shoulder, and escorted her out to the open arena teeming with rodeo fans.

He waved to fans shouting his name and blew a kiss to his mother. Minton had gotten them seats up front. She looked terrified as well. Brock and Luke had joined Cam, Jackson, Scott, and Clif at his assigned chute.

"Hey, you gotta get out to the field. They're announcing the current leaders in every event." Scott pointed to a small group gathered in the center of the dirt. Brushing another kiss across Summer's lips, he headed that way, more than anxious to get down to business.

"You okay, sweetheart?" Luke asked Summer as she stared after Austin heading out to claim his current title.

"Not really. I don't know what happened to me in the last year, but I hate watching him do this. Scares me to death."

"And pisses you off as well, I'm betting."

Summer grinned in spite of herself. "How'd you know that?"

"Makes Mama madder than an old, wet hen when he rides. I've seen Hope chew Brock's ass several times for doing something where she thought he might get hurt." He elbowed Brock, who chuckled and gave her a kind smile.

"I kinda think it comes with caring about someone so much if they hurt you hurt. I lit Hope up a few weeks ago for trying to balance on a chair she'd put a stepstool on top of instead of asking me to get whatever it was she couldn't reach." He shook his head. "I walked in the kitchen and saw my pregnant wife on her tiptoes on top of the contraption she'd built, and I almost lost my mind. Scared me to death, but then I felt bad for yelling at her." Brock shook his head and then searched the crowds until he located Hope. Summer watched her give him a knowing grin, almost as if she knew what he was confessing.

So love is apparently worrying. Great.

"But he'll be fine. He's pretty damn good at all of this. Been practicing and riding as long as I can remember," Luke assured her. "First time he got thrown hard off a practice bull, he shattered his collarbone. Mama and Daddy thought that'd break him of wanting to keep going, but it only made him more determined. He'd sneak and practice with the brace on. Thought Mama was gonna strangle him, but he worked his ass off until he had it down to a skill." He gestured to Austin standing in the middle of the Cheyenne Arena. "Wouldn't of made it this far if he didn't know what he was doing."

"He always been so sure about what he wants?" Summer couldn't help but ask. She'd heard his mama and Holly out. Now, she wanted it from his brother's perspective.

"Yep," Brock and Luke answered simultaneously.

"He don't take no for an answer, either. Only takes a split second, too. He sees something he wants, and goes after it 'til he gets it. He didn't want to go back out on the circuit this year, but to him, he ain't got that PBR buckle yet, and it won't be over 'til he does." Luke was mighty chatty. Summer knew she should take advantage of it, but her stomach roiled with barbed nerves tearing through her gut. She tried not to see Brant standing at Chute 12 with that damned bull and a rider than looked scared shitless. *Maybe Austin won't ever have to ride him.* There was a chance of that. It was all in the luck of the draw. Seemed like Austin usually got what he wanted. She tried to reassure herself, but was failing miserably.

Brant's eyes narrowed in on her. His glare whipped through her like a cold black wind in the humid arena. Cocking her jaw to the side, she turned so he could see *Camden* displayed right across her breasts from the T-shirt Clif had given her to wear that night. The enraged look on his face was priceless. She wished she'd taken a picture.

Before she could revel in Brant's obvious irritation, the announcer began, "Welcome to Cheyenne Frontier Days!" The crowd roared. "It's time for the Cinch Shoot-Out qualifying round for all of our riders. This is the best of the best, ladies and gentlemen, but if they don't make the scores tonight, it'll all be over. Let's hear it for the current champions."

He worked his way through the team ropers, steer wrestlers, and the tie-down champ. When Deena Chisolm, the current barrel racing champ, stepped to the center and waved to the crowds, a twinge of jealousy turned in Summer's belly. She was better than Deena, always had been, always would be, but that no longer mattered.

Smiling and whistling a moment later, she blew Austin a kiss when the announcer bellowed his name. He returned the gesture, having eyes for no one but her. How the hell had she gotten so lucky? He'd come along at just the right moment. Maybe it *was* meant to be. Maybe he really was her hawk. She'd certainly felt like she'd been swinging by that damn rope forever. *Let go of the rope. I've got you.* Ekta's story wouldn't give her peace.

Had he already saved her, or was something else coming? Maybe she *should* just let go of the doubt and be in this. Glancing down at her T-shirt, and then up at J.J. in the stands with the rest of the Camdens, she smiled. She was already pretty much in it. Might as well go with it.

Another glance in Brant's direction dissolved a little of her fledgling confidence. She hadn't brought it up yet, but she couldn't exactly move to the Camden's ranch until she had custody of J.J. She couldn't very well live in Nebraska and get him back and forth to Dallas every other week.

Austin might be her hawk, but she doubted he'd be willing to fly J.J. that far twice a month. Maybe she could try to get the custody hearing moved up. She could prove to Austin that she wanted to be with him, but what happened if the hearing didn't go her way? She'd only be speeding up losing her son. Bile singed her throat, but just then Austin returned to the chute while the crowd continued to shout his name.

The bull riders always got the crowds going. He swept her up in his arms, branded her mouth with one of those kisses that melted away her every hesitation, and made his announcement to every single cowboy in a hundred-mile radius that she was his.

Travis Anders, a prick she'd met back in Tulsa, was riding first. She knew he was lagging in second, way behind Austin's forty-point lead. He'd also hit on her repeatedly until she'd told him to fuck off. He wasn't man enough for her. Hell, he reminded her way too much of Brant—a brat that pitched a fit when he didn't get his way.

Leaning against Austin, they watched his ride. When the timer buzzed, he was barely hanging on and had shifted to the right, lowering his score to a seventy-eight. Austin seemed to settle in after Travis's ride. The next three riders were thrown before the timer and were out of the Cheyenne competition.

The minutes seemed to be timed with every frantic beat of her heart. She touched the macaw pendant and whispered another prayer to any god willing to listen as she watched his fine ass go up over the chute gate and his boots stomp down onto the bull. Jackson was already dressed, his face painted, and out in the field working. Cam handed Austin's ropes down.

Her heartbeats shot upward from her chest to her throat. Luke offered her a kind grin. "He'll be all right."

Brock nodded his agreement.

She gnawed her lip. *Ransom Paid* was a massive brown bull, already angry Austin was on his back. He shifted against the chute, ready to buck. She searched Austin's face for fear or even concern but came up empty. Determination chiseled every plane of his gorgeous features, and gall burned in his eyes. Realization settled on her. He was out to show Brant tonight, show him who she belonged to, show him that his little stunt with the horse that morning hadn't rattled his cage.

"Let's get this done." Austin's husky growl vibrated against her skull. His nod to the gate-man snared the air in her lungs and held it captive.

Instinctively, she reached and grabbed Cam's bicep when *Ransom Paid* lit out of the gate like someone had set his hide on fire. Cam grinned at her and wrapped his arm over her shoulders but never took his eyes off Austin. "He'll be fine, sugar. Ain't you seen the way he looks atcha? Not gonna let anything keep him from you."

Three seconds, four seconds, she gasped for breath, five seconds, six. Expertly, with unparalleled precision, he rode the hell out of that bull. Leaning in to his bucks and guiding himself with his free hand. He damn near made it look easy.

"Look at him go, folks! Incredible!" sang from the announcers.

Luke, Brock, Clif, and Scott went wild. Summer beamed. She couldn't stay still. Jumping up and down and screaming his name, she heard the timer sound, but he didn't let go. The roaring crowd all but lost their minds. Everyone single person in the stands was shouting *Camden*. At 9.3 he bailed off, landing on his feet. He raced away faster than he'd rode. Jackson leapt in front of the bull's horns without an ounce of hesitation and distracted the furious beast.

Bolting away from his team, she dodged the crowds and other riders and made the twenty-yard distance to where he was climbing out in a split second. He was panting for breath but didn't let it stop him from lifting her off the ground.

She wrapped her arms and legs around him, squeezing him for all she was worth. He spun her around and she let her eyes close, enjoying the ride. His euphoria in that moment was so potent it crushed even more of her doubt. They'd figure it out. Whatever it was, she just wanted to be with him.

"Ms. Sanchez certainly knows how to celebrate a ride like that," the announcer chuckled as Summer gripped the sides of Austin's face and half-mauled him with her impassioned kiss. "Looks like we have another reigning rodeo couple. They'll be telling their kids it all happened in Cheyenne, someday, folks. They're still going!"

Laughing at that, Summer finally lifted her head and beamed as Austin held her with one arm and waved to the crowds with the other. When he finally set her down, they walked hand in hand back to his team. Luke and Brock were all over him, and a minute later his scores were heralded to the crowds. "That'd be a 94.2 for Camden and the Minton Chaps team. That's an arena record. Give him another round of applause, ladies and gentlemen, not many men can ride like that."

Austin and Jackson performed some kind of high-five routine they must've come up with as kids before he was all over her again. When he finally settled down, he gave her his customary, devilish smirk. "Remember what I told you about me riding and then winning?"

She grinned. "Something about it making you want to go all night."

"Hell yeah, baby. You ready?"

Leaning in, she longed to palm the bulge she could feel pressing against her jeans. "I'm more than ready. I love it when the beast is hungry. Makes me so wet I burn for you. You just set an arena record, cowboy, seems like the beast deserves some kind of special reward."

His rumbled growl worked through the surrounding noise of the arena. "Be careful, honey. Once the beast is loose, I don't plan on reigning it in until you can't walk. I have several rewards in mind, and I plan on indulging in every single one, starting with those gorgeous tits and ending with that sweet little rosebud that tempts the hell outta me every time I smack your ass."

Her entire body seized in ardent desire. Oh, hell yeah, this was a man, a real man that could have anything he wanted from her until she passed out in the pure ecstasy of being in his arms.

"Now," she demanded in a breathy plea. He covered his groan with an edgy chuckle.

"Got a few things to do first. Namely, seeing my folks, accepting the big-ass check they're about to write me, and then getting little-man to bed."

"Okay, but I don't want to see Dallas Devil's ride. I can't watch anyone else get hurt."

Austin sighed. She watched him work his jaw.

"What? What happened?"

"I found out when I was out there with the other category leaders apparently Dallas Devil butted up against the chute and broke some kid named Trey Landon's shin bone and ankle this morning in the Slack events. He's out for the rest of the season."

"Why were they bull riding in the Slack events?"

"Not sure. Had some cowboys that aren't on the PBR circuit that wanted to compete. Decided to add it in last minute just for hoots and hollers, I guess. Brant managed to get Dallas Devil in, and his rider tonight was all about it, thinking he'd be tired. Brant musta licked somebody's balls for them to let the bull be ridden twice in one day."

"Of course he did. He's loving that his bull's gonna end up winning the title this year. His daddy's probably eating it up." The nausea returned. It'd serve Brant Jr. and Sr. right if they figured out he was doping that damned bull, but that wouldn't heal all the cowboys he'd already injured. Greg St. Cloud had just gotten thrown in a four-second ride, and Dallas Devil and his rider were up next. Summer couldn't stand it.

"Why don't we go get my stuff? He's about to ride. We'll stay in the locker room 'til it's over then go sit with Mom and Dad," Austin soothed.

She took off with Austin hot on her trail. A shocked gasp erupted from her lungs when she flew into the locker room. Austin's bag was overturned on the floor and his equipment was strewn everywhere. "What the hell?"

Sighing, Austin quickly lifted the overturned bag. "Town's full of people, sweetheart. Not all of them are gonna be nice. There wasn't really anything in there worth much. I had a feelin'. Half expected this. I gave Luke my wallet and phone back at the cabin. I told you my gut's never wrong."

"But..." She studied the area around her. There were a dozen other tack bags completely undisturbed lined along the walls and on the benches. "Why did they only go through yours?" *What if it was Brant?* The haunted question was one she longed to ask but didn't.

"Probably either got caught or got scared they were going to. Mine was on the bench closest to the doors, and let's be real, I've been winning all season. The fact that I probably have cash on me isn't far-fetched. It wasn't Brant, baby. He's been up there with Dallas Devil and his team the entire time we've been here. Get that thought right outta your head. It couldn't have been him. Besides, he's worth a hundred times what I am."

"No." She shook her head and then raced back into his arms. "His bank accounts are fatter than yours, but that doesn't mean anything at all. He's not even half the man you are, Austin."

Summer's own vow settled her a little. She had seen Brant standing at the chutes as soon as they entered the arena, and he hadn't left his post. All of his smarmy friends were with that devil beast of his daddy's, too. Security was pretty tight. You were supposed to have a pass to get down there. Maybe it was one of the other riders. It couldn't have been Brant.

Austin made quick work of picking up his gear. "They didn't take anything. It's all here. Ride has to be over by now, let's get."

Before Austin could escort Summer back up to the stands with his family, sirens filled the air.

"Oh, no." Summer gripped his hand. Setting his bag down and having no desire for her to see whatever had just happened, he turned and drew her into the sanctuary of his arms. Keeping her safe was all that would ever matter.

Brock and Luke appeared a moment later.

"Don't take her back out there," Luke mouthed silently.

Keeping Summer's face buried in his chest, Austin gave one single nod of understanding. To his chagrin, she lifted her head and glared at all three men. "I'm not a little kid. Tell me what happened."

"Uh, the bull from Preston Cattle threw his rider and then went after him. He...got trampled," Brock eased cautiously.

"I've never seen a bull act that way," Luke said. "There's crazy and then there's something else entirely. That was more than crazy."

"Yeah, well, if you give an animal steroids, they tend to react that way," Summer fumed.

"PBR is out there now talking to your ex."

"Good, but they're not gonna do anything. His daddy will buy his way out. He always does."

"Not sure his daddy's gonna be able to talk his way outta that." Luke tried to sound reassuring.

Determination formed on Summer's features, and Austin wondered just what was going on in that head of hers.

"If someone wanted to prove Brant was doping that bull, how would they?"

"No," Austin bellowed.

She rolled her eyes. "Answer the question. You went to vet school or something, right?"

"Uh, yeah," Luke eyed Austin cautiously. "Best way to tell if a bull's being drugged is to do blood work on the beast in question. Beyond that you'd need the prescriptions he has or the actual syringes and medication. For a bull that size you'd be looking for something with Trenbolone in it, and he'd have to be giving him quite a bit."

"Summer Malia Sanchez, you will not go near Brant or that bull ever, do you understand me?" Terror seized Austin's gut every time he thought about her being in striking distance of her ex.

Eventually, the qualifications were over. Austin had indeed come out on top. He mentally added the ten-thousand dollar bank to his mounting winnings. He'd spent very little. There wasn't anything he needed other than the woman on his arm and that little boy that needed a daddy worth having.

The poster-sized check he accepted with Scott and Clint was a little over the top in his book, but he put on the show, posing for pictures with Summer, J.J., the Minton team, and his chute team, all with the check.

"Tell us what you're gonna do with the prize, Mr. Camden?" One of the Frontier Day event organizers thrust a mic in front of his face.

"Uh..." Austin lifted his hat and ran his hands through his hair. He certainly had plans for the money, but he wasn't ready to share them just yet. "I'm not sure. Have to see just how much Ms. Sanchez will let me spoil her. 'Spect that'll buy a bunch of diapers, as well." He gestured to J.J.

"Well, if that ain't true love, I don't know what is. He's got it all ladies and gents, and that was one helluva ride. He's the man to beat this season. I feel certain we'll be seeing you in Vegas." The man shook Austin's hand. Summer shot him an incredulous look.

"What's that look for, darlin'?" He wrapped his arm back over her shoulders, drawing her closer as the crowds started to dissipate.

"You showing off for all the cowgirls, talking about buying diapers. They're all wishing they were lucky enough to be standing where I am." She leaned up and whispered a kiss on his jawline that he swore he could feel all the way in his groin.

"I only show off for you and occasionally for my mama, and I didn't say anything that wasn't true."

"You are not spending all of that money on me and J.J., cowboy."

He grunted his disdain. "Ordering me around might get you in a heap of trouble, doll baby. Don't get in over your head. You know when you get to arguing with me with that smart mouth, it drives me crazy. Might take you back to the locker room, have you up against the wall, and not give a damn who sees me."

"I'm ready and willing, stud, but your mama is standing right over there, and I just bet you won't drag me outta here with her standing nearby."

"Pretty sure I've more than shown you that nothing stands in my way when there's something I want. I'm already hurtin' for you, so don't tempt me." Austin tried to blink the lusty haze from his eyes when a fan wanted a photo with him.

"Minton's buying everyone a round of shots at the Buckin' A, and Austin and Summer can have the first dance. I think he probably deserves that," Scott goaded the crowds. They broke out in another round of applause, and Austin sighed. Dancing at the Buckin' A hadn't been in his evening plans. Glancing at Summer, he chuckled. The disappointment was evident in her eyes.

"You're cute when you're pouty, but you keep frowning like that people are gonna think you don't want to dance with me," he whispered in her ear.

She spun in his arms and stared him down. Her tongue slowly licked over her full bottom lip before she let her teeth make the same gentle path. His cock twitched, and his breaths picked up pace. Her eyes were full of darkened fire, anxious and craving. He swore the whiskey heat beneath those long lashes branded his body with pure yearning.

"I don't ever mind dancin' with you, cowboy. I'd just prefer to be doing it naked in your lap, or maybe dancin' naked on your face. Hard to do that at the Buckin' A."

Austin eliminated the space between them, pressing her body to his. He cupped her ass and gave a discreet thrust against that sweet heat he could feel from the crotch of her jeans. "You feel what you're doing to me?" His low growl elicited a broken gasp of breath from her as she nodded. "You're gonna take care of it for me over and over again tonight, so let's go dance and tell my family good night, because as soon as I get you back to the cabin and we get J.J. in his crib, I'm not letting you out of my arms 'til morning. I want to hear you scream for me tonight, honey. I'll let you ride on my face, mark me with your scent, and then I'll let you ride on my crotch, get me nice and slick with those creamy juices that drive me wild, but that'll just be the beginning."

As the night wore on, he spun Summer around the dance floor, keeping their dancing entirely PG since half the saloon was full of families that night, all keeping an eye on him. It seemed he'd just become their hero, or that's what they kept telling him anyway.

"Being such a gentleman tonight. I miss my beast," she purred in his ear as the lights lowered just a little more. He pulled her closer.

"It's taking everything I've got in me to keep from throwing you over my shoulder, flipping off every cowboy in here that stupidly thinks I don't see them admirin' you, and making sure you know who you belong to."

Her pouty little smirk only served to further tighten his groin. He already felt like he was being strangled.

"Bet we could show them all where my loyalties lie, cowboy. Slip your hands down to my ass." Too far gone not to be entranced by her directives, he followed her orders. Cupping the perfect curves in his hands, he began to massage as she proceeded to grind against him. He'd been at half-mast for the last two hours. To say he was craving and tired of being patient would have been a severe understatement. "Kiss me."

He took her mouth and her breath, stealing them all for himself in a kiss that ignited the very air enveloping them. He fed her his tongue softly and thoroughly, mapping her mouth with his own. Keeping his left hand working her ass, he brought his right hand up and let his fingertips gently trace over her cheek, down the delicate column of her neck, and to that vulnerable hollow just above her collarbone.

His thumb teased the tender skin. His mark was branded there, just under the collar of the Camden T-shirt she was wearing. They both knew if he moved it slightly to the side the whole bar would see his brand. She shifted against him, lost in his touch, in his kiss, in him. He continued to tempt her with his thumb, exposing mere millimeters of the marked skin to brief seconds of air and then moving back to keep the secret hidden from view.

Her breaths eluded her. She gripped his neck tighter as he turned his head and extended the kiss. The wolf-whistles and applause ripped them forcefully from the evocative world where they so longed to go.

"Let's get out of here, sugar. I'm outta patience."

She lifted her head from his shoulder and nodded her agreement. Laughter and a few more whistles rang out when they headed toward Holly, sitting at a table holding a very sleepy baby J.J. Summer lifted him into her arms. He hugged her fiercely and then nuzzled his head into her shoulder and began to suck his thumb.

Feeling bad they'd had him out so late, Austin waved to the crowds, thanked his sister for playing babysitter, and dragged Summer out to the truck. He'd called the Cheyenne Medical Center to check on the trampled rider a few hours before. He was casted head to toe but was expected to make a full recovery. Austin's overturned bag in the locker room was all but forgotten as he navigated their way back to the ranch cabin. Finally, mercifully, they were alone.

CHAPTER SIXTEEN

Summer quickly changed J.J. into his pajamas and settled with him in the chair. Austin handed her a warmed bottle of milk. "Can you just make sure it isn't too hot? He's really too old for this, but I love snuggling with him at night, and the warm milk makes him sleepy."

Contemplating for a moment, he shrugged, held the bottle in front of his own mouth, and squirted a little milk inside.

Summer covered her mouth to keep from laughing at him outright.

"What? It's not too hot. It's good." Austin handed her the bottle.

"You can just test it on your arm," she snickered.

The little guy had inhaled a huge supper with Austin's parents before the Cinch Shoot-out, so he only downed about half of the bottle before he was sound asleep and the nipple slipped from his lips.

While Summer was getting him in the crib, Austin decided to be a gentlemen and at least shower off before he did some decidedly ungentlemanly things to his girl in the bed.

He turned the water on hot, shed his clothes, and stepped in. The water stripped away the dirt from his skin and the tension knotted in his muscles. He ran his hands over his face and tried to get his head straight. He wanted her, needed a fix, was desperate for her hands on his fevered skin, and for that sexy little snatch of hers to wrap him up so tightly he walked a tightwire of sanity before he lost it all. But if he didn't get it together, he was gonna blow long before he was ready.

She made him potent, brought him back faster than anyone ever had, but there were so many things he longed to do to her that night. They'd been playing out in great detail in his mind all damn day. She was too much.

His cock throbbed against his abs, and he considered. As soon as he saw her laying in his bed swollen, wet, and begging, he'd be rock-hard again. There was no doubt. He could make it last for hours as soon as he'd blown off a little steam. Before he could wrap his hand around himself, he felt her naked breasts press against his back and watched her hands, slick from the water, slide upwards from his thighs and over his painfully hardened ridge.

The satin-covered steel of his cock made Summer ache. There were so many things she wanted from him that evening, and the shower was the perfect place to start. A low craving growl echoed from Austin's lungs. "Need a shower, darlin'?" He throbbed against her hand.

Delighted with his reaction, Summer wound both hands around his cock and indulged herself in the feel of his thickness and rigidity as she milked him.

"Dammit, woman, I'm not gonna last this first time. I've been thinking about you all fuckin' day, how good you feel, how bad I need you. I swear I'm right there," he grunted.

Her entire body throbbed with need. She slid her nipples up and down his back, making him shudder against her. "Good." She pumped him harder. "I want it all over me."

Before she quite knew what he was doing, he spun, turned her, grabbed her hands, and plastered them to the tile shower wall. "You wanna be marked, darlin'? Say it. Tell me where."

"Yes, God, yes. I told you the beast deserves a prize. Your choice, cowboy." Giving him control tapped into a well of longing she'd never known was housed deep within her soul. She'd never been with anyone she trusted like the man currently pressing her to a shower wall. It was intoxicating.

She'd never felt more alive than when she was in his arms, and never more content than when she answered his body's demands with her own. Every single thing that had ever gone wrong in her life dissolved in the blazing heat of his intense gaze and his possessive arms.

"I ain't in the mood to be gentle, Summer, so if you want me to stop or to slow it down, I need you to fucking speak up now."

"You know exactly what I want, and it ain't your gentlemanly side. Now fuck me...hard."

"Keep your hands up." His fierce command made her moan. Her body rolled against his, desperate to feel the electricity that sparked between them. He dragged his cock up and down between her ass-cheeks, making her squirm as a rushed heat of wetness coated her pussy. "I don't have any lube in here with me, sugar, but very, very soon I'm gonna have that sweet little puckered rosebud around my cock."

"Yes," hissed from her lips. "Take me, please." Nothing else mattered nothing but being owned, being filled to capacity with him. "So hard I feel it in the morning, so hard I know I'm yours every time I move."

"You okay with me not wearing a condom? I swear I'm clean. I've never done this with anyone else. This is for you, for us. I'm gonna pull out and come all over you. I swear, baby. I'd never do you wrong. You know that."

She considered, but she wanted to be owned by him completely, something he'd never shared with another woman. She wasn't ready to have another baby, but if she ever did want more children, she knew beyond a shadow of a doubt she wanted to have them with Austin. He wouldn't come inside her. She knew he'd keep his word. Her doubts sluiced away from her body with the pouring shower water and fled down the drain. "Yes, I want it all. I want it all with you."

On his next low groan, he pulled her back over his cock, feeding himself into her pussy in one quick motion. She gasped from his sheer size and the lack of foreplay.

"I said I wasn't in the mood to be gentle. I wasn't lying." He pounded into her. She rocked with him, her entire body quaking and desperate for a release. Tensing her pelvic muscles around him, she reveled in his impatient moans.

"Damn, that feels good. Keep doing that," he ordered.

Austin took her faster, helpless to resist. God, nothing had ever felt so good. The silky ripples of her pussy tugged in perfect rhythm. She fit him like she was made for him alone. His blood spiked with the creamy scent of her musk, ripe and potent, as it permeated the steamy air he forced into his lungs.

He'd never felt her so tight, so warm against him. He throbbed fiercely, watching her body consume his. Hell-bent on spraying his cum all over her sexy ass and up her back, he'd had no idea how fucking fantastic it was going to feel without the Trojan. Suddenly, she was coming. Her body milked at his with frantic spasms. He wasn't going to last. It felt too damn good. Jerking out of her, he unloaded all over her lower back, and watched his seed drip down the perfect hills of her ass. Running his fingers through the semen, he brought them to her mouth. "Suck them for me, sugar. I wanna taste myself inside your mouth."

She lapped up his offering, aftershocks of her orgasm still rocketing through her. He spun her around and devoured her mouth, holding her steady in his arms, letting her body enjoy the release he provided. Dipping his tongue deep, he feasted on the mix of his seed and her saliva. Perfection, and he would never get enough. One lifetime that she hadn't even agreed to yet wasn't going to cut it. She'd let him take her without protection. That was something. It was the first time in his life that he had no concerns. If he got her pregnant, so be it. He wanted that with her and no one else.

"I'm far from finished," he admitted as he washed the remnants of semen from her back.

"Good. 'Cause I'm ready for more." She let him finish cleaning her up and climbed out of the shower. He shut down the water and wrapped her up in a towel, drying her thoroughly before he haphazardly ran the towel over himself.

Letting the thin towel hang loosely off of her body, Summer backed toward the bed while Austin advanced on her. Her favorite expression burned in his eyes, scorching her skin. The one that said he was going to fuck her senseless.

His every move was laced with keen intention. Carnal hunger pulsed in the air between them. The raw masculine scent of him, leather and rosin spiked with sex, ripened the air. He didn't speak. He didn't need to. The white-hot fire in his eyes said it all—the beast had shattered its chains. His spectacular win, the hours they'd been stalled from this, and their shower must've been more than the cage of his soul could contain.

Summer's nipples throbbed anxiously against the threadbare terry cloth. Her mouth watered, so hungry for whatever he might provide. Her body longed to fly with his. His cock thickened and grew as she watched. She longed to run her hands over him again. The feeling of his rock-hard strain made her weak with desire.

Austin reached, took hold of the corner of the towel, and stripped it from her grasp. "I want to see your beautiful body, every square inch. It's all mine."

A moan spilled from her mouth. Her eyes goggled as he proceeded to tear the towel in two vertical strips with ease. "What are you...?"

"I'll buy them another one. You mean what you said about not wanting plain, vanilla sex?"

Understanding sent another wave of euphoric excitement spiraling through her body. "Yes. Damn you, yes, Austin. I told you this. I want whatever you're about to do. I want it. I want you, all of you."

A low rumbled moan thundered from his tensed chest. "Good. I knew you were the perfect woman for me. Look at me, Summer."

Swallowing down a slight case of sudden nerves, she stared him down.

"Does all of that wanting me mean you trust me?"

"Yes." She never hesitated. The answer came from her soul, her heart, most certainly not her head. Her head was opposed to her trusting anyone ever again, the very reason she couldn't seem to admit that she'd already fallen in love with him. She'd been hurt far too many times. But she had no time for those thoughts currently. Her heart and her almost painfully swollen, fevered pussy were running the show. She rubbed her legs together, trying to bring herself some relief to no avail. She needed him. He was now a requirement.

"Completely?"

"Yes," she nodded frantically.

"Good. Lay down on the bed, honey. Don't make me tell you twice."

Trying to still the slight shiver of her body, she glanced down at her chest to make certain the frenzied race of her heart wasn't actually evident to his eyes.

Reclining on the bed, she watched him work. His fingertips slid from her right elbow out to her wrist. He brushed a tender kiss there in the hollow against her racing pulse, inhaling deeply of the cheap drugstore perfume she'd sprayed on before they'd left for the rodeo. She'd been wearing it for years. It had become a part of her natural scent.

Another kiss, a gentle spin of his tongue made her squirm before he gently wrapped her wrist in the towel and secured it to the headboard. Any cowboy worth his salt could work a lariat with ease. His skill with a shredded towel was rather impressive; not that she was surprised.

"That feel okay? Not too tight?"

"It's fine," she managed in a breathless pant. If she'd needed to, she could've pulled her own wrist free. He'd left plenty of slack. Her beast had the biggest heart this side of the Mississippi. Her body rolled impatiently as he secured her left arm.

"I need to do your legs, too, darlin', or can you be still for me?" His smirk spoke volumes directly to her overly-heated core, desperate for relief. She ordered herself to still and to enjoy the way he stared at her like she was some kind of delectable buffet prepared all for him. "So fucking gorgeous, all spread out there for me. My God, you are perfection. Relax for me, baby. Let it feel good for me, because I'm about to thoroughly enjoy you."

"Yes! Now, Austin, please." She fought not to squirm, but she was beginning to wonder if the man was a sadist.

The mattress lowered under his weight, only making her more

anxious. "Damn, I like you greedy for me. Beggin' and achin' all for me. Hurts doesn't it? You need it so bad it hurts." With the callused tip of his index finger he traced a looped path over the swollen rise of her mound. The ragged nerve-endings there quivered under his touch. Heated drips of her need worked their way between her thighs. A thundered groan sounded in her ear. "I barely have to touch you to make you drip for me, sugar. You're so hungry for me, so damn perfect."

Her chest rose and fell in quick pants. Heat scorched through her veins. "More, please."

"Oh, I'm gonna give you more. Don't you worry. I have so many plans for you tonight."

"Well, get on with them, cowboy. I'm about to lose my mind."

A sinful chuckle was his only audible response.

She thought she was about to lose *her* mind? She had no idea the kind of torture he was enduring, looking at her laid out, tied to his bed, dripping wet, her body a landscape of feminine perfection all for him, and making himself draw this out. Austin's mind scrambled with the onslaught of things he longed to do to her, what he wanted to make her feel, how perfect they were together, and how much he loved her.

The temptation to keep her tied there until she flat out agreed to move back to Pleasant Glen with him crossed his mind, but trying to keep Summer Sanchez tied down any longer than she wanted to lay there would work about as well as trying to baptize a cat. Plus, she'd be twice as hissy and scratchy, and damn if that didn't make him even more horny.

He began his feast with her kiss-swollen lips, flushed ripe and raw. He leveled her body with his own, letting his cock tempt her pussy as he sucked her tongue into his mouth and nipped her bottom lip when she pulled it away, gasping for breath. He continued his drugging kisses, ravaging her mouth, weakening her resolve.

"All mine, honey, and I'm about to take everything I want."

"Yes." Another decadent roll of her body against his made him groan. He nuzzled his face between her breasts, so plump and full he left whisker burns between them in his thorough care. She damn sure would feel something in the morning. He'd make certain her entire body was aware that she'd been owned in entirety. She'd feel his presence, his possession, his greed with every step she took, every time those cute little panties she wore rubbed in just the right places, and every time her diamond-hard nipples throbbed out their remembrance of his pleasure.

He drew her right nipple into the heated hunger of his mouth, sucking and licking, tonguing the stiff peaks until they were raw and she was begging him in broken syllables of pleasure. He nipped her captive nipple before sucking away the pain. Chill bumps skittered across her chest following the fiery trails his lips blazed from one nipple to the other. Moving down her body, leaving bites and nips along her abdomen, he settled between her legs and looped them over his shoulders.

"Keep 'em spread nice and wide for me, honey, I'm gonna be here a good long while." He trailed his tongue up the right lip of her pussy and down the left, making her vibrate in anticipation. Opening his mouth over her, he let her feel his teeth against the slick, wet silk coating her. A desperate cry spilled from her lungs and she thrust upward in his face, urging him onward. His lifted his head, staring her down. "Be still, Summer."

A whimpered groan shook through her body, but she complied. He buried his face between her lips, pressing his tongue in her opening and bathing her until he was thoroughly marked with the heated scent of her sex, ripe and potent. Lifting her hips with his hands, he dropped lower than she'd expected. Her shocked gasp elicited a chuckle from him, but he continued.

"Oh my God. That feels so good," she panted.

"I know it does, honey. It's all mine. I'm gonna make everything feel good." He circled her puckered opening with his tongue, and her entire body tensed. A muted scream from her open mouth came out as a breathy mewl of longing. The bed shook with the primal urgency of her pulling at the restraints. Unable to draw it out any longer, he worked his way back up to her clit and wrapped his mouth over her throbbing pearl, fully distended, so needy for him. He lapped up the juices pouring from her, tenderly dragging his teeth against her drenched tissues, and then began to suck that perfect little bud, blooming in his mouth with frantic pulses against his tongue.

"Come in my mouth, sweetheart. I want to drink you." He suctioned his mouth to her clit, keeping the pressure ever-building. She spiraled over with a harsh cry of his name. Her body bowed taut before the aftershocks dissolved her into a quivering mass of beautiful curves and perfection. Complete and utter perfection.

He lifted his head, making certain she watched his every move as he licked her honey from his lips. She shook with another wave of carnal desire. "So damn good. Sweet and spicy, just like my girl." Giving her hips and legs a break, he settled them back on the mattress, moved to her side, and forged his way up her body with his hands and his lips. Up on his knees, he straddled himself just below her tits. Her eyes goggled, that fire he loved still a roaring blaze in their whiskey depths. Pressing his hips forward he brought his throbbing cock to her mouth. "Get it nice and wet for me, darlin'." Since she had no access to her hands, he grasped himself and dipped the head of his cock between her welcoming lips carefully. "That's it. Can you take a little more?"

"God, yes."

His low, guttural moan echoed around them as she turned her head to the side and traced up the throbbing veins of his cock with her tongue. "Suck me," he commanded, dipping himself in her mouth again, following the rhythm she set.

Grabbing the bottle of lube he'd left on the TV tray serving as a bedside table, he drew his cock out of her mouth and covered her tits with the lube.

"I've never done this before," she confessed.

"Oh yeah? Watch my cock slip and slide between your gorgeous tits, honey."

Summer doubted this would really do much for her, but once again she was shocked. She loved that she could give him this. He ran his hands over her lubed breasts, cupping and pulling, massaging and readying her more. It felt incredible. Yet another hungry moan poured from her lungs when he pinched her nipples with a great deal of restraint, given the strength of those hands. As she arched her back in invitation, he rubbed his palms over her nipples, making them throb. He massaged with more vigor.

Finally, he drew her breasts together, and she watched his cock glide between them. His head fell back as he picked up pace, moaning in reverence.

"My God, so fucking good," he grunted. His eyes glazed with lust. His muscles tensed and flexed, and his groans filled the air. Rivulets of sweat formed on his neck. She wished she could lick them away, taste his salt and his musk. His gorgeous body moved back and forth over her. She longed to run her hands over his chiseled abs, straining and pulling as he simultaneously felt her up and fucked her tits. He held them tightly together as he worked.

Leaning her head down, she brandished the head of his massive cock with a drowning kiss when he neared her mouth. His growl reverberated through her veins. "Damn, baby, that feels so good."

Giving this to him, letting him take what he wanted, was the most fulfilling and erotic thing she'd ever done. Love and lust fought for dominance in her brain. She had no idea how he made this feel so good, but he did.

She'd driven her own life right into hell. Letting him drive for a while was freeing, not restraining. Why was she being so stubborn with him anyway? This man knew things about her she'd never known. Why couldn't she just go with it?

"Austin this is...so...amazing," came out in panted breaths. "Thank you." Her thankfulness seemed rather stupid since his cock was currently still sluicing between her breasts. *Just shut up and enjoy this Summer. You can tell him you loved it and him later.*

He smirked and released her breasts. In one split second, he had a condom on, bracketed himself between her hips, and thrust hard, parting her in one quick move that made her weak. "Believe me, sweetness, the pleasure was all mine. Now, just lay there and take it for me. My God, you feel so damn good." He grunted as he pulled away and pistoned back, faster and faster with each pass. Her body shook. His heated musk marked her skin and filled her lungs. His body formed a protective sanctuary over hers. She succumbed to him completely.

"Look at me, baby." His voice strained out the demand. Letting her eyes flutter open, she stared into the onyx depths of his. Love. It was right there, glowing in the ignited fire. Verbalizing the very look in his eyes, he thrust again. "I love you, Summer," he grunted. "So damn much." Lowering his head, he kissed her, letting his tongue take on the rhythm he'd set with his thrusts.

A moment later he sat back and lifted her hips, holding her legs up in a V. She shook as his lube-covered hand slipped up her overly-sensitized inner thigh and rubbed over her clit as he took her with more force.

"God, I love to watch my cock pound into you, honey. Love to watch your cream cover me, and your face when I take you like this."

The gruff strain of his vow sliced her resolve into ribbons, freeing her. The orgasm bolted out of her core in a mass of heat that pulsed through her veins. The binds at her hands somehow loosed the ones restraining her soul. She was his. The beast inside him gave a thundered, guttural growl when her pussy milked him in quickening pulses that drained him completely. He collapsed against her. "I love you. Please say it back for me, honey. That was incredible." And the beast returned willingly to its leash, because she held the restraint. She owned the beast. The heady power of love quaked within her as the orgasm finally freed her of its staggering waves.

"I love you, too."

He buried his fact in her neck, nuzzling her gently as he used his hands to release the towel-restraints. Tossing them away, he drew her up on his chest as they both chased their breath.

"That was incredible, Austin. I've just...never been in love before. This still scares me."

"I know. I've never been in love before either, honey. But I told you, scared doesn't work for me. So, it's been fast. Who gives a shit as long as it's right?"

"Yeah, you're right, I guess."

"I may need you to write that down for me so I have proof you told me I was right about something." He kissed away a hint of glistening sweat dewed at her hairline.

"Shut up, cowboy. I just told you I love you. Now, let me go check on my son, since the beast gets mighty loud when he shoots off."

"I'll check on him. You lay there and look thoroughly fucked. Damn prettiest thing I've ever seen when I get you hot and sweaty for me."

When he returned, they decided another shower was in order since she was covered in sweat, lube, and his cum. Summer was exhausted by the time they returned to the bed. Her legs were barely able to hold her up, something Austin seemed highly pleased with.

He settled her on his chest once again. "I have a request."

"Beyond me letting you tie me up, fuck my tits, and basically having your way with me?"

"Yes," he laughed.

"What else does the beast want?"

"Beast is sated and sleeping, doll baby. Damn near whipped after all that. It was incredible."

"And when does the beast make his return?" A sleepy giggle slipped from her lips. She could barely hold her eyes open.

"As soon as I wake up with you in my arms, generally. Can I make my request now?"

"Do it quick. I'm about to fall asleep."

"Go out with me tomorrow night."

"Um, I'm pretty sure we've moved beyond the dating stage of this lightning round of our relationship."

His chuckle said he loved that idea. "Yeah, I know, but let my folks keep J.J. tomorrow night and let me really take you out on a date. I may not be any good at it. Haven't done it since I was a teenager, but you keep saying Cheyenne makes you feel young again. Figure I ought to indulge myself in all of that."

"That sounds so fun, but are you sure your parents won't mind keeping him?"

"Already cleared it with them. They're all thrilled. Brock, Luke, Hope, everyone volunteered to help out. He'll be the best watched toddler on the planet. We'll spend all day playing with him tomorrow and then head out around sundown, that sound good?"

"I don't want him to spend the night with them, though. Is it okay if we pick him up when our date's over?"

Disappointment clouded the exhaustion in his eyes. "Yeah, it's fine," he lied.

She started to change her mind. J.J. would be perfectly safe and happy with the Camdens. He seemed to adore them. Picking J.J. up after their date clearly hadn't been Austin's plan, but she couldn't bear to spend one more night away from her son than she was forced to by that stupid custody agreement.

CHAPTER SEVENTEEN

Summer laughed as she watched J.J. use Austin as his own personal playground. Austin was extended flat on the floor of the sitting room. For the last hour, J.J. had been crawling over him and slobbering kisses all over his face then seating himself on his chest to applaud his own actions. Austin seemed to be having almost as much fun as her little boy.

Austin was so excited about the date he'd planned for that night, Summer decided to explain why she couldn't move with him to the ranch after Cheyenne the next day. It felt cruel letting him go on for the next week thinking she was going to go home with him when she couldn't, but she didn't want to ruin their night. The words she would have to say tumbled around in her head constantly. She would promise to move to Pleasant Glen, Nebraska as soon as the custody hearing was over. There was no other way. She'd have to return to Dallas at the end of Cheyenne, as sick as that thought made her. She had no choice. Secretly, she prayed that Austin would volunteer to move with her temporarily, but the selfishness of that idea overwhelmed her with guilt. That would mean his family would have to continue running his portion of the ranch when they'd been counting on his help after Cheyenne.

They could do the long distance thing for a while, she told herself. He'd made a ton of money lately, and she knew he'd fly out there often for her...for them. Maybe she could fly up to Nebraska when it was her turn with J.J. occasionally.

It was only until September. The incoming loss was already taking vicious blows at her psyche. Watching Austin with J.J. made her deliriously happy and profoundly sad at the same time. She didn't want J.J. to have to do without him, either.

J.J. crawled up over Austin's face and Austin lifted his T-shirt to blow raspberries on his round belly, making him laugh hysterically. Summer squeezed her eyes shut, memorizing that sound and the image before her.

Austin grabbed his cowboy hat and brushed a kiss across Summer's cheek at the same moment. "Be back in a few." He settled the hat on his head.

"To pick me up for our date?" she laughed.

"Yes, ma'am, so be ready. I've got to get a few things prepared."

"What are you up to, cowboy?" The mischievous suspicion in her eyes made every bit of this worth it.

"Don't you wish you knew, sunshine?"

"Yes, so tell me."

"Not a chance in hell. Be good. I'll be back." Grinning over his plans, Austin slid into his truck and headed out onto the main drag through town. If they were going to pretend to be teenagers again, he had to do this right. Getting on 25, he made it to the liquor store in under ten minutes. Searching for what he needed, he tried to recall the last time he'd actually purchased any alcoholic beverage this cheap.

Chuckling to himself, he hoisted two six-packs of Pabst Blue Ribbon and a bottle of Boone's Farm strawberry wine onto the counter. Damn, it had been years since he'd had either. Probably tasted like shit, but he couldn't recall the flavor of either. He recalled kissing Miranda Harper while they split a half bottle of Boone's between them, sitting on the tailgate of Luke's old F-150 parked out at the reservoir. Neither the girl nor the wine had made much of an impression. Even as a teenager, he knew he wanted someone full of heat and sass, someone exactly like Summer. Luke had been busy in the cab with Miranda's older sister, Indie. She'd been Luke's *main mount* all through high school. Everyone thought they'd end up together. Austin shook his head at the memories.

Cashier, with as much gruff in his voice as gray in his beard, climbed off the stool where he was seated, eyeing Austin and his purchases. "Usually have to card everyone who buys this shit. You look a little old for Boone's Farm. You ain't buying this for kids, are ya?"

"No sir, I promise. Just doing a little reminiscing with my girl."

"She old enough to drink, son?"

Scowling at that insinuation, Austin huffed. "Plenty old enough. Do I look like a pervert to you?"

"Well, you show up with this sweetened paint thinner, and she might not be your girl too much longer."

"I'll take my chances."

Old man shrugged and rang up the order.

"Can I get a Styrofoam cooler and a bag of ice as well?"

An hour later, he listened to Summer list out a thousand contingencies for every conceivable possibility for J.J. to his parents.

"And there's infant Tylenol in the diaper bag. Here, I'll set it on the counter."

Austin halted her progress. "Babe, Earth will not end tonight. Baby boy will be fine. They have put kids to bed before. Almost all of us are completely normal. And Holly's smart, she's just weird, probably from that time I dropped her on her head."

"Hilarious." Holly rolled her eyes. "We're gonna have fun tonight, aren't we J.J.?" She held him up over her face, swaying him back and forth until he laughed and then promptly drooled in her eye.

"Yeah, he's cutting teeth." Summer cringed.

"He'll be fine, honey. You go have a good time." Austin's mother mopped up Holly's face with a cloth diaper and rescued her from J.J. "I promise we will call if we have any questions."

"I'm sorry. It's just…"

"You're being a great mom." His mother squeezed her arm reassuringly. "Go on. I promise you have nothing to worry about."

Summer kissed J.J.'s face a dozen times and finally let Austin lead her out to the truck. She settled in as they made their way toward town. "So, where are we going on this date?"

"We're going back to our roots, sugar. Gonna start with something to eat. Since we're going old school, I figured we'd get hot dogs at the A&W. Then we're going to the midway. You have to ride The Zipper. Then, I thought if I played all my cards right, you might let me take you parking see if we can't steam the windows up a little."

Laughing at him, she beamed. "Did you get Luke to buy us some Boone's Farm, too?"

"Nah, I don't need him to buy it for me anymore, but it's in the cooler in the back."

"Are you serious?" She spun in her seat and lifted the lid of the cooler situated beside J.J.'s car seat. "Oh my gosh, you are serious. I can't believe you did all of this."

"Told you I haven't done this since I would've thought this was a great date. I'm rusty, but I want you to let all the shit with Brant and life go for a little while tonight. Just hang out with me. Let's have some fun."

Heat bloomed in her cheeks, and her beautiful smile expanded further. "This is perfect. You're amazing, but you might not have liked me so much when I was sixteen. I didn't let anybody get too far back then."

Chuckling at that, he tried to envision a younger version of Summer Sanchez, without a daddy screwing her life up and without an ex hell-bent on destroying her. Happy, loved, and free, just the way she was meant to exist. "Oh yeah? I'll bet you were one hell of a cock-tease though."

"Ha!" She dissolved in a fit of laughter that said he was right.

"I knew it. Rubbing up on some poor dude, grinding in his lap, kissing with tongue, letting him play with those titties, thinking he's getting somewhere, making him ache, then leaving him high and dry." He feigned insult. "How many guys still nursing the case of blue balls you left them with?"

"You sound like it might've happened to you a time or two there, cowboy." She stuck her tongue between her teeth, still giggling.

"God, more than a few times. Came in my jeans more times than I care to admit."

"Aww, you want me to see if I can recreate that for you tonight?"

He arched his left eyebrow. That sassy mouth of hers was going to be his undoing one day. "Hell no, honey. I'm getting lucky tonight. I mean, I went all out; hot dogs, shit wine, PBR, getting you sick on a roller coaster. Hell, I'll even win you a pink teddy bear at the carnival. What more do you want?"

She doubled over laughing. He beamed. If he got to listen to her do that for the rest of his life and he got to be the guy holding her in his arms every night while she fell asleep, he'd die a happy man.

"Wow, a teddy bear. That might get you all the way to third base, cowboy."

"Damn straight, it will. I'll use my rugged good looks, my smooth moves, and my '*I'm a professional bull rider, darlin'*' line to get me the rest of the way."

"Oh, is that what you think?"

"S'pose if that doesn't work I could always tie you up in my bed again." He waggled his eyebrows.

"You know, I think it'd do you good *not* to get your way, occasionally."

"I like gettin' my way."

"Don't I know it."

"Plus, I'm damned good at it." He winked at her.

Her dramatic eye roll made him laugh. "You're also full of shit."

"I really wish people would stop telling me that. It's gettin' insulting." He parked near the A&W and leapt out of the truck. Opening her door for her, he offered her his hand as she climbed down.

"Being a gentleman doesn't always get you in a girl's panties, you know."

"Oh, I know. Tried that gig a dozen times. But you're worth it, even if I don't get lucky tonight. How's that, Miss Sanchez?"

"Don't I feel special."

"You should, 'cause I put a lot of thought into this. I should at least get a hand job or something."

Shaking her head at him, she let him guide her inside the burger joint.

After they'd ordered, he picked up the tray of their food and brought it to the table she'd selected outside in the glow of the full moon and the neon lights of Cheyenne. When he slid onto the metal bench seat beside her, she plucked one of his chili cheese fries from the paper dish and popped it in her mouth.

He huffed, "Only girls that put out get to eat my fries."

She cracked up again. This date was already perfect by his estimations. Staring at him in challenge, her beautiful grin lighting the flecks of gold in her eyes, she lifted another fry, slathered in liquid cheese, and brought it to her lips. "The things I'll do for chili-cheese fries."

He let a low rumbled growl sound in her ear as he leaned over and brushed a kiss on her cheek, then took a nibble of her ear lobe, making her shiver.

While she slurped up the last of her half-vanilla half-chocolate milkshake, he threw away the trash from their hot dogs and fries. "You ready, sugar?" He offered her his arm and a sly grin.

Standing, she looped her arm through his. "You know, a week ago, give or take, you took me out to that steakhouse in Cody, smiled at me like that, and all I could think was, oh shit, I'll never make it out of this alive."

Chuckling at that allowance, he draped his arm over her shoulders, pulling her closer as they headed toward the midway. "Oh yeah? Well, I wrapped my arms over you to keep you from committing murder in the first with witnesses, and all I could think was that I'd finally caught the thing I'd been searching for half my life. I swear, Summer, I knew then and there I'd never want anything else."

"Really? You really knew right then?" She nuzzled her head against his shoulder and the hazy summer night settled in peacefully around them.

"I knew right then." Home, to Austin, had always been the squeaky hinge on the rusty Camden Ranch sign at the south entrance to the ranch, the slap of the screen door in the spring on his mama and daddy's house, the expanse of grassland dotted with grazing cattle in the noonday heat, and the stacked lightning in the clouds of the summer storms that swept through Lincoln county while the sun set beyond the fields.

At that moment, he understood *home* would forever be wherever she was. All he needed was her in his arms. He'd be her home as well. He'd construct a protective harbor for her with the might of his body. He'd keep her safe. He'd make her his, the sooner the better.

"Hey, you never told me exactly what made you go after Brant that particular night. Was he just being his usual douchey self, or was there something in particular that got my girl so ornery that night?"

Her cheeks flushed a thousand shades of pink evident in a sunset, and she rolled her eyes. Damn, but she was beautiful.

"It just got to me that night. He was out partying with the buckle bunnies, and it was his week with J.J. He never spends any time with him. He just gets him and shoves him off on his mama, the wicked witch of the west. I'd been stewing on it for weeks, plus I was exhausted, and I just wanted my little boy. I overheard his mama on the phone telling whoever she was talking to that she was gonna prove that I was an unfit mother as soon as I ran out of money. Tell the courts how I didn't even have a home, but I don't have a home because of them. I had to let my crappy apartment go because I had to be on the road with Brant because of the custody agreement she got the judge to agree to." She shrugged. Austin hated that her smile had faded and that look of desperate terror had returned to her eyes.

Stopping outside the entrance to the midway, he turned her and cradled her to his chest. When her hands fisted his T-shirt, he swayed her gently in the setting sunlight. "Listen to me, I've racked up close to two-million dollars this season, and I haven't finished Cheyenne or ridden Vegas yet. That's on top of the money I'll make when my cattle's ready to sell. You ain't gonna run out of money on my watch. When we get back to Pleasant Glen, I want us to both talk to your lawyers and see what we can do to get J.J. with us permanently. I know his daddy has a right to see him, but it ain't gonna be this every-other-week shit you've got going on now. But tonight, for me, try to let it go, okay? J.J. is perfectly safe. He's with us and we have him until the end of Cheyenne. Let's enjoy that and worry about tomorrow, *tomorrow*."

"That sounds really good." She squeezed him tighter, and he kissed the top of her head.

"I'll always take care of you both, baby. You're mine. I told you, I take good care of what belongs to me."

Austin made quick work of purchasing them bracelets that allowed them to ride whatever they wanted. He secured Summer's around her wrist and guided her toward the long line already formed at The Zipper.

After Austin's vows, Summer's smile returned to her. She'd been beaming most of the evening. Contentment was a heady sensation to a girl who'd never experienced it before. The colorful lights of the midway danced on the trampled grass underfoot. The air was thick that evening with the scent of corn dogs, funnel cakes, and cotton candy. Country music from a cover band on an outdoor stage at one end of the midway intermixed with the ringing bells and buzzers from the carnival games and enveloped them in the nostalgia of Cheyenne.

She tucked herself tighter against Austin, making him grin as he strengthened his hold of her. He winked at her, making her heart beat disjointedly for a moment. She wondered if his reassuring wink coupled with that sexy-as-sin grin would ever stop turning her inside out. She highly doubted it wouldn't always affect her. Everything about him both stirred her soul and settled it simultaneously. So, maybe love wasn't just worrying over someone. Maybe it was this feeling that despite all of the shit going on in her life, she was the luckiest girl in the world because he was there.

There were a hundred questions she desperately needed to ask him. What happened if she didn't get full custody of J.J. even with his money behind her? What would that mean for them? She told herself there was no reason she wouldn't at least obtain primary custody. Beyond that, the time Brant could see J.J. could be worked out. She knew if it were up to Brant, he'd sign J.J. away and probably never think of him again. It was his mama that wanted J.J. to be raised up in the Preston way of life. *Over my dead body.* Summer's jaw tensed. She would fight for her son, and now, she actually had someone willing to fight with her.

Packing those thoughts away for the moment, she stared up at the golden orange glow of the wild carnival ride they were about to embark upon.

"Uh, what are the chances someone might puke on this?" She wrinkled her nose.

Laughing, Austin edged her forward in the line. "You worried all my chili-cheese fries you ate might make a reappearance midride, darlin'?"

"They were good," she teased.

"I wouldn't know."

No one had ever made her laugh the way he did. She broke out in another fit of giggles. "I promise I'll make it up to you."

"Says my little cock-tease." He lowered his voice so only she could hear him.

"Your cock seemed pretty happy last night, cowboy," she whispered in his ear.

His shuddered growl hummed from him. "That was fucking incredible. I'm still thinking about it. Hoping for a repeat performance."

"Thought we were going parking. Hard to do all of that in your truck."

Austin feigned confusion. "Sorry, all I heard was *hard* and *in your truck*."

She elbowed him rather hard.

"Dammit, woman, don't do that. I've got a gut full of milk shake and hot dogs."

"Oh geez, please tell me you're not gonna puke on me while we ride this thing."

"My brothers and I rode it at least a dozen times every summer when we came out here. I'll be fine, but we don't have to ride it if you're *scared*," he goaded.

"I am not *scared*, cowboy. I just don't want to have to clean you up when it's over."

"No worries, darlin'. I'll be ready to go again...just like I always am." He waggled his eyebrows.

She rolled her eyes. "It's a good thing I wore my shit wadin' boots, cowboy. It's gettin' deep in here."

"What? I was talking about the ride, sweetheart. Always thinking about my crotch. I'd tell you to get your mind out of it, but I sure as hell love it when your head's down there."

Before she could come up with an appropriate comeback, she was laughing again. When he sealed them inside the caged seating for the ride, she gripped his bicep.

"I've gotcha." He laced their fingers together. "But you're not scared, right?"

"No, it's just... I'm fine."

"Uh huh," he chuckled as the ride lurched forward. Unable to help herself, she cringed into him. He laughed at her outright, but then the ride really took off. She screamed, but she was having a ball. The ride whipped and jerked them through the air. For a split second, she could see the entire midway and the town surrounding them. Austin's whoops of delight added to her euphoric joy as they flew through the air. Her stomach bottomed out and she squeezed her eyes shut, reveling in the zing of anticipation whirling through her veins.

When they finally jerked to a stop back on the ground, all she wanted to do was ride it again with him. He indulged her through three rides and then insisted they play some games. After the third time around, she was a little unsteady on her feet. Grinning at her, he wrapped her up in his arms letting her re-center and find her balance.

"Better?"

She shook her head and hugged him tighter. He seemed to know that she was lying. She'd regained her balance—she just didn't want to let go of him just yet. "You wanna go, baby? I love holding you, but I might could do it better in the bed."

"No, I'm fine. I just want to stand right here." She buried her face against his T-shirt again, inhaling deeply of his masculine scent, that leather and rosin heat that made her feel safe and loved.

"As long as you want. I'm right here." He rubbed his hands up and down her back, not minding at all that people were having to dodge around them as they raced for more games and rides.

Eventually, he got her a massive bag of cotton candy, and they settled at one of the outdoor picnic tables near the Ferris wheel. He proceeded to feed her the cotton candy with his fingers and then kiss the sticky sugar from her lips repeatedly.

His tongue traced her lips and coaxed her mouth open with every bite she accepted. The taste of spun sugar and him, that perfect heat and pressure he applied with his lips, the possessive demands he made with every kiss, everything about it was perfection. She never wanted it to end. Her nipples puckered painfully against the lace of her bra. Her panties were uncomfortably wet. She wanted him to take them off and lap up the cream her body made so readily for him. She longed to feel him press into her, opening her all for himself.

Scooting closer to him, she trailed her hands down his chest, desperate to get back to the truck so she could run her hands over his zipper-line, make him throb and pant. She loved the way his entire body responded to her touch.

"Whatcha thinkin' about, baby doll? You got that look in your eyes that makes me crazy wantin' you. You needin' something more than some sweet kisses? That little snatch gettin' juicy for me again? Needin' me to make it feel better?"

Summer shuddered against him. *Yes. Please. Now.* "You have a filthy mouth, cowboy."

"I have a filthy mind, darlin'. Hasn't seemed to bother you yet."

The heated moment shattered around them when, "Are you Summer Sanchez?!" rang through the air. A young girl, no more than fifteen or sixteen, descended on them with her folks trailing behind her.

"Uh..." Summer jerked away from Austin, blinking away the lust that had certainly formed in her eyes. "Yeah, I'm Summer. Who...are you?" She forced a grin, trying to remember to be polite.

"My name is Dakota Alvarez. I'm sorry. I didn't mean to interrupt anything. I'm just such a huge fan of yours. I've watched all of your rides on YouTube a hundred times. You were the best barrel racer there ever was. I'm up from Oklahoma. I barrel race back home. I want to do it professionally. I'm riding in a teen event here tomorrow afternoon."

Summer beamed at her. She recalled that innocent light shining in her own eyes many years ago, long before reality had broken her thoroughly. "It's nice to meet you, Dakota. This is my boyfriend, Austin Camden."

Dakota offered Austin a nervous smile. Her father stepped forward and shook Austin's hand. "Saw you ride last night, son. That was something else. Impressive as hell."

"Thank you, sir. I do what I can. Plus, I had my good luck charm with me." He held Summer's hand in the strength of his own. Dakota's parents chuckled.

Dakota sat down next to Summer. Okay, so she was a little intrusive. Summer and Austin both understood admiring riders when you were a kid. They were like superstars that had accomplished exactly what you wanted to do. They shared a discreet grin, and Austin backed off to let Dakota have full access to Summer.

"How old are you, Dakota?"

"I'll be sixteen in three weeks."

Summer nodded. Three weeks to a license was a huge deal. She remembered that, as well.

"Do you have any tips for me? Anything that might help me get better? Like maybe your top ten tips for up and coming riders." Dakota edged closer.

"Top ten, huh?" Summer considered that. Truthfully, she wanted Dakota to go back to her horse and leave Summer with Austin. She wanted the entire world to exist for only them that evening. "Uh, well, you need to ride every day, but don't always do the barrel pattern. Your horse'll get bored. Take good care of your horse. That's the most important thing, and when you're competing, keep your eyes on the pocket, not the barrel. Horse is gonna go where you're lookin'. You stare at the barrel, they'll ride into it. Other than that, control your speed when you're rating. Trotting a barrel horse builds muscle better than flyin' with 'em sometimes. Change it up and figure out what works for you and your horse. Do it every day, but don't get cocky. I never really started believing the buckles were gonna be mine until I rounded the heck outta the third barrel on my final ride of the night. Was that ten?"

"I keep telling her that the boys need to come after the buckles," her father huffed.

Dakota rolled her eyes just out of her father's line of sight. Austin chuckled quietly, and Summer nodded her understanding. "Don't be too hard on her. You only get to be sixteen once. Just don't let any boys become more important than the buckles if that's what you really want."

"It is. I swear. Thank you so much." She threw her arms around Summer, startling her. She accepted the awkward hug, but before she knew what was happening Dakota snapped a photo of the two of them with her phone.

When her family was out of earshot, Austin laughed. "You know that picture's gonna be all over Snap-Face-Twit-Tube or whatever the hell it is they're all into now."

Summer joined his laughter. "She was sweet."

"You're incredible, Summer. It kills me you haven't been able to ride. Soon as I get you to the ranch, I'm putting you on a horse and watching you fly."

"That sounds amazing. I miss it so much."

There was something she wasn't telling him. Austin could tell. Something she needed to say, something about moving to Camden Ranch with him. His gut roiled with the notion that she might decide not to go. He was pretty sure that wasn't it, but there was definitely something worrying her.

"What's going on in that head of yours, beautiful? Something's nagging my girl."

"I'm fine. I just kind of wish Cheyenne could go on forever. I love being here with you. I don't want it ever to end."

"Doesn't have to end. We'll just take it about two hundred miles due east of here."

She nodded but dropped his gaze. Deciding to let it go for the moment since she definitely didn't want to talk about whatever it was and he'd promised her a night off from all of the complications of their relationship, Austin stood. "Believe I promised you a teddy bear, Ms. Sanchez."

She laughed again. Had he never heard those sweet gasps and moans she gave him when he had her under him in his bed, he would've thought that was the most heavenly sound he'd ever heard. "You don't have to get me a teddy bear. I'll still let you get to third base."

"Nah, come on. I like it when you make me work for it." He guided her to the milk bottle game, rather liking his odds.

"Austin, those things are almost always rigged. They put sand in the bottom bottles so they won't fall over and break or something."

"Uh huh, and that might concern me if I didn't hang onto two-thousand-pound bulls for a living. Now hush up, and let me win you something. Makes me feel manly. I might even beat my chest." He winked at her as she giggled and shook her head at him.

God, if he could just keep her doing that, everything would work out just fine. Every single time he made her laugh, he fell more and more in love with her.

He accepted the three ridiculously-soft softballs from the attendant and watched them stack the bottles. "Shatter all the bottles on the first try and win the little lady something pretty, mister."

"That's my plan." He narrowed his eyes and studied the bottles. "Do me a favor and go slide the one on the right back in line with the one on the left. It's about a half centimeter off, and cheating a cowboy's bad luck."

Irritation creased the lines in the man's forehead, but he did as Austin asked. One on the bottom left was obviously heavier. Austin wound up and aimed. Name of the game, when it was rigged, was brute force. He had that in spades. He sailed the ball between the bottom bottles. Every one of them fell.

Summer gasped and threw her arms around him. "How did you do that? I've never seen anyone win before."

"I'm good, baby. You know that."

The attendant looked like Austin had just pissed in his Cheerios.

"Whatever the lady wants," Austin demanded.

"Oh, uh, let's get J.J. that big monkey. He'll love it."

Austin nodded for the man to follow her instructions. He handed off the monkey, and they headed back to the truck.

"Thank you for winning this. J.J. will be thrilled. He can crawl all over it."

"My pleasure, and now for the next portion of our evening, I'm hoping you're gonna crawl all over me."

He popped his hand on her ass as she crawled up into the truck. Seating herself, she cocked her left eyebrow upward. "If I crawl all over you, do you promise to keep doing that?"

"Oh, hell yeah, darlin' 'til your sweet little ass is blistered pink all for me, then I'll kiss it and lick it 'til it feels better."

As he drove them out of town away from the crowds, his little vixen got impatient. She snaked her hand over his crotch, palming him through his jeans, making him grunt eagerly.

A seductive catch in her breath said she felt his cock twitch out its approval. "You keep that up, honey, I'm real likely to run this truck off the road. Either that, or we'll get arrested for indecent exposure when I pull over, tear your clothes off, and let you feel how hard you make me up close and personal."

"Getting arrested might not be too good for the current PBR champ, so speed it up, cowboy. I'm horny."

"Damn, I love a woman that knows what she wants."

Fifteen minutes later, the truck bounced along a one-lane dirt road, largely hidden in the shade of massive trees and brush, that led to the banks of Crow Creek. He parked at a low creek bed, right on the shore.

"Do I want to know how you found this place?" She smirked.

"Drove around a little when we left Ekta's, and I might've been out here a time or two in years past."

"Figured that."

"Here." He popped the top on two of the cans of PBR. They both took a sip and cringed simultaneously.

"Can't say I've missed that." She wrinkled her adorable nose.

Setting both beers in the cup-holders, he hauled her into his lap. "Come here to me."

Grinning at him, she shifted and straddled her legs over his, aligning their groins and bringing those luscious tits to his chin.

"Now, what should we do?" Her inquisition took on a breathy tenor when he traced his index fingers over her exposed collarbone and then over her nipples.

"I was thinking I ought to get you outta that little tank top, so you can bounce them titties in my face."

"You sure no one can see us out here?"

"We might give a few fish an eyeful, maybe an owl or two, but I sure as hell don't share, honey. We can put on a show for those hawks on that cottonwood right there, but beyond that, you're all mine. For my eyes only."

"There are hawks over there?" She spun, brushing his clean-shaven cheek with her cleavage. He ordered himself not to strip her down, jerk his jeans down enough to get the job done, and slide her down his cock. Shaking himself, he nodded.

"Yeah, two red-tails on that tree just out of the headlights. See." He pointed high in the tree. "Red-tails mate for life. Their nest is probably nearby."

"I didn't know that." She looked genuinely intrigued. He tried to redirect the blood flow back to his brain. Sorting through years of 4-H, Young Farmers, and Young Rodeo, he landed on another fact he could recall.

"Yeah, they mate for life, but even bonded pairs still flirt and court each year before they make babies. They'll fly together, put on a show. It's pretty cool to watch."

"Yeah, that is cool." Emotion chafed her tone.

His brow furrowed. "You okay?"

"Yeah, just made me think of how Ekta keeps saying you're my hawk. I like that they mate for life. Makes me happy that there are animals that do that."

"Look at me, Summer."

She turned back and stared into the depths of his eyes.

"I'm in this for life. If you want to fly, I'll fly right beside you. Forever."

She blinked away what must've been liquid emotion. "Pretty sure you didn't bring me out here to give me a bird lesson."

"Something else you wanna talk about?"

Once again, she buried whatever was bothering her. She was mighty good at that. Once he got her settled in at home, he was gonna have to put a stop to it.

She ran her hands over his face, tracing his jawline. "Did you shave just for me?"

"Thought a guy should clean up a little since he was getting to take you out."

"Mmm, I don't know. I think I like you scruffy." She lifted her shirt over her head, and he moaned from the sway of her full breasts that had him instantly mesmerized.

She pressed her hips forward, let her eyes close, and sank downward, sliding her pussy against the fierce bulge in his Wranglers. His growl covered the slight pop of her bra as he released it and dragged the straps down her arms.

Braiding the fingers of his right hand through her long, dirty-blonde hair, he guided her lips to his while he teased the underswell of her left breast with his other hand. The feeling of her silky, warm skin against his callused hands undid him every single time he had the pleasure of touching her.

"You like it when I leave whisker marks on you, don't cha, darlin'? My girl likes it when I mark her." Using his chin, he separated her breasts, brushing tender kisses on each. He spun his tongue between them, tasting the salty tang of her, then marking the underswells on each side.

"Yes." She thrust upwards again, burying his face between her tits, grinding hard against his cock over and over. Every move threatened to destroy him.

"Jesus Christ," he grunted. "Lesser man woulda lost it right then and there."

"Good thing you're such a stud then. Bring me, Austin. Right here. I need it. Put your mouth on me and make me come."

"And if I suck your beautiful titties 'til you cream them panties, whatcha gon' do for me, darlin'?"

She considered for one split second while he cupped her breasts, massaging and priming her for his mouth. "I'll let you taste it off my fingers, then I'll give you a surprise."

His thundered groan filled the truck cab. "Oh, hell yeah, baby." He drew her body upward and lifted her breasts until he enclosed the bare tip of her right nipple in his mouth and suckled. Alternating between bathing his tongue over the puckered bud and sliding his teeth over her, he jutted his hips forward, aligning his painfully rigid cock in the center of her pussy as she continued to ride him.

Using his dexterity to his advantage, he popped the snap of her jeans, eliminating one layer of fabric between their groins.

"Yes. God, that feels good," she gasped.

"Keep going, sugar. Hard as you like, but if you make me come in my jeans, you're cleaning it up with that sassy mouth."

A whimpered moan escaped her as he engulfed her left breast this time, suctioning his mouth to her forcefully, pulling until her nipple pulsated against his tongue and his cock throbbed against her mound.

"So close. Please, please don't stop." She shook.

Holy hell, he was gonna lose it all in his boxers just like a green kid. She was too much. He nuzzled his face between her breasts, feeling them bounce and nurture his face. Ordering himself to remain in control, he gave another few latched sucks and then tore his mouth from her left breast and returned to her right while he circled his thumb over her clit, pressing the damp cotton against her.

She didn't have to worry about anyone or anything seeing them. They'd steamed the windows of his truck up with the blaze of pure heat they created whenever they were together. Sliding his teeth along her right nipple, he applied the pressure she required and nipped. She came in a storm of shuddered gasps and wild cries of his name, clawing at his arms and T-shirt, strands of her hair clinging to her passion-flushed cheeks. Damn, but watching her give it up was prettier than any natural wonder of the world he'd ever seen a picture of.

She collapsed against him, panting for breath. He wrapped his arms around her, cradling her on his shoulder while he chased his breath as well. He cracked the windows of the truck, providing them a little fresh air. Nuzzling his neck, she tucked closer to him still.

Yep, perfection. He'd searched his whole life and all over the freaking country for this feeling, that moment when she buried herself in the safety of his embrace, when she cuddled closer to him in her sleep and sighed contentedly. When she gave herself over to him without inhibition, that light in her eyes when he'd been gone and returned to her, or J.J.'s sweet grin when Austin played with him or rescued him from his crib. That was what he'd been looking for forever.

'Told you it was never about that buckle, man.' Swallowing down shock, Austin continued to try and steady his racing heart.

'Dude, talking to me while I'm getting it on, not cool.' So, now he was mentally arguing with his dead best friend. Yeah, that wasn't weird at all.

Summer sat back a full minute later. "You do amazing things with that mouth, cowboy."

He smirked. "Believe you promised me a taste and then a surprise."

With a sly grin, she arched upward on her knees and stuck her fingers down her panties. A rumbled growl reverberated through his lungs as he lowered them as far as he could and stared unabashedly. She swirled her fingers between her slit and his body bucked without his permission.

She brought her fingers to his lips and he licked and suckled her offering.

"More," he commanded. The moonlit reflection of his eyes, dark and greedy, met him in the rearview mirror.

She repeated the gathering of her own spicy nectar and fed him again.

"I need more, Summer. God, I need it all. I'm taking you home and burying myself inside of you."

"We're not going home yet. I still have to give you your surprise."

Trying to quell his frustration, he grunted, "I figured I was getting a blow job. I'd rather soak down the walls of your pussy in our bed."

"I'll give you a blow job after we go skinny dipping," she chanted as she popped open the truck door.

"Uh, sugar, you don't wanna..."

"What? Is my big bad cowboy afraid of going skinny dippin'?

Thought you didn't do scared." She slid off his lap, landing on the soggy ground on the banks of the creek.

"Oh, I ain't afraid, darlin'. I just don't think you..."

"Just come on." She tugged on his arm.

Before he could climb out of the truck, she had her boots, jeans, and panties off. He caught the pile when she tossed them toward him. Sighing, he set them in the truck. She was headed straight for the moving creek off of the South Platte River, and judging from the wild look in her eyes there was no stopping her. He went ahead and dug behind the backseat for his quilt-lined Carhartt jacket and an old blanket he kept back there for winter emergencies.

"Summer, baby, don't..." She was on the edge of the water now.

"Get nekkid and catch me, cowboy," she dared.

"Dammit, Summer, do *not* get in that water." He grimaced as she leapt in without a care in the world. Biting his lips together to keep from either shouting at her or laughing at her outright, he shoved his jeans down in his boots, and headed to the water. She bobbed back up, gulping and screaming like a banshee.

"Oh my God! It's freezing!"

"Uh huh." He shook his head and waded out to the tops of his boots. Reaching out, he lifted her shaking body up into his arms. Her teeth chattered so hard he was worried she might chip them, and she was blue from head to toe. "I tried to tell you."

She shivered with more vigor, whimpering constantly now.

"Here." He settled her on the bed of the truck, and wrapped the blanket around her. "This ain't New Mexico, darlin'. This is Wyoming. You can't leap in a moving creek off of a river even in July and not freeze your tits off. Same goes for Nebraska. You'd do well to remember that. We're in the mountains."

Her blood seemed to have heated enough for her temper to flare. He'd been expecting this. "You coulda stopped me, damn you."

Austin huffed, "And I quote, 'Is my big bad cowboy afraid of skinny dippin'?' You and your stubborn little ass coulda and shoulda listened to me."

She ground her teeth but then wilted in the blanket, unable to stop shaking. "Okay, fine, I should've listened. Ugh, everything hurts."

Shaking his head at her, he crawled up on the tailgate with her and lifted her onto his lap still wrapped in the heavy blanket. "Come here, let's get you dried off." He gently eased the blanket against her skin until she was as dry as he could get her, then he unwound her. She whimpered and tried to cling to the blanket. "I know it's cold, baby. Give me the blanket. It's wet. It's just gonna make you colder. Let me dry your hair with it then I'll get you dressed."

While she continued to shiver, naked in the bed of his truck, he dried her hair and carried her to the cab. Helping her back into her clothing, he swathed her in his Carhartt and turned on the heater.

When her body calmed and her skin resumed its normal olive tone, he eased back down the dirt road toward civilization.

"You can quit biting holes in your tongue and go ahead and call me a dumbass." She pouted.

"I would never call you a dumbass. I'm not an abusive fucker. I'd just appreciate it if you'd at least acknowledge that I *am* always trying to take care of you."

"I know that. I'm sorry. I just…I felt like… I don't know. Never mind."

"You felt like being a little reckless, letting it all go?"

He got a single nod in response.

"That's what this whole night was supposed to be about, honey. No issues with any of that. You just occasionally leap before you let me look out for you."

"No joke," she sighed. "I'm just not used to anyone looking out for me. Not an easy thing to get used to."

"Well, I figure we have the next sixty or seventy years together, so maybe by the time we're in the old folk's home, you'll have gotten used to it."

"I can't believe you're so sure you want to marry me after just a week." He opened his mouth to explain yet again, but she held up her hand. "I know, I know, you have a gut thing and you're never wrong or whatever. You do know most of us take things a little slower though, right?"

"You wanting to slow things down?"

She tucked herself deeper in his jacket. "Truthfully, no. Well, maybe. I don't know. I either want to stay in Cheyenne forever, never let the next week end or to fast forward six months, be sure you're really gonna be happy with me and love me and J.J. forever and have settled into a new life. It's this in-between part that scares the shit out of me."

"Sounds to me like it's the unknown scares the shit out of you. I get that, believe me, I do, but if that stupid wreck taught me anything, it's that you can't take one day for granted. If you see something and you want it, you go after it with all your heart, and if you get it, you cherish it and take care of it every moment of every day. That's how I plan to handle our relationship for the rest of our lives.

"I just don't think it can possibly be as complicated as everyone would like you to believe. I get up and I make damn sure you know how much I love you before I saddle up. I ride. I work. I come home and have supper with you, listen to you tell me all about your day, or if I'm real, real lucky, you come out and ride with me and we work together. We have supper. We take care of the youngins. I put you to bed and make sure you know that my every single action is for you. Season in, season out. I take care of you, and of J.J., and any others we might up and create. And if all goes well, when I'm too old to do much else, I get to sit in a rocking chair on a front porch somewhere on the ranch with you while we watch our youngins do the same thing with their families. I can't think of a better life, Summer. So, it's gonna take a little figuring and work. Good. I like hard work. I'm in this."

"You really think it can all work out like that?"

"Yes, I do." He grinned. She couldn't stop yawning. Jumping in subzero water was rather exhausting. He knew from experience.

The rapid click of the parking brake, startled her. She'd dozed off as he'd driven back to the ranch cabins. "We're back, Sleeping Beauty. Want me to carry you in?"

"No, I'm fine." With another deep yawn, she slid out of the truck and let him guide her inside their cabin.

Holly was dozing in Luke's lap, and Hope was asleep in Brock's. Austin's parents were sitting in the rocking recliners watching TV. Their brows furrowed when they took in Summer's damp hair and the fact that she was wrapped up in Austin's Carhartt in the middle of July.

"Summer decided she might like to discover just how cold the South Platte is about this time of year." Austin chuckled.

She glared at him, but was too exhausted to do much else.

His parents both laughed. Holly sat up and rubbed her eyes. "Did you throw her in?"

"If I'd thrown her in water that cold, I wouldn't be around to tell you about it. She'd have maimed me at the very least."

Austin's mother shook her head. "All right, you two get some rest. J.J. was good as gold. He's been asleep since about nine."

"Thank you so much for watching him, Mrs. Camden." Another shiver worked through Summer.

"It was no trouble. We're gonna see the sights tomorrow. Let your daddy play in the Frontier village, but we'll see all of you at the pancake breakfast Friday, right?"

"Yeah." Brock yawned. "We're gonna play in Cheyenne tomorrow, then after the breakfast Friday, I'm taking Hope on to see Yellowstone. We'll be back at the ranch Saturday, though."

"We'll be at the breakfast Friday, Mama. Then I've got a practice session from 10:00-2:00. Y'all are welcome to come before you head out," Austin reminded them.

"That was our plan. You know how your mother loves to see you thrown off of bull after bull," his father chided.

"They're practice bulls. I'll be fine." Austin brushed a kiss on his mother's cheek. He took Summer's hand and guided her toward the bedroom while his family saw themselves out. Stripping her out of her clothes, he grabbed one of his T-shirts and a pair of sweatpants he'd located in the bottom of his suitcase for her to wear.

"Thank you." Her blinks extended in length as he tenderly re-dressed her, laid her in bed, stripped himself, and climbed in beside her. He cradled her against his chest and brushed her damp hair behind her.

"See, I knew you were a cock-tease."

"I'm sorry," she fussed sweetly.

Chuckling, he brushed a kiss on her forehead. "Don't be sorry, baby. I was teasing you. Just go to sleep. We have the rest of our lives to be together."

CHAPTER EIGHTEEN

Friday morning, after stuffing themselves full of Kiwanis club pancakes and waving goodbye to Brock and Hope, Austin led his family, his girl, and their boy to the practice arena.

Hidden a few streets over from the throngs of people already crowding the main thoroughfare in Cheyenne proper, the practice arena was a bare bones operation kept out of the eye of the fans. Far more function than form, there were four chutes, but only two were in use and loaded with practice bulls. Fourteen bull riders had made it all the way to Cheyenne. Only five had qualified. All five were practicing that morning in the diminutive arena.

Lummis Ranch provided the practice bulls for Frontier Days. They had their men out loading the pens. Jackson met the Camdens on the north side of the small arena. Each rider provided one bull fighter, since practice bulls weren't near the brutes rodeo bulls were. They'd throw riders, but didn't usually see any need to go after the rider once they'd dispensed with him.

Despite that, the pancakes in Austin's gut churned ominously. He couldn't figure what was wrong. Summer seemed fine. J.J. was fussy, but that was probably because he hadn't slept well the night before.

"Let's do eight this morning," Austin instructed Jackson as he handed J.J. off to Summer. He recognized the tense set of his own voice.

"Yeah, I knew that's what you'd want. I already told Mr. Lummis that. He says they've got you four ready, but Anders and Ryan Cogburn, each put in for six, and Colton Jones, and Bill Youngers want four, and they were all here first. You're gonna have to get in line and cycle through. Gonna be crazy around here for a while," Jackson explained.

"Always is. It'll be fine." Austin took in the riders, their bull fighters, the stock contractors, and a PBR rep sent to keep an eye on everything. There were two dozen people where normally it would have been just him and Jackson along with the practice bulls. He'd have to deal if he wanted to practice. His next ride was the following night, and if something bad was coming, he needed a full session to prepare.

Of course he wants eight. Most riders took four at a practice. The most intense, or most insane, depending on your perspective, took six. Summer sighed inwardly. She would rather beat her own head against a brick wall than watch Austin get his ass thrown in the dirt eight times in a row. Bouncing J.J. on her hip, she shared a sympathetic gaze with his mama. They both knew they couldn't stop him. They just wished they didn't have to watch it.

Austin and Jackson sauntered off to where the Lummis boys were loading stock.

"Everett, did he say eight?" Jessie demanded.

"Honey, since the moment he started walking, he hadn't ever done anything the easy way. You know that." Ev sighed.

Summer couldn't help but grin. She reminded herself that her coaches would ask her to run the barrel pattern ten times, and she'd go twenty.

"He's been doing eight at every practice session since he was fifteen, Mom," Holly reminded.

They stood by and watched Travis Anders ride, and then Bill Youngers. Only one bull was allowed in the arena at a time, so loading and unloading ate up most of the practice session. Austin and Ryan

Cogburn took turns next. Austin's bull wasn't doing much bucking, so he dismounted, landed on his feet, and ordered a different one.

Colton Jones was next as they continued to work through the bulls. Summer willed the minutes to go by faster. She chatted with his mama and Holly, but felt her stomach turn every time it was Austin's turn to climb in the chute again. At least the activity all around them made it seem a little less intense.

He returned to the gates while Youngers went again.

"Smile for me, sugar. They're just practice bulls." He planted a kiss on her lips.

She sighed. "I know. I just love you. Remember, you don't have to be scared. I'll be scared for you."

His parents beamed. She watched Austin's neck contract as that sinfully sexy grin formed on his face again. "I love you, too. We still eating with Ekta tonight?"

"Yeah, she called this morning. Can't wait to talk to the hawk."

Chuckling, Austin wrapped his arm over her as two other riders were thrown and more bulls were loaded into the chutes. "I'll try not to disappoint. I'm up next. Be back in a few."

Summer was momentarily distracted by a waving Dakota Alvarez, standing by a horse trailer where several horses were being led out. Dakota joined Summer and the Camdens at the fences.

"They're doing the junior barrel racing event here this afternoon. That's my horse, Wildfire, coming off now."

Summer stared longingly at the beautiful calico, a perfect fifteen hands high, with a shimmery coat, bright attentive eyes, and braided mane.

"Looks like you take great care of her." Summer smiled.

"She's kind of my best friend," Dakota admitted. Summer understood that only too well. "Would your little boy like to pet her?"

Nodding, Summer carried J.J. to meet Wildfire. J.J. gasped and oohed over the horse, who leaned her head down sweetly for him to pet her. Summer grasped his little hand to keep him from smacking the horse's neck in an attempt to love her. "Easy, buddy. Be gentle."

"She's completely bomb-proof. She won't hurt him," Dakota assured as she kept hold of Wildfire's reins.

"I can tell. She's a great horse."

"I'd be honored if you wanted to ride her while we're here. She'd love it."

"Oh, you're so sweet. I better not. Austin will be practicing for a while then his family's going back to their ranch. We're having dinner with a friend of mine tonight."

"Too bad. I was hoping you might come see me ride and tell me everything I'm doing wrong."

Summer hated to hear Dakota down on herself. "I'm sure you're great. As long as every ride is better than the one before, that's all you need to worry about. Compete with yourself, not anyone else."

"Thanks." Dakota beamed at her.

Summer let J.J. pet the horse for a few more minutes. Her heart lurched to a stop when the Preston Cattle trailer ambled up the dirt road behind the arena. She didn't recognize the truck pulling it. Furrowing her brow, she braced herself, not certain what might be coming.

She offered half smiles to Bill Youngers and Colton Jones, who lifted their hats to her as they left the arena. Supposing there was some kind of gentleman cowboy code for other riders' girlfriends, Summer tried to be polite. They'd only requested four bull rides and were finished for the day.

Other bulls were still being loaded in from both chutes for Austin and the other riders.

"Oh, careful there, little guy," Dakota eased. J.J. was reaching for Wildfire's mane.

"Sorry." Summer shifted J.J. to her other hip away from the horse. A cold sweat dewed on the back of her neck. Her heart beat frantically, but she had no idea what was wrong. Studying the area again, she couldn't locate Brant's trailer. It had disappeared. The hair on her arms stood up stiffer than her spine.

"Uh, good luck today, Dakota. I need to get back. Austin's practicing."

"It was good to see you again. Your little boy is adorable."

"Thanks." Summer waved, but before she made two steps she heard Holly's gasp.

"Austin!"

Dakota and Summer raced back to the chutes.

"Ev, do something!" Mrs. Camden pled.

Austin was in the center of the ring with not one, not two, but three bulls surrounding him, and one of them was Dallas Devil.

"What happened?" Summer demanded.

"Austin was on that bull on the left. He made it almost ten seconds then bailed off. They were slow getting him back in the chute and the other gate opener let the next rider out. He bailed and climbed out so there wouldn't be two in the arena at the same time, but then Dallas Devil busted through that broken chute door on the opposite side. He's got a flank strap on, and he's mad as hell. None of 'em are happy the others are there. I gotta get Austin outta there." Luke threw his leg over the metal gate.

"Oh my God!" Summer panicked. There was no way he could escape all three bulls all hell bent on killing each other.

"Hold him." She thrust J.J. in to Holly's arms and raced back to Wildfire. "I need to ride him."

A wide-eyed Dakota managed a nod as Summer hurled her leg over Wildfire's bare back. "Kee-yaw!" rang from her lungs as she rushed the horse through the rider entrance of the practice arena.

Holy fucking hell. Austin kept his eyes on the devil and backed away while Jackson tried frantically to get one of the other bulls back in the chutes. They'd all seen each other and were about to show each other who was dominant with Austin in the middle of it all. The Lummis boys stared on dumbfounded. Travis and Ryan had ridden their sixth and left the arena.

"Austin, get away from him," Jackson shouted.

"I'm fucking trying."

"I'll get the one on the right. You move left." Luke's low voice sounded from somewhere behind Austin. If he took a split second to gauge his brother's location, Dallas Devil would charge and he'd be a dead man. He was already pawing the ground. Dirt rose under his hooves and permeated his breath as it curled up from his snout. His snarls pounded against Austin's skull.

Suddenly, the thunder of hooves distracted the three men in the arena.

"Summer! What the hell?" he bellowed, but she was undeterred.

"Climb out," she ordered as she circled the horse around Dallas Devil, infuriating the bull but distracting him from Austin.

"Holy hell." Jackson raced in and shoved the bull Austin had been riding hard. He turned on Jackson, and Luke leapt in. Together they guided him back into the chutes.

"Summer," Austin shouted.

"Get the hell out," she screamed.

The next bull tore away from Jackson and headed toward Dallas. Summer cut between them. Fury and terror surged through Austin. His gut roiled. He was going to be sick. What the hell did she think she was doing? She was going to get herself killed.

He'd never seen anyone ride like that. She circled Dallas Devil again, taunting him. If she survived this, Austin was going to kill her when they all got out. "Get the hell away from him. Right now!"

Narrowing her eyes and honing her focus, she extended her body to the right, barely holding onto the horse with her legs, and jerked the quick-release knot holding the flank strap, but it didn't untie.

Dallas reared back and she pulled hard to the left, just missing his horns as he came down where she'd been on the horse a half second before.

Turning the horse back, she circled him again, confusing him. She spun the horse like the master rider she was. Before Austin could blink, she was behind the devil again. Her next extended reach was good; the flank strap released, and the devil shook but stopped bucking.

Luke and Jackson had managed to get the third bull back in the chute. Summer circled wide.

"Get everyone out of here," she bellowed. "Brant can get his damned bull himself." With that, she flew back out of the arena, his savior, undaunted.

Clenching his jaw so tightly it ached, Austin paced while Summer returned Dakota's horse to her and brushed off everyone's shock over her skilled riding and her bravery.

When she finally returned to him, he ordered himself to maintain control while he gripped her shirt and half-dragged her to the locker room. "What the fucking hell do you think you were doing? You could have gotten killed."

"You were gonna get killed, Austin! My God, are you really that arrogant? I just saved your ass and now...ugh...what happened to your bag?"

Unable to see anything beyond the infuriated haze of his own anger, Austin hadn't noticed that once again his tack bag was overturned in the practice locker room. Tack was strewn everywhere.

Before he could process it all, Summer shook her head. "We're breaking up. I can't go to the ranch with you. I can't ever be with you. Take me back to Cody. I need my truck." Tears welled in her eyes, and she shook in an effort to keep them from cascading down her trembling face.

"What?" This had to be some kind of horrible dream. Too many things had happened for him to understand any of them. How the hell had that devil bull ended up at the practice arena? "We are not breaking up. I love you."

"I love you, too, Austin." She convulsed. "That's why we have to. I can't do this to you. He'll never let me go. This is all my fault."

"Okay, I know that was scary, but just come here to me." Austin reached for her, but she jerked away from him.

"No. No, I'm not letting you hold me or kiss me, and I won't let you tell me it will all be okay because it won't. And if I let you touch me, I may not be able to... Just no. I have to go back to Cody. I have to get my truck. People don't fall in love in a week, anyway. This was all too good to be true, and I knew it. Brant will never let me go. He tried to kill you."

"Brant did not do that," Austin tried to shout but his voice was a half whisper laced with haunted misery.

"Yes, he did. There were prod marks all over that damned bull's hide, Austin. I saw the trailer pull up. He put him in the chute and used a hotshot on him to make him even angrier. He waited until you were the only rider left. Don't you see? I cannot get you killed. And in the middle of all of that, he went through your bag again."

"We are not breaking up."

"Yes, we are. You can't just decide that you want something and refuse to live in reality. We cannot be together." She broke down and he tried again to touch her, to comfort her, but she shoved him away.

He dammed back his own tears with the clench of his jaw. Aware that his brother and sister were standing in shocked silence at the entrance to the locker room, he tried to work through the hellish pain that tightened its vice grip on his chest and come up with some way to make her stay.

"I can't take you back to Cody," was the best he came up with.

"You can't keep me here."

Closing his eyes and praying for help, he ordered his chin to stop quivering. "I have to do a chute tour in a little while and I have to ride tomorrow night. I can't take you back until after that." Two days. I have to fix this in two days. "I'll quit." The idea avulsed from his lungs like a single lightning strike that set an entire field ablaze.

"What?"

"I'll quit. I'll drop out right now. I won't ride ever again. Brant can't hurt me, Summer, but if that's what it takes to keep you with me, I'll quit right now."

"No. You will not quit for me, and he still has custody of J.J. He'll never stop. I can't have a life ever again. I'm so sorry, Austin. I never meant to hurt you." Another storm of tears streaked her face.

"Please, Summer, just please don't do this." His voice was weak and hollow, but he wasn't above begging, not for her.

"Don't make this harder than it already is. Just take me to Ekta's. Thank you so much for the past week. I never knew it could be this way, but I can never see you again."

She turned from him, and took J.J. out of Holly's arms. "Summer, you don't have to do this. We can all help you with Brant," Holly pled on his behalf.

"You can't, but thank you. I need to get out of here." She tucked J.J. to her chest and fled the locker room. Austin's feet were rooted to the concrete floor. He couldn't breathe. He couldn't see. He wasn't certain he even wanted to. He wanted no part of this life without her.

"Austin, man..." Luke gently reached for his shoulder but he jerked away.

"Get the hell away from me." He flew after Summer.

An hour later, he still hadn't gotten through to her. Somehow, he was driving her and J.J. to Ekta's. How the hell had this even happened? He still couldn't figure it. "You're breaking my heart. Killing me. You know that right? I don't even want to go on without you."

Her jaw clenched tighter, and she turned farther in the seat, refusing to look at him. "At least you will be able to go on. Better than being dead."

"Being dead can't hurt near as bad as this does. Dammit, if I'd known this was coming, I mighta let that motherfucking bull have his way."

That vow earned him a half glance. He slowed the truck. "I will do anything, Summer. Hell, I'll run away with you and never look back. We'll never see Brant again. Just please."

"Stop. Just stop it. Do you think I'm not just as heartbroken as you are, Austin? This is killing me. I ache. My whole body hurts from this. I am in love with you. I'm pretty sure I will always be in love with you, but I won't get you killed."

"He cannot hurt me."

"You have no idea what the Prestons are capable of. When I was living on their ranch, there was this city councilman that didn't get along with Mr. Preston. He denied some kind of tax exemption on part of the ranch land or something. It was gonna cost the family a bunch of money in taxes that they should have been paying anyway. Two days after the ruling, the councilman's car was run off a bridge on Loop 12. The story barely made the papers. It just went away. That's the kind of people they are."

"And you think I'm just gonna walk away and leave you to wolves like that?"

"You can't save me."

"What about the hawk thing? What about what Ekta said?" To his dismay, somehow he'd driven them to Ekta's cabin without any conscious memory of actually getting them there.

"It's a story. You can't save me. I had to save you, and now I have to leave you. Just go, Austin, please." She threw open the door to the truck, had J.J. out of his car seat, and her suitcase in her arms before he could stop her.

He flung himself out of the truck. "Summer, don't do this."

Ekta appeared on the porch. Tears marred the deep lines of the old woman's face. "Whirlwind, this is not meant to be."

"Shut up, both of you." Summer bolted inside the cabin.

"Your story is not at its end, Hawk."

"What the hell does that even mean? This isn't at all what you told her about Sapana or whoever it was. I thought *I* was supposed to be the one that saved *her*. She just ended everything. What am I supposed to do now? I can't...I won't..." He tried to maneuver the words around the rock-like enclosure in his throat. "I need her with me...always."

"Did it ever occur to either of you that Sapana had to swing from that lariat long enough to believe herself worth saving? I prayed it would not come to this, but the storms are restless and coming. She cannot stop them, and neither can you. You will have to save her, Austin, if you can, but you must let her swing for now."

"I don't want to let her swing. I want her safe in my arms," he pled to the woman as if she could actually change his fate.

"I know, but she has never loved before. She doesn't feel she deserves your love now, and she believes that her love is cursed because of her past. She's showing you love the only way she understands it. Give her time. Your story does not end here."

With that, Ekta turned and followed Summer's path back into the cabin. Austin stared after them both, still unable to believe what had happened.

CHAPTER NINETEEN

"You didn't have to stay." Austin tried to rid his tone of the scorn and irritation over Luke not returning to the ranch with the rest of his family.

The sun was setting behind the mountains now. He hadn't eaten since breakfast. Apathy over his own well-being filled him instead. It was nearing supper time. He needed to help Summer cook and to get J.J.'s hands washed. He was supposed to be setting him in his highchair thing and buckling him in. Putting on his bib, and watching Summer brush her hair out of her face while she served plates.

Instead, he sat on the back deck of the ranch cabin, staring out into nothingness. Everything inside reminded him too much of her. It just hurt too badly. Her scent still clung to the sheets of their bed. He couldn't sleep there ever again.

"Grant said the corn's all in. I got nothing but time." Luke handed him a flask. Austin downed the bourbon, trying to feel the burn, but his chest was hollow. There was nothing there to ignite. "We could go into town. See if we can't scare up Preston."

"He didn't put that bull in there. I keep telling everyone it wasn't him."

Luke's nod said he didn't believe that any more than Summer had. "Any idea who did it then?"

Austin shook his head.

"Hey, uh, Clif called, said to tell you not to worry about not showing at the chute tour. They got another rider to do it. Said if they can find out anything about who did this, they'll call you."

"Clif can fuck the hell off with everyone else."

Uncomfortable silence filled the cool evening air. Austin wanted to run away. Run from the pain. Run from the images ingrained in his head. Run from the memories of her hands on his body, the feel of her clinging to him. Run from the scent of her. It filled his lungs constantly. He couldn't rid himself of it. The recollections adhered themselves to the very air he breathed. He had to move. Something deep inside of him spurred him on.

"I'm going for a walk." He stood and stepped off the porch in one quick move.

"You want me to come along?"

"No. I'll be back sometime. Don't worry about me." With that, he took off across the pastures attached to the ranch cabins, trying desperately to clear his head. He had less than two days to fix this, and that depended on him coming up with some way to keep her from Cody. *Two days.* The words became his mantra. Every strike of his boot on the hard earth spoke the time. His cadence sped until he was sprinting away.

He glared at the oppressive darkness as it engulfed him, blotting him from the fields.

"You said it was her. You said it wasn't the buckle. You said I was supposed to get her!" he shouted into the moonlit nothingness. He'd never spoken out loud to Max, certainly never attempted to summon him from the heavens.

"You were." Max's voice reverberated through the Austin's hollowed ribcage.

"What the fuck happened then?" He tripped over a tree root and landed on his hands and knees. He had no desire to stand, no fight left, so he sat on the cold dirt and stared up at Heaven. Hadn't he lost

enough in one lifetime? Maybe this was the punishment he'd always felt he deserved for getting his best friend killed.

"You can't have us both, and I wanted to tell you that it's okay to let me go. Actually, you've got to let me go. I wanted to tell you good-bye. I'm good, man. Really good. Let me go."

"What?"

"When you have her, you'll let me go. You'll finally forgive yourself for something that was never your fault, and I'll go."

"But I don't have her, and I don't know how to get her back."

"The Arapaho woman told you the story is not over."

"What do you mean, you'll go? I carried your casket. You're gone. You're the one that kept talking to me all these years."

"You've never let me go. You kept chasing me, trying to bring me back. Summer's separation from you is not permanent, but mine is. I brought you out here to tell you good-bye, my friend."

"Max, dammit, I don't understand. How do I get her back, and why the hell are you leaving me now?"

"The Zuni people believe that the macaw brings forth eternal summer for the people. Birthed from the staff of Yanauluha the priest. The strongest of the people rushed to the largest eggs they thought would take them to summer. Their impatience birthed only ravens. Those with patience and wisdom chose the small eggs and birthed the macaws. Her people make their feathers from the plumage, red, yellow, and blue. It is her beauty. You must give her time. Impatience and brute force brings the raven. It won't be long. You will indeed be her hawk and someday you will fly together."

"Max, what the hell are you trying to tell me?" Austin was half certain he must've hit his head when he fell.

"I'm trying to tell you good-bye, Austin. Your summer is coming. Cling tightly to that. Your fight has just begun. Fight with your mind, not your fists. Find your patience. You've never been too good with that. She needs you. Thank you for always being my friend."

———

Luke Camden

"Austin!" Luke jerked upright. He must've dozed off as the sun was coming up. His phone danced on the coffee table, vibrating its impatience. "Austin? Where the hell are you? I'm coming to get you," spilled frantically from his lips.

"This is Scott. Austin isn't there with you?"

Rubbing his hands over his face, Luke tried to think. "No, he never came back last night. Took off at sundown. I'm going out to look for him."

"I'll go with you. Listen, I talked some chick over at the PBR board into pulling Austin's day sheet for me. He's been paired with Dallas Devil tonight. I called to see if you thought there was a chance in hell he was up to that. I'm guessing not."

"Tell you God's truth, I really don't give a damn who Austin's paired with tonight. I'm going to find my brother."

"Maybe he's with Summer. Maybe they got back together. You know how he is when he wants something. Maybe he talked his way back."

Wrenching the crick out of his neck, Luke considered that. His gut said Austin wasn't that lucky, but he *was* damned stubborn. Never let anything go. He wasn't gonna give her up without one hell of a fight. "I'll call her."

"I'll drive around town. See if I can find him. Call me if you hear from him."

"Will do."

Easing back onto the couch, Luke debated how to proceed. Taking the easy route first, he called Austin's cell. No answer. He tried again a minute later. Nothing.

Was that a good sign? His mind ran through a thousand scenarios, everything from Austin shutting his phone off because Summer had taken him back and they were busy...reuniting, to his brother lying face down dead in a ditch somewhere played out in his head.

Standing, he began to pace. If he wasn't with Summer, Luke's call was only going to scare her more. It was painfully obvious that's why she'd done this. She was terrified of that ex of hers. Luke felt terrible for thinking she was after Austin's money. Obviously, this was real love, as fucked up as it was currently.

He stared at his phone and willed Austin to call. When it remained silent, he drew a deep breath.

"No time like the present." He repeated the adage, buying himself a few more seconds. He had Summer's cell number from the night he'd helped watch J.J. She'd wanted everyone to have it in case something happened. Grimacing, he touched the number and prayed Austin might answer.

"Hello?" Summer ordered her voice to sound somewhat normal. She'd cried most of the night. Her entire being felt raw. The single word clawed at her arid throat.

"Uh, Summer, it's Luke. Any chance Austin's there with you?"

"No, he isn't here." Blinking several times, she tried to rid her swollen eyes of emotion. "He's probably pulling his papers or blowing off some steam." The thought of him drowning the pain she'd inflicted on him in another woman made her sick. She swallowed down bile and vomit.

"He never came back last night. Scott called. They pulled his paperwork already. He's paired with Dallas Devil tonight. Listen, I'm gonna go out and look for Austin, but if there's any way we can prove Brant's doping that bull, now's the time to do it. Austin ain't gonna back down now. He's gonna want to stick it Brant, and he's a disaster. He can't ride that bull tonight and not get himself killed."

Panic surged through her veins, engulfing her entirely. What part of her heart that remained intact pushed her to move. "I have to go."

"Uh, okay, I'm gonna go out and see if I can't find him. If you can think of a way for us to get something on that bull, let me know."

"Good. I'll call you if I think of something."

She would not let Austin hurt himself because of her. That would make all of the pain they were enduring useless. She'd prove Brant was pumping that damned bull full of steroids, get him disqualified, Brant arrested, and save Austin, then she'd figure out how to get back to Cody and let him go on and win his buckle. He didn't need her messing up his life anyway.

"Ekta, J.J. and I are going into town," she called as she strapped J.J.

into his harness carrier. This had to work. She'd seen people on TV breaking into hotel rooms. People never suspected moms to be up to anything. She'd figure out the rest when she got there.

"Take my truck, Whirlwind. You'll need it."

Ekta handed her the keys to her Chevy truck, circa 1980.

"How do you know I'll need it?"

"I can hear the thunder now."

Summer furrowed her brow. The sky was perfectly clear. It was a beautiful Cheyenne morning, not that anything would ever really be beautiful to her again.

"The thunder in your soul, Whirlwind. It beats its call for him. His wings are strong enough now. There was a weight he had to let go of, and he has done that. Take your things with you and take my truck. You will not be returning to me. The buzzard will return my truck to me when I need it." Ekta hugged her, but Summer pulled away.

"I am going to prove Brant is doping that bull, then I'm coming right back here. You were wrong about me being Sapana. I have to save him, not the other way around. Look, I don't have time to argue with you. I have to find something proving Brant's an asshole and get it to the PBR board in time to get Dallas Devil disqualified from tonight's rodeo. I love you. I'll be back in a little while."

"Take your things and J.J.'s things, just to make me happy, Sapana."

"Fine," Summer hoisted her bag into her arms. "But stop calling me that." When she'd loaded J.J. and all of his stuff into the old truck, she hugged Ekta good-bye. "I'll be back in a little while."

Ekta simply waved. "Remember, Whirlwind, you are made of things the world can never take from you. Even when all seems lost, the macaw and the hawk will fly together. It is time."

Sick to death of hearing about Native American bird legends, Summer finally got Ekta's truck to crank. "Okay, little man, we have to find prescriptions, or papers, or the actual shots, or something in the hotel room. I need you to help Mommy." She tried to remember the name of the steroids Luke had told her about when she'd asked a few days ago.

"Ma-ma," J.J. babbled beside her. "Tin."

Her heart sank. He'd started doing that a few days ago whenever

Austin was around. "Yeah, I miss him, too, but we have to save him. He needs us."

She sat in the parking lot of the Cheyenne Suites Hotel and debated. Everybody anxious to show off their money always stayed there. Mostly Wrangler and Stetson execs and stock contractors. She could go in with J.J. in his carrier, tell them she was Brant's wife—she gagged from the thought of ever having to voice those words again—and tell them she lost her keycard. There was a better than decent chance that people at the hotel had seen Brant taking his whores back to his room though. Things could get dicey quickly.

Plan B was most definitely illegal, but she wasn't backing down now. Brant's truck wasn't in the parking lot, nor was her ex-mother-in-law's Cadillac. She decided that was a stroke of luck.

Parking Ekta's truck near the door to get in and out quickly, she strapped J.J. back in his carrier and prayed he'd be quiet. Cheyenne was already alive with people that morning. The hotel lobby was busy. Now, she just needed to figure out which room was Brant's.

Approaching the front desk, she racked her brain.

"Can I help you, ma'am?"

"Uh...yes. Um, well, I need to know which room Brant Preston is in. I'm...meeting him here."

"Oh, my gosh, are you Summer Sanchez?"

Hopefulness welled in Summer's chest. "Yes, I am."

"My daughter is such a huge fan of yours. She was so upset you weren't riding anymore. We're saving up to buy her a horse. She's working out at the Colbert's stables, saving her money and practicing when she gets a chance. Would you mind if I got your autograph for her?"

So much for anonymity. "Oh, I'd be happy to. What's her name?" Trying to force a smile, Summer scribbled her name on a hotel notepad.

"I'm really not supposed to do this, but since we're friends... Just don't tell my manager." The woman began typing on her computer.

Slumping against the counter in relief, Summer glanced at the front doors to make sure Brant wasn't coming back. Hopefully, he'd landed himself in a pot of scalding water after the incident with Dallas Devil.

"There's a room registered to a Jean Preston. Is that the one you're looking for?"

"Yes, ma'am. That's his mama."

"They're in room 318."

"Thank you." Summer raced to the elevators. She hit the three and then realized that she had no real idea how to get in a room without a key card.

'This one's on me. Take care of him for me. Fly high, macaw. He needs you.' The words in a mischievous male voice echoed up from her soul, but she and J.J. were the only ones on the elevator. A gasp stole her breath. Chill bumps skittered across her entire body. Who was that?

"Bye-bye-bye," J.J. began waving to no one. "Bye-bye."

"Shh," Summer soothed. The elevator doors opened, and she stepped off. Scanning up and down the hallway, she followed the Rooms 315- 345 signs.

Keeping her head down, she scooted past Brant's room when a maid parked her cart beside room 316. Pretending her room was farther down the hall, Summer kept a close eye on the hotel maid. The woman had a universal keycard on a stretchy bracelet attached to her wrist. Her mind offered her no good way to get the bracelet from the woman, however.

Another mischievous chuckle in that same male tone shook through Summer. The woman pulled the bracelet off and set it on top of the cart after opening the room next door. Unable to believe her luck, Summer swooped in, grabbed the card, unlocked Brant's door and tossed the key back on the cart. Whoever was helping her was a really, really good friend.

Slipping into the room, she scowled at Brant's luggage. Everything about him made her want to vomit all over his clothes and then rub them in his bed, but there was no time.

She went through his toiletry bag and then all three of Jean's make-up bags, looking for a syringe case or bottle of meds from a vet's office. Nothing. The maid would be in his room next. She had to hurry.

Heading to Brant's suitcase, she cringed as she dug through his nasty-ass clothes. She patted the bottom of the cases, making certain there wasn't a hidden compartment or anything. Where would he keep the steroids? Surely not on his trailer. Bull loaders would be in and out of that, as would the PBR reps that checked the animals.

Her eyes landed on Jean's Louis Vuitton suitcases. Of course. He would let his mother take the fall for it. Carefully unzipping the first case, she dug through the designer jeans and western wear. Bitch had some of J.J.'s clothes in there. She forced herself not to take them. No one could know she'd been in there. Trying to be quick and thorough proved difficult, so Summer slowed her frantic search, but nothing appeared to be in Jean's duffle bag. Hoisting her suitcase onto the bed, she carefully unzipped the front pockets only to reveal a pair of gaudy-ass cowgirl boots. Moving onto the main compartment, she threw the top back and dug through clothes, J.J.'s blankets, and a pack of diapers. Grinding her teeth over the obvious attempt to make her buy J.J. things he needed using up what little money Brant gave her, she started to unzip the interior zipper pocket when something caught her eye.

"Bingo," she whispered as she lifted a manila folder out of the very bottom of the case. It would've been better if she could've found the actual bottles he was using, but this would have to do. Brant would have been methodic about the prescriptions and receipts. His father would've insisted. She sat on the bed and flipped open the folder.

Stumbling bleary-eyed onto the main drag through Cheyenne, Austin pulled his hat lower to cover his bloodshot eyes. He wasn't certain how'd he gotten there. He'd wandered around all night long, slept for a few minutes in somebody's pasture, then got up and started walking again. Max hadn't said another word to him, and he had to get it together. He had to get Summer back today before she demanded that he take her back to Cody for her truck.

Forcing himself to put one boot in front of the other, he slunk into Paramount Coffee. Having to clear his throat three times before he could make audible words, he refused the barista's concerned gaze. "Large black coffee."

"You okay there, cowboy?"

"Been better."

The woman offered him a smile and poured his coffee. "Would you look at that." She gestured out the large plate-glass windows that constructed the front of the coffee shop. "I thought those were wood-peckers at first, but they're macaws. Must've escaped from somewhere. Look at 'em go."

Austin blinked rapidly, trying to bring the red-plumed birds into focus. "I'm a bit of a bird watcher. Have dozens of feeders all over my yard," the woman explained.

All right, Max, what the hell is that supposed to mean?

Silence. Max's voice seemed to no longer be housed in his soul.

Means two birds escaped from a pet store west of here. Get it together, you moron, he ordered himself.

"Thanks," he lifted the coffee in appreciation and left the shop. His eyes landed on the PBR tent at the Frontier Days Western entrance. Without any real thought, he headed that way, downing the coffee as he went. His gut offered him nothing. He couldn't get a feel for his upcoming ride, if he even chose to attend. Nothingness closed in on all sides, consuming him.

He'd downed enough of the coffee by the time he reached the tent to at least make out faces. Travis Anders was in line awaiting his day sheet. Two PBR reps were speaking in heated whispers just outside the tent. Austin didn't have the wherewithal to make out their discussion.

Colton Jones approached. "Hey, man, you okay? I heard what happened yesterday. That's crazy. How the hell did that bull get in there?"

Austin couldn't answer. His eyes zeroed in on Travis Anders's hands. *There were prod marks all over that damned bull's hide.* "It was you," he choked. Grabbing Anders by the collar, he jerked him away from the woman handing him his paperwork and shoved him hard on the ground. "It was you! You motherfucking asshole, do you realize what you've done?"

"Mr. Camden, calm down," the attendant reprimanded.

Incensed rage burned through Austin's veins. He jerked Anders's right hand upwards. "Those are prod marks from the hotshot he used on Dallas Devil. It was you. I knew it wasn't Preston. He'd never endanger his daddy's prized possession like that. How'd you do it? How'd you get him out there?"

Anders jerked his hand away, but the reps from the PBR that had been outside the tent were on him in an instant.

"Got in a hurry trying to get out of practice and get the bull down the chute before someone saw you, grabbed the wrong end of the prod. I'm gonna kill you!" Austin roared.

"What the hell?" Luke raced into the tent. "Where have you been? I've been looking everywhere for you."

"It was him. I told you it wasn't Brant."

"Mr. Anders, we have a few questions." One of the reps hoisted Anders to his feet before Austin could pound his revenge into his skull.

"I've got to get to Summer. It wasn't Brant." Half-crazed, Austin sprinted out of the tent with Luke hot on his trail. "I need my truck."

"Fine, but let's take mine for now." Luke gestured to his.

CHAPTER TWENTY

Summer's hands shook as she stared down at the documents. She willed herself not to be sick. Her heart struggled to beat. She cradled J.J. to her and tried to figure out what to do next. *'I will do anything, Summer. Hell, I'll run away with you and never look back. We'll never see Brant again. Just please.'* Standing and working on instinct alone, she took the forged copies of her son's birth certificate and social security card, closed up the folder, returned it to the suitcase, and left everything just the way she'd found it. She may not be worth saving, but J.J. was. Slipping from the hotel room, she debated going straight to the police station. *"Remember, Sapana, you are made of things the world can never take from you. Even when all seems lost, the macaw and the hawk will fly together. It is time."*

"Tin," J.J. whispered as the elevator doors closed, seeming to understand that something was very wrong.

"That's right." Summer convulsed as she folded the only proof she had and kept the papers fisted tightly in her hand. "We're going to find him, and tell him that we need him, and that I never should have run away like that. And that I love him so much. And I can't do this without him. We're going to keep you safe. I promise, J. I promise."

Flooring Ekta's truck, she tried to see through the hot tears pouring from her eyes. She made it to the ranch cabins just as Austin leapt from Luke's truck.

"It wasn't Brant," he bellowed as she flung herself out of the truck and flew into his arms. He wrapped her up so tightly she almost believed that together they could save her little boy.

"He's going to take him. He's going to kidnap him. I found the this." She thrust the paperwork into Luke's hands.

"What?" Austin released her just long enough to cradle her face, wipe away the steady stream of tears, and brush a tender kiss on her lips. "Please say you're here because you need me as badly as I need you."

"I do, but Austin, listen to me," she pled. "He forged a birth certificate saying I'm not J.J.'s mama."

"Where's the real birth certificate?" Luke asked.

"I have it," Summer clung to Austin. He hadn't let her out of his arms yet, and that was perfectly fine by her.

"Is the birthdate the same?" Luke quizzed.

"Yes, everything is exactly the same except my name isn't on it."

"This one isn't signed. No one's name is on it." Austin swallowed harshly as he studied the documents. "Why wouldn't Brant go ahead and sign it? There's not mother's or father's signature."

"Well, he's the kidnapper. Guess he figures he can sign it anytime." Luke continued to pace. The way he constantly watched out the front of the ranch cabin made Summer shiver.

"There were passports, too, but they weren't forged. I think they were gonna take him out of the country and then bring him back in a few years. They have family in Ireland."

"You left the passports there?" Austin's voice was rough and rigid, but it was the only thing that soothed her at all.

"Yes, I left everything I could. I thought maybe they wouldn't notice the paperwork was gone for a few days. Give us a head start; that is, if you still want to run away with me. I have to get J.J. away from him, Austin, and I can't ever come back."

"I would run away with you in a split second, baby, but we're not running from this. We've got him right where we want him. Hard to maintain custody if you're in prison. We're loading up my truck and heading to Pleasant Glen. We'll talk to the sheriff there and then to the federal agents if we have to. Kidnapping isn't exactly something his daddy can buy his way out of. He's gone way too far this time, and you just found plenty of rope to hang his sorry ass with."

"This is why he sent Dallas Devil out in that arena yesterday. He didn't want me to have any help when he took off with J.J." She shuddered against him, and he tightened his hold on her.

"He didn't put that bull in the chute, sugar. He had no idea you were going to find this paperwork. It was Travis Anders. I was trying to tell you. I knew it wasn't Brant. He's not going to risk more trouble with the PBR, especially with this. He wouldn't want anyone paying too much attention to him. I'll bet he was gonna sell off Dallas at the end of Cheyenne, make a shit ton on the prize bull, and run."

"So, Anders was what, trying to get you killed?"

"Trying to keep me from competing at the very least."

"If Anders just wanted you out of the competition, why did he keep going through your bags? I mean, that was him too, right?" Summer asked.

"No." Realization of everything that stood to do them harm settled harshly in Austin's gut. His heart had finally located a steady cadence as soon as she'd raced into his arms, but now he had to protect her with his very life if that was necessary. "Holy hell that *was* Brant. He was after my phone. I've got a recording of him saying that we get J.J. until the end of Cheyenne. I'll bet that's what they were after. You were supposed to give him back tomorrow per the custody agreement. I got him to give you a few more days."

"It wasn't Brant." Summer buried her face in his neck again. "It was either Jean or one of the stupid lackeys that work for his dad. Brant never left Dallas Devil at the qualifications, remember? I told you they were evil. We need to get away from here, right now." She climbed out of his lap and that sense of panic that had been his constant companion returned immediately.

"Give me your phone, darlin'. I get to call you that again, right?" He still couldn't find steady ground. Everything had happened too quickly.

Her broken smile was far worse than her tears. "I'm so sorry, Austin. I was just so certain I was ruining your life, and now I really am."

"You haven't ruined anything. I will fight day in and day out for you, and together, we will fight for J.J. No matter what it takes, we fly together. You promise me you'll never run away again."

"I swear, Austin. If we can really get Brant put in jail, and I know J.J.'s safe, I'll marry you whenever you want. I just can't do this alone."

"You never have to be alone. Now, let's get back to the Glen where everyone knows me and my family, and everyone will help me keep you safe. We're out here in Brant's territory, and we're just asking for trouble. Give me your phone."

Summer handed over her cell phone. "What are you doing?"

"You need anything off of here? Numbers, email addresses, anything?"

"No, I know Ekta's number, and my mom's, and my grandmother's by heart. I don't even have email, and I never call anyone else. Hey, we could go to my grandmother's. The Zunis will keep us safe."

"And that's the very first place he'll look. Everyone on the circuit thinks I'm from Oklahoma where Minton's home offices are. By the time they've figured out where the ranch is, Brant will be rotting under the jail."

He dropped Summer's phone on the laminate floor and stomped it with the heel of his boot until it was in a million unrecognizable pieces.

"Why did you do that?" she gasped.

"Because he pays the bill on that thing, meaning he can easily have the location pinged. I'll buy you a new one once we're out of Cheyenne."

"What about yours?" Luke inquired.

"He's got my number since I made him leave that message, but he'd have a harder time getting someone to trace it since he doesn't pay the bill on it. I need to get in touch with Mom and Dad so they know what's going on. I have to talk to Minton. I sure as hell won't be riding anymore."

"Okay, just hear me out," Luke edged closer. "I've been thinking. I should stay here. I can keep an eye on everything and keep up with Brant. I'll stay outta sight, but I can give you the head's up when he figures out what she found. Switch phones with me. If they ping your number and find me, who cares? Brant doesn't have any idea who I am and would never suspect that I have your phone, so the message will be safer with me. You get them home and hidden. I won't leave Cheyenne until Brant does."

"You would really do that for me?" Summer sounded astonished.

"That's what family does." Luke shrugged.

"Thank you." Austin's emotions kept strangling not only his voice but his thoughts. Not sleeping all night wasn't helping. "Okay, we need to think. Assuming it'll be a few days before they realize them papers are gone, how do we get out of here without my absence being noticed by too many people?"

"Austin, what about your contract with Minton? I don't want you to give everything up for me. I just don't know what else to do."

"Come here to me." He had to put a stop to all of this back and forth. Embracing her in the strength of his arms, he kissed the top of her head. "Last night was by far the worst night of my entire life, and that includes the night of the wreck. Bull riding's all or nothing, honey. The moment you get to thinking you'd rather do something else, you should. I've been thinking that all season right up until the moment I met you. I told you I knew right then."

"Apparently, that's a Camden thing," Luke sighed.

Summer grinned against Austin's chest.

"It's a hell of a thing, I'll say that. Like being struck by lightning and never wanting it to end. I don't want to be a rodeo hero anymore. I want to be *your* hero," Austin pledged.

"You are my hero," she vowed adamantly.

"Then stop thinking that I'm giving up something. I'm keeping my girl and my little guy safe, giving them a home, and doing what I was put here to do—be a cattle rancher."

She squeezed him tighter. "Thank you. I don't know what I did right in my life. I swear I've screwed most everything up, but at some point I must've done something right. I met you at just the right moment. Like..."

"Fate," Austin supplied with a glance at the few loose strings of white clouds on the horizon over the Laramie Mountains. One of them looked decidedly like a wound lariat. *'Thanks, man.'*

"Yeah, I guess. I still feel like I fell into your life and turned everything upside down."

"I kind of think you fell into my arms and set everything to rights. Perspective, sugar. For now, let's go with mine and get the hell outta Dodge, so to speak."

"While you two were professing your fated love or whatever," Luke chided, "I've been working on a plan. Austin you should go out in town, act like an asshole. God knows you can when you ain't gettin' your way. If you find Brant or any of his wagon trail groupies, let on that Summer left you after what happened with Dallas Devil yesterday. Tell anyone who'll listen that you flew her back to Santa Fe. If you can put on like you're hung over or injured even better."

"Why injured?" Austin had followed right up until that point.

"Then no one will wonder why you don't show tonight to ride."

"I don't know. I think we should go on. I want to talk to the police as soon as possible. A few days from now, Brant can charge me with kidnapping instead of the other way around," Summer reminded them.

"No, he's right." The longer Austin stood there with Summer close enough for him to absorb her scent and her essence, the easier it became for him to think clearly. His mind reengaged as he began to understand that she was never leaving him again. "I've got some places in mind we can hide out if it came to that, but I'd much prefer we get to stay on the ranch. The longer we can keep Brant away, the better. Even if he realizes you found that proof, if he thinks you're in Santa Fe and heads that way, that's perfect."

Summer's nod was visibly forced. "I don't want you to go," escaped her mouth in a quiet confession, just before she sank her teeth into her bottom lip to make herself stop talking.

Austin closed his eyes, reveled in the fact that she needed him, and swayed her back and forth. "I'll be right back. I can make the whole damn town think I'm an asshole in record time, sugar. You know that. Stay here with Luke and get J.J. ready for the trip. I don't want to stop once we head out. If you can get him some food together that he can eat on the way, that'd be good."

"What if he already knows those papers are gone? What if he's already freaking out, and he comes after you or gets one of his daddy's goons to find you?"

"There's a pistol in my glove box. I'll be fine."

"He shoots better than Mama, and that's saying something," Luke tried to help.

"You got her?" Austin raised his eyebrows as he gestured to Summer.

"I'm gonna help her get everything ready and then we might go out and get lost 'til you're ready to go. Not a great idea for her to be seen here, since it's floating around that you two broke up, and there's four dozen other families staying in these cabins. I'll call Mom and Dad once we're out of here, bring her to meet you along 80 somewhere, then I'll double back."

Austin let the plan register in his mind. The contingencies were eating at them all. They needed to be in action. They could stand around debating the day away or they could get on with this. "I'm going into town to see how much trouble I can russ up. You help her get everything ready and get out of here. 'Bout thirty minutes due east on this side of the state line is a little one-horse town, Burns. Exit 386 I think. Get off there and cut back West. There's an old gas station there I had to fill up at once. Little dirt road runs behind the station. I'll meet you off of that road. Park as soon as you're outta sight of the station. No one'll see us loading up my truck."

"There any cell service out there?" Luke was already shoving some of J.J.'s toys into the diaper bag.

"Probably not. So don't vary from what I said. I don't want to waste all afternoon trying to find you."

Suddenly, J.J. crawled to Austin's boots and pulled up on his Wranglers. Grinning, Austin lifted him up. "I missed you, little man. I'll be back to get you and Mama in just a little while. You take care of her for me." He brushed a kiss on J.J.'s temple. He batted Austin's face away with a giggle.

"Tin."

"That's right. Aus-tin." Summer gazed at them sweetly.

"Tin," J.J. repeated.

Though it pained him to do so, he handed J.J. back to Summer and tried to think of the fastest way to get attention in a town full of cowboys. Wrapping his arms around both of them, he tried to let that feeling of having them in his embrace tide him over for the next hour or two. "I'll be back quick."

"Austin." He watched Summer's graceful neck contract with her swallow. "Please be careful. I'm so sorry I pushed you away. I love you, and I swear I'll make all of this up to you somehow."

"You loving me, marrying me, making a life with me once we take care of this is all the making up I need. 'Til I get you in bed tonight, anyway." He winked at her. There was his sunset glow in her cheeks again.

Luke rolled his eyes. "Get," he ordered.

Summer watched Austin's truck pull away and she sank down on the sofa, trying with all her might to make sense of what she'd found and how her entire world had been turned upside down in one week. Brant didn't even want J.J. Why was he doing with this?

"You okay?" Luke's impatience perforated his tone.

"I'm really already packed. I just need to change J.J.'s diaper and fix him some cups of milk and juice for the cooler. I just...need a second." She let her head fall into her hands, trying to summon courage from the mountains and prairies surrounding them.

"It's a lot to process. Take a few deep breaths. I know I don't know you that well, but Austin's my kid brother. I'd give him the shirt off my back if he needed it, and he'd do the same for me. I've always looked out for him. Took care of him. I swear I'll keep you and J.J. safe, too."

"I know you will. Thank you." *Because you're the buzzard.* She both hated that Luke ended up being a scavenger bird and that her story had aligned precisely with Sapana's, just like Ekta had said. She should have known.

"Uh, just out of curiosity, in case this goes way further south than I'm sure it ever would, you ever shot a pistol?" Luke quizzed as he dragged two of Austin's suitcases out into the sitting room.

The acid in Summer's otherwise empty stomach swirled to a maelstrom. "I'm not intending to be shooting anything, but yeah, I have a few times."

"You a decent shot?"

"I once shot a rattler slithering towards my horse, Vixen."

"How far away were you?"

"From where I'm sitting right now out to that first hay bale out there." She pointed to the hay, baled mostly for show in the Ranch Cabin pasture, a good 30 yards away. Luke looked impressed.

"How many times it take you to hit it?"

"I hit it on the first shot, but I fired twice 'cause it pissed me the hell off he was messing with my horse. Nobody messes with my horse, or my little boy, and lives to tell about it, or Austin either, for that matter."

"Understood, and you and my brother are either a match made in heaven or hell on wheels to anybody that crosses your path. Think I'm glad I'm on your side." He winked at her. It reminded her of the way Austin winked at her to remind her that he loved her and to reassure her that he would always be there for her, but didn't have anywhere near the same effect. He certainly hadn't meant for it to. The reassurance was there, but not the love.

"All right, let's get, darlin'. I don't like the idea of Brant or his mama causing trouble out here in front of all these people. You got everything you need?"

"Just give me one minute." Summer headed into the kitchen, filled all of J.J.'s juice cups and a couple of bottles just in case they needed him to be quiet at some point. Flinging Austin's toiletries from the bathroom into his case, she made quick work of the rest of her preparations and stayed inside the cabin per Luke's instructions while he discreetly loaded his truck.

"Ready?" Luke held the door open. With a quick prayer that Austin was safe and would meet them in Burns in just a little while, she rushed out the door.

CHAPTER TWENTY-ONE

Cursing the traffic and scanning the local hangouts up and down Frontier Park and what had effectively been dubbed Cowboy Triangle, Austin was debating how to proceed when he found what he was after.

He still couldn't believe everything that had happened in the last twenty-four hours. Damn day felt like it had deducted a decade from his life. His body still ached from the pain of being without her and stumbling around in the dark all night. The rigid chill that had set up in his bones had gone as soon as she'd raced into his arms, though, so in his book, life was looking up.

He just had to get Summer to the ranch, tuck her up nice and safe in his house, get those papers to Wes Wilheim, the sheriff in Pleasant Glen that had been friends with the Camdens for years, get Brant's sorry ass locked up in a federal prison for attempted kidnapping, and life would be beautiful. *That's a lot of ifs there, Camden.* It occurred to him just then how much his own consciousness sounded like Max. Refusing fear was something he was more than accustomed to. He refused to believe that all of it wouldn't work out. Brant's number was up. He'd messed with the wrong girl this time. He was going down, and if Austin got the chance, he intended to see all of the Preston Cattle corporation go with him.

"Bingo," he huffed. Three maroon F-250s with the Preston Cattle logo on the doors were in the parking lot of The Albany Bar. Studying the parking lot, making certain this was as safe as it could be, he barreled in and parked diagonally across two spaces with a tire over the curb. His brakes squealed on cue, and he tried to hide his grin and get into character. Swallowing down the bile brought on by forcing himself to remember what it'd felt like when Summer had left him, he stumbled out of his truck.

Pulling his hat low, he made a show of tripping through the front door and bumping into a waitress, making her spill a pitcher of water.

"Sorry, ma'am," he tried to steady her.

"Go home, cowboy. You're drunk," she spat angrily.

Shoulda been an actor. The restaurant wasn't full, but every patron noticed his entrance.

Three of Brant's lackeys were at the bar. They eyed him suspiciously and leaned in to inevitably discuss his appearance. As he was still wearing the grimy clothes he'd had on since yesterday, he'd definitely dressed the part.

Ignoring the Please Wait to be Seated sign, he flung himself onto a nearby stool.

A manager approached cautiously. "Can I help you?"

"Uh, yeah." Austin rubbed his head and squinted his eyes at the sunlight, though he'd never been more stone-cold sober. "What time is it?"

"11:30, Mr. Camden. Maybe you ought to get on back to your room and sleep it off."

Perfect. They knew who he was. "It Sunday yet?"

"It's Saturday. Maybe I ought to drive you back to your room. Where you staying?"

"Nah, I'm good. Friday, you say? Am I s'posed to ride tonight?"

Brant's boys snickered.

"It's Saturday, and yeah, there's a rodeo tonight. You're the main show. How 'bout a coffee?" The man, who was being rather kind, poured Austin a cup. "Bull's gonna kill you if you get on him drunk, man. Come on, sober up."

Shaking his head, Austin shoved the mug away, sloshing the coffee on the tile floor. "Give me one of them Suffering Bastards." He burped loudly. Three waitresses scowled. "Feels about right, just skip the lime juice and the ale, and keep 'em coming."

"That's just straight up bourbon, Camden. It's 11:30 in the morning. I ain't mixing you liquor. Drink the coffee or hit the road."

One of Brant's douche-nozzles was texting somebody fast and furious. Austin took a sip of the coffee to hide his grin.

"Heard our bull made you his bitch, Camden," another one jeered.

Cutting his eyes to the asshole in question, Austin huffed, "I can't believe her. You ever seen her ride? Damn," he sighed longingly, putting on one hell of a show.

"Who? Summer? Yeah, we seen her. Only a pussy needs a woman to save him. Loser."

"You say it was your bull?" he feigned confusion.

"Yeah, it was Dallas Devil. You're riding him tonight, soon as Brant gets him out of quarantine. Nice knowing you, Camden."

Quarantine. Well wasn't *that* interesting. "What's he quarantined for?"

The Preston Cattle boys could apparently clam up faster than a jack rabbit on speed. Debating how to proceed, he motioned to a nearby waitress who approached him warily.

"I got one hell of a headache, honey. Just give me a shot of something to take the edge off. Put it on their tab. Manager won't know."

"Our tab!" one of Brant's boys bellowed. "He ain't drinkin' on our tab. Mr. Preston'd shit a solid gold brick. Buy your own damn liquor, Camden."

"They owe me a drink. Drove my girl away." Austin shook his head in despair.

"Drove her away? He's off his tits. We didn't do nothing," the third huffed.

"You hush up. I heard you put that bull in that ring that tried to kill him." To Austin's shock the waitress came to his defense.

"We didn't do that. They caught one of the other riders this morning with hot shot marks on his hands. It was him. Now we're all in trouble for it, though."

"I didn't hear nothing about that," the woman spat. Austin kept his eyes on the marbled pattern of the bar, listening intently.

"What do we care what you heard, honey? Refill my drink and keep your mouth shut."

"You're about twenty pounds of bullshit in a ten-pound bag, Denton McCoy. If you can find it, you can ride your sad little whiskey-dick straight to hell," she came right back, and Austin laughed harder than he probably should have, but this was taking way too long. The trouble needed to speed it up, and whatever had happened between the waitress and McCoy was ripe with opportunity.

Heat flooded McCoy's cheeks. "What are you laughing about, Camden?" he bellowed.

Austin spun on the stool but before he could make a retort, "Thank God! There he is," rang through the restaurant.

Fuck it all to hell. Austin cringed as Scott, Jackson, Cam, and Clif surrounded him.

"Get him another coffee," Clif demanded of the hot-headed waitress.

"He ain't finished the one he has. Nursing a broken heart. Poor thing. These idiots goading him on." She threw another glare at McCoy. Scott sized up the situation.

"Why don't you three settle up and get. Heard the Devil might be out of competition tonight. Bet Brantley's some kinda pissed."

Austin bit his tongue to keep from asking how they'd heard that. Clif seated himself on the barstool beside him and put his arm on his shoulder. Clearly looking drunk wasn't something he struggled with. He wondered if that was a bad thing.

"Listen, let's get you back to your cabin. Get you to bed. You'll be all right. PBR's had Dallas Devil since he busted through that chute gate yesterday. Brant's raising hell about it since they caught Travis Anders with hotshot marks on his hands. Preston had Anders arrested, still claiming that he stole the trailer with Dallas inside. He's at the jailhouse, but they won't release the bull."

Still feigning confusion, Austin measured his words carefully. He didn't want to give anything away. "What's all that mean for tonight?"

"If they don't release him before noon, he won't be allowed in the rodeo tonight. You can skip if you want, or take a ride on an unranked bull," Clif explained.

A ride on an unranked bull meant Austin's score would automatically be lower since 50 of the possible 100 points were up to the bull. The rides from Cheyenne were all on top ranked bulls. This was supposed to be the best of the best.

"Maybe he oughta skip. Look at him. He looks like hell," Jackson fussed.

"Thanks," Austin muttered.

"Have you talked to Summer?" Scott looked bereaved to ask.

Here was his chance. Captain Whiskey Dick and all of his cohorts leaned closer. "Not since I took her to the airport." He hung his head.

"The airport?" Clif and Scott both cringed.

"Where'd she go?" Cam gasped.

"Back to Santa Fe. Said she never wanted to see me again. Said we were done for."

"I'm sorry, man. I've never seen anyone ride like she did yesterday. She's something else," Jackson vowed reverently. Irritation ticked in Austin's blood. Jackson sounded just a little too admiring for his liking.

"I'm sorry, Austin. Maybe it ain't over. She loves you. I could tell," Cam vowed.

Jesus, bless this cowboy. It was as if Cam had been given a script.

Scott tried to elbow Jackson discreetly. "Let's get you back and cleaned up. Little coffee and some protein and you'll be good as new. Take the ride on an easier bull, then at least you'll have a score for tonight."

If Dallas Devil was still quarantined and Austin skipped, it wouldn't land him with a score of zero. He would just have fewer scores to make his Cheyenne average.

"I ain't riding ever again. Cam's right. It ain't over. She loves me, and I have to get her back." That statement required very little play-acting on his part.

"Come on, Austin, you don't mean that," Clif pled.

"She's not worth you giving up when you're so close to the belt," Scott huffed. Austin's fists clenched of their own accord. He tried to remember to fight with his brains and not his brawn, but Scott would pay for that remark someday.

Shaking his head, Austin stood. "Shut the fuck up, Scott. I'm going to Santa Fe. I can't believe I let her leave without me. God, I'm such a dumbass." He turned toward the entrance.

"You can't leave," Clif demanded.

"Watch me. I gotta get her back. Nothing else matters." With that, Austin bowed out the front doors and headed to his truck.

Now, if only he could figure out what the hell Brant and his mama were up to currently, he'd be golden. Brant was more than likely up at the PBR office screaming about his bull. Austin couldn't exactly show up over there, and he had no idea where the she-bitch hung out.

Strolling through the hotel lobby would be far too obvious, but he'd bet a good ride she was lounging by the pool, as long as Brant hadn't figured out what Summer had stumbled upon trying to save Austin.

His heart swelled again. He didn't have time to go on a wild goose chase looking for Jean Preston anyway. He needed to get his ass on to Burns and get what was soon to be his little family on the way. Backing his truck out of the Albany Bar parking lot, he pulled out on Capitol and joined the throngs of cars trying to get through Cheyenne.

To his absolute shock, she-bitch herself waved him down, walking right out in front of his truck. Damn it all, if that wasn't a temptation straight out of hell. He methodically applied the brakes, though a decent portion of his brain longed to floor the truck.

Rolling down the window, his heart vibrated against his ribs. Why the hell was she looking for him? Whatever the reason, it couldn't be good.

"Mr. Camden, Mr. Camden." She waved a handkerchief like she was some kind of southern debutante in a hoop skirt made out of the draperies. She didn't look frantic, just more her typical puckered-at-both-ends-with-her-hair-on-fire appearance.

"Yeah?"

She stood on her tiptoes to see in the cab of his truck. "Where's Summer?" Austin searched her eyes, trying to figure out what exactly she knew.

"Not real sure, to tell you the truth."

"Well, when you see her again tell her that I've arranged for J.J. to have a proper Stetson fitting. They're making him one special, just from me and his granddaddy. Then I'm going to have his picture made tomorrow afternoon at 1:00...at a studio nearby." She stumbled over the lie, but never dropped his gaze. "I'll be picking him up this evening. It's Brantley's turn again."

Oh she *was* good. He had to give her that. He just bet she was having J.J.'s picture made, probably at a drugstore that made passport photos. "Doubt I'll be able to tell Summer anything or that you'll be able to get J.J. a hat made since she's long gone. Probably half way to Santa Fe by now." He wasn't quite the liar she was, but he made do.

"What?"

Well, at least he knew she hadn't figured out what was missing from her suitcase just yet.

"I took her to the airport 'bout an hour ago. Told me she never wanted to see me again."

"But...she can't...how dare she!"

Austin shrugged. "She might be on her way to her mama's or the reservation. I'm not sure. I gave her some money, and she knows she gets to keep J.J. until after Cheyenne." *Take that, bitch.* He watched fury sizzle in her eyes behind her ridiculous plum-tinted sunglasses she was wearing.

"Well...Brantley gets J.J. back...after Cheyenne, since that's what you tricked my son into saying on your phone."

Gall throbbed in Austin's entire being. He gripped the steering wheel tighter, longing to inform her that he knew she'd been after his phone since they'd gotten to Cheyenne, but he refused to break character. "I'm sure she'll be in Dallas by then. It's me she don't wanna see."

"She just better be."

"Where is he?" Summer turned in the passenger seat of Luke's truck, searching for Austin. With every passing moment, panic crawled over her skin and tightened its choke hold around her.

"Give him a few minutes. He ain't bad late yet."

"What if Jean or Brant already know, and they had Austin arrested or hurt him or something? The Prestons are bad people, Luke. I swear." She couldn't bring herself to say what truly terrified her. What if Brant Preston and all of those morons that work for Preston Cattle and lap up Brant Preston Sr.'s shit just because he signs their paychecks had Austin—or had already murdered him?

"Darlin', you don't have to tell me they're bad. It takes some pretty nasty blood to steal a kid away from his mama. That's low down. To me, even the good Lord himself can't be too forgiving of that, but I'm telling ya, Austin can handle himself. Give him time to get the job done right. He'll be on in a minute."

Handing J.J. a few more Cheerios, which he was happily devouring, she tried to think of anything but what might be happening to Austin all because of her. "Tell me about the ranch. Please. Just talk."

Luke appeared startled, but nodded. "Uh, well, Austin's land borders mine. We all work the cattle and the haying and everything together, but the ranch is divided out into two halves, then into six different parcels. My dad and my uncle were supposed to run the two halves and divide their halves amongst their kids, but my uncle's a sonuvabitch and he and his wife only had Brock. We used to work that half as well, but Brock married, got himself straightened out, and took over his half back in the winter time."

"Did that make anyone upset? I mean, didn't all of you lose money?" This was good. Now, she could think beyond the sickening chill that kept overtaking her body.

"Nah, we love Brock. We all came up working the whole ranch together. There's the Camden family accounts, which is where we put all the money we make off the cattle anyway. Each kid plus Mama and Daddy take out an allotment to live on after we sell, so it's not like Brock gets a ton more than we do. We all like it that way.

"Money makes people crazy, and Mama ain't having a bunch of squabbling kids. That ain't how we were raised. We do all have separate cattle brands just so we can keep up with them all. Mom and Daddy's cattle have the original Camden brand. Ours are mostly our initials with the arrow like the original.

"Austin usually bolsters the family accounts with what he wins on the circuit because we work his cattle for him while he's gone; course he's won ten times this year what he has any other. Not sure what he might want to do with all of that. Anyway, we divide out the earnings, leaving plenty in the family accounts for the next season, new equipment, stuff like that, and then we go on our way.

"Austin's house is closer to mine than any of the others. We got houses and outbuildings all over the ranch. He wanted one of the log cabins my great-great-uncle built back when his daddy ran the ranch. It's not fancy or anything. Mama and Daddy have the biggest house, since they had all of us youngins. But Austin's house is nice. He redid it with some of his winnings a few years ago. Stays nice and warm in the winter storms, positioned good on his land. He can see for damn near miles. On a real clear day when the wind ain't kicking up the dust, which ain't too often, we can see each other from our side porches. You gotta squint, though."

"I don't need a big fancy house. I've never even had a house that was my own in my whole life. I'd be happy living in a barn as long as I have Austin and J.J., and I know they're safe." Summer checked the side mirror again, willing Austin's Silverado to drive up.

Luke chuckled. "Doubt Austin'll let you live in one of the barns. I got the impression he kinda likes knowing you're warm, and safe, and fed."

"Well...uh..." she fumbled for another piece of information that might interest her enough to keep her relatively calm. "What kind of horses do you have?"

"Ranch horses are all quarters. Austin's main mount is a jet black gelding he named Lusty, 'bout seventeen hands high, mighty thing that really only listens to him. We leave him be while Austin's gone, but you watch when he gets you to the ranch tonight, Lusty'll be in the west stables, waitin' on him to come out. We can't get the blasted horse in the stables all summer long, mind you, but that horse would do anything for Austin."

Summer knew that feeling. She even grinned over the horse's name. "He named his horse Lusty. Sounds like Austin."

Luke laughed and nodded. "We run twelve horses between us. Couple of calicos, several copper colored ones. Holly used to ride competitively. She's good, not near as good as you, but decent. She's finishing up her masters next year, working towards her doctorate in psychology, so she sold off two of hers to help pay for State. She isn't running cattle for the time being, so we use her land for our herds, meaning we can all run larger herds. Without her land, we all make less money. See, it works out as long as you think like a family and not like a bunch of assholes." Glancing in the rearview mirror, he grinned. "There he is." Relief played heavily in Luke's tone. He could tell her not to worry all he wanted, but she knew better.

"Thank, God." She leapt from the truck and waited on Austin to pull beside Luke's truck on the dirt lane that ran behind Roscoe's Filling Station. Roscoe must've taken the day off because there was no one around. With magnetizing force, she raced into his arms, colliding with the wall of muscle that constructed his chest. She steadied in his strength, and he cradled her head on his shoulder.

"I've got you, sweetheart. Everything's gonna be just fine. Let's get home, okay?"

She managed a nod. "That sounds really nice. I don't think I've ever had a place I called home before." Her emotions lived far too close to the surface currently. The dull ache in her gut eased in his embrace, but tears continued to taunt her eyes. She refused them. She wouldn't be weak, not in front of him. Look at everything he was giving up for her. She would fight with him, right beside him, no matter what.

"You do now, sugar. Climb in. I'll get little man situated. I filled up in Cheyenne, giving credence to the tale I spun about following you to Santa Fe."

Staring at his truck, Summer's stomach roiled. This was it. They were running away. He may have been going home, but she was running from every mistake she'd ever made in her life, running from Brant and the Prestons, running from the life she'd been living for so long she'd forgotten what it might be like not to be a rodeo gypsy and actually have somewhere warm and safe to lay her head every night. *Home.* Yeah, it was gonna take some getting used to. Closing her eyes and touching the macaw pendant she'd tied around her neck when she'd left for Brant's hotel that morning, she promised herself that she would be the wife he always needed. He'd given her one week of a real life, real love; she'd more than happily give him a lifetime as long as he was hers.

CHAPTER TWENTY-TWO

Austin squeezed Summer tightly for one moment then released her. Wishing she could ask him to hold her longer, she reminded herself that they had to get on the road.

"Okay, Dallas Devil was quarantined by the PBR when Anders pushed him through that chute gate yesterday. I hung around until I found out for sure that he was being held past his qualifying time. Fate's being far too kind with us. Little nervous it's gonna run out at some point, but no one will expect me to ride tonight. I took a pass instead of playing at riding an unranked bull.

"Here are all of my passes to the rodeos, the midway, concerts, everything." Austin handed those to Luke. "No one's figured out Summer found them papers. Keep a close eye on Preston and his mama, though. She ain't hard to miss, since she dyes her hair old-lady-orange."

A slight giggle escaped her despite the situation. "She calls it Rose Autumn 47. Buys cases of it from the beauty supply store and makes one of their maids pull it through one of those cap things all the time. Makes her look even scarier than she does regularly."

"Right, like I said, day-fucking-glo orange. Their room's at the Cheyenne Suites."

"Yeah, I was thinking I'd see if I can't get myself a room there. Seems to me if anything's going down, that's where I'll see it."

"Agreed, and I'll pay you back."

Luke rolled his eyes. "I ain't worrying about it. Get her on home. I'll call you when I get situated and if I see anything."

"Thanks, man."

Summer grinned when Luke and Austin hugged. Not something you saw cowboys doing all that often. Longing took fierce hold of her. What would it be like to be a part of a real family? She still couldn't believe she might get the chance to find out, if this really all worked out. That seemed horrendously far-fetched, however. She just wasn't that lucky.

Austin carried J.J. in his car seat to his truck and buckled him in. Next came their bags, his stroller, and the booster seat for him to eat at that Ekta had insisted she pack that morning.

"Let's get." Austin climbed up in the seat. "I'd like to be home before dark if we can."

"Will we be able to talk to the sheriff tonight? I don't want to wait."

"I know, darlin'. I'm gonna do my damnedest, but it's all gonna work out. I swear."

"Is that an Austin Camden gut feeling or is that just wishful thinking?"

He debated far too long for her liking. "Gut feeling."

"You lying to me don't make me feel better."

"I'm not lying to you. We'll figure this out one way or another."

Summer didn't want to ask what "another" meant exactly.

Austin wished to hell he did have some kind of gut feeling about this. If it was going downhill, he'd change course and disappear with her for as long as it took to get her ex in prison. His gut offered him very little, so he barreled down I-80, praying that the ranch could be their safe haven for a while.

If it weren't for all the shit going on, he would have been thanking his lucky stars. He was going home with Summer by his side. He couldn't wait to get there, but willing the miles to go faster just wasn't working.

"I'll try not to have to pee too much." Summer cringed.

Chuckling at her and lacing their fingers together, he considered. "Truthfully, I would kind of like to not make appearances too many places, especially once we cross the state line. Seems like every ranch family in Nebraska knows my family. Just a precaution. If anything should come up, I'd rather fewer people know I'm heading home. But I swear, darlin', we're gonna show Wes the papers you have and they'll arrest Brant, and hopefully his good for nothin' mama. It'll all be over with tomorrow at the latest."

"I hope you're right. My life never quite works out that easy though."

"I'm gonna call Dad and tell him what's going on. That okay with you?"

"Of course. Please tell them how sorry I am about...everything."

Austin squeezed her hand and called his parents. He tried to quickly work through what had happened the day before, since they were there for most of it. Luke had already phoned so he was able skip the parts about Summer breaking in Brant's hotel room.

"I've already spoken with Wes, son. How far out are you?" Ev asked.

"Got another three hours, Dad. I'm not too interested in any cops knowing where we are until we've given the forgeries to Wes, so I'm keeping it to 70."

"I'll have Wes out here when you arrive. You're probably going to have to talk to someone at the NSBI, though. I don't think the Pleasant Glen sheriff's department is quite equipped to handle kidnapping. I knew them Prestons were sacks of horse manure, but even I'da never guessed they'd do this."

"I quit, dad. I'm not going back on the circuit. I'm coming home to stay." There, he'd said it. It hadn't even hurt. Peace settled in his mind. For one split second, everything felt right.

"I know, son. I'm so damn proud of you, Austin."

"I'm gonna go get your house ready for Summer and the baby, honey. I put an extra roast on this morning. Just had a feeling we might need more tonight. You'll be here for supper, right?" He could almost hear a smile in his mama's voice. Of course she'd known. She always seemed to. Austin couldn't help but smile. God, it was so good to be going home.

"Thanks, Mama. We'll be there for supper unless we come up on a storm."

"You be careful, and tell Summer we're so happy you two found each other. We'll get that sack of shit she married put directly in jail and then we'll get you all settled in. I'm just so thankful...you're both coming home." Austin's heart pricked over his mother's vow. Emotion now played heavily in her voice. He could count on one hand the number of times he'd seen his mama cry. The night Brock's mom and daddy had taken him from the ranch and moved him to North Carolina, the night Max was killed in the wreck, and the day she'd miscarried a baby, a couple of years after Holly was born.

"Me too, Mama. We'll see you in a little while." He ended the call from Luke's phone and pressed the pedal just a little harder.

―――――

Luke Camden

Luke glanced up again from the copy of *American Cowboy* he was pretending to thumb through. From his vantage point in a darkened corner of the Cheyenne Suites Hotel bar, he could see from the entrance doors all the way to the elevators. Knowing what room Brant was in had proven quite helpful. He'd made up some shit excuse about being in for a stock show and needing a room on the third floor for good luck. The woman looked at him like he was crazy as a loon, but gave him a recently-available room right next to Brant's.

Asshole himself had stormed in about an hour before, looking ready to strangle a puppy. He'd gone up to his room, and ten minutes later was back in the bar downing shots like he was getting paid. He was still on the barstool with one of his right-hand men, drowning his sorrow over Dallas Devil being out of the rodeo that night.

Luke's ears pricked when the man beside Brant glanced around nervously. "Well, what are they *doing* to him exactly?"

"Checking those damn hotshot marks is all they'll tell me," Brant growled. Didn't seem like Brant was worried about anything but the bull. Figuring that he probably didn't go through his mother's luggage too often, Luke assumed he didn't yet know what Summer had found.

His entire body tensed when what had to have been Brant's mama, the frosted orange queen of Dallas, flew into the room, pouncing on Brant like a fly on the bar. She smacked the back of his head.

"What the fucking hell do you think you're doing?" Brant bellowed. "She. Took. Him!"

Luke sank lower in his chair.

"Who took what, Mrs. Preston?" The man that had been drinking with Brant seemed to have vastly more patience for Brant's mother than her own son did.

"Summer took J.J. She took him back to Santa Fe. That ridiculous hillbilly bull rider she's taken up with gave her money," she raged. "What are we going to do now?"

Feeling his pulse race and his jaw tighten, Luke leaned in just a little closer.

"Why the hell would I give a shit what Summer's done? Good riddance. I've got bigger things to worry over than where Summer is. I didn't give a shit when I *was* married to her—why would I now?"

Interesting. Very, very interesting. Luke didn't dare even flip the page on the magazine. He tried to blend in as best as he could with the wallpaper. He glanced at his watch. Nearing 4:30. Austin and Summer should've been almost through Ogallala. They'd be in the Glen within the hour and on the ranch around 6:15.

"Well..." His mother huffed and puffed, but couldn't seem to blow her son off of his bar stool. He genuinely didn't seem to give a shit. "This is all your fault. If you hadn't agreed to call his phone and leave that message, we'd have J.J. with us tomorrow."

Brant rolled his eyes so hard Luke almost laughed. "Why do you care? So, she took him to Santa Fe. Only thing that tells me is maybe she ruined Camden, and he'll be out of the competition. Beyond that, I don't give a gnat's ass."

Mrs. Preston's face turned the approximate color of her hair, rose autumn 47. She vibrated in her fury. Luke prayed she wouldn't put two and two together and go check that folder in her suitcase. When she unhinged her jaw, she fumed, "Why aren't you at the rodeo?"

"I ain't got a dog in the race, and currently, I ain't allowed down there. I told you this. What is wrong with you?"

"What do you mean you aren't allowed down there? Did you phone your father and tell him this?"

Brant shook his head. "I'll get it taken care of. They'll release Dallas Devil tomorrow, and we'll be back in the competition."

"I saw him break through that chute gate. He wasn't hurt. Why do they still have him?" she demanded.

For the first time in the entire exchange, Brant turned and stared his mother down. "What the hell do you mean you *saw* him? Why were you down at the practice arena?"

Excellent question, Preston. Luke was darn near proud of him. Maybe he wasn't quite as dumb as a sack of hammers.

"Well, I mean...I didn't see it... I *heard* Dallas Devil wasn't hurt."

"No one was hurt, but that don't mean the PBR ain't crawling all over my ass about it."

"I thought that other rider took him. Trey...whatever."

"Travis Anders. They let him go without charging him. Said the marks on his hand are circumstantial, whatever that means."

Luke rolled his eyes. Maybe the sack of hammers scenario wasn't too far off, after all.

"I'm going to go lay down. Have a whiskey sour sent to the room, Brantley. And come check on Mommy when you're finished with that drink. I'm feeling a little faint."

Fuck. Luke was out of luck when it came to conversations in their room. He'd have to do his best to keep an eye on 'em once Brant headed upstairs. To his shock, Brant watched his mother leave, downed his shot, and left the hotel, headed out into the streets of Cheyenne.

It was just after five when a broad grin spread across Austin's face as they finally passed Merle's, the local feed and seed, and crossed the railroad tracks into the tiny town that had raised him. He slowed on Main Street as they passed Saddlebacks, the only honkytonk around, the post office, the Cut 'n' Curl hair salon, and the Methodist Church. The library, the new coffee shop, and the CVS were on the other side.

Summer had been steadily gnawing her lip ever since they'd come out of Ogallala. "That sign back there said Pleasant Glen."

"Yeah, baby, this is it. Welcome home."

She attempted a smile but it came out much closer to a haunted frown. "You keep saying that. I've never even been here before, Austin. It's a lot of pressure."

Nodding, he debated what exactly to say to her. They'd shared so few words on the long trip he was worried she was regretting her decision. "Okay, I've told you I'm really no good at relationships. I half expected you to be pissed as hell at Brant and the whole situation and to kind of take it out on me. Then I felt stupid that I'd thought that because I realized that you're scared to death. I know. I should've figured that out sooner, but would you mind just talking to me, sugar? Screaming at me. Crying. Do something besides sitting there looking like you really wish you were anywhere else."

"I hate it when I cry. I'm not a baby." She crossed her arms over her chest and sank down in the seat.

"No, but tears are kind of a natural reaction when life gets shitty. I'd say finding out Brant is trying to steal J.J. is about as shitty as it's ever gonna get. Crying doesn't make you weak, Summer. Makes you human. I'll deny it to my grave, but trust me, when you left yesterday, that wasn't just Wyoming dust in my eyes."

"I'm so sorry. And why would I be mad at Brant and take it out on you?"

Unable to hide his smirk, he chuckled. "Not sure if anyone's ever pointed this out to you, darlin', but you got more than your fair share of temper, and you're stubborn as hell. Perfect woman for me, like I keep saying, but I ain't used to this quiet Summer. I'll get used to it. I know there's sides to you I haven't gotten to know yet, and I know I'll love them all or I'll learn to, but after last night," he shrugged, "this scares me a little."

"Thought you didn't do scared, cowboy." She leaned over in the seat and brushed a kiss on his cheek, righting every ache he'd endured and easing the worry that had set up shop in his gut.

"I didn't used to. Swore nothing would ever scare me again after that wreck. Being scared made me feel weak and that pissed me off. See, we have that in common, but yesterday when you ran in Ekta's cabin, I was terrified I'd never see you again, that I couldn't get you back. Think I'm still a little afraid this isn't actually happening. Maybe I'm dreaming or something, and I'm gonna wake up and you're not gonna be in my arms. I don't ever want to wake up like that again. So, yeah, I do scared when it comes to you and J.J. Losing either of you scares the shit out of me."

"I'm scared, too. I'm terrified that your family will hate me for bringing all of this on them. I'm scared you're gonna wake up with me in your arms in a few years and wish I were someone else. We haven't been doing this very long, and this is pretty rocky ground to be starting on. I'm scared I don't know how to be your wife. That I'll screw something up again. I'm terrified that I'm going to lose—" She shook and then finally gave in.

"Hey, okay, come here to me." He pulled off on the five-mile dirt road that would ultimately lead to the entrance of Camden Ranch.

"I'm so scared, Austin. What if Brant takes him from me? What if...?"

"I will not let Brant take J.J. from you. I won't. I promise you. And, baby, I kind of think marriage has to be a little like learning to ride a horse. So, we climbed on a green horse, fell in love, and got thrown a time or two. We'll probably get thrown some more. That's life. You climb on the beast and you ride. As long as we're learning together, we'll figure it out. Day in and day out, just like I told you. We decide to fight for each other and never against each other, and we'll figure the rest out."

Suddenly, J.J. tossed his juice cup against the back windshield of Austin's truck and started screaming.

Summer immediately jerked away from Austin and tried to settle him.

"He's sick of being in the truck. We never got him out. His diaper's probably soaked," Summer lamented.

"All right, let's get him home, then. We're almost there, buddy." Austin cranked the truck again and continued down the dirt lane. The volume of J.J.'s wails increased with every passing moment. Summer tried the pacifier, a bottle of milk, and his stuffed animal horse. They all ended up smacking the rear windshield when J.J. hurled them away.

Austin would have found that mildly amusing had his nerves not already been fried. He'd promised the kid he was good at trials by fire. Seemed J.J. was putting him to the test. Austin's ears were ringing when he finally drove under the Camden Ranch entrance sign. He considered driving on to his parents' house, since it was closer, but he doubted anyone was there. They'd all be at Austin's getting ready for them, so they were in for another ten minutes of screaming.

He'd intended to point out some of the barns, stables, and outbuildings to Summer on their way across the ranch, but she wouldn't have been able to hear him. When he finally pulled in his open garage, they bolted out of the truck and tried to calm the baby.

His parents appeared immediately.

"What did they do to my boy?" Austin's father lifted J.J. from Summer's arms. They'd been wanting grandkids. Austin had never had any intention of being the one to provide them, but life had been throwing him curve balls endlessly as of late. He was learning to just go with it. He didn't even recognize the man he'd thought he was six months ago. The man he was currently felt far more real anyway.

J.J. abruptly stopped his protest and studied Ev. "That's it, big man. You needed to be let out to run, didn't cha? They kept you up in that truck for too long. Little guys need to be outside running just like big guys. I'll get on Austin about that." Everyone chuckled as Ev settled J.J. on his feet, let him grasp his fingers, and walk out of the garage to the endless expanse of grass surrounding Austin's log cabin.

J.J. seemed delighted with this arrangement and took off. Summer collapsed against Austin's chest, while Holly, Brock, Grant and Jessie beamed at them.

"Long trip. Hell, this might've been the longest day of my life," Austin tried to explain.

"Figured that." Grant offered Austin his hand and then pulled him in for a hug.

"Uh, Summer, baby, this is my big brother Grant. You already know everyone else, I think."

"It's nice to meet you. And I'm so sorry for everything I did...and said...and all of this." She pled to Austin's mother.

Jessie looked startled. "Well, darlin', you have absolutely nothing to be sorry for. Let's see here, you tried to keep my son safe. You worried over him at your own expense. We all get a little off track every now and again, but you didn't do anything wrong. We'll get this whole mess taken care of. You brought my baby boy home. I know you understand what that means to me. You certainly don't owe anyone an apology."

"Hope really wanted to be here. She's up at the library today. Should be home in a little while. Said she was going to bring home some legal books on the best way to handle, uh, custody issues." Brock grimaced.

"Hope is Pleasant Glen's one and only librarian. If you need a book, she's your girl," Austin explained to Summer.

"It's fine. Tell her thank you. You all didn't need to go to any trouble on my account." Summer looked uncomfortable with the attention.

"Natalie went to Lincoln last night. Spending the day with Gran and picking up supplies from Orscheln. She won't be back 'til tomorrow," Grant explained.

"My great-grandmother is in assisted living in Lincoln. Natalie is my other sister. You can meet her tomorrow." Austin played interpreter once again. "Is Wes on his way?" At the moment, he didn't particularly care where Hope or Natalie were. He knew Summer wouldn't relax until the police had those papers and assured her that they would take care of Brant.

"Said he'd be here after supper. Called someone this morning that he said could help," Jessie explained. "So, why don't you two get settled? Your daddy's heading back with little man now." She gestured out the garage door. Ev and J.J. appeared to be having a meaningful conversation as they slowly meandered back to the garage. "When you're unpacked, head up to the house and we'll eat. I put clean sheets on your bed and some groceries in your fridge. Cleaned everything up a little."

"Sounds good, Mama. Thank you."

Summer lifted J.J. up into her arms. His mood had turned for the better as soon as Ev had taken him out to toddle around the yard. Her little cowboy through and through. He needed wide open spaces and hated being cooped up, just like his mama.

"We'll be up there in a little while." Austin waved to his family as they headed back the direction of Ev and Jessie's house, Summer assumed. Trying to steady her racing heart, she followed Austin inside the expansive log cabin that apparently was going to be her home. She still couldn't wrap her head around it. How had this even happened to her? Two weeks ago she'd been sitting outside Brant's hotel room night after night, making sure J.J. was okay, and now...

Shaking her head in disbelief, they entered through a large mudroom. He had a simple washer and dryer in there, along with a wall of shelves. Most were empty, but a few contained old deer skin gloves, loose spurs, a spare bit, old work boots, a worn pair of chaps, and empty travel coffee mugs from Wrangler, Orscheln Farm Supply, State Farm, and Carhartt.

Suddenly, Austin halted and spun at the doorway between the laundry room and the kitchen. "This is a little weird, right?"

"Yeah, more than a little." She squeezed her eyes shut and tried to figure out what the hell she was even doing. She'd fallen in love with a rodeo cowboy without ever having been inside his house. This was insane.

"Okay, so we'll figure it as we go. Obviously, this is the laundry room. I keep supplies in here that I need before I get to the barns in the morning. But we can change it if you want."

"I don't want to change anything. Looks like it works great. I don't want to come in and mess up your house, Austin."

"Our house," he corrected.

"This must be how them mail-order brides felt."

Giving her that grin that always made her feel like things would be okay, he nodded. "My Great-great-great Granddaddy got himself a mail order bride back in the day. Obviously, I didn't know them, but Dad says they were deliriously happy and died in each other's arms when they were old. Had a great uncle that met and married my great aunt, basically so he could fuck her for two weeks before he got on a ship heading to the Sea of Japan, in WWII. Same deal. He came home. Moved her and their kid up here to the ranch. They actually got to know each other, and were married some sixty-odd years before he passed. There's a pew up at the church house dedicated to 'em. We can do this. Let's just take it one step at a time, okay?"

Nodding, Summer clung tightly to those stories. People used to do this all the time. She was absolutely irrevocably in love with the man showing her his house. That was all she needed.

There was a massive great room and a small kitchen, open to the living area. Sturdy beams that must've been over a hundred years old held up the roof. The walls were stacked stone in some places and roughhewn logs in others.

A stone fireplace took up most of one of the wall opposite the kitchen. Two bedrooms with a bathroom between were on the other side of the living room. They both grinned when they saw that one of the previously empty rooms now contained an old crib, small dresser, and a basketful of old baby toys.

"That was my dresser when I was a kid, and I'm guessing that was Holly's crib. I'm sure she scrubbed them toys. He can play."

J.J. was already wiggling out of Summer's arms. She set him on the carpet and they watched him crawl frantically to the basket of toys to dump it out.

"This was so sweet of them. I'll never be able to pay them back for helping me."

"Sugar, you don't have to pay them back. They already see you as family. Please stop thinking about life with a tally sheet. Okay?" He drew her into his embrace and let her feel his steadying strength.

He guided her into the substantial master bedroom. The king-sized bed had fresh sheets and quilts on it. A folded blanket lay on the end. Another stone fireplace constructed the wall across from the bed.

Summer ran her hand over the bedding, needing to feel something, anything, to prove she was really there. Two dozen rodeo buckles were framed and hung on the wall beside the master bath.

She stared out one of the windows to the beautiful ranch in the setting sunlight. If she'd allowed herself, she could've believed that nothing could touch her there, that she was finally safe here, miles from anyone or anything else, except Austin and his family, people she cared about and that cared about her.

Everything about the house reminded her of Austin. Constant, reliable, and steady. Safe and cozy with just an edge of raw, hardened cowboy that fought hard for the life he wanted.

Swallowing down another round of emotion, she felt the warmth of Austin's chest on her back as he secured his hands around her waist. "I've got you, sugar. I'm right here. We're gonna get everything figured out. This is where you belong."

"It's beautiful here. I've never really been anywhere I felt safe, but I think I might be able to feel that here...eventually."

"I'm not gonna stop until you know you're safe here. I won't rest until I've made you understand how badly I want you here with me."

Summer let his vow wash over her, a warm tiding of calm.

"Wanna see the best part?"

She grinned and felt a little piece of herself restore while she was in his arms. "I've already seen your best part, cowboy. Besides, I'm not sure I'm up to that right now."

Laughing, Austin squeezed her tighter. "There's my girl. I knew she was in there somewhere. Shoulda known my cock could bring you outta hiding. Don't worry, he's real, real fond of you, too." He stuck the tip of his tongue between his teeth, still chuckling, as she spun out of his arms.

"You can tell Austin Jr. I've had a hell of a day and that he's an arrogant *little* thing," she chastised. God it felt good to flirt and bicker with him again. She'd missed it more than she ever would have allowed herself to imagine.

"Ain't nothing about me that's *little*, and you know it. I am hornier than a three-balled tomcat, but we'll get to that later. I was talking about my favorite part of the house, sweetness."

She smirked at him, which expanded his grin, while he took her hand and guided her out onto an octagonal deck off of the master bedroom. Immediately understanding why this was his favorite part of the house, she sighed. The view from the back deck was truly beautiful.

"Sun comes up right over those fields every morning, and there's no better place on the entire ranch to see it."

Wrapping her arms around his neck, she nuzzled her face against his chest. "Thank you for everything. Thank you for falling in love with me and everything you've done for me."

"Uh, sugar, you're welcome, but let's not forget that you saved my ass from three bulls couple days ago, or was that yesterday? I swear, I can't figure out what day it is. You also broke into your ex's hotel room trying to keep me from getting killed on his bull. Anyway, we saved each other, Summer. Now, let's go get little man ready and head up to Mama and Daddy's. I'm half starved, and I want to talk to Wes before I bed you down tonight."

"I guess you really are my hawk." She still wished that wasn't the case.

"Then climb on and let's fly."

CHAPTER TWENTY-THREE

After a delicious dinner with more food than Summer had ever seen on one table, she laced her fingers in Austin's and watched two men in their early forties enter the Camdens' kitchen, one in a Pleasant Glen sheriff's uniform the other in a suit. Everything about the second man said federal agent.

The sheriff greeted Austin and the Camdens heartily. He offered Summer a kind smile. "Ev, Jessie, this is a good friend of mine, Alan Miller, with the NSBI. He's doing me a personal favor cutting through the red tape and taking this investigation on quickly. Attempted kidnapping wrapped up in forgery is a little outside of my typical wheelhouse," Sherriff Wilheim explained as they settled at the kitchen table. Holly and Grant were playing with J.J. in the living room.

"What's the NSBI?" Summer reviewed every word in her mind.

"We forget not everyone came up in Nebraska. It's the Nebraska State Bureau of Investigation, Ms. Sanchez." Detective Miller offered her his hand and a kind smile.

"Sorry, let me finish introductions. Alan, this is Austin and his parents Everett and Jessie. Camden family built and established the Glen. Salt of the earth, the lot of 'em. So, you understand why I went ahead and called you." Sheriff Wilheim smiled.

"I gotta be honest, when Wes and I were coming up together in Ogallala, we cut our teeth watching rodeos. PBR channel is the only thing ever on my television. When Wes called me up and told me Austin Camden and Summer Sanchez needed my help, I left Lincoln to get out here in a hurry. I'm a huge fan of you both," Detective Miller grinned.

Austin gave Summer an encouraging smile. If her barrel racing days could help save her son, that was just fine by her.

"If you can get this taken care of for us, I'll call in any favor I've got left after quitting and get you tickets to Vegas," Austin vowed.

"I'm much obliged, but I have a proposition for you. If I can get this taken care of for you, will you not quit? You got the skill, son. I more than admire what you're doing, and understand that she's worth walking away for. Hell, I left the Corps for my wife before I got that twenty-year retirement package they promise everyone. I loved being a Marine, but not near as much as I love her. Corps didn't matter anymore. It wasn't worth being away from her. I get it, but I hate to let some low-downs from her past keep you from your buckle."

Shock tensed the chiseled form of Austin's face. Confusion, intrigue, concern, a thousand emotions played in his coal black eyes. "Think I'd rather get this taken care of and see where we land before I make anybody any promises. She's all that matters."

"Understood. Like I just said, I spent 10 years in the Corps, so I'm not much on beating around the bush. Let's get this done. Wes says you have the forgeries on you?"

"Yes, sir." Summer pulled the forged birth certificates and Social Security card from her purse. "These are the fakes and here are the real ones." She handed him a folder she'd remembered to bring from Austin's house from the diaper bag.

A low whistle slid between the detective's teeth. "Changed his name and everything." He drew a deep breath. "All right, as much as I'd love to call up the Laramie County force and get to rightin' wrongs, I need a whole lot more information. First, tell me exactly where you found these."

Summer supplied every single detail she could possibly remember, including all of the bags she'd gone through first and how she'd broken into the hotel room. She only left out the part about the male voice she'd heard in her head, since she didn't want the cops to think she was insane and making everything up.

"Let's maybe not tell the breaking into the hotel room portion of the story to anyone else except maybe your lawyer," Detective Miller said.

"Do we need a lawyer? I mean it's pretty cut and dry," Austin huffed.

"I wish it were, but it really isn't. You're likely gonna need a lawyer," he sighed. "Ms. Sanchez, did you happen to take any photographs of the bags or passports or anything?"

"No. Once I found the folder, I just...I didn't know what to do. I put back everything I could, hoping my mother-in-law wouldn't notice anything was gone from her bag, and I got out of there."

"Never tell anyone I said this, but I half-wish you'd taken the passports. I'm glad you didn't, since that's a federal crime, but it is hard to get out of the country without 'em these days, in case you do have to give the little fellow back to his daddy."

"What?" The entire world around her stopped spinning with those words. The air in her lungs seized. "I'm never giving him back. Ever. You got that?"

Austin's arm settled on her shoulders keeping her seated. "Why in God's name would we turn J.J. over to someone obviously trying to kidnap him?" He gestured to the papers.

Detective Miller grimaced. "Because..." he glanced at the Sheriff. "Listen, I believe you, completely. If Wes vouches for you, you don't have to convince me, but to the courts all I have is a faked birth certificate and social in her possession. Her ex can easily explain this away and pin it on her. Say she was trying to frame him. It could get ugly."

"It will not get ugly because it will not be happening. You're the detective. You want me to compete? You figure this out," Austin demanded hotly.

"Son," Ev sighed. "I'm sure we can all figure this out. What needs to happen so that the actual criminals are the ones that end up behind bars, Detective?"

"Well, several things. I did a little research on the Prestons after

Wes phoned me this morning. They got a big time cattle operation down in Dallas. Not real likely they're gonna want to lose that. I can get the Texas Bureau to scare the shit outta all of them. Let on that we have more on them than we do. See where that gets us. Flip side of that is Brant Preston Sr. employs about a dozen lawyers. I got no use for a man like that. What's a cattle rancher need that many lawyers for if he ain't trying to get away with something? If his lawyers get in on this, they'll shut him up quick, and Ms. Sanchez could be looking at arrest."

Summer shuddered. She knew it wouldn't be as easy as Austin kept saying. She should have just run away. She was going to have to anyway. She couldn't have a family and a real life. She couldn't be a Camden, no matter how much she loved Austin. No ranch, no horses, no raising J.J. around good people that would love him. None of that would ever be in the cards for her. She should have known.

Austin strengthened his hold of her. "I will not let anyone take J.J. from us. I don't care what we have to do." His soothing tenor only made this worse.

"Don't panic, and don't run yet, Ms. Sanchez, there are other things we can do as well." This at least brought a ragged breath back to her lungs, though she didn't like the idea that a detective already knew she was planning to run away. "This is a decent forgery. Whoever had this done paid good money for it, meaning there's probably a well-known document forger behind it. Problem will be locating the forger and offering him a bargain if he'll supply information on who paid him. I'm gonna start in Dallas. I'm doubting she had this done while they were on the circuit."

"Why would a man who does something like this confess?" Ev leaned closer.

"In my experience, and I've worked more than a few kidnapping cases, forgers are actually easier to turn than just about any other crimi-nal. First of all, they inevitably have many, many clients. They don't need any one of them. They can always rely on the others, especially a one-time client. Brant Preston strikes me as the kind of man that prefers to win his battles with hot-tempered intimidation, not the cool burn of precaution. You seek a forger as a means of precaution in a scheme you've been working on for a while. I'm doubting whoever did this gets much business from the Prestons. This isn't going to be someone employed by Preston Cattle or any of their subsidiaries. In lieu of me arresting the forger and exposing all of his other clients, he'll very likely turn over the payment method used by the Prestons, which will be all the proof we'll need in court. It'll also get me access to their bank account records, which Mr. Preston will not want. That alone may be enough to get them to sign your son over to you, Ms. Sanchez. I just have to find the forger, and finding men that don't want to be found *is* my specialty."

"Well, what happens if you can't find the forger?" Summer demanded.

"There's more than one way to get to Rome, so to speak. Tell me when you're supposed to give your son back to the Prestons per the custody agreement."

"Well, at the end of Frontier Days. Technically that's only four days from now, depending on if you count the last rodeo as the end, or the day after."

"That does make things more difficult," Detective Miller sighed.

Summer squeezed her eyes shut, damming back the tears.

"I said difficult, not impossible. Give me tomorrow. I can call in a few favors in Cheyenne. Good buddy of mine is the sheriff and I have two good friends in the Wyoming Bureau. We all went through boot camp together. Might be that we can scare Brant Jr. into talking about his daddy. Like I said, he's got a whole lot to lose. We can float it to the wife that her husband could be indicted in all of this, and they could lose everything. In my experience the wife can probably get through to him quicker than the police can. If we make a showing in Cheyenne and get people talking about the Prestons, it might get us where we're going real quick-like."

"Wait..." Summer let that idea tumble around in her brain. She currently felt like she was drowning. Her head was weighted with guilt and terror. She couldn't catch her breath. "You think Brant's daddy is behind this?"

"Well, he holds the money. Everything, and I mean *everything* is in his name. I figured he at least paid for the forgeries, but tell me why you asked me that. I'm guessing you don't think it was his daddy?"

"That never even occurred to me. Brant's father has never even seen J.J. He doesn't care about him any more than he cares about Brant. I'd left Brant before I gave birth to J.J. Brant himself had only seen him a handful of times when I got that court summons when he was about four months old. My gut tells me it's Brant and his mama. I'll bet his dad doesn't even know about this. It's Jean that pushed the custody agreement through."

Austin cut his eyes to hers and smirked. "Thought you didn't believe in gut feelings," he whispered in her ear.

"Good. Okay, good. Keep talking. Tell me everything that happened with Brant Jr. from the moment you found out you were pregnant until right now," Detective Miller urged.

Swallowing down any kind of pride she might ever have had, Summer detailed how she'd ended up with Brant, his abusive behavior, the fact that none of the Prestons had even been at the hospital in Santa Fe when she'd given birth. How she'd gotten a job at Walgreens when she was five-months pregnant and had been saving up and had just gotten a tiny apartment near the Pueblo reservation when she'd gotten the court summons from Dallas. Then she told them how she'd been dragged around from one rodeo to another, rarely having enough money to get a hotel room when Brant had J.J. "Then I met Austin." She shrank in her chair, trying to blend into the oak spindles, and wishing she never had to look any of these people in the eye again. Her world wasn't one they were even aware existed.

Ev looked sickened. Jessie wiped away tears, got up from her chair, pulled Summer up into her arms, and hugged her tightly. "We are going to get this taken care of and keep you and J.J. safe. You just believe me when I say that, okay?"

Summer managed a nod, but she wasn't certain she *could* believe that.

"Sweetheart, I am so sorry. I promise you it's not just gonna be Austin fighting for you," Ev pledged. "We'll figure this out. You'd be surprised what a resourceful cowboy can do when he's pressed to, and any man that would hurt his wife ain't a cowboy."

"I know, sir."

Austin guided her into his lap this time, tucking her into his substantial embrace, not seeming to care who was in the room with them. "All right, I personally can tell you that Brant Jr. is nothing more than a bully. You call him on the carpet, make like you're not scared, he'll tuck his tail and run. Maybe I ought to go back to Cheyenne and confront him," Austin challenged.

"I don't recommend that, because bull riding doesn't come with a badge. If you think we can intimidate him into talking, I'll get some guys looking for the forger while we have us an old-timey showdown in Cheyenne. I can get uniforms to show up conveniently wherever he might be. Hell, I can arrest them both with the forgeries as evidence. I'm just not sure without the forger we're gonna get a conviction. If they make bail, which wouldn't tax them in any way at all, they can still enforce the custody decisions and that would make them all the more ready to up and run. Now, you mentioned that you weren't wanting Mrs. Preston to know you have the forgeries. If I see if I can't scare one of them into making a move, she's probably going to go through that folder to see what the cops are sniffing around for."

"We don't have any choice do we? We have to get something done now," Austin demanded.

"Be great if we could. Be a damn miracle if we can, but we won't know until we pull the trigger on something. Like I said, let me call in favors tomorrow, show up in Cheyenne on Monday. Meanwhile, I'll put Dallas PD on known forgers in the area. If we haven't gotten anything out of anyone by Tuesday, I'll think about arrest warrants, but I hate to jump to that so quickly."

"We need to know something before Tuesday." Austin's grip on Summer strengthened with his frustration. The desperate desire to run coursed through her veins. If his stable hold hadn't felt so damn good, so certain, she would've taken off and never looked back. She wouldn't have stopped running until she and J.J. were so far away from Brant he'd never find them.

"We will, Mr. Camden. I promise you. This isn't all or nothing. Cases like this take a little time and a little patience, but we'll see something as soon as we arrive in Cheyenne, Monday. Let me do my job, okay?"

Summer lifted her head to see Austin's single nod. The same determined nod to his own destiny he gave the chute gate opener just before he clenched his jaw and rode the hell out of a bull. He hadn't been thrown since they'd met. Maybe, just maybe, she *was* his lucky charm. Maybe together they could hang on for dear life and come out of this alive. Maybe.

"I have a few requests." Detective Miller edged closer.

"I'm listening." The fierce tension locked in the solidity of Austin's muscles both steadied Summer's racing heart and made her feel secure.

"Fewer people know where you are, the better off we all are. Looks like you got enough land to get good and lost *on* this ranch. If our goal is to keep Brant Jr. from getting J.J. back, let's not give him a roadmap to you, okay?"

Austin and Summer both nodded.

"Do not run...yet." Detective Miller sighed. "Look, if it were my kids, I'd be considering the same thing. I can't sit here and tell you I'd trust the system because I wouldn't, but give me a chance to do this the right way, please."

Austin's jaw tensed as he studied Miller. "Let's see what we find out Monday," was his only concession.

CHAPTER TWENTY-FOUR

"Talk, sugar. Say something," Austin begged her as they ambled slowly from his parents' house back to his. The warm summer night was almost perfect. She told herself to relax, but occasionally a cool breeze would whip through her hair and make her shiver. The cool air seemed determined to keep her on edge. She willed it away and went on with what she had to tell him.

"I don't know what to say. If we'd been together longer, it would be easier, but Austin, I'm not going to just hang around here waiting on Brant to show up and take him, or the police to come arrest me for not giving him back. You have an entire life here, and I know you're about to tell me that you'll run with me, but I don't want you to have to do that."

Halting abruptly, Austin kept tight hold of her hand. Begrudgingly, she turned to face him. J.J. had fallen asleep in the stroller Austin was pushing. "What's it gonna take, Summer? What's it going to fucking take to make you understand that I am in love with you? How long are we going to go on with this back and forth? I want to be with you. If we have to run, guess who's running right beside you? Hell, if we have to change our names and move to Canada, guess who'll be taking you shopping for snow pants? Come to think of it, you're gonna need those here for winter, but that's beside the point. You are amazing. You are worth saving and worth loving, and I, my God, I am so in love with you I can't see straight. I didn't even know I could love something as much as I love you. If you could just let me get that through your stubborn head, we could figure out where to go from here."

"But..." she tried, but he lifted his hand from the stroller, and cradled her face.

"Hush." He captured her dogged protests with his lips, melting a little more of her resolve. His tongue traced her bottom lip before he turned his head and breathed over the heated skin he'd just ignited. "You're all mine. Think I've proven I ain't going down without a fight. Close your eyes, sugar. Kiss me."

A breathy moan escaped her as he parted her lips with gentle pressure. "That's it," he spoke in broken intervals between the impassioned motions he used to take ownership of her mouth.

Tenderly, his callused hands slipped from her face. One traced the delicate hollow of her neck, the other teased the side of her left breast. Her breath tangled in her throat. The night before, she'd been certain she'd never have the pleasure of feeling his hands on her again, never be able to taste the hungry masculinity that resonated from his lips. Her entire body responded like he'd pulled her from the deluge and breathed life into her lungs. She drank in his tender care and the fortitude his love provided.

After several long breath-stealing moments, he pulled back and rested his forehead against hers, sporting that damned grin that got her every single time. "Gotta make one quick stop between here and home, but this isn't over. I'll make you forget you ever even heard Brant Preston's name."

"Please, Austin, please I just can't keep freaking out and thinking about what might happen. I just..." She couldn't seem to verbalize exactly what it was she craved.

"Need me to make the world go away for a little while." He knew what she required. He always did. "I'm gonna take such good care of my girl. I promise you. I'll fuck you so thoroughly, honey, all you're capable of is falling fast asleep safe in my arms. I'll take it all away."

She managed a nod as her body swayed anxiously.

"Come with me." He took her hand again and used his other to slowly guide the stroller toward his home. When he turned northbound in their eastern trek, her brow furrowed.

"Where are we going?"

"Somebody I want you to meet." A stable surrounded by a gated paddock came into view. A large jet-black horse was nickering and snorting as they approached. He kept his anxious black eyes locked on Austin and raced once around the large paddock.

"I'm guessing that's Lusty."

"Who told you about Lusty?"

"Luke told me. He's beautiful."

"He's one hell of a horse. If we hadn't come up here, he'd likely have shown up in the kitchen. Knows my truck. Whenever he sees it, he comes back to the paddock, otherwise, unless you're feeding him, he can't be bothered."

Lusty neighed loudly. "Hey there, boy. You miss me?" Austin patted the horse's side and let him nose at his chest before he pulled a pack of sunflower seeds he must've taken from his parents' house from his pocket and fed them to the horse.

When he was finished with his snack, he eyed Summer, swishing his tail.

"Sizing you up." Austin chuckled. "She's so damn pretty isn't she, boy?"

Summer rolled her eyes, but a grin spread across her face. Lusty gave her a grunt of what sounded like begrudged acceptance and lowered his head so she could pet his muzzle.

"Where's Whirlwind, boy?"

"I'm standing right here," Summer huffed.

Laughing at her outright, Austin brushed another kiss on her lips. "We have a calico named Whirlwind, sugar. Fate wasn't gonna leave us wondering about the two of us. When you told me Ekta called you Whirlwind and about Vixen, I almost fell outta my truck. Whirlwind's not an easy mount. She'll toss ya, if you don't know what you're doing, and she's got no time for going slow. She's Lusty's girl, though. They hang out together. Makes me regret making him a gelding." He gestured his head to Lusty.

Glancing skyward, even Summer had to admit that the fates seemed pretty damned determined. If they wanted her and Austin together so badly, they better step up their work on who got to keep J.J. Suddenly, she heard the thunder of hooves steadily coming from the back fields somewhere.

"There she is." Austin grinned when Lusty turned and neighed softly. A fiercely beautiful calico cantered into the open paddock and nudged Lusty almost flirtatiously. Summer's breath caught. Memories of flying on Vixen filled her head. Back when life wasn't so damned complicated.

Whirlwind let Austin and Summer pet her before she took off, and Lusty went after her, returning to the fields since it was plenty warm enough for them to sleep outside. They'd have to be brought in tomorrow morning for work, she assumed.

They walked on hand in hand, heading back to Austin's house. She couldn't call it her own, even in her mind. Not until she knew she'd be able to stay. He gently parked the stroller in the garage and eased J.J. up into his protective embrace. Her poor little guy was worn out.

"Does he need his bottle?" Austin whispered as they headed inside.

"He can go on to bed. He's exhausted, and it's late. He's never slept in a crib though. I'm not sure he'll like it." She debated asking if they could put the portable crib in the room with them, but the starry night tucked around them. No one knew where they were. Surrounded by miles of ranchland on all sides, no one could get to them. For the moment, she let the serenity console her tattered nerves.

Concern creased Austin's brow as he headed into the room Jessie had set up for J.J. and expertly laid him in the crib. Summer retrieved his blanket from the diaper bag and covered him in it. He never even stirred.

They'd barely made it two steps out of J.J.'s room when Austin swept her off of her feet and into his arms. "It's time to put my other sweet baby to bed."

She searched his darkened eyes and the firm set of his jaw expecting to see the intensity she'd come to know as her Austin. The beast seemed absent from him that night. She tried to prepare herself for the heat and the ferocity, but instead he settled her gently beside his bed while he turned on lamps, whose low light gently warmed the room.

"Look at me, Summer." His voice was a husky whisper, smooth as whiskey, and just as intoxicating. She lifted her eyes to his. "Be with me, baby. Be right here with me. All I want you to do is think about how good we feel together."

She shuddered and tried to kiss him frantically, wrapping her arms over his shoulders, scratching at his shirt. She tried to stir the beast into ravaging her up against the wall, on top of the window bench, or on the hardwood floors fast and furiously. Anywhere that would strip her of the insanity that had become her world. Why wouldn't he comply? Why wouldn't he just fuck her until she couldn't think anymore. "Please, Austin," she whimpered.

"Shh." He placed his index finger over her lips. "Nice and slow, sugar. We're doing this nice and slow tonight."

"But..." She lowered her eyes, unable to look at him and lie. Her stubbornness made a valiant effort to conceal her true desires. "I don't want slow. I want the beast."

"No, you don't. Not tonight. Some other night, when things are settled, we'll do whatever you want." He nuzzled his face between her shoulder and the heated skin of her neck, brushing a tender kiss on the thin sensitive skin. "Tonight we're going to make love, slow and thorough."

"But I need..." She panted for breath.

"I know what you need, Summer, and it ain't what you're asking for. You're mine, and I know precisely how my girl needs to be loved tonight." With that, he slowly worked his fingers through the buttons of her shirt while he kissed either side of her mouth and then centered his lips over hers in a seductive glide that melted like a sweetened confection against her tongue. Tenderness and vulnerability weren't things he showed anyone else. This was all for her.

When he'd loosed the final button, he broke the kiss and slipped behind her. His fingertips gently teased at the nape of her neck as he slowly lowered the sleeves of the shirt, letting every inch of her skin from her shoulders to her wrists feel his callused caress before the garment fell to a cloth puddle on the floor.

"I could, you know." His lips brushed the side of her neck. His whispered words teased her heated skin. He encountered one of the fading marks he'd left on her shoulder and spun his tongue there, kissing the love note he'd written so perfectly on her skin. "I could be inside of you in a minute flat. Could take you up against the wall, wrap your legs around my hips, bury myself inside of you until you're coming around me while I take you hard and fast."

"Yes," she groaned as her eyelids fluttered closed. She was lost in the thrumming notes of his rumbled tone. "I want..." she tried once more, already lost in his tender care.

"You'll want this more."

His lips kissed along the shoulder strap of her bra before he released her breasts from their lacey enclosure. They spilled forward into his capable hands, rough calluses against the heat of silky flesh. "So damn beautiful," he groaned.

When he'd dispensed with her bra, he traced his fingers down her spine, making her back arch and her entire body quake with need. His left hand feathered across her stomach while his right cupped her breasts, drawing her body to his. Using the arch of her back, she laid her head on his substantial shoulder and slid her ass against the fierce bulge she could feel behind the zipper of his worn Wranglers. His belt buckle abraded her lower back, cool friction against her fevered skin.

"Summer," slipped from his lips in a craving growl.

His hands skated down her abdomen until he'd popped the snap of her jeans. She stepped out of her boots as he worked the denim down her legs. Some part of her mind wanted to protest the fact that she was naked and he was fully clothed. She wanted to see his gorgeous body tensed and hardened as he stared at her, wanted to admire the lean musculature that constructed him so perfectly.

Austin's eyes zeroed in on the patch of wet heat gathered in the cotton crotch of her panties as they lay open in the jeans he'd just removed. He'd been so terrified he'd never have her like this again. Never have the ripened scent of her sex fill his lungs, the taste of her climaxes on his tongue. Never be able to caress her satin skin in his hands. Never be able to feel her delectable little body tensing and tugging at his fingers. Never have her under him, swollen and wet with a need only he could fulfill. If it took all night to get his fill of her, of this, to make up for the one day she hadn't belonged to him, so be it.

He cupped her mound, memorizing the feel of the damp curls covering what belonged only to him with one hand, and let his other map her right breast and feel her nipple pucker for his care as he swayed her body with his own. Unable to help himself, desperate to take her all in, he lifted her back into his arms and carried her to his bed.

Settling her in the white cotton sheets, he stepped back to admire the stunningly beautiful creature that had turned his entire world upside down. She stared up at him anxiously. Her quick breaths swayed her ample breasts in a mesmerizing dance all for his eyes.

"You are so gorgeous." He brought his lips to a fading hickey he'd left between her breasts. He kissed each purple marking, tenderly reminding her body of his ownership. "I was so scared I'd never get to see my marks on you again. So fucking terrified I'd lost you for good." He trailed his tongue to the next marking, tracing and tending while she writhed underneath him.

Moving on to the marks he'd left just over her bellybutton, he continued to the light stretch marks that ran low along her abdomen. "God, your body is so beautiful, honey. It's incredible." He kissed the thinned skin from her right side to her left, tending the marks on her hips as well. He allowed himself to imagine her body swollen full of his child. Her breasts ripe and her belly round with his seed, with what they made together. His mouth on her, loving her, worshipping her, caring for her endlessly.

Brushing a kiss on the wet curls covering her mound, he tempted her clit, circling his tongue at the top of her slit. She shook against him, keeping her legs tightly together. Terrorizing fear over losing her son, the frantic desperation they'd both felt when they were apart, the world around them that continued to try and destroy them left her raw. He'd never seen her react with such sensitivity. Every single side of her he was learning made him love her more. Her breath caught and she tensed.

A whimper hung on her lips. Her eyes sought his frantically. She didn't appear to understand why her own body seemed to be betraying her. She was his wild girl who liked it rough and dirty. Perfection, except that wasn't what she needed tonight. She'd clearly had sex more times than he cared to think about, but she'd never been worshipped. She'd never made love. Neither had he. This was an entirely different world he'd navigate for her and with her. She just had to let him be her guide.

"I'll be gentle, sugar. I know you're tender. I know you're scared. I'm right here. I would never let anything hurt you. Just spread your legs for me. Let me take it all away." He kept his voice calm and in control as he eased her legs apart. "Just like that."

Her thighs tensed in a protest that was nothing more than an act of confusion. "I've got you, honey." He ran his fingertips down the most sensitive parts of her inner thighs, feeling her quiver as she allowed him to explore. "So beautiful, so sweet." He let his index and middle fingers glide on either side of her slit. It wept for him. Pure silken heat seeped from her pussy.

A ragged moan rumbled from low in his gut. "Nice and easy. Relax for me," he breathed as he dipped his fingers inside of her, letting her body take him at her own pace. She shook from the pent up need as he lowered his head and tongued her clit at the same moment.

Summer's entire body honed in on how insanely good the heat of his mouth and his softly stroking fingers felt. Her hips rocked in desperate approval. Everything about this was unexpected and different. He'd never been so gentle with her.

She expected his command for her to be still, but everything about him that night was without demand. She'd been certain slow and easy wouldn't be as good as when he freed the beast all for her, but the love in his reverent care was otherworldly perfection. She'd had sex with him repeatedly. Each time had been better than the time before. He made other men she'd encountered seem like mere boys, but this, this wasn't something she'd ever have recognized before—feeling what it was like to be truly loved. This was more than sex, more than making love, this was being worshipped. Her mind ceased its badgering reminders that her entire world could be torn apart. When she was in the safety of his arms, she knew he would hold her together, never allowing her to be rent in two.

Her abdomen trembled. She rocked her hips against him in constant rhythm. His tongue softly coaxed her hood while his fingers stroked her G-spot without hurry. Finally, mercifully, he drew her clitoris into his mouth and sucked.

"Oh God," she groaned, tensing her thighs against his stubble.

"There it is." He blew cool air across her overly heated flesh, making her writhe as his fingers strummed faster. "It's so close, isn't it darlin'? So close I feel it coming. It's right there. Relax and give it to me, Summer." Her back arched off of the mattress. She shook. Her core flexed constantly. Her body drenched his fingers as she came hard and fast. "There's my baby." She quaked, and he gently eased his fingers away, seeming to know how sensitive she was that night. "Feels better now, doesn't it?" The orgasm continued to crash through her in constant waves that rolled with her body, leaving her unable to do anything but beg for more.

With the sheen of her release on his lips, he mapped his way up her body, kissing and licking his way to her breasts. He settled his hand on her trembling belly, loving her. "So soft, sugar. My God, you are just so perfect."

He whispered soft sweet kisses on the upper swells of her breasts. She arched her back, desperate for his mouth on her nipples, but he only chuckled. Dragging his lips and his tongue along the sides and working his way under her right to kiss and taunt between them.

"Austin, please," she groaned.

"You have the most beautiful tits, honey. Swollen so pretty for me. Let me enjoy them tonight." He circled her areolas, teasing each raised bump with his thumbs but avoiding where she most wanted his touch. He ignored her nipples' adamant requests, spinning his tongue between her breasts again instead.

Her body rolled against his. The soft cotton of his shirt, the thick metal of his belt buckle, and the rough denim of his jeans sent a frenzy of euphoria over her skin. Every nerve ending from the top of her head to the tips of her toes begged for more of him. She wanted him naked, wanted to melt into his heated flesh as he pierced through her, making her his own.

She begged, knowing he wouldn't give in until he was finished worshiping her breasts. Finally, he swept his tongue closer to her painfully turgid peaks, zeroing in on where she most wanted his mouth. Heated breath caressed her areola. He cupped the weight of her right breast, bringing it to his mouth as he began to suckle. A reverent moan hummed against her flesh. Tending her left with his hand, his fingers taunted her nipple, rolling and squeezing, slowly adding to the pressure until she was certain she would lose her mind.

Her head shook back and forth, she wrapped her legs around his denim covered thigh and gave herself over to the sensations. She was so close, on raw edge. She ground against him.

His mouth suctioned harder to her left breast. His fingers continued their torture on her right nipple. A moment later he nipped the nipple he'd primed with his mouth and gently pinched the one in his hand. She came in a quickened gasp of breath. Her fevered body shivered when he stood, removing his heat from her skin. She lifted her head and watched him shed his shirt. A moan escaped her when his belt loosened from his jeans. A half second later, he'd sheathed his cock with a condom from the bedside table drawer and hovered over her again.

"Please, I need you, Austin."

"I've got you, darlin'. Relax for me." Austin gripped his cock and dragged it through the slick heat coating her pussy. Bracing himself on the mattress over her, he pressed himself inside slowly, allowing only a scant inch of his cock to succumb to the awe-inspiring feeling of her body absorbing his own. "Look at me." He breathed his command over her lips.

Her eyes fluttered open. "More, please."

Allowing himself to gain another inch, he groaned from the torture of holding himself back. "You're all mine, forever, baby. Say it for me. Tell me who you belong to."

"Yours. Please, please, give me more." She writhed. "I'm all yours."

"That's right, honey. All mine." He gained another inch. His body begged to be taken to his entirety, but he denied himself the rapture he so craved. "No more running from me. Never again. If we run, we run together."

"Yes," she panted her vow. Her body writhed, drawing him farther in. Giving in, unable to resist, he thrust his hips, burying himself past his hilt before he withdrew and pressed in again. Their bodies aligned, chest to chest and groin to groin.

"I love you, Summer. I've imagined taking you like this since the first time we made love. Look at me."

"I love you, too," she cried out for him, locking her eyes on his as he held her, quivering, her body frantic for release. So many questions held in those beautiful whiskey eyes. He'd answer every one of them. There was no room for doubt between them. Tending and reassuring her became his only goal.

He pressed in and pulled away with constant steady pressure. The heat they created when they were one rose around them, bringing the perfume of her and of sex to his lungs. A fireworks display of lights popped across his line of vision. "Feel me. Feel me take all of you." His cock throbbed fiercely. He wasn't going to last much longer. "Feel how much I love you."

On his next greedy claim of her, she broke free, trembling around him. His name sang from her lips, shattering his resolve. "My God, you're so beautiful when you come for me." He lost it all on a breathless grunt. Cum shot in hot, heavy spurts, filling the condom, making him wish there was nothing between them. He longed to bathe her walls with everything he was. He gripped her body to his, refusing to let go until their climaxes freed them from the ecstasy of being together, a sensation he never wanted to end.

When the heavenly draws of her pussy on his cock waned and she'd drained him of every ounce of tension and fear he'd carried for the last forty-eight hours, he withdrew, dispensed with the condom, and eased beside her on the mattress, keeping her skin in constant contact with his own.

She turned and tunneled farther into his protective embrace. "I love you," she spoke into his chest. He reveled in the vow and the sensation.

"I love you too, sugar. So much."

"That was incredible. I've never felt anything like that, but I swear I think that every single time you take me to bed." It seemed he'd broken through some of her stubborn shielding. He'd take every confession she'd give up.

"We're incredible together, Summer. It wouldn't be like this with anyone else."

"I know." She nestled closer once again.

"Then promise me that you meant what you said. No running without me. You got that?"

"There's my beast." She eased back and gave him a heart-stopping grin.

"I'm tired, woman. Worn out after all we've been through and what we just shared, but I could come up with enough energy to wear your bottom out. Now promise me, Summer. No more thinking about taking J.J. and bolting because you think I shouldn't have to give up my life here."

She stared up at him. "Thank you for loving me enough to leave all of this. I have to believe that we won't have to run away or I'm going to make myself insane, but I promise, Austin. I couldn't make it without you anyway. I guess we really are meant to be together."

Allowing himself to draw a full breath, he finally relaxed. "Thank you, and just so you know, I do have a few places we can go if we need to buy Detective Miller more time. I will not let Brant find you or J.J."

"Thank you. I've been racking my brain trying to think of where to go that Brant wouldn't know about. Thing about marrying the asshole is he did play nice long enough to know where I was born and bred. Do you really think we'll have to run to Canada? I don't even have a passport."

"Nah, we can disappear most anywhere, sweetheart. I need to figure out a way to get a bunch of cash out of my accounts without my card alerting everyone to where we are. Might get Grant or Dad to make several withdrawals from the family accounts for the next few days. Not enough to tip anyone off, though."

"I never even thought of all of that. I suck at running away, apparently, which is crazy, because I swear, before I met you, running away is all I ever wanted to do."

Gently, Austin brushed his lips over hers. "I told you I've got you, and you know I take care of what's mine. Now, are you ready for bed, honey? I'm beat."

"Are you going out to work cattle with them tomorrow?" There was a worried edge to her tone. He cradled her closer and kissed the top of her head.

"I'm not leaving you or little man until Brant's in prison. Good thing you kind of like me, 'cause I'm going be all over you until we get this all taken care of."

"Never thought Brant would be good for anything. Guess I was wrong about that, too. I kind of like that you're not gonna leave me alone until the asshole is in prison."

Letting that tiding continue to content him, he chuckled. "Let's get some sleep."

"Would you mind if I took a shower? I feel kind of rough."

Austin considered. Every fiber of his being needed to care for her constantly, needed to prove that he'd never let her down. "How about I give you a bath?"

"I'm not a baby. You don't have to do that."

"You are my baby, and I want to do that. Plus, it's not all that selfless or anything. I'm getting in with you. Holding your wet, nekkid body up against mine." He gave her a low growl. "Nothing chivalrous about that. It's just a bonus it comes off that way."

Letting the melody of her laughter further soothe him, he headed into the bathroom to turn on the jetted Jacuzzi tub he'd added in when he'd redone the master bath a few years ago. He'd installed the large tub to ease the abuse bull riding rendered on his body, but nothing was going to feel as good as holding Summer in his arms while he washed away the world from her sweet little body.

Suddenly, she was behind him pressing her breasts to his back clinging to his waist as he stood from testing the water temperature. "I can't believe you take baths. I figured you were a macho cowboy, too cool to relax in a tub."

"You don't sound disappointed to find out I'm not." He spun and held her in his arms. "Any bull rider tells you he doesn't take a long soak after he gets his ass thrown six ways from Sunday is an outright liar. We'll play like nothing actually hurts us for the crowds, but trust me, any rider lucky enough to have a girl he calls his own likes it when she fusses over him after a ride."

"You wantin' me to fuss over you, cowboy?" The sparkle in her whiskey eyes said she'd always take care of him.

"Always, sugar, but tonight I'm fussing over you. Hop in. Water's just right." He took her hand and guided her into the half-full tub. "You want any of this shit?" He held up her toiletry bag.

Giggling, she nodded. "Yeah, just some soap and my shampoo." Austin dug around in the bag until he located the current bar of hotel soap she'd been using. Rolling his eyes, he tossed it in the trash. "No more hotel soap. I really hope I get a half-second with Brant Preston before they cart his ass off to jail for me to let him know exactly how I feel about the way you were living before we met. Here, I've got real soap." Digging in one of the drawers, he skipped over the Lava he normally used and located a bar of Dial. Grabbing her bottle of VO5, he headed toward the tub. "This the one that makes your hair smell like strawberries?"

She nodded and turned off the water so they wouldn't flood the bathroom when he climbed in.

"Good. I like that. You're allowed to keep using this." He set the soap and shampoo on the side of the tub and drew her back against his chest, allowing himself one long moment to revel in the feel of her slick skin against his and the way her ass cradled his cock to perfection.

"You think you can just up and tell me what kind of soap I can use, cowboy?" Her stubborn side stirred his blood. It always would.

"You like using that hotel shit?"

"No."

"So, you just wanna argue."

"Maybe."

Smirking, he proceeded to lather his hands with the Dial and work them over her shoulders until a slight moan escaped her. "Yep, I think

I can just up and tell you what kind of soap to use." His hands roved farther down her back, working out the knotted muscles and taming the tension there as well.

"This isn't fair," she whimpered. "God, that feels good."

Chuckling, he worked his hands back to her shoulders and then rubbed the soap over her breasts and belly. He cupped water in his hands and rinsed them thoroughly. She groaned as he submerged his hands to massage her ass and thighs.

"You can't...just tell me...what...to do..."

"Damn, sweetheart, you shoulda told me your hips were hurtin' like this. I would have given you a massage a few days ago."

She groaned as her head lolled on his chest. "I wasn't aware that was an option. Believe me, I'll tell you from now on."

"That mean you got the arguing out of your system, and you'll go to the store and get whatever soap you want instead of using the hotel crap?"

"But then you get your way."

"I told you I like gettin' my way, and I believe I've proven yet again that I'm damn good at it."

A half-hearted grunt was her only answer.

"Spin around for me and let me rub your feet and calves."

She eased away from him and turned to recline against the other side of the tub. "If you insist."

"See how good it works for you when you just comply?" Winking at her, he lathered his hands again and ran the strength of them up and down her calves, draining them of any tension as well. When he moved to her feet, he centered in on her arch with his thumbs. Her entire body was lax. Her eyes at half-mast.

When he brushed a kiss on the top of her right foot, her breaths sped. "Careful, cowboy, I might come again."

"Mmm, definitely have to remember this." He drew her two smallest toes into his mouth and sucked.

"Damn you." She shuddered. "Why do you have to be so good at everything?"

Another dark chuckle escaped his lips, but he was mesmerized by the sway of her tits when her back arched. *Not tonight, Camden. She ain't up for another round.* He made a valiant effort to quell his erection as he moved on to her other foot.

When she was thoroughly bathed, they stepped out and dried off. He took a moment to thank the good Lord up above for what he had in his arms, in his bed, in their home as she fell asleep curled up on his chest.

The parts of the night before he could recall played in his mind. He hadn't heard Max's voice all day. Hadn't had that same damn nightmare since the first time he'd taken her to bed, and somehow that night, finally knowing she was his for good, he couldn't seem to access the guilt that had been his constant companion for the last twelve years.

CHAPTER TWENTY-FIVE

Scooting upward in bed, panic seared through his veins. *Dammit, Summer. Where are you?* Bolting from the bed, he checked the bathroom and blinked twice before he could read the clock. 2:38 in the morning.

His heart thundered to a sprint as he raced into the kitchen. The house was dark and entirely too quiet. She wouldn't have stolen a truck. If she ran, it would have been on foot, and there were only two ways out of Pleasant Glen. He could catch her, somehow.

Heading to the bedroom-turned-nursery, his hand landed over his heart trying to slow its frantic beats. There she was. Wearing nothing but one of his T-shirts and the moonlight streaming from the windows, she stared down into J.J.'s crib, softly rubbing his back.

"He okay, sugar?" Austin kept his voice to a hoarse whisper.

She nodded. Her chin trembled, but she valiantly refused any further signs of emotion.

Joining her at the crib, he tucked her back against his chest and watched J.J. sleep soundly.

"I heard a noise. It scared me. I just wanted to check on him." Her voice was a half-haunted whisper.

"You'll get used to the noises here. Barn doors'll bang in the wind sometimes, and the horses and cattle stir occasionally. No one knows we're here. He's safe. I will never let anything hurt him."

"I know." The tremble of her voice shook his soul.

"Want me to bring him back to bed with us? You'll know he's safe, and you can get some sleep."

She shook her head. "No, he's sleeping so well. I just..."

"I know."

They stood there for several long minutes. He wouldn't rush her back to bed. She wouldn't have slept anyway. When she finally turned and paced back to their room, he debated sitting in the room with J.J. so she could sleep. He didn't want her to think he was worried too, though, so he followed after her and cradled her on his chest in his bed. "Go back to sleep, sweetheart. I will never let anything hurt either of you."

Summer was up at the crack of dawn, in the kitchen making coffee and breakfast. Since she hadn't really slept, Austin wasn't surprised. With J.J. in his lap, still groggy, they watched her whirl around the kitchen like someone was timing her.

"She used to do this at your old apartment, little man?" He yawned.

Summer laughed but never stopped. She filled the coffee mugs and scrambled eggs simultaneously. J.J. sighed and nuzzled his head on Austin's shoulder, babbling occasionally while still sucking his thumb.

"I told you I missed cooking, and I need something to do so I'll stop freaking out. Cooking makes me calm."

"Oh yeah, *calm* is precisely how I would've described you." He rolled his eyes.

After they ate, Austin got Summer to show him how to get J.J. in the baby carrier he could wear on his back and he dragged her to the stables. Admitting to himself that even *he* could not fuck her constantly for the next few days straight to keep her mind off Brant, Austin knew the next best thing to keep her occupied. Nothing made the world fly away like saddling up and going for an endless ride across the prairie.

Grant was on the Gator bringing in the horses for work. Lusty was leading the pack, anxious to get back to it now that Austin was home. Whirlwind was at his flank. When they headed into the paddock,

Austin indulged Lusty with several rubs and nuzzles. J.J. bounced in the carrier, excited to see the horses. Grinning, Austin was more than ready to train up a new little cowboy.

"Figured you wouldn't leave her long enough to work today. We got it. You can stay back," Grant offered kindly.

"I ain't riding this morning. She is."

"I am?" Summer looked astonished. She tried to hide her excitement.

"Yep, you are. You aren't gathering cattle, though. You're just gonna ride until life makes sense again."

"That may take all damn day," she sighed.

"So be it. I got little man. We'll figure out lunch. Maybe take a Gator tour of the ranch. I'll show him around his new home."

"Are you sure?" She was all but bouncing on her toes.

"Climb on in there and see if Whirlwind will let you saddle her."

"You promise you will not take him anywhere near your Mighty Bucky thing or have any discussions with him about becoming a bull rider."

Laughing at her outright, Grant and Austin shook their heads.

"I don't even know where his old Bucky is. Probably out in one of the barns. I'll keep an eye on 'em. If he tries to put the baby on one of the calves, I'll personally skin his hide," Grant vowed.

"And I'll help him," Brock chuckled as he joined them at the paddock, pulling on a pair of gloves.

"Thank you." Summer planted a kiss on Austin's lips and then one on J.J.'s cheek before she ducked under the low paddock fence.

Trying to remember that Whirlwind didn't know her, Summer ordered herself to calm. She hadn't ridden for fun in far too long. Austin knew her so well. He'd known this was the one and only thing she might could do outside of his bed that would make her forget all of the troubles looming on their horizon.

Keeping her head low, she extended her hand to Whirlwind who eyed her cautiously. She allowed herself to be sniffed and the horse eased closer. "Good girl." Summer gently stroked down the horse's neck then ran her index finger tenderly down the slight groove in her muzzle. She gave a soft neigh of appreciation as Summer's finger teased her nose. Moving on, Summer scratched under Whirlwind's chin, grinning when the horse leaned into her, desperate for more. "Gets itchy there doesn't it, girl?"

Austin, Brock, and Grant looked on. The grin on Austin's face spoke directly to Summer's heart. She swelled with pride. When Whirlwind closed her eyes, Summer understood immediately. Flattening her palms, she gently rubbed the horse's eyes, probably tired of the dusty wind constantly blowing in them.

Whirlwind gave another neigh and nuzzled Summer's neck.

"What's she doing?" Grant huffed.

"Teaching your ass how to get a horse to love you forever," Austin supplied with more than a note of pride in his voice.

Loving Whirlwind long enough to get her to trust her, Summer left her wanting just a little more so she'd come willingly the next time. Guiding the horse into the stable, she took the saddle Austin pointed to and saddled her expertly before she mounted her. Whirlwind seemed very pleased.

"Have fun, sweetheart. Several miles each direction you'll come up on a fenced tree line that separates our land from the other ranches. Cattle in several of the pastures, but the paths are clear. Stay on this ranch," Austin commanded.

"I will." Summer certainly didn't need that reminder. As much as she always loved riding, she still wasn't entirely sure of her surroundings. "Okay, if I want to ride *away* from Wyoming, which way do I go?"

Austin, Brock, and Grant all chuckled as they simultaneously pointed to the right.

"Got it." With that she leaned in, clicked her mouth, and they were off.

A minute later, her hair whipped out behind her as the ranch itself spread its arms before the horse and let them fly. Letting her eyes close in an extended blink, she felt her soul settle. Whirlwind's rhythmic gallops ate up the unending expanse, and she reveled in the sanctuary she'd been provided.

Her entire life raced through her mind timed to the thunder of hooves. All she'd been through. How she'd found herself here on a horse that spoke directly to her heart. *I was never going to fall in love with a rodeo cowboy.* She couldn't help but grin. There were a lot of things she never thought would happen, and yet they had. She was never going to have children, and now, she loved her little boy more than life itself and found herself wanting to have more with Austin. Her hawk. He'd rescued her from that damn swinging lariat. She'd never felt more secure. Now, they had to save J.J. Determination timed itself with every strike of Whirlwind's hooves. They would save him from Brant and create a life together. If this all worked out, she swore she'd live through every shitty moment of her past just to get herself here again. They could do this together. She refused to doubt that. This was going to work.

"She would whip your ass up one side and down another, and that's before Mama got a'holt of you." Grant laughed as Austin joked about getting on the old Bucky with J.J.

"Well, what she doesn't know wouldn't hurt me, but since I haven't actually gotten her down an aisle yet, maybe I'll save that for his second birthday." While Austin was in the process of switching J.J. from his back to his front to take him for a ride on the Gator, his cell rang. Forgetting for a moment that he'd switched phones with Luke, he wondered how on earth he was calling himself. Shaking his head and calling himself a dumbass, he answered. "Tell me something good."

"Wish I could. I don't know who's more insane, Preston or his mother, but I'm leaning towards his mom."

"The ass-wipe ran me off a horse. He's a kidnapping douche-nozzle. His mother is insane."

"Yeah, I hear ya. I followed him around Cheyenne last night. Mostly from one bar to another 'til he stumbled back to the hotel. His mother's wound tighter than a nun's nancy. She tried to have one of the waitresses fired from the hotel café because her eggs were overdone."

Austin chuckled. "Not surprised, but you don't think they know Summer found them papers yet do you?"

"Not that I can tell. Brant headed out about early. Went back to the PBR office. They released Dallas Devil back. He's set for the rodeo Wednesday night, but Brant still ain't happy."

"You're good at this."

"Well, if the whole cowboy slash playing vet around the Glen don't work out, maybe I'll become Walker, Texas Ranger."

"Figured that's where you got your skills." Austin laughed.

"Well, from there and that time when we were kids stuck at Grand-daddy's house during that blizzard and watched four seasons of *McCloud* 'cause that was all we could get through the antenna."

Smirking as he cranked the Gator, Austin asked, "You found you some pretty girl to be your counterpart for this particular episode?"

"Keeping up with the Preston psych-ward patients is taking up most of my time."

"Thanks for doing this. We talked to a Bureau detective last night. They're looking for the forger because the actual forgeries aren't enough to send Brant to jail."

"Why not?"

"Something about Brant being able to say Summer framed him or something. It was a bunch of bullshit. Anyway, they're looking for the guy that makes a living forging documents to prove her ex-husband is the low-life everyone knows he is. That makes sense, don't it? They're planning on having a police presence all around Brant and Jean tomor-row. I'm very interested to see how they react to that. You mind staying out there 'til then?"

"Nah, I'm good. Kind of looking forward to something going down. I'm tired of just spying on the two of 'em arguing."

"What are they arguing about?"

"Yesterday, she came storming in the bar up in arms over Summer being in Santa Fe." Luke gave nothing away. "He basically told her to fuck off. Acted like he didn't give a shit about Summer at all, which don't make sense to me, given that he was pissed enough to knock you off a horse over her."

"That was a pissing match. He doesn't want her, love her, or give a shit about her. He just don't want me to have her. He doesn't want her to be happy. That's about as far as his field of shit is plowed. Hence the one and only reason he's trying to take J.J. He just wants to make her miserable. Trust me, he doesn't even want his own kid."

"Nice guy."

Austin grunted his disdain.

"Oh, hang on a sec," Luke said.

Austin heard the phone crackle. A moment later, Luke's chuckle was audible. "They're towing his mama's Caddy. She parked it on the curb of the hotel right by the entrance. The detective have anything to do with getting it towed?"

"Nope, but karma *is* a bitch. High time she learned that."

"Let me go, Aus. She just came off the elevator, and she's about to blow."

———

By Sunday night, Summer was bordering on hysterical. Luke hadn't reported anything all that odd other than Brant had downed more liquor than was held in most distilleries in the last two days. Detective Miller was in Cheyenne preparing to let their presence be known the next morning.

The Preston Cattle crew had shown at the big stock show, but Brant hadn't attended. Since Summer insisted that Brant loved nothing more than showing off for people, she'd seen this as a bad sign. Austin tried to discreetly make plans for them to go somewhere else if nothing came out of the next day. Most every member of his family had gone to the bank for him and taken out cash from the family accounts. Twenty-thousand dollars was currently in his wallet, which would get them by for a while. He'd vowed to Summer repeatedly that the police would either have found the forger or gotten Brant to confess in a few weeks' time. She didn't seem any more certain of that than he really was.

Currently, Summer was in the bedroom repacking the bags Austin had just gotten her to unpack. Shaking his head, Austin captured her with his arms and held her to him. "Come on, darlin', you're spinning like a rope. You're a bundle of nerves with great tits. Deep breath for me."

She jerked out of his grasp. "Austin, this isn't going to work. I just know. Nothing except finding you has ever worked out for me. I *did* find you, so now all my good luck has run out. We're gonna have to run away."

"Can we please wait and see what happens tomorrow before we completely freak out?"

"No."

Before he could continue his futile argument, his cell rang. "It's Detective Miller."

Summer halted her frantic packing as he answered. Miller launched into the reason for his call immediately. "Dallas PD thinks they found the forger," Austin mouthed as he continued to listen.

Summer's eyes goggled before she squeezed them shut in what he assumed was a prayer.

"What happens next?" Austin demanded.

"They aren't going to bring him in yet. Two uniforms are going out to talk to him. He's been in trouble before and does a fair amount of work for the Dallas elite. Well known around the country clubs. I prefer to scare 'im and then leave 'im to think while we keep an eye on him. Nothing as cruel as your own guilty conscience."

Austin highly doubted that any asshole who'd willingly forge a kid's birth certificate had much of a conscience at all, but he didn't argue.

"If he turns on Brant Jr., that'll give me enough to get warrants for the Preston checking accounts, and we'll have him. I told you just to give me a little time. We got eyes on Brant right now. Bet my badge on the fact that he's both guilty and feels the pressure of it. Looks like hell. Paranoid and wiggling like a worm on a hot dock."

"My brother says he's been making friends with Jack, Jameson, and Jim Beam lately."

"Nothing new about that," Summer quipped under her breath.

"Yep, I'm sitting in the hotel bar. I'm assuming your brother looks just like you, only a little taller, with lighter eyes."

"Light brown Resistol cowboy hat?"

"Yup."

"Yeah, that's him."

"K, I got eyes on him and Preston. Your brother's not a half bad detective, but he's been sitting in here too long. Needs to leave and come back."

"He's afraid he'll miss something."

"Tell him I'm much obliged. I'll call tomorrow. We'll be in the hotel lobby asking about 'em when they come down tomorrow morning, and then at the PBR tent and anywhere else Jr. might like to go. Should be interesting."

"Yeah, well, we're losing our minds here, so updates would be good."

"Understood, but I ain't gonna risk a call to you if I'm on to something or I might out one of my men. I know you're worried, but try to relax. Let me do my job. I'll talk to you tomorrow."

"What did he say?" Summer demanded as soon as Austin ended the call.

"They're sending cops out to talk to the forger, and that Brant looks guilty as shit."

"He *is* guilty as shit. He's a motherfucking asshole. Too bad you can't be arrested for that. I'da had his ass in prison day after I married him."

"Nobody's doubtin' that he was one sperm that shoulda been swallowed, honey, but Miller sounds pretty confident about tomorrow, so please relax for me." Gently, he tugged a pair of J.J.'s pajamas out of her hands and set them in his suitcase. "Come on. Tell me your favorite movie. I'll download it."

"Is there a movie about a kidnapping, motherfucking, ex-husband that gets his ass blown up in his car and trampled by his own bull while the mother of his kid laughs hysterically? Because I want to watch that one."

"Might could find the car blowing up thing, but the bull is gonna be hard to come by. You're getting too specific." Austin removed the suitcase from the bed and climbed on. He beckoned her with his index finger, smirking when she rolled her eyes and begrudgingly crawled on beside him.

CHAPTER TWENTY-SIX

Up for chores even if he was in Cheyenne and not Pleasant Glen, Luke slowly sipped his second cup of coffee and kept an eye on the Cheyenne Sheriff's Deputies stalking the front entrance of the hotel. *Should be interesting.*

Stock contractors were supposed to be having a meeting at 9:00 that morning with the Frontier Days officials and a few of the sponsors about the final rodeo. Luke had learned this bit of information when Detective Miller had knocked on his hotel room door at midnight the evening before. He'd expected to be told to go home, but Miller told him everything they'd found out and how to improve his detective game. Apparently, they needed all the help they could get.

Despite the meeting being in an hour, neither Brant nor his mama had made an appearance at the hotel restaurant for the deeply discounted breakfast.

"Can I get you anything else, good lookin'?" The waitress that had been flirting with him all morning made another approach. Cute little brunette with a nice plump backside he wouldn't have minded running his hands all over. God, he loved a woman with real curves. The black waitress apron she was wearing, along with the bandana tied in her ponytail, left him with all kind of ideas he really had no business considering, given the gravity of what he was supposed to be doing. In her early to mid-twenties, she was a little young for him anyway, but he was flattered nonetheless.

"I'm fine, darlin'. Take another coffee when if you get a minute."

"You got it. You need some sugar?"

"For my coffee?" He gave her a half grin and lifted his left eyebrow in intrigue, watching her turn redder than strawberry wine.

"For wherever you want it," she came right back. His cock twitched its intrigue, but Brant chose that moment to slink off the elevators. Guy really was a rat-bastard.

Giving her a wink, he gestured to his half empty coffee cup. "How 'bout in my coffee...for now."

His breath caught, but she beamed at him and he relaxed. He would have hated himself if he'd hurt her feelings.

The deputies entered from the front doors just as Brant rounded the corner. Luke ran his thumb along the rim of the mug, trying to discreetly watch the interaction.

As soon as Brant spied the uniforms, he spun and headed out the back doors by the pool. Miller and Luke shared a quick glance. Miller grinned and gestured for his deputies to follow Brant.

The sheriff himself entered next. He gave Miller a quick nod, and took a seat near the doors.

Mrs. Preston barreled down a little after ten. Luke had gotten up and walked around Cheyenne at 9:15, keeping an eye out for Brant or the cops. His ass had been getting sore sitting in that hotel. He didn't know how Austin had done this for months at a time. He already missed the ranch. Taking a different table and pretending to read a book on the Cheyenne people that had lived in Wyoming prior to the Civil War, he watched Jean Preston march right up to the sheriff.

Biting his lips together to keep from guffawing, he leaned closer to hear.

"I sincerely hope that you're here to do something about the noise at night. That ridiculous midway is going constantly, concerts every night, and I can hear people talking and even singing of all things when they're coming in from the rodeos. I won't tolerate it. This is the nicest hotel in Cheyenne. There are those of us who shouldn't have to put up with such things, and I expect you to do something about it."

"The midway shuts down each night at twelve thirty, Miss...?" the Sheriff played his part well.

"Mrs. Brant Preston Sr., of the Dallas Prestons. I feel certain you've heard of my husband, and my son is the supplier of Dallas Devil, *the* highest ranked bull of the season."

"Oh, I've heard plenty about the bull. Just didn't know who *you* were. It's Frontier Days ma'am. Things are gonna get loud. People are having a good time. I'm Sheriff Dillon, *the* sheriff of Cheyenne. I was sent out here to talk with a Jean Preston, actually. I'm guessing you're Jean?"

This took her aback. Luke gripped his mug tighter.

"Why on earth would you want to talk with me?" Chancing a glance, Luke noted her usual sanctimony staging an uprising with all-out panic in her eyes.

"We have a few questions about your son, if you have a minute."

"Oh." She clutched her chest. "Brantley is a good boy. I do not know why the PBR is being so harsh with him. He supplied an outstanding bull, and now everyone's upset about it. I told him just last night if these cowboys were half the man he is, they'd stop all of their complaining and ride. That's what bull riders are supposed to do, after all. Good day, Sheriff. If *you* can't do something about the noise, I'll find someone who can." With that, she marched out of the hotel.

If he were a betting man, Luke would say there were at least four or five entire cornstalks, not just cobs, shoved up her self-righteous ass.

Miller and Sheriff Dillon sank down at Luke's table as soon as Jean disappeared.

"We can't find Brant. He took off." Miller sighed.

"Come again?" Luke huffed.

"We'll find him, but he didn't attend that stock contractor meeting. We're checking the bars he's been frequenting."

"Since they're both gone, can't we tap their room or whatever that's called?"

Miller and Dillon both chuckled.

"Well, that's illegal, and we'd both lose our jobs, but I like the way you think. We do have a few other ideas." Dillon sighed. "We show up enough places that they are today, and something'll come out of the chute, so to speak."

"Well, pardon me for pointing this out, but you can't even find Jr. Think I'll go see if I can't locate him. I promised my brother I'd keep up with him." With that, Luke joined the throngs of people out and about in Cheyenne.

On a gut feeling he rarely ignored, he located Preston just before noon at an A-frame biker bar in the industrial section of Cheyenne. He could see him at the bar through the plate-glass windows. His profile was outlined by the red glow of the Budweiser sign. Weren't too many cowboys bellying up, however. Brant was either up to something or had already done something and didn't want to be found. Luke's boots were gonna stand out in a crowd of black leather and chains, no doubt about it. Instead of entering, he parked his truck across the street, and called Miller. "He's at the Eagle's Nest."

"How the hell did he get all the way out there?"

"I'm guessing he didn't want to be found. Seeing as how he's trying to kidnap J.J., that makes sense to me."

"Yeah, yeah, I know. We're on our way."

By Monday evening, the cops had shown up at the bar, which Brant had slithered out of faster than shit off a shovel, and again at the hotel, then finally down at the PBR tent where he was getting his ass chewed for missing the meeting that morning.

They'd eaten lunch at the Chop House with Mrs. Preston and a few other women she'd apparently met poolside at the hotel a few days before. She eyed them cautiously, but continued on with her show for her counterparts. When they'd followed her out, she'd spun around in the parking lot and demanded to know why she was being followed.

After informing her that they still had a few questions about Brant, she'd made up a hair appointment and had raced away.

Brant had returned to his post at the hotel bar at five. Nothing too interesting seemed to be happening, so Luke ducked back into his room to phone Austin.

"Summer's about to lose her fucking mind. We haven't heard anything all damn day. What the hell?" Austin bellowed furiously.

"Miller didn't call you?"

"No one called. You ever tried to keep a mother whose ex is trying to kidnap her kid off a ledge? It's a bitch, let me tell you."

"I'm sorry. I was trying to play detective and make sure the actual detectives were following Brant. They lost him for a little while this morning. That's probably why they didn't call. I'm sure no one wanted to tell you that. Brant's ducked out on the cops several times now. They're being careful not to push too hard since Miller wants him scared."

"Yeah that seems to be his tactic with everything. I'd prefer him go in shooting and leave the scaring for later, but that's just me."

"I'm gonna take a quick shower. Got Cheyenne dust all over me from following him around town. He'll still be on that bar stool when I get back. Tell Summer I'm sorry no one let you know anything. You think she can hold on another day or two?"

"We don't have two days, and I don't know. She's ready to run right now."

"Sometimes it's better to know *where* you're running to before you take off," Luke commented while he braced the phone between his shoulder and cheek so he could rid himself of his jeans.

"I know where we're going, but I ain't telling anyone, not even her. Once we run, I don't want anyone getting grilled by the cops."

"Bet my *left boot* I know where you're going, but I'd take it to my grave. You know that."

"Yeah, I know." Austin's nervous chuckle said Luke's guess was correct.

"Try to get Summer to simmer down. Like I said, Brant's running and his mama's looking loonier than usual, which is saying something. Maybe tomorrow one of 'em will crack."

"God, I hope so."

An hour later, Luke begrudgingly returned to the hotel bar. *Fuck.* He ducked behind a column in the lobby. He was too late.

"Right now, Brantley! Right this very moment!" Mrs. Jean Preston,

Miss Rose Autumn 47 herself, was effectively losing her shit in the bar of the Cheyenne Suites Hotel, complete with stomping her feet.

Detective Miller pulled his hat lower and shot a quick glance at Luke.

"Fuck the hell off, Mother. I don't have time for this."

When her face reached the approximate shade of her hair, she started spluttering and shrieking for Brant to come to the room with her. Brant, Miller, Luke, and the entire lobby area of the hotel turned to stare in shock.

Clearly embarrassed, Brant escorted her to the elevators, looking thoroughly confused. Luke and Miller caught the next one up. The Prestons' door slammed just as they stepped into the hallway.

"What the hell is wrong with you?" Brant's deep bellow could be heard through the door, along with muffled crying. Luke gestured to his room, hoping they could hear more through the adjoining wall.

Miller followed him inside, keeping the door from slamming shut and alerting anyone to their presence. Luke pressed his ear to the wall, but couldn't make out anything but blubbering. Miller was frantically texting on his phone. Everything went silent. Time seemed to drag on endlessly. Able to hear nothing but his own heartbeats, Luke pressed his ear closer. *What the hell is going on next door?* Frustrated with the cat and mouse game, he had half a mind to march in over there and demand to know, but suddenly the wall right in front of his face bowed with an echoing boom. The wall studs reverberated the blow as if they were just as shocked over the impact as Luke.

Jerking his face away, Luke's eyes goggled. Miller's mouth hung open as they stared at the dent clearly created by Brant Preston's fist.

The next hour offered nothing but Miller pacing and occasional muted shouting from next door. Luke had no idea what to do. He ducked in the bathroom to give Austin an update. Miller quietly talked to Sheriff Dillon and the officers assigned to the case, but there was no sign either Brant or his mother left the room. Dillon had deputies downstairs in the lobby that confirmed neither had made an appearance.

"You've been following them all damn day telling them you wanted to talk to Brant. Go knock on the door and demand to talk to him now," Luke finally ordered.

"Patience, Mr. Camden. We have no idea if all of this even has anything to do with Ms. Sanchez. I'm not upping the ante until I know I have a winning hand. Not when it comes to kids. We can't afford one misstep."

Austin's gut was ravaged with nerves. Something was coming. He could feel it. He'd spent all damn day trying to get Summer to relax, but he couldn't fight it anymore. His gut had never failed him.

Luke's call had come ten seconds after he'd decided they were loading up, even if they weren't going anywhere yet.

He hurled another cooler full of food into one of the old ranch trucks. Summer frantically buckled J.J.'s car seat in the front. They nearly collided on their way back into the house.

She reached for him. "We won't have to run forever, right? I mean, once they have the forger or get Brant to confess, we can come back. Please just say we can come back."

Wrapping her up in his arms, he kissed the top of her head. "We'll be back, honey. I swear to you. We just need to give the cops a little more time."

"Why won't you tell me where we're going?"

"Because I don't want to tell Mama and Daddy. I don't even want to say it out loud, okay? Just trust me, please. I'll keep you safe."

"I know you will. I don't understand what's happening. Jean's always so worried about what everyone thinks of her and the Prestons. She'd never cause a scene that she didn't think made her look important. I can't believe she freaked out in a hotel lobby."

"Yeah, I got a feeling we need to get out of here soon. Something's not right."

Luke and Miller passed each other in their relentless pacing that wasn't accomplishing anything other than wearing out the hotel carpeting.

There'd been another argument between the Prestons, but they'd been unable to make out any distinctive words.

Miller's cell phone buzzed. He answered it immediately. Luke halted his trek to nowhere and listened.

"Cab just pulled up in front of the hotel." Miller explained quietly. Cabs weren't too common in Cheyenne, especially during Frontier Days. This sure as hell wasn't New York City. The cool slivered slip of a door closing from Brant's room ricocheted through Luke's head.

"Hey, someone just left their room. Presumably coming downstairs. Let's keep eyes on whoever it was. If they get in the cab, follow it. I need to know where they're going," Miller ordered.

Debating phoning Austin again, Luke decided a play-by-play probably wasn't necessary. It was highly likely that Brant was going on another bender and had decided to get a cab from the beginning this time.

With the minutes stalling his heart, he resumed his pacing. Miller's phone buzzed again two minutes later. "Dillon says it's Jean. She called the cab. They're following it. Okay, just give me a call when you can. Don't lose that cab."

Thirty minutes later Miller's phone buzzed yet again.

"Turn the thing on speaker so I can fucking hear," Luke commanded.

Miller complied. "You're on speaker. Go ahead, Dillon."

"This whole situation just shot way over my pay-grade," Dillon sighed.

"What happened?" Luke was rapidly approaching panic. His gut swirled ominously.

"Cab just pulled into Cheyenne Regional Airport. Apparently the Prestons have their own jets. Seems the Missus summoned one up from Dallas. We're trying to pull the flight plan now, but she's already boarded. I have no idea where she's going, but if it's to that tiny ranch town where you've got your rodeo heroes stashed, I'd tell them to get somewhere else quickly. That's a Cessna Citation. Wherever she wants to go, she can get there quickly. It's barely an hour flight time on a normal jet. He's got maybe a half hour to get as far away from that ranch as he can."

"But she may not be going to Nebraska. Austin floated it that Summer was in Santa Fe," Miller contended.

"Yeah, but she might be. Thought we were in this to keep that little boy safe? From what I've seen, his daddy is a drunk with a real bad temper, and his grandmother is crazier than a shithouse rat. If it was my kid, I'd get the hell out of anywhere anyone might think to look for me, at least until we figure out where the hell that plane is flying."

"You're right. I'll call Austin. Let me know as soon as you figure out where she's heading."

"I'll call, Austin," Luke corrected.

Austin answered the phone before it finished its first ring. "What's wrong?"

"Listen, get Summer and the baby and get the hell wherever you're going for at least tonight. Jean Preston just took off in some kind of private jet. Nobody knows where she's going, but given the events of the night she's probably figured out what Summer found and is on her way to demand the baby before the law catches up with her." Luke's intonation was frantic. Austin had never heard his big brother sound frightened before. He swallowed down bile.

Luke stopped talking but Austin could hear another man's voice in the room. "Who is that?"

"Detective Miller. Hang on a sec."

"Go get J.J. Put him in his seat. We're leaving right now. Hurry." Austin barely managed the order to Summer. Abhorrent pain broadcast from her as she gave him a single nod and raced back inside their home. His mother dammed back tears with the close of her eyes. His father continued to pace, shaking his head.

"Okay, Miller says he's given the order for the forger to be brought in. They're getting him now. But we're still not 100% he's the right one. He also says to leave my phone on the ranch and pick up a throw away once you're out of town so no one can trace you."

"Okay, I'll get one tomorrow. I want to get where we're going tonight. If Jean Preston is coming to the Glen, I don't want anyone seeing me leaving. I don't want to be followed."

Luke was silent for the length of one heartbeat. As if the cell phone held some kind of telepathic link, Austin knew precisely what he longed to say. He still couldn't quite understand why Austin was willing to leave it all for Summer.

"Be careful, Austin. Call me when you can. We'll figure this out and get both of you back home." Luke sighed.

"I know you don't get it, man. I really do, but I have to do what's right. I'll...uh...see you later."

"Yeah. Hope so."

Trying his damnedest not to feel anything at all, Austin offered his parents one last wave as he drove off of the only home he'd ever known, the lands that had raised him, and his family.

"Austin, you don't have to do this. Just let me go. I'll find my way back to you somehow when all of this is over. Please, you can't leave here. I can't let you do this," Summer pled.

He shook his head, unable to speak.

"Austin," she tried again but emotion consumed her voice.

"Not right now, okay. Just turn on some music or something."

Biting her lip, she turned on the old radio and buried her face in her hands.

———

Everett Camden

Everett Camden caught his wife as she fell into his arms sobbing. God, it tore him up to see her cry. They watched the back of what had once been Ev's old Ford drive off the ranch. That was the very truck they'd brought Austin home from the hospital in. It was more than Ev could stand, and far more than he would allow. "I know where he's going, honey, and I intend to bring them home."

"He told you?" A glimmer of hope played in Jessie's beautiful emerald eyes.

"No, but I know my son better than I know my own hands."

"How are you going to bring him home?"

"I'm gonna do what I should've done when they got here a few nights ago." He lifted his cell phone from his pocket and scrolled through the numbers his old friend Heath had provided. Ev and Heath had gone to school together. They'd rebel-roused the hell out of Nebraska-Lincoln back in the day. Heath had returned to his family's lands just outside of Dallas when his father's health had gone down. He hadn't finished his agriculture degree, but Ev had sent him all the coursework when he was finished with it. Back then, knowledge meant something, and to cattle ranchers knowledge would always mean more than any piece of paper. Ev had flown down for his daddy's funeral. Heath had come up when Ev's mama passed. Few years after that, Heath had gone on to get his veterinary degree from A&M. He'd tested out of most of the bachelors' classes because he'd done the course work Ev provided. Ev had called to get a phone number, but Heath had provided so much more. He always did. That was how they worked.

Lifting the phone to his ear he considered his words carefully.

"Preston Cattle, this is Ginger speaking, how may I help you?"

"I need to speak to Brant Preston, Sr. Now."

"May I tell him who's calling?"

"Sure, tell him Everett Camden's calling from Camden Ranch deep in the heart of Nebraska. Friend of Dr. Heath Hotchkins. You might also tell him that Heath has a few questions about the prescriptions his son Brant Jr. requested a few months ago."

"Yes, sir."

————

"You know what, you can sit in here on your pansy-ass and not do jack shit, but I'm going over there and finding the hell out what that woman is up to. I'm not gonna let my brother go down for kidnapping and be run out of his home." Luke left a shocked Miller standing in his room and stormed next door. He pounded on the door. "Dammit, Preston, I know you're in there. Open the fucking door."

Nothing. No answer, no noise at all.

"Here." Miller joined Luke in the hallway and lifted his phone to his ear. "Yes, this is Nebraska State Bureau Detective Alan Miller. I have reason to believe that there may be a person in distress in hotel room 318. I need the room opened."

Two hotel managers got off the elevator less than a minute later. They rushed to open the door. Luke shoved them aside as he stepped inside, but the room was empty. Brant must've escaped when the cops downstairs left to follow his mother's cab.

Luke took off. He flew to the elevator and then out of the hotel, methodically scanning every person in the streets of Cheyenne that night. He went in every bar and when those turned up empty, he got in his truck and headed back to the Eagle's Nest to check there.

CHAPTER TWENTY-SEVEN

"Why are we slowing down?" Summer's own voice shook through her weary bones. They hadn't spoken in over an hour. Austin never took his eyes off the road. She'd watched the tiny ranch towns fly by and hadn't asked why they were driving back toward Wyoming. He clearly had a plan. If it had been up to her, they would've been well past Denver by now, but she didn't question him. For once in her life, she was going to listen to someone else and do it their way. He was leaving everything for her. She still couldn't believe someone could possibly love her enough to do what he was doing.

"We're almost there, honey. I'm sorry. I know I'm acting like an ass. I didn't mean to scare you. Just trying to keep everything in my head."

"It's okay. It's just when you talk it kind of makes me feel better."

"My family has a tiny fishing lodge on Lake McConaughy. Grew up camping out there. Dad finally bought the cabin 'bout ten years ago. A few of us come out to fish occasionally, but no one's used it in the last few years. Grant, Dad, and Nat love to fish, but the rest of us prefer to tent camp on the prettier side of the lake. Cabin's on the side of the lake where the tourists don't come. Better fish out that way. Covered up with bramble and weeds. You can barely make out the cabin, which seems like a good place to hide for a while. It's not lush.

There's a foldout couch and place for a camp stove. No heat or air or anything."

"I don't need anything lush. We'll be fine. I spent the last six months camping in hotel hallways. It'll be an upgrade from that." She tried to sound positive and knew she'd failed miserably.

The truck bounced as it climbed over tree roots and rocky dirt. Summer could see the moon reflected off the largest lake she'd ever seen. It looked like an ocean from what she could tell. Tree limbs licked at the windshield and scraped past her window making her cringe from the high-pitched howl they made against the glass. He drove on.

Finally, he pressed the emergency brake and studied her. "You okay?"

"No."

"Yeah. Stupid question. How about are you as okay as you could possibly be right now?"

She managed a nod.

"K, I'm gonna take one of the flashlights and make sure no one's here. Stay in the truck."

Summer watched Austin climb out of the truck. Narrowing her eyes, she saw him methodically searching the front and eastern side of the tiny cabin then he disappeared around the back.

Left Boot Lodge had at one time been painted along the concrete walls. The truck lights bathed the chipped blue paint.

Just prior to her officially losing her mind, Austin returned. "Come on. Let's get J.J. settled for the night. Then we'll figure out where to go from here."

Trying not to turn her ankle on the tree roots and slip-rocks, certain she was going to have to run fast as some point, Summer carried her sleeping little boy inside the cabin. The smell of fish hung in the hot humid air, hitting her lungs with a repulsive blast as soon as they were inside. She fought not to gag.

"Sorry about the smell. You'll get used to it. We'll open the windows. It'll help some." Austin cranked the ancient windows open. She would never have complained, so she went on with helping him set up.

———

At two in the morning, Cheyenne became a ghost town, and Luke stumbled from his truck, headed back inside the hotel. Brant was nowhere to be found. All Luke knew to do was to go back to the ranch. If Preston thought he was coming to Camden Ranch and taking anything at all, Luke would have something to say about it. No one was gonna run his brothers off of their land and live to tell about it.

Miller and Dillon were at the airport making sure Brant didn't escape by plane. Colorado, Wyoming, South Dakota, Kansas, and Nebraska police departments were on the lookout for his truck as a possible accomplice to a forgery involving a kidnapping. No one had seen him. The elevator doors parted. Weighted with all that had happened, he stopped at the soda machines and purchased two Dr. Peppers. He was gonna drive all night.

Drawing in a weary breath, he headed to his room but stopped short. His eyes goggled. Brant Preston Jr. himself was sitting in the hallway between their hotel rooms.

"What the fucking hell?" Luke demanded.

Brant's body jerked as he lifted his swollen red eyes to Luke's. He'd either been drinking or crying or both. Slimy fuck-whistle slithered off the ground. He swallowed harshly as Luke ground his teeth.

"Look, I know you're Austin's brother, okay. You're not that great of a detective, and you two look just alike. Plus, the Camden brothers are kind of legendary around here. I know you all don't let anyone mess with the other. I just didn't know why you were following me... until tonight." Another anxious swallow.

Luke's biceps flexed of their own accord. It would be so fucking satisfying to drive his fists hard and fast in to Brant's face.

"I also know Summer ain't in Santa Fe. She's been angry at her mom ever since she told her to go on and marry me. She wouldn't go back there. Plus, I saw how she looked at your brother. She never looked at me like that. She's with him back at your ranch. I know, but I swear I never told nobody I knew where they were. Can I please talk to you? I swear I'll give Summer anything she wants including our son. I just...please...can we go somewhere and talk?"

"You expect me to believe one fucking word that comes out of your ugly face? You ran my brother off a horse over her."

"Yeah, well, if that were the biggest problem I had, believe me, I'd be kissing your boots. Austin galled me from the very beginning. He was the only rider I thought might ride Dallas Devil, and it pissed me off. Then he took up with Summer and..." He shrugged. "I guess I'd let you or Austin beat the shit out of me over all of it, if it would make all of this go away. Go ahead. It ain't like you couldn't, and God knows I deserve it, but please, I'm begging you. I cannot go down for *kidnapping*." His voice lowered to a frantic hiss. "Just please hear me out. I swear I had no idea what she'd done."

"Who's *she*?"

"My mother."

Luke opened his hotel room door and directed Brant inside. "Just so you know, there's a Colt Commander in my room, and I'm not in a real good mood. Don't get cocky."

———

The sun was just coming up when they hit the Lisco city limits. Luke had come the long way to Ogallala since that would land them closer to the cabin. His cell rang. Keeping an eye on Brant, who'd been a decent riding companion, Luke answered his father's call.

"Left the airport about an hour ago, heading that way," Ev supplied. "You be careful getting out of your truck. Your brother's real likely to shoot."

"Don't I know it. Wish I could call, but Miller told him to leave his phone. You got what you went to Lincoln to get?"

"More than that. Whole damn thing's crazier than I ever even imagined."

"You're okay though, right? He ain't tried nothing?" Luke gave nothing away. Brant could walk into his own fire. Dumbass that he was.

"Well, your mama ain't put that pistol up yet, but we're fine. You've seen her shoot. Ain't gonna be me that gets hurt if they get stupid." His father's warning tone made Luke grin. It was somehow comforting when you weren't the one being threatened. He ended the call.

"Hey, do you want me to drive? You could just give me directions. You look exhausted," Brant offered.

"Do I look dumber than a stump to you? You sit there and keep it shut. We'll be there in a little while."

———

Austin's head jerked upwards. He ran his hands over his face, trying to stay alert while wondering how on earth this was ever going to work. He'd stayed awake most of the night. J.J. had woken up crying just before sunrise. Currently, he was wiggling on the couch between Summer and Austin. How the hell did you disappear and not forever be looking over your shoulder? How were they supposed to exist like this?

J.J. pulled up using the back of the couch for support. He desperately wanted to go get in the water he could make out beyond the cabin. Austin wished he could go for a swim himself. Lake Mac always soothed his soul, but no one could see him there. Soon as the fisherman pulled up their lines for the day and people were out and about in town, they were driving down to Denver to buy throwaway cell phones, maybe stay the night there, then come back.

Lifting his arms over his head, trying to ease the tension that had taken up residence in muscles he wasn't even aware he had, another yawn overtook Austin.

"Want me to make some breakfast?" Summer's tone sounded nothing like her. Broken and weary. It shattered his heart.

"Yeah, if you want." Maybe doing something would help her.

Since it took less than three steps to get to the kitchen portion of the cabin, he watched her crack a few eggs and turn on the propane tank on the camping stove.

"Da-Da," J.J. babbled quite coherently. "Da-Da, Da-Da." He pointed frantically towards the dock.

The bowl of eggs in Summer's hands shattered on the concrete floor. "What?"

"Get him," Austin ordered as he pulled his Browning from one of his bags. "Stay in this cabin." He headed out the front doors but stopped short. Four police squad cars pulled up behind a truck he couldn't quite make out. *Fuck.* He hadn't planned on spending eternity in hell.

"It's me!" Luke bellowed frantically with his hands in the air. "Put the damn pistol down. You gotta hear this." Luke and Brant walked side by side toward him.

"Yes, you do," Austin's father urged. His parents were approaching from the other side of the cabin, along with Jean Preston and a man he'd never seen in his life. His mama had a pistol trained on Jean with her eyes narrowed.

"What the hell?"

"Austin, I swear I'm not here for J.J. I'm sorry. I was horrible to you, and I was horrible to Summer since the moment I got her down that stupid aisle. Just don't shoot." Brant's plea made him sound like the child he was.

Summer flew out of the cabin. "You'll never take him from me!" Her scream shattered the quiet morning.

Austin pulled her to him. "They're not here for J.J." The fact that his family was escorting Brant and his mother toward them was enough credence as far as he was concerned.

Detective Miller climbed out of one of the squad cars. He raced toward Brant and Luke.

"What the hell are you doing here?" Luke demanded of Miller.

"We left Cheyenne about fifteen minutes after you did. I saw him climb in your truck when I was coming back to the hotel to tell you that Dallas got the forger to confess. Truthfully, I was anxious to know where the heck the two of you were going together. Didn't want to spook you by turning on the lights. We're here for Brant Jr."

"Wait, please. Let me at least tell her what I did and sign J.J. over to Summer before you arrest me," Brant tried to negotiate with the cop.

"He ain't being arrested for kidnapping." Austin's father reached him first and dragged him into an unexpected hug. "Deep breath, okay. It's all gonna be just fine."

"Well, what *is* he being arrested for?" Summer huffed.

"Wrangler, Ford, the Frontier Days committee, and the Professional Bull Riders association are pressing charges for the fact that

Dallas Devil had Trenbolone via Finaplix-H steroid solution in his bloodstream. Brant just cost them all a whole lot of money. He basically threw the entire season," Miller explained. "The tests came back this morning, and the PBR got a call last night from a vet in Dallas willing to testify that Brant threatened to have his clinic shut down if he didn't write a prescription for three times the normal limit given heifers."

"Oh, just wait 'til you hear the whole damn story," Luke supplied as he joined everyone on the concrete porch.

The cops agreed to wait and let Brant explain himself if they could record his testimony. "I had no idea my mother was trying to take J.J. from you, Summer. I would have stopped her long ago. I couldn't figure out why she was so pissed about me letting you have him for all of Frontier Days, about that phone message you made me leave." He gestured to Austin. "I swear. I had no idea. I don't know how you found what you found, but I'm actually glad you did. She figured out what you had and told me last night."

"That's why she was pitching a fit in the hotel bar," Luke explained. "But she wasn't ever flying here. She ran back home to Dallas."

"Yes, well, it isn't her home anymore," the man Austin didn't know bellowed angrily.

"Who the hell are you?" Austin huffed.

"That's Brant's daddy," Summer whispered.

"Seems my wife found out I was planning on filing for divorce a few months ago. Working under some bizarre delusion that if she got custody of J.J., I wouldn't go through with the divorce, she went to the courts and demanded another custody hearing after the baby was born. When I pulled my lawyers off of the custody hearing, because through all of this I believe the boy belongs with his mother, she apparently contacted some half-wit forger who now threatens to take down my entire cattle operation.

"Summer, I had no idea she'd done this. I am truly sorry for everything that happened to you either at the hands of my wife or my son. When your father asked me to get you off the circuit, I'd foolishly believed Brant was in love with you and that you might be something he would actually work for. I should never have made the deal I made.

I certainly do not expect your forgiveness, but I would like to give you some peace of mind. Our family will not interfere with J.J. or you ever again. Everett phoned me last night and explained what was going on. When Jean landed in the jet, I knew he was telling the truth. Before we flew back up here to explain, I had my lawyers draw up custody documents giving you sole custody of J.J." He held out a manila folder. Mutiny flashed in Mrs. Preston's eyes just before she began crying.

Summer was shaking too violently to have accepted the papers, so Austin took them on her behalf.

"Mr. Camden explained that you'd expressed interest in marrying his son and had truly fallen in love. I had them draw up two sets of papers. If you'd like to make Austin J.J.'s legal father, those documents are in there as well. Brantley will sign anything you'd like."

"I swear. I will. Just, please, I can't go down for attempted kidnapping," Brant begged.

"Mrs. Jean Gentry Preston, you are under arrest for the attempted kidnapping of Jahan James Preston." One of the officers slapped cuffs on Mrs. Preston's wrists. Austin almost felt sorry for her. She was pale and drawn. Terror paled her eyes.

"Brant, are you just going to stand there and let them do this?" she demanded of her husband.

"You used my money to hire a forger that willingly talked to the cops. What do you want me to do, Jean?"

Austin rolled his eyes. So, that's why he'd done all of this. All in the name of the mighty Preston Cattle of Dallas, Texas. It struck Austin as odd that he'd never thought to ask what J.J. stood for. His brow furrowed as he turned to Summer.

"Jahan means the entire world. Because before you he was my whole universe."

"Let's get them papers signed and my children back to their home where they belong." Ev put his arm around Summer in a fatherly embrace, supporting her still-trembling body. "I'm done with this whole blasted thing. If you have to lie, cheat, or steal to get something, it ain't worth having." He bellowed Brant's direction. Neither Brant nor his father seemed to agree with the sentiment, however.

Brant cringed when the cops added cuffs to his wrists. "Listen,

Camden, you know how it's gonna work. I'm out. Dallas Devil's season's scores will be removed from all of his riders. You haven't missed anything but your ride with him. If you wanted to go back to Cheyenne and finish, you could. You deserve the buckle, and everyone knows it."

CHAPTER TWENTY-EIGHT

Las Vegas, Nevada ~ November

"All right, now, I'm gonna be a daddy...again...so make me look good," Austin taunted Bruiser, the bull he'd been assigned for his final ride.

The roar of the Vegas crowds no longer fed his blood. He was there to finish a job he'd started. Beyond that, the only thing worth having was standing by the gate with his brothers trying to grin at him. The terror of this still made her ornery as hell. He'd take care of that as soon as he got her back to their hotel room.

"Camden swears this is his final ride, ladies and gentlemen. Let's see if we can't make him stay," one of the announcers bellowed.

The crowds chanted his name, but he shook his head as Bruiser shifted against the gate. Jackson was already in the ring. Cam handed his ropes over. Clifton and Scott were smiling, pleased that Minton Chaps was about to become the sponsor of the PBR champ.

"It seems Ms. Summer Sanchez has captured our bull rider's heart, Jim. Looks like Mr. Camden might be busy raising up another little bull rider next season," a PBR official commented into the sound system for all the arena to hear.

"That's right and I was informed that she's no longer Summer Sanchez. He made her Summer Camden this afternoon right here in Vegas."

Blushing as a broad grin spread across her face, Summer turned to let the crowds see her big beautiful belly. The diamond engagement and wedding rings on her finger sparkled in the arena lights as she rubbed her hand over their youngest son's current locale. J.J. was on top of Ev's shoulders, waving for the cameras. Austin beamed. Soon as he got the hell out of that arena, life would be perfect.

This time his destiny was right beside him, so with one final nod, he pulled up on the ropes and held on. This ride wasn't for Max, or Minton, or to show Brant. This ride was for Summer, for their boys, for his family.

Bruiser shot out of the gate, and Austin held on for all he was worth. Held on for all he'd endlessly fought for. Held on for her, for their sons, for the life he'd always wanted but had been too damn scared to believe he deserved. This was it.

Time slowed. With each frantic buck and spin of the bull, images flashed in his head. That bar in Cody. That ranch cabin in Cheyenne. That first night with her on the ranch. Signing the adoption papers. The positive pregnancy test. The diamond he'd slipped on her finger. The first time J.J. had called him "Daddy." And stepping out of The Little Church of the West that very afternoon when he'd finally made her his wife. Eight seconds. Eight moments that would always make his life worth living.

The timer ripped through his concentration. His seconds were up. Life was waiting on him.

"That was a near perfect ride for Camden. You're looking at this year's champion, ladies and gentlemen."

He let go of the rope and bailed off of the bull. Jackson slid in beside him as the other fighters pushed Bruiser back in the gates. "You did it, man! You did it!"

Austin turned and winked at his wife. Obvious pride swelled within every curve of her beautiful body. She was beaming as she shook her head at him and held her hands out. She was too round to run to him anymore. Perfect by Austin's estimations. "Yeah, I sure as hell did." He bolted towards the gate and had Summer swept up in his arms a half-second later.

––––––––

Staring out at the glow of the Vegas strip reflected off the cool, navy-blue night sky from the top-floor suite of The Venetian Hotel, Austin cradled his wife in his arms.

She grinned. "Well, you did just win spectacularly, cowboy. PBR champion buckle and all. We'll have to work around my belly, but I still think the beast deserves a prize."

Austin waggled his eyebrows. "I like working around your belly, darlin'. Lets me be creative. But my parents have J.J., and I've got lots and lots of plans for my bride on our wedding night. We can take it nice and slow."

Intrigue and that wildfire he loved burned in her eyes as she smirked. "We really were idiots."

"Hey, I told you I was potent first time I took you to bed. Just didn't know I was quite potent enough to get you pregnant in that shower back in Cheyenne, but coming all over you in the shower here, sounds like a good start for our evening, Mrs. Camden."

"Guess I can't get more pregnant." She giggled.

Chuckling, Austin slid the maternity jeans over her bump and down her legs. Barefoot and pregnant. Yeah, life didn't get much better than that. "Have I mentioned how much I like these elastic jean things? So much easier to get 'em off of you."

"You're still full of shit." A soft sigh accompanied her taunt as he fell to his knees and kissed his way over the tattoo she'd gotten a few days after they'd returned to the ranch, safe and fully in custody of J.J. His cattle brand, an AC with an arrow between, was permanently affixed to her lower back and the top of her ass cheek. An answer to the broken feather on her other side.

"Fucking sexiest thing I have ever seen," he vowed reverently as he spun his tongue over his mark.

"I'm rather fond of yours, too, you know?"

Standing, Austin pulled off his undershirt and tossed it on the floor.

She ran her fingers over the large tribal hawk he'd had inked across his chest. "Thanks for always being my hawk and for always being my hero."

"Forever, baby. Thanks for always being my girl."

FOREVER WILD - CHAPTER 1

THE NEXT BOOK IN THE CAMDEN RANCH SERIES...

"She's a wild one, with an angel's face. She's a woman-child in a state of grace," sang loudly from Indie Harper as she flew up I-80 in her '68 Camaro Z28 in toreador red. Faith Hill sang on, so did Indie. *"She's a wild one, running free."* Her long, dark auburn hair whipped out the open windows. "Woohoo!" she chanted as she flew past the Nebraska state line. Oklahoma and Kansas were now behind her.

She was going home, and for all of the complications and shit sure to come from seeing her mother she couldn't wait to get there. At least that's what she kept telling herself. Nerves tingled up her spine, but she made a valiant effort to ignore them. This would be good. She hadn't been home since the Christmas before, over a year ago.

Her baby sister was getting married. She could endure her mother long enough to get her fix of Pleasant Glen, see her daddy, love on her sisters, and ride her horses. After that, she'd head back to Oklahoma City and get back to wrenching cars.

In a matter of moments, the scents of sweet corn and hay coupled with manure. The breathy memories filled her lungs. Her grin expanded. Had to be a Nebraskan cowgirl to get off on the smell of home.

Slowing as she came up behind a ranch truck hauling cattle, she listened to the radio DJ. "We're throwing it way, way back this Memorial Day weekend. That was Faith Hill's 'Wild One' from 1993. Up next we've got your farming report. You're listening to Husker's Radio KXNP."

Switching off the farming report, Indie frowned. "It's not way, way back. It wasn't *that* long ago." Okay so, maybe she wasn't exactly a woman-child anymore. Staring down 33 decidedly made her more woman than child. Glancing in the passenger seat, where she'd slung her duffle bags since her tool boxes and spare tires were in the trunk, the corner of that damned reunion invitation taunted her.

How the hell had she been out of high school for fifteen years? She could've sworn she was eighteen like two weeks ago. Leave it to Melony to follow their mother's orders and plan her wedding one weekend before the reunion, leaving Indie without a good reason not to attend. Indie adored her little sisters, but Melony's endless desire to make their mother happy galled her to no end.

Their daddy always said Indie got the portions of rebelliousness that were meant for her twin sisters, plus an extra shot. Grinning again, she floored the accelerator and shot around the truck, over the double-yellow line. An oncoming Pontiac laid on their horn. She whipped her Camaro back and flipped them off for good measure. God, it was good to be home.

Fifteen miles outside of Pleasant Glen, her car began its customary lurching clunk. She should've replaced the tires before she left, but she'd figured she had a few hundred miles left on them, and she'd switch them for the Hoosier CO6 radials she'd been eyeing when she got to her father's shop. The Goodyear E70's weren't a great match since she'd cut the quarter panels. Flats were something she was growing quite accustomed to. "Just couldn't wait 'til I made it to Daddy's, could you?" Sighing, she pulled off on the shoulder and hopped out.

Not in any way surprised that a truck pulled in behind her, she tried to hide her eye roll. She *was* in the land of well-bred cowboys, after all. Hauling her jack and wrench set out of her trunk, she didn't stop until her eyes landed on Grant Camden climbing out of his F-250.

Shit.

"Can I give you a hand, ma'am?" Concern thrummed in his tone. She lifted her head, and a broad grin spread across his face. "Indieanna Harper, is that really you, darlin'? My God, it's been a day or two since you showed up back here in the Glen, hadn't it? We missed you, girl. It's good to see ya." He scooped her up into an all-encompassing hug.

"More than a day or two. How are you?" Tension tightened in her throat as she hugged him back. So, maybe there was one other ginormous reason besides her daddy and her horses that Indie was looking forward to being back home.

"I'm good. I'm guessing you don't need my help with that tire, though."

Forcing a chuckle, she grinned. "I know it ain't in the Camden way of doing things to leave me here, so stand back and watch me work, cowboy."

"You got it." Grant held his hands up in surrender, a hearty laugh accompanying his broad grin.

When she rolled one of the spares she carried to the flat, she waggled her eyebrows. "Time me."

Still laughing, Grant checked his watch. "All right, go."

Letting the timer drive her, she whipped off the lug nuts, had the car jacked up, and the tire replaced in minutes. She lowered the car and tightened the nuts before standing. "How'd I do?"

"Seven minutes, fourteen seconds. Damn, girl, if Luke wouldn't lay me out flat when he beat the shit outta me, I'd propose." He winked at her.

And there it was. *Luke.* Her heart sped frantically. Luke Camden. She'd never been more than a friend to Grant, but his big brother Luke, well, there was enough history there to fill every textbook back at Pleasant Glen High. "You admitting your big brother could knock you on your ass, Grant Camden?"

"Don't tell him I said that out loud. He'd get way too much pleasure outta that."

The words *pleasure* and *Luke* rolled through her mind and sent a flash fire of heat spiraling down to her breasts. It didn't stop its collision course until it had taken up residence between her thighs. She'd been back home at least two-dozen times since she and Luke had ended their five-year relationship, when they were freshman at Nebraska-Lincoln. Every single time they were within a hundred miles of one another they sought each other like moths to a flame. She'd knock on his door late the last night of her typical weekend visit and spend several long, delicious hours allowing her body to be worshipped by his. God, it was like nothing else she'd ever experienced.

They never really talked about anything of any importance, never did much more than set his bed sheets on fire, reminisced a little, and promised to call and text more often. She'd wait on him to go to sleep, spend a few hours absorbing the heavenly contentment he offered just holding her in his arms, remind herself why she could never stay there with him, and then she'd run away again.

"Deal." Indie grinned. "How is Luke?" *Geez, anxious much, Indie?* She'd gone far too long without a tryst with him, and it was clearly getting to her.

"He's good. I'm guessing you're in for the wedding. You staying for the reunion, too?"

"Not sure yet. We'll see how long I go without wanting to pulling my mama's hair out and fileting the mayor."

Laughing again, Grant nodded his understanding. "Carolyn's got the whole damn state coming to this wedding. She's in her element, I'm assuming."

"Oh, I'm sure." Indie rolled her eyes. "Speaking of Nebraska's pearl-clutcher-in-chief, I better get to the mansion and get this over with. Tell Luke I can't wait to see him."

Grant smirked. "Sure thing. See ya 'round, Indie."

Climbing back in her car, she was left with nothing but memories that scalded her throat with regret. She'd followed Luke to college. Okay, so that had been his dream, not hers, but the way it had ended, God, what she wouldn't give to go back and ... *And what, Indie?* Luke Camden is too good for you, too stable, too secure, too ... *rancher*. He was tied to the land that was tied to the Glen, and that was far too many ties for Indie. She'd always be in love with Luke, but sometimes love wasn't enough. She couldn't stand Pleasant Glen, couldn't stand her own mother — who was married to the freaking mayor of the town she despised — and couldn't erase the past any more than she could ever settle down and become a rancher's wife.

———

"So, Indie's due back in town for Tuck and Melony's wedding. I'm figuring that's why you're dancin' around here like you gotta gnat in your sac. You change the sheets on your bed and clean up your shit or you figure it'll take her a day or two to come knocking on your door?" Austin Camden, Luke's little brother, laughed.

Luke rolled his eyes. "Fuck off, Austin."

"Oh, come on. Don't even act like you aren't playing the part of the three-balled tomcat in this situation. You two get so loud we all have a cigarette afterwards."

Even Luke's father, Ev, joined in the laughter over that. Luke slung another hay bale in the back of his truck. When Grant's truck pulled up, he knew things were only going to get worse. No one but his family and Indie's father knew of their late night trysts whenever she came back to the Glen. Since he shared his family's ranch with his parents, cousin, brothers, and sisters, it was next to impossible to have someone in his home without everyone knowing. The ranch was massive, yet somehow his family always knew when Indie's Camaro headed through the front gates.

Grant's shit-covered boots hit the dirt. Something had clearly happened. Grant looked far too pleased for Luke's liking.

"Never guess who I just ran into," he chuckled.

"Oh, I bet I can," Luke sighed. Every one of the 198 people that lived in Pleasant Glen had inquired as to the possibility of him and Indie getting back together permanently, since everyone assumed she'd be in town longer this trip than she ever had before.

"Indie Harper had a flat out on Route 410. She was heading into town. I pulled over to see if she needed any help," Grant explained.

Luke grunted at the very idea of his Indie needing any help with a flat tire. It was preposterous.

"Yeah, yeah, I know, but I didn't know it was her at first. Anyway, girl changed that tire in under eight minutes. She's something else. When she was leaving, she said to tell you she couldn't *wait* to see you." He stuck the tip of his tongue between his teeth and laughed.

Luke stared his brother down. Grant was lucky they were related. Two days ago when Sloane and Ashley Patrick had droned on for the better part of a half-hour about how Indie was surely coming back to the Glen for Melony's wedding *and* their high school reunion, and how *great* it would be if Luke and Indie got back together in time for the reunion and she stayed this time, Luke had decided to place a well-aimed fist in the mouth of the next person that spoke Indie's name to him. Seeing as this was his brother, he only ground his teeth.

"I ain't pulling your chain, man. Those were her words. All I'm saying is you ain't over her, and apparently she can't *wait* to see you."

"I ain't deaf. I heard you the first time." Luke let that information tumble around in his head. At one time he'd known Indie the way the stacked lightning knew the mid-western storms, the way the ocean knew the shoreline's kiss, the way the Cottonwood trees sought the silt banks of Nebraskan streams — because they knew how to survive.

Awareness of her always sank in long before anyone had to tell him she was back in town. He could sense her presence long before he laid eyes on her beautiful body. His mouth watered as he considered every single thing he knew about Indieanna Harper. The taste of her musk, wild and ripe, the sweet spun sugar of her lips, the way she gasped on his first thrust, the raspberry heat of her nipples when he swirled his hungry tongue around their stiff peaks, the dark fire in her eyes when she wanted more. The way she came with a whimpered cry of his name.

"All right, both of ya. Leave him be," Luke's father commanded. "Austin, if you're taking your newest little one into Lincoln for that doctor's appointment, you need to get a shower. Grant, we still got a dozen heifers that ain't calved yet, and I'm getting worried. You and Brock go check 'em."

Luke was well aware that his brothers and cousin were being sent away so his father could join the throngs of people who had an opinion on how he should handle Indie's return. He made no effort to hide his eye roll. Clearly, no one in the Glen thought he had a brain. The fact that he'd graduated with a master's degree in veterinary medicine and took care of every animal in the local area clearly meant very little.

"Quit rolling your eyes and let me say my piece. You're nearly 33, son, and God knows I ain't gonna fuss about anything you and Indieanna Harper want to do, but I will say this: you've been in love with her since the first day of ninth grade. There hadn't ever been anyone else. You knew she was the one from the moment you saw her. That's how the Camden men work. You know that, too. So, it seems to me she's gonna be here for a few weeks. You're both gonna be in Tucker and Melony's wedding. Maybe you ought to take the opportunity the good Lord's seen fit to provide ya, and see if you can't make her amenable to staying this time."

"You really think I haven't thought of that?"

His father, his brothers, and the entire town of Pleasant Glen needed to butt the hell out. Yeah, he had a plan. Indie wasn't running away from him this time. He'd make her see that he could be everything she needed. He'd make up for her mother's constant disdain and the affair that had torn his baby completely apart. He'd make up for the hell this town had put her through, and most importantly he'd make up for being an idiot when he was nineteen. *'You keep me sane, Luke Camden, and I'll keep you wild'.* That was how they'd always worked until he'd dragged her to college with him. Somewhere she had no interest in being, while her life here fell completely apart. And then, to ice the cake of stupidity he'd baked, he'd begged his mother for his grandmother's engagement ring and had proposed. He'd put their entire relationship in a pressure cooker and had turned up the heat. Trying to tie Indie Harper down was the very last thing in the world she'd needed at nineteen years old. So much for keeping her sane. He'd done nothing but make her run. There was one thing it had taken him years to understand: without her wild soul, he had no sanity.

This time he'd show her how they were two sides of the same coin that couldn't exist apart. He'd keep his normally calm head on his shoulders and see if he couldn't bring a little sanity back into both of their lives, and then he'd show her just how wild she always made him. She always brought out his most primitive instincts, his savage soul, when she took him to bed. He'd prove to her that he never wanted to tame her wild being. He wanted to sate her in every possible way. There'd be no more caging her in. He knew better now. If she wanted to run this time, he'd fly with her.

As it stood, every single time she came knocking on his door, he inhaled her like a junkie too long without a fix. His body took over his brain. He rushed, desperate to absorb the seductive heat that clung to her curves like nothing he'd ever experienced before. This time he was going to take his time and show her that he'd learned a thing or two since they were a permanent fixture in the Glen. He'd drowned his sorrows in dozens of other women in the last fifteen years; none of them had any hopes of measuring up to Indie. Now he had to show her that he knew precisely how stoke her fires in a slow burn that would last forever.

"I figured you had. I just wanted you to know if your mama or I can help, we want to."

Guilt quelled a little of his ire. Tucker Kilroy, Luke's best friend and the guy marrying Indie's sister, had already offered his help, and so had his brothers and sisters. Hell, even Indie's daddy had vowed to do anything he could to help Luke talk Indie into moving back home. He begrudgingly admitted that everyone that had inquired about Indie's return to the Glen had, in one intrusive way or another, offered their assistance as well. That was the thing about living in a tiny ranching town. Everyone knew everything about everyone else. That was the part Indie hated most, but generally they did all mean well.

"She hates this town, Dad. Not sure what I can do about that."

"I 'spect it's her mama she don't care for, and it's the memories of the town that keep her away, son. Given what all of them put her through growing up, and when her mama up and made off with Mayor Jenkins, I can't say as I blame her. Maybe you could show her that most everyone's over the affair and that all those kids that were so cruel to her have grown up as well."

Continue reading...

ABOUT THE AUTHOR

Bestselling author, Jillian Neal, was not only born 30 but also came accessorized with loads of books and adorable handbags in which to carry them, at least that's what she tells people. After earning a degree in education, she discovered that her passion could never be housed inside a classroom. A vehement lover of love and having maintained a lifelong affair with the awe-inspiring power of words, she set to turn the romance industry on its head. Her overly-caffeinated, troupe-spinning muse is never happy with the standard formula story. She believes every book should be brimming with passion, loaded with hot sexy scenes, packed with a gut-punch of emotion, and have characters that leap off the page and right into your heart.

Her first series, The Gifted Realm, defines contemporary romance with a fantasy twist. Her Gypsy Beach series will leave you longing to visit the sultry shores of the tiny bohemian beach town, and her erotic romance series, Camden Ranch, will make you certain there is nothing better than a cowboy with some chaps and a plan. The sheer amount of coffee required to keep all of those characters dancing in her head would border on lethal, so she unleashes their engaging stories on page after page of spellbinding reads.

Jillian lives outside of Atlanta with her own sexy sweetheart, their teenage sons, and enough stiletto heels, cowgirl boots, and flip-flops to exist in any of the fictional worlds she brings to life.

For more information...

jillianneal.com
jillian@jillianneal.com

ALSO BY JILLIAN NEAL

THE GIFTED REALM SAGA

Within the Realm

Lessons Learned

Every Action

Rock Bottom

An Angel All His Own

All But Lost

The Quelling Tide

GYPSY BEACH

Gypsy Beach

Gypsy Love

Gypsy Heat

Gypsy Hope

GYPSY BEACH TO CAMDEN RANCH

Coincidental Cowgirl

CAMDEN RANCH

Rodeo Summer

Forever Wild

Cowgirl Education

Un-hitched

THE GIFTED REALM: ACADEMY

Free, web serial

71258416R00217

Made in the USA
San Bernardino, CA
13 March 2018